AETHER RISING

CECILIA DOMINIC

<h1>ABOUT AETHER RISING</h1>

The only place to hide could be behind the truth.

No one can lie to Louisa Cobb. It's her gift. Her curse. Magic her stepfather has no compunction about using to gain the upper hand in business. But when Parnaby Cobb presents her with her latest mark, she realizes he's testing her loyalty.

Her target is Patrick O'Connell, an Irish tinkerer and scoundrel who stole a kiss—and her heart—years ago. Should she betray her stepfather to set Patrick free, she'll be cut off without a penny to her name.

Patrick knows exactly he's been captured, why he's struggling to lie into Louisa's sky-blue eyes. He's invented a device to stabilize and direct the mysterious Eros Element. If he fails to recreate it for Cobb, his closest friends' happiness will be at risk.

Back in Boston, as Patrick stalls for time and Louisa uncovers secrets of her tragic past, the two of them engage in a treacherous dance on the edge of love and danger. Where one wrong step could condemn them both to everlasting heartache—and unleash an unimaginably powerful force that could destroy their world.

LOOK FOR THESE TITLES BY CECILIA DOMINIC

Steampunk:

Aether Psychics Series

Noble Secrets

Eros Element

Light Fantastique

Aether Spirit

Aether Rising

The Inspector Davidson Mysteries

The Art of Piracy

Mission: Nutcracker

Urban Fantasy:

The Lycanthropy Files

The Mountain's Shadow

Long Shadows

Blood's Shadow

Dream Weavers & Truth Seekers

Truth Seeker

Tangled Dreams

Web of Truth

ISBN: 978-1-945074-12-7

Edited by Holly Atkinson and Angel Durham

Cover by Karri

ACKNOWLEDGMENTS

I'm so thankful for the opportunity to finish the Aether Psychics series. The feedback that I've gotten from you, my readers, has been so supportive and encouraging. Writing can be a lonely business, and when a reader tells me how much they enjoy my books, it helps me to remember that my words connect me to so many amazing people.

I also need to thank my angel investor, who immediately leaped in with an offer to finance this venture when I fretted about having to crowdfund it to finish the series. Thank you so much for believing in my writing!

Books can't come to fruition on their own, and I'm blessed to have such a great team helping me. Thank you to my editors Holly and Angel for fixing my mistakes and making this book shine.

And finally, to my family and friends who put up with my absent-mindedness, especially to my husband Jason, I am as always grateful for your love and support.

CHAPTER ONE

Danielsville, Tennessee 10 March 1871

Louisa looked up from her magazine when the men entered the train car. Their heavy steps made it bounce, and she pursed her lips in what she hoped was a pretty but effective show of annoyance at the interruption. Then her mouth passed puckered to make an *O* of surprise when her stepfather's pet thugs ushered in an extra person.

A familiar person, and she couldn't stop looking at him.

Something heavy plopping to the red velvet cushions on the bench beside Louisa made her jump. Her stepfather wiped his brow even though it was cool outside. He gave her his "business smile"—lots of teeth but no crinkles at the corner of his eyes.

"I need you to talk to Davis," he said. "He's hiding something. Something doesn't feel right."

"Yes, Father." She willed him to continue, to explain what the tall redheaded and bearded man standing between his two current favorite hired muscles was doing there. Cobb had said they were going down to Tennessee to pick up a talented inventor since Paul Farrell had only gotten so far with the aether. Louisa didn't know what she was doing there—her place was charming business associates and their sons in drawing rooms and ballrooms, not on messy trains—but now she wondered. Was Parnaby testing her?

Her heart accelerated like the train, moving from a steady chug to panicked clip.

"Oh, and I believe you've met our guest, Patrick O'Connell. It was so long ago you may not remember."

She leaned into the pillow behind her, tilted her head up, and flashed a coquettish smile. "Have we met? You look familiar. Oh!" She clapped her hands. "You're that tinkerer from Claire McPhee's ill-fated birthday party." She squeezed a careless laugh through a too-tight throat.

The Irishman filled the train car, moving so naturally with its easy sway he could have been part of it. Not like her on trains and boats, which made her dizzy and nauseated. The only vehicles she could stand were carriages if she was facing to the front and airships as long as the weather was clear and calm.

"Aye. Hello, Miss Cobb." He ground the word out through his teeth. He'd matured—they both had—and his brawny frame dwarfed the men beside him. In spite of his caged animal air, he could have broken free, at least before the train started moving.

What was going on? And what was her stepfather up to?

The two handlers pressed him to the bench across from Louisa and Parnaby, and everyone eyed each other in uneasy silence. His red hair and beard blazed with the afternoon light that slanted then dappled through the windows as the train moved from open country to forest.

Louisa's stepfather nudged her foot. He was letting her take the lead, as he had promised her he'd do. This was a test.

She swallowed. *Not here. Not with this man.* But she had to.

"Remind me of your name again?" she asked as if it hadn't haunted her dreams—both the nocturnal kind and the girlish day kind—of the past six years.

"Patrick O'Connell."

She opened her fan. In spite of the car no longer being in direct sunlight, her cheeks heated.

"Oh, right. And how is your friend, the negro doctor?"

"He's well."

"Yes," Parnaby said. "He helped O'Connell here pioneer a new kind of therapy device similar to the electroshock helmets the neuroticists use for melancholia."

"Oh?" Louisa fanned herself. "What is the new device for?" She looked over the lace at O'Connell.

He bit down, but the words came out anyway. "We don't know yet, it's only been used to help young women recover from disturbing experiences."

"Don't try to lie to her," Parnaby said. "No man can."

"And what about women?"

Parnaby laughed. "Oh, right, you're clever. No *person* can lie to her."

Louisa bit her lip. She'd hoped to reveal her special ability in her own time to this man whose lips she remembered all too well. In fact, if she closed her eyes and smiled just right, she could still feel the kiss he had stolen from her at the party. She had no doubt she'd finally be able to get the truth of what had happened that night from him, but she was more curious about whether he remembered her like she dreamed about him.

It was an improper question, and did she really want to know the truth?

———

The first and last time Patrick had seen Louisa Cobb before this odd train trip was when she had been fifteen. He thought surely she'd be married by now, six years later. But if it was impossible to lie to her, well, what kind of relationship would that be?

A damn good one.

Unlike his parents, who had fought over his father's drinking and skirt-chasing. He'd been honest, but in an unrepentant way, and Patrick had often wished his father hadn't been so brutal with his retellings for Patrick's mother's sake. But for a society miss like Louisa, whom men just wanted to pat on the head and visit in bed, forced honesty would be a disadvantage. Or was Cobb just waiting to wield her at the right man, like a business rival's son?

That ain't right.

He almost smiled at the expression that popped into his head, the one that had shocked Chad. It was a good reminder that he was more than he seemed, but he needed to hide behind the stereotype, ensure Cobb underestimated him.

"So you're probably wondering why we invited you to join us on our journey back to Boston," Cobb said.

The train shifted as their track joined another one, and Louisa hid her face behind her fan. An unladylike belch, then moan came from behind the lace.

"Just a few more minutes," Cobb told her and patted her hand. "Does the aether device do anything for motion sickness?" he asked Patrick.

"Perhaps you should have her ask me." He regretted his flippancy when she emerged from behind her fan with pinched lips that told him she was fighting not to vomit.

"I'll take it the answer is no," Parnaby said. "You might be an Irish brute, but you're not going to withhold help from a suffering woman."

"From a suffering anyone," he said.

Cobb sat back with a smile, and Patrick mentally kicked himself. He'd seen enough of the entrepreneur to know how he operated—he was a master manipulator and exploiter. Patrick had just revealed a weakness, whereas his intention had been to withhold as much as possible about himself.

No, that wasn't right. Neither was forcing him to reveal trade secrets, especially regarding a device powered by an element they didn't understand fully and that carried unknown risks.

Patrick met Cobb's challenging gaze. "I'm not sure what you want me to do with it. Are you suffering from melancholia? Perhaps some sort of neurasthenia or delusion?"

Now when Louisa ducked her head, Patrick was pretty sure it was to hide a laugh. *Interesting.* So she wasn't so enamored of Cobb that she'd jump to his defense or be offended at Patrick's teasing.

"Never mind what I want it for. I just want you to perfect it so that the influence can be spread over a wider area, like in the theatre."

"Are you looking to manipulate theatre-goers' emotions?" As an entertainment strategy, Patrick could see how it would be very effective, but then an icicle of realization formed at the base of his skull. What of other influence, like at an emotionally charged political rally or protest? Mobs couldn't be controlled. Or could they?

"I won't do it," Patrick said. "It's too dangerous."

"Oh, I think you will. You see, I know what concerns you the most."

"And that is...?"

"Your friends' happiness. As you said, you won't let them suffer. You want Doctor Radcliffe and his precious Claire McPhee to marry, correct? Interracial marriage is still illegal except in special cases where dispensation is granted by the government. I can ensure they find all possible obstacles to their happiness."

The train slowed, and Patrick glowered. But then he remembered Davidson's hasty admonishment to cooperate with Cobb even if it didn't make sense. It was the only way for them to see what Cobb was truly up to. He only hoped Davidson could get him out when it was time. And that Louisa didn't ask about Davidson.

If she knew him as Davis, would that negate or attenuate her talent? Patrick could honestly say he didn't know a Davis.

His head fogged with the layers of deception. The train emerged from heavy forest into a field, where Cobb's airship waited, and rolled to a stop.

"Ah, here we are, my dear," Cobb said and stood. He helped

Louisa to stand. She still swayed as though the train moved, but at least she looked less sick. "My men will show you to your room on the airship, Mister O'Connell."

The thugs hauled Patrick to his feet, and they followed Parnaby and Louisa out of the train. When he saw the field only contained the airship the *Blooming Senator* and Cobb's men, any hope Patrick had that Davidson might engineer a rescue before Patrick was truly out of reach evaporated like the steam that hissed from the train's funnel. As much as he would have liked to break free and run, his promise to Davidson to spy on Cobb and his obligation to his friends for Cobb to leave them alone kept him doubly shackled in a figurative sense.

Patrick recalled the attack on the *Blooming Senator* that had dropped the aetherist Edward Bailey and the others into his and Chadwick Radcliffe's lives. Although he hadn't seen the airship itself, his tinkerer's brain wouldn't allow him not to look for signs of what had occurred. First he noticed the dirigible had been repainted, but if he looked closely enough, his trained eye could see where glass had been replaced and other subtle scars.

The air isn't necessarily the safest place.

The thought chilled him. With one last look at the early spring world around him, Patrick allowed the henchmen to shove him on to the ship.

———

Louisa's stomach settled once the airship rose above the clouds and gained forward momentum. She missed her stepfather's former maid Marie, who would make ginger tea with honey and lemon. Marie was the only one who could make it with just the right proportions to settle a dancing stomach. Not that Louisa travelled with her stepfather on most of his journeys to Europe and beyond—and she didn't think she could handle the turbulence she'd heard was over the oceans—but she would always associate Marie's tea with the treat that was a calm domestic trip.

Once Louisa could move about without holding on to the walls, she wandered into the hall. She'd last seen Patrick O'Connell being bundled into the airship behind her, but she didn't know where they'd taken him. This level was all bedrooms. She suspected that her father wouldn't just let a talented tinkerer like Patrick O'Connell wander about unguarded, but she also didn't see any guards posted outside any of the rooms. She ascended the narrow stairs to the next level, which held the library, ballroom, and laboratory.

Ah, the guards were in front of the lab. Parnaby stood and spoke with one of them. He turned and smiled at Louisa—this time with crinkly eyes and no teeth.

"Feeling better?"

"Yes, much, although I miss Marie's tea."

If she hadn't known Cobb so well, she would have missed the flicker of pained annoyance that flitted across his face. She braced herself for his snappish retort and wished he would just say what was bothering him.

"You're an adult. You can make your own tea."

"You're right, I can."

But I won't apologize for bringing her up. Your stupidity and selfishness lost her and inconvenienced me.

Louisa assumed a neutral expression, folded her hands in front of her and looked from the henchman to her father. "Is that where you're keeping O'Connell? Aren't you afraid he'll find something in there to blow us all up?"

"I had the room cleaned out while we were on the train. Don't worry about him—he has the bare necessities to be comfortable for this journey."

"Oh, I'm not." She waved a hand. It was amazing how easy it was to lie to others in spite of the fact they couldn't intentionally deceive her. And it wasn't too much of a lie. She was more concerned about how her own emotions seemed in danger of taking over when she was with the Irishman.

How could one stolen kiss mean so much?

"Good. It's tea time. Go up to the dining room. I'll meet you there."

Louisa dipped her chin so she'd seem to be meekly acquiescing to his command, but she ground an imaginary bit of dirt between her back teeth in frustration at being ordered about.

Once she reached the stairs, she climbed quickly to the spot in the middle where an air vent relayed the words from the hallway below.

"...make sure he doesn't speak to her," Cobb was saying to the guards. "I'd underestimated the influence of the history between them."

A blast of hot air added to the heat in Louisa's cheeks, and her stepfather's admonishment only added to her resolve to see if O'Connell remembered her the same way she remembered him and determine if any feelings for her remained.

And what if he says there are?

She smiled and ascended the stairs at a more ladylike pace.

Then things will get interesting.

CHAPTER TWO

Somewhere over the Eastern Newly Re-united States, 10 March 1871

Patrick stood at the counter by the window and watched the world pass beneath him. Or, rather, he caught sight of the land through breaks in the clouds and tried to determine his location.

For what? I can't alert anyone to rescue me.

At one point he thought he saw a flash of gold, the glint of sun on a brass device, but he couldn't find it again. It would make sense, though, for the Clockwork Guild to be following them. He didn't believe for one second what Davidson had told them, that Cobb and the Guild had come to some sort of amicable agreement. More likely, they pretended to, but neither side trusted the other, and the guild had one talent—spying.

And here he was trapped in the air and headed to Boston, where he'd be kept in a cage of some sort and made to work on something that would enhance peoples' emotions, but that he didn't understand well enough to put safeguards into, while waiting for some sort of release from a man he hardly trusted.

A different shape caught Patrick's attention, a bird of some sort. It was too small to belong this high up in the air. He tested the windows and found that one would open, although not far enough for him to squeeze through. He left it slightly ajar, and the strange object came at the airship arrow-straight. When it got close enough, Patrick saw it wasn't a bird, but rather some sort of brass device shaped into a metal dragon-type creature. Its wings, each about the length and breadth of his two hands side-by-side with fingers outspread, flapped with mechanical rhythm, and its multifaceted green eyes glittered.

The airship's engines changed pitch, and Patrick held on so he wouldn't be thrown to the floor when it accelerated. Cold air whistled through the open window, but Patrick didn't shut it. He couldn't stop watching the creature, which pursued them with relentless determination. The hiss-pop of steam rifles going off above him made him press himself to the back of the room, and the creature shuddered as though hit. It opened its mouth and let forth a small plume of sparks. That was enough of a message —the gunfire stopped lest it decide to latch on to the hydrogen balloon. The wyrm reached Patrick's open window, detached its wings, and fell through the crack, now a clockwork worm that telescoped into itself around a wax message cylinder. After closing the window, Patrick picked it up and stuck it in his pocket just before his door was flung open.

"Did you see it?" This was the thug Patrick had named Monkeyface because the man had ridiculously protruding ears behind long side whiskers.

"See what?"

"The dragon." Monkeyface moved his arms with similar undulating motions to the ones the flying clockwork displayed.

Patrick enjoyed how ridiculous the man looked before answering, "Yes, I saw it."

"Did you see what happened to it?"

Patrick practiced talking around the truth rather than lying. "It looked like you shot its wings off, and it fell."

Monkeyface sagged, his grin revealing he must not like his teeth much considering how many were missing. "Oh, that's good news. You never know what sorts of creatures you'll encounter over the mountains. Spies're everywhere."

"I don't doubt it. Now if you're done panicking over strange clockworks, please tell Mister Cobb I'm ready for my tea."

Now the thug scowled. "You won't be telling Mister Cobb what to do. It doesn't even work for his own daughter, and little girls is s'posed to be able to wrap their papas around their littlest finger."

"Then please tell him I accept his invitation to join him and the lovely Miss Cobb." Patrick straightened his shirtsleeves and tried to walk past the guard, but Monkeyface elbowed him in the solar plexus. Patrick fell to his knees with a wheezing breath.

"Nice try, Red. You'll get your tea when he says you can get your tea."

Patrick coughed, and the door slammed behind the guard. Patrick wanted to know what the creature left him, what message was on the cylinder, but he would have to wait for a more secure place than the laboratory. And rig up something to listen to it with. He remembered Marie's stories of Parnaby or his men spying on their airship guests. He hoped no one had seen his delivery. He suspected that everyone was watching for the creature and lost sight of it when it approached the airship.

———

Iris peered through the telescope up at the *Blooming Senator*, but the same clouds that kept them from being detected obscured her view.

"Do you think he got it?" she asked her husband, Edward. He stood beside her and looked through binoculars.

"I think so. The wings have just dropped, so it attached to something on the airship."

Iris screwed her one eye into an unladylike squint, but it didn't clarify the image through the lens or help her see the falling canvas wings of the modified clockwork worm, now wyrm. With a sigh, she lowered the device and blinked to clear the afterimages. She was more accustomed to and comfortable with peering into underground places, not the open, sunny sky.

"If he wasn't the one, we're all in trouble." She leaned into Edward, who now sported a rakish tan. He put an arm around her and pulled her close.

The desert had been good for him. The sun and wind cleared the gloom that had fogged his brain in Paris before they had realized the aether gas could affect emotions. He had confided in her the depth of his melancholia and just how close he'd gotten to—well, she wasn't going to think about that.

They were back in the States—the reunited states, thanks to Patrick O'Connell and Chadwick Radcliffe—and about to rescue their friend from the clutches of Parnaby Cobb.

Sometimes it was difficult to focus on the present when her mind was used to pondering the past and the ancient danger that still lingered.

The ship descended into the mountains and slipped further under the heavy gray clouds. When it landed, Edward opened the door of the observation deck and lowered the ladder, stairs being too heavy for a smaller vehicle such as the *Skycatcher*. Iris followed him, not able to resist caressing the soft material of the left air chamber on the way down and grateful once again that the Ottomans had no problem with women wearing trousers, at least not when they crewed ships. Getting up and down would have been difficult if not impossible in her skirts.

Marie and Johann met them at the bottom. The *Skycatcher*'s nets had been retracted, but Iris was still careful not to step on any strings that might have escaped.

"Did it work?" Johann asked. Mist clung to his blond hair, and dark curls escaped from Marie's braid. They each held up a wing. "They caught these in the nets."

"I think so," Edward said. "Now we just have to reach Boston on time."

"I hope it got to him," Marie showed Iris the wing she held. A bullet had pierced the canvas. Iris pressed the ribs, but no images or impressions came through. Her talent had grown stronger, but she still needed someone to have had real contact with an object for her to glean emotions and images from it.

"The wings wouldn't have detached unless the wyrm managed to latch on to something," Edward reminded them. "We tested it, remember?"

Iris nodded and rested a hand on his arm. "Waiting is always the hardest part."

Edward checked his pocket watch. "That reminds me. It's almost time for tea."

Johann rolled his eyes. "Please tell me that after all we've been through—"

Edward grinned, and Iris laughed. "He's just teasing." Then her stomach rumbled. "But I have to agree with him this time."

They entered the lower gondola, and the rumble of the engines made the entire thing shake as the ship took off. Once it achieved the air, the *Skycatcher*'s feel smoothed out.

———

Louisa looked up from her magazine and the article titled, "What to Do When You Meet an Old Beau" when she heard the shots. Of all the rooms in the airship, she preferred the smaller, more informal dining room, which was interior and therefore allowed her to convince herself she wasn't in a moving vehicle. In fact, she likely wouldn't have heard the pops from the steam rifles had she been truly engrossed in what she was reading, but her mind kept wandering to a certain captive Irishman and a party long ago. Regular etiquette advice didn't seem to apply as well to him.

She closed her eyes and tried to feel if the airship was losing altitude—which would indicate they had been fired upon and hit—and the thought of plunging through the clouds to the jagged peaks of the mountains below made her stomach quiver. No, the airship seemed to remain steady, and her curiosity piqued. Sometimes the men took shots at birds flying nearby, but they should be higher than any natural creature could fly.

So that leaves unnatural creatures or attackers. And there would be more shouting and firing if we were under attack.

A conference room sat behind a wall that could be retracted to open up the space for dinner parties too large for the dining room. She rose and moved toward the door, her ears alert for any signs of further conflict. There were legends of large flying creatures over the mountains, and if one approached the airship, she wanted to see it.

The conference room door opened for her with a squeak, and she was relieved to see the room was empty. The sky shone light blue without any variation in color from clouds, and she could almost convince herself it was merely glowing wallpaper or a screen, like on a stage. A glance to her left told her the door to Parnaby Cobb's office was cracked open, so she moved slowly so as not to alert him to her presence with the rustling of her skirts.

She reached the windows and deliberately kept her gaze straight ahead or up so she wouldn't look at the ground. Alas, there was nothing at eye level or above, so she squinted her eyes and peeked downward.

In spite of the sun hitting the windows, the glass radiated cold. Its bite gave her something to focus on other than the sensation of her stomach falling to her feet and beyond when she saw the clouds and the patches of dark brown and green that showed in the gaps. She chewed the inside of her cheek to forestall her stomach's progress toward nausea and forced herself to look for anything unusual.

"Louisa?"

Cobb's voice made her spin around too fast to face him, and her stomach lurched. She covered her mouth with her hand and chewed on both cheeks. She drew in deep breaths through her nose while focusing on a knot on the conference table.

"What are you doing in here? You know you can't handle the view," he said. "And it could be dangerous."

"Why?" Her voice sounded like a squeak because she dared not open her mouth too far.

"Because a strange clockwork creature was sighted."

"The Guild?" She allowed him to steer her out of the room and into the dining room, where she sank into her chair. She closed the magazine with a snap.

"I'm not sure." He didn't meet her eyes, and she wondered if he and the odd organization had fallen out. He had brought her along to their most recent meeting that she knew of, and the man, who wore a mask, hadn't been able to say three words. At least not three honest ones. Relations between Cobb and the Clockwork Guild had been strained since.

Or worse—had he seen what she was reading?

"What was it?" Although her stomach settled, she couldn't help the little ladylike burps that escaped with every other breath, so she kept her questions short.

"Some sort of flying dragon creature, but not large." He held out his hands. "About so big."

"Spying?"

"Or delivering something. Morlock is talking to O'Connell now to see if he received anything. Perhaps I should let you question him."

The thought of the lab with all its windows extinguished the flare of excitement at seeing O'Connell again. Was Cobb toying with her? He'd told his men to keep her and Patrick apart.

"I need a few minutes for my stomach to settle."

Cobb patted her on the shoulder, but she noticed the corners of his mouth draw tight with disgust under his whiskers. She hated these moments that made her look like a weak female, but she couldn't help it. Motion sickness and fear of heights had followed her since she was a child.

"I wasn't serious. Do you need your laudanum?" he asked.

Louisa shook her head, which made it spin more. Why had she allowed her curiosity to get the better of her?

"Yes, I believe I do. I have some in my chamber. I'm going to lie down."

Morlock appeared at the top of the stairs. "He says we shot the wings off it, Sir."

"And you believed him?"

Morlock shrugged. Louisa drew back from his smell—body odor and sickly sweet pipe tobacco—and chewed her cheek again.

"We'll watch him, don't worry, Sir."

"Good. Can you accompany Miss Cobb to her room? She's not feeling well."

"I can make it on my own, Father," Louisa said and kept her voice even with every ounce of her will.

He knows how that man's smell turns my stomach. Does he want me to vomit in his airship?

"Very well," Cobb said. "Back to your post, Morlock. Let me know if you need a physician, Louisa."

"I should be fine." *Unless your doctor can cure me of these irritating sensitivities I inherited from Mother.*

She clasped her hands together so they wouldn't shake and waited for the two men to leave the room. Her tea had cooled, but it calmed her stomach better lukewarm than it would have hot. After sufficient time had passed for Morlock's smell to depart from the passage, she rose and made her shaky way two levels down to the hallway with the bedrooms. Lying on her bed brought her some relief, but footsteps above her kept her from sleeping.

The Irishman paced in his prison.

CHAPTER THREE

Somewhere over the Atlantic States, 11 March 1871

The *Skycatcher* kept pace with Parnaby Cobb's airship. Below the clouds, Iris tried to sleep snuggled in Edward's arms, but even the comfort of having her husband hold her close wouldn't calm her mind.

What did Cobb want with Patrick? Was it the aether weapon? Was it the therapeutic device Radcliffe had started working with? Was it something else more sinister than any of them had imagined yet?

Knowing Cobb, it would be something on the evil end of the spectrum. That was part of what drove her to distraction about the whole situation—he'd always been there behind the scenes, pulling the strings. And now, after she'd discovered what the aether could do. Yes, it could heal, but carried too far, it could have deadly consequences.

She shuddered, and Edward stirred. She forced herself to lie still, her breathing even. Not that she couldn't talk to Edward, but he'd heard all her worries before. She envied his ability to take everything to its logical—not worst case—conclusion and his newfound confidence that all would work out. They were intelligent. Therefore fate would cooperate with them.

Iris wasn't convinced. History was full of the worst case coming true, like Paris. They'd escaped just in time, before the Commune government took over and executed the emperor and thousands of innocent Parisians. Her mind ticked off the reasons for her anxiety like a litany.

History never treated the innocent well.

Her mind wandered back to the temple of Apollo Smithneus —Apollo "of the mice"—which had hidden the secret of a force more destructive than any mere weapon. The site had originally been carved out of the earth by a culture older than the temple, probably from before the flood that appeared in myths across the globe. The tool's outer sign, Greek fire, the secret weapon that had allowed the Greeks to take over an empire and the Romans after them, also called Apollo's flame, had gone down in history as a weapon of light, but with a dark shadow cast on those who had used it. She hoped Zokar would keep his promise to destroy the temple, to finish what the Felis cult of long ago had started.

Of course he would. He was trustworthy, wasn't he? He was Marie's uncle and wanted the best for his niece, for all of them. But at two o'clock in the morning, everything seemed worse.

Convinced that sleep would elude her and stiffening from trying to lie still, Iris gently extracted herself from Edward's sleeping form and substituted a pillow to support his arms. Like many academics and tinkerers, his shoulders would hurt after bending over books and contraptions, and she remembered her father's trick of supporting his arms at night so they wouldn't mimic the collapse of the day. Irwin McTavish had still been mostly straight-shouldered when he died.

Iris had lost track of the number of times she'd wished her father was still alive to consult with, but then he would have ended up going on their first expedition, not her, and she never would have met Edward. Or if she had, it would have been in passing, and she wouldn't have come to know him as she had.

The "what if?" track was a different, less useful, path to madness.

She would make some tea and try to put the events of the Ottoman Empire and the knowledge she now had out of her mind.

When Iris arrived in the *Skycatcher*'s small galley, she found she wasn't alone. Marie looked up from the burner, on which a kettle whistled.

"Is your stomach bothering you?" Marie asked. "I have enough water for an extra cup if you need some peppermint tea."

"My stomach is fine. I seem to have finally gotten my air legs. But I would love some peppermint tea if that's what you have made. Couldn't sleep."

She watched Marie go through the ritual of making the herbal tea. They both rocked along with the subtle motion of the airship, and Iris tried to breathe along with the engines' rhythm. Once the tea had steeped, she accepted a cup from her friend, who poured one for herself. Marie extinguished the small lamp after double-checking to make sure the burner was off. They opened the door and walked into the passenger compart-ment, which was furnished with two small tables and chairs.

"Is something bothering you?" Marie asked once they sat where they could see out of the windows, which showed them nothing but blackness. Still, Iris noticed that both of them kept checking to ensure nothing would surprise them out of the dark.

"Just the same old stuff," Iris said. "Who's flying?"

"Johann." Marie grinned. "He's like a child with a toy. Armand set us on the right coordinates, so if he steers straight, we should keep pace with the *Blooming Senator*."

"Oh, Edward's going to be jealous. It's been his dream to fly an airship someday."

"Perhaps tomorrow. Cheers." Marie raised her cup, and Iris did likewise. As her eyes adjusted to the lack of light, Iris picked out the furnishings of the small space. Compared to the *Blooming Senator*, the *Skycatcher* was toy-like, a small piece in a large game.

But true games don't have people's lives at stake.

"So why are you up?" Iris asked Marie. "You were awake earlier than I was this morning." She needed the conversation to keep her mind from wandering in uncomfortable directions.

Marie shrugged. "Too many reminders, I suppose. And I can't be comfortable this close to..." She pointed upward, indicating Parnaby Cobb in the sky above them.

"Do you think he still wants to bring you back into his employ?"

"No." Marie blew across the steaming surface of her tea. "I believe he wants to punish me for refusing him in Paris. I know too much about him and the *Blooming Senator*. That he hasn't tried shows he doesn't realize I'm in the country."

"Ah." Iris searched for words of comfort, but she couldn't find any. Her logical mind said Marie was likely correct.

"We won't let that happen," Iris finally said.

"I believe you'll do your best not to, but some things can't be prevented. This is one area I'll have to rely on myself."

"And Johann. He'll protect you with his life."

"That's what I'm most worried about." Marie looked away, but Iris noticed the tight set of Marie's shoulders.

"Would you feel safer in Paris?" Iris asked, then bit her tongue. They'd been isolated from the news while traveling, but once they had landed Stateside and gotten hold of a newspaper, they'd found that Paris had devolved into bloody chaos with its new government, keeping Marie from returning. And Iris couldn't go back to England since someone had falsely tipped off the authorities that she'd had greater responsibility in Jeremy Scott's death than she actually had.

"Not for the moment." Marie looked out of the window into the darkness.

"We're both women without homes," Iris said. But what could she do about it? Edward would need to find an academic position at some point, so perhaps not being tied to a place for the moment was a good thing. Although he was being a good sport, he would be happiest back in a situation that allowed research and provided routine. Plus, did England really hold anything for Iris beyond familiarity?

Marie's lips curled into a Cupid's-bow smile around the rim of her cup. "Isn't this how people become pirates? I could get used to life in the air."

"I wouldn't have the stomach for it. Plus I haven't given up on my dreams of becoming an archaeologist. I just need an area of specialization that's not so dangerous."

And there went her mind in the direction she didn't want it to go.

"Do you think you would be happy being an American?" Marie gestured to the still-invisible world outside the window. "It's big enough that if you got bored in one part, you could move somewhere completely different, and the frontier is still exciting in parts."

The lack of scenery allowed Iris to imagine the universities and opportunities they might be passing over, places where she and Edward might both be employable. "I might have to be. Would you?"

Marie shrugged in a classically French actress manner. "I can fit in where I need to. In fact, once we rescue Patrick, I count on being able to disappear."

"That will be difficult. Johann needs to perform just like Edward requires his research."

"That can happen across the country as easily as it can in Boston." But Marie didn't sound sure. She tipped her mug up and finished her tea with two long swallows. "Or we can go back to Europe. Well, I should get some sleep. Good night."

Iris squinted against the galley light before Marie closed the door, and then she sat alone. Rather than comforting her, Iris's conversation with Marie only gave her something else to worry about. Parnaby Cobb once again proved to be a shadow looming over them.

If I was a different sort of woman, I would use what I know to elim-

inate the man. But she'd seen evidence of what happened to those seduced by that path. No, even if they could manage to rescue Patrick, they were well and truly trapped, but they at least had to try.

———

Louisa lay awake and listened to Patrick O'Connell pacing like a captured animal above her, which he'd done all afternoon and evening, and then into the night. Burying her head under her pillow muffled the sound but hadn't done anything to ease the vibration of his footfalls. Had Parnaby planned it this way? She knew enough of him to not dismiss his ability to manufacture any kind of torture, and he wasn't happy with her.

Or perhaps he'd underestimated O'Connell's ability to remain awake and alert.

Either way, Louisa needed the tinkerer to settle down. They'd be landing in Boston at lunchtime, and she needed to be fresh for the afternoon's meeting. No one would question it if she slept in. She just had to get to sleep, and that infuriating man wouldn't sit still. She thought about moving to a different bedroom, but she suspected the unused rooms were locked and not heated, and she didn't want to risk running into Morlock on his rounds. He'd never spoken to her, but he looked at her like he raped her with his eyes, and she had no doubt he would take advantage of her and ruin her if he had the chance. Some men couldn't resist their greatest temptation.

She knew O'Connell would treat her as a gentleman would. Or she thought he would. He had in the past.

I can't start thinking of him as a hero even if I do want to find out if his kiss is the same as I remember it. It can't be. We were both just children. Or I was. And I need to sleep.

But what to do? The men had been instructed not to allow her to speak with O'Connell, and Cobb would have a guard stationed at the door. Louisa wouldn't even be allowed to get close to him. Plus, even if she did decide to go up and have a word with him, there was the Morlock problem.

She flipped on her back and tracked O'Connell's footfalls across the ceiling, from the spot above her head to the closet that formed a partial barrier between her chamber and the water closet, then over the water closet and beyond. The laboratory was one of the larger rooms in the airship, but also one of the few that didn't have two entrances, which made it the logical place to store a prisoner since the *Blooming Senator* didn't have a brig.

Louisa slipped out of bed, going to the closet to grab her wrapper and put it on over her sheer nightgown. The footfalls sounded different there.

She frowned. When Cobb had commissioned the airship at the Van de Venden plant, he'd brought Louisa with him. She'd been a young teen at the time and hadn't paid much attention, but she did recall one of the salesmen saying that each room needed at least two methods of egress—which she'd heard as egrets and thought was funny until Cobb smothered her urge to giggle with a look—and the windows didn't count. Cobb had told them it didn't matter, that American standards were different. The salesman had nodded and made a note, but Louisa suspected he did so to humor Cobb. The Belgians were smart and would maintain their standards even if they had to sneak in second exits to some rooms. So where was the laboratory's?

A moment of blessed silence made Louisa realize O'Connell had stopped pacing. Then she realized he stood right above her, and he was scratching at the floor. She climbed up on her trunk so she could better listen to him and wished she had some sort of light to illuminate the closet ceiling. The sound of his nails prying apart something heralded a shower of dust and wood shavings. She sneezed and blinked to clear the sawdust from her nose and eyes.

When she could finally see again, she found herself looking up at him. He grinned as though he was delighted to see her.

"Why, Miss Cobb, I had no idea I'd find you down there."

"It's about time you stopped pacing. Some of us need to sleep." She hopped off the trunk and tried to brush as much of the mess off as she could.

He dropped through the hole and stopped her.

"They can't know about the trap door," he said. "I promise, I'll just be down here for a few minutes while I—" He stopped and clamped his mouth shut.

"While you what?" She narrowed her eyes at him.

"Listen to the tube my friends sent me," he choked out. He pressed his lips together, fury deepening the lines at the corners of his mouth and drawing his eyebrows together.

"Why couldn't you listen to it up there?"

"They'd hear me. The guards. Thankfully the trap door is in the corner they designated as my W.C., and it's behind a partial wall."

"So you didn't need to come through." She crossed her arms. Something about him being so near made her cold in spite of her being covered. Or that was what she thought. Why else would her nipples be tightening?

"No, but I wanted to see you again. I heard what Cobb said to the guards."

Louisa's mouth dropped open. She closed it again when a piece of sawdust fell on her tongue. She picked it out of her mouth and glared at him.

"If you don't want to know the answer to your questions, don't ask them," he said. He stepped closer to her. If Morlock had moved like O'Connell was, Louisa would have screamed or slapped him or something, but she lowered her eyelids.

This was her chance. She could discover if he still had the magic in his lips that she remembered. Not likely. Again, that had been a long time ago, and she had to let go of those silly girlish fantasies.

"What are you thinking, Miss Cobb?" He ran his hands over her, gathering up the bits of sawdust and holding them, presumably so they wouldn't make a suspicious mess on the floor. She shivered at his touch although his fingers were efficient, not tender. When he walked behind her and ran his hands through her hair, loosening her braid, she closed her eyes and swallowed against the sensations gathering at her core.

"This means nothing," she murmured to herself.

"What was that?" His voice, now in her left ear, had dropped into a low, resonant octave that made every one of her nerves come alive, pushing her to reach for him and close the frustrating distance between them.

"Did you find it all?"

"Find what?"

"The sawdust. I'm going to have to take a bath in the morning now."

"I don't know about that. I think I found most of it, but I need to check a few more places, save you that bath."

He moved her hair aside to bare her right ear, and with one calloused knuckle, he traced the curve of her neck down to the ribbon that tied her wrapper at her throat. Her knees and hips tried to turn to liquid, and she swayed but straightened her backbone.

"Just one or two more places," he said, and his lips followed the same path his hand just had. She'd expected his whiskers to be wiry, but they brushed over her like a soft paintbrush. If she shivered any more, she'd fall apart.

"Mister O'Connell," she squeaked, but she leaned into him. He loosened the ribbon, and the sound of the silk moving through his fingers made her joints buckle.

"Call me Patrick," he said as caught her against him. He was fully dressed and she in her nightclothes—her thin, wispy nightclothes—but she could feel him, his hard muscles against her hands, which explored his chest of their own volition. Her wrapper fell around her ankles, and he felt around the lower neckline of her night dress with the hand that wasn't holding her.

"Find anything?" she asked. She couldn't do anything but cling to him.

"Oh, aye, but no sawdust. You'll want to send that wrapper to be cleaned."

"What an eminently practical suggestion," she said, but her voice wouldn't obey her and be normal. She didn't recognize the breathy, husky tones, but he didn't seem to care. Again, his mouth and whiskers found her collarbone, chest, and the swell of her left breast. She wanted something so badly but didn't know what, only for him to keep going. She found herself oddly disappointed he wouldn't move lower with his mouth but again wasn't sure why. The thought occurred to her as she tangled her fingers in his oddly long hair and tried to guide him to center. He straightened and pressed his forehead to hers.

"I can't keep going, Lass. I can't ruin ye." His Irish brogue had thickened, and she found it to be exotic.

"Ruin me for what?" she asked, but her daze lifted, and she recognized she stood in the arms of a man she didn't know, an enemy of her stepfather's. And her nightdress was damp, but not just in the places he'd kissed. She stepped back but kept her hands on his chest because they wouldn't release him.

"Good lass. I shouldn't have come down here."

"No, you shouldn't have. And don't speak to me like I'm a puppy dog." Her heart still pounded and with every beat, disappointment warred with a need that had settled low in her abdomen. And he hadn't even kissed her. Well, he had, but not like she wanted, not on her lips in the way that would let her release her memory of him.

"What can I do to say I'm sorry?"

"Kiss me," she said, recognizing she still held him in her power and his own control hung on just barely.

"What?" The surprise on his face was almost comical.

"I. Need. You. To. Kiss. Me." She blinked, determined not to let her frustration come out in tears, but her voice cracked with her next words. "Now. So I can forget you."

CHAPTER FOUR

Somewhere over the Atlantic States, 11 March 1871

Patrick had many things on his mind, not least of which was the feel of Louisa's shoulders under her silky night shift and how her hands trembled on his chest, but he was definitely not interested in kissing her and forgetting her. Or allowing her to forget him, not again. He could at least accommodate the first part of her request—no, command.

He trailed the fingers of his right hand along her shoulder and collarbone, up the side of her neck, and to the back of her head, where they tangled in her tumbled curls. She watched him with her wide sky-blue eyes, the ones he'd dreamed about when he felt things were about to go horribly wrong.

She'd been looking at him with the same sense of wonder when Aidan had run into the party and shouted, "There's been an accident. Claire's hurt."

Chad and Claire had put the accident behind them. It was time for Patrick to do so as well and to finish what he'd started that night, heal the memory of the first and only time he'd met her. He pulled her head to his, and their lips came together in the natural fit he remembered with all the attendant sensations he'd put out of his mind because he thought he'd never feel them again. He pressed her lips open with his tongue, and she reciprocated his passion.

No, he wouldn't forget her.

Her hands went around his back so her arms almost encircled him. He pulled her more tightly to him, wanting to touch as much as possible, and the peaks of her nipples pressed through the fabric of his shirt and vest. He knew she could feel him as well, that part of him that wanted to bury itself inside her and make her his. His mind mapped out the most efficient way to get her into the bed, lay her back, and—

He couldn't. He was no gentleman, being of Irish peasant stock, but she was a lady and a virgin and deserved to be treated as such. Although she was the daughter of his enemy, he had no complaint with her and couldn't take advantage of her, no matter how badly she wanted it. How much they both wanted it. With more regret than he'd ever felt, he pulled away again and held her at arm's length. She opened her eyes, and her eyebrows drew down into a look of fury.

"Was that enough of a kiss for you?"

"Why did you stop again?" She crossed her arms and rubbed her hands over her shoulders. He, too, felt the absence of the warmth they'd created together.

"Because you're a young lady from a good family, and you need to save yourself for your future husband."

"Ha! What future husband? My stepfather hasn't found anyone who offers something good enough to trade me for." She turned and grabbed the blanket from the bed. She wrapped it around her, and rather than hiding her appeal, it made her look like a Celtic goddess in a cape.

"Still, you're a virgin." He frowned, a suspicion forming in his mind—had she rebelled? "Aren't ye?"

She sat on the bed with a huff. "Yes, I'm a virgin. Of course I am. Do you think he would let anyone near me like this?" She gestured to the small distance that separated them. "He wants me pristine for my future master."

The hopelessness and resignation in her voice resonated with his own. They were both stuck in their situations.

"Do you want to be married?"

"If I could make a love match, yes. Like Claire McPhee. And if he would be someone not like my stepfather."

Patrick thought of Edward and Johann, both of whom were happily married to spirited women. "Not all men want to rule their wives."

"No, but most gentlemen do."

He didn't have an argument for that. Plus, she wasn't in the mood to view her situation positively, and he didn't like the thought of her being married off as part of a business deal.

"Listen to your message tube," she said. "Here, I have a player. Sometimes music helps settle my stomach." She pointed to the corner, where she'd set up her equipment. "I'm going to put myself back together." She rose and went into the lavatory, shutting the door behind her.

The quality of her sound would be better on her equipment than on the makeshift player Patrick had fashioned from the clockwork wyrm. He put the tube in and cranked the handle until he found the right speed to make the words on the cylinder sensible.

"We're following below you. Will come for you at 0600 while most of ship asleep. Look for double-chambered cruiser and take escape compartment. Will pick you up."

Patrick glanced at the clock—five thirty. That gave him half an hour to wait and plan. But did he want to escape? Cobb would sabotage Chad and Claire's chances of legally marrying.

But he had enough information to pass on to Davidson, perhaps enough for him to make an arrest or at least investigate further and shed suspicion on Cobb. Plus, he didn't want Cobb to get hold of the aether device or anything like it. He could deceive Cobb, but not Louisa, and he had no doubt Cobb would wield Louisa and her talent against him.

No, making a break for it would be the most logical thing.

He hated that he had to balance his friends' needs against his own and those of innocent people, but he didn't have a choice. He grabbed the cylinder and two of the pillows from the bed, threw them through the trap door, and jumped on the trunk and hoisted himself through. He listened for noises outside the room and was pleased to hear snoring. That would make things easier. He placed the pillows under the blankets on his cot so at first glance he would seem to be asleep. Then he went back. He tossed his bag down first but came upon a problem.

Closing the door behind him proved to be difficult, as it lacked a string or handle. Obviously it had been designed as an emergency means of exit. Could he leave it open? No, he didn't want Louisa to be accused of complicity in his escape. Nor did he want her reputation to be at risk. Patrick acknowledged his ruthless side, but it was nothing compared to Cobb's, and women tended to be blamed for men's actions against their purity. Patrick would have to hold the door with one hand and lower himself with the other as he pulled it to behind him. He managed to do so, but the drop to Louisa's trunk was longer than he remembered, or maybe his arms were fatigued. Either way, he tumbled into Louisa's bedroom, and the trap door slammed shut behind him.

———

Louisa heard everything through the thin wooden door between the bedroom and water closet. She braided her hair and splashed water on her face to calm the furious reddening that came to her cheeks when she thought of what she'd wanted—still wanted— Patrick to do to her. When she heard him exiting, she dashed out and to the closet just in time to see his feet disappearing.

What is he doing? And where did my pillows go?

Still wrapped in the blanket, she watched and waited for him to reappear, which he did momentarily with a loud thud. He wore his vest and jacket, and he carried his bag.

"What are you going to do?" she asked. "And could you be a little louder? You'll have the guards upon us."

He took her hands, and hers were small and cold in his large ones.

"Don't worry. I'm going to slip out and hide until it's time for my friends to pick me up. I closed the door so they wouldn't know you were involved."

"But you took my pillows. They're monogrammed, you oaf."

"Right. I didn't think that through."

"Your friends had a lot of faith you'd be able to escape," she said and tried not to make it sound like a barb.

"Come with me. You've time to dress if you're fast. I promise I won't watch."

The tension had disappeared from his jaw with the promise of freedom. She was tempted. What would it be like to drop away and start a new life with a new family? She'd done it before, when her mother married Parnaby Cobb when Louisa was a child.

But she knew Parnaby. He wouldn't let her go that easily. Her talent was too valuable to him.

"I can't."

"Why not?"

She couldn't help but think he'd asked her many more questions at this point than she'd posed to him, which was unusual. But then, there wasn't anything "usual" about their current situation.

"Because I'll be a danger to you and your friends."

He brushed a stray curl behind her ear. "You can just join Marie, then. Cobb has been after her since she claimed her talent in Paris."

"Marie's back?" Louisa clasped her hands. "Oh, that's wonderful! I've missed her, although I doubt she's thought of me."

"She never mentioned you, no." Her little clock chimed five-forty-five, and the door to the laboratory above them opened with a squeak. Patrick grabbed his bag.

"Are you coming or not?"

She bit her lip. It hurt that Marie hadn't mentioned her, but she hadn't ever treated the maid like a friend. What would it be like to be equals? Would it feel awkward? And Louisa was angry with Cobb for treating her like a treasured pet, not a person, but he'd given her security when her mother died. Could she leave that for an uncertain future with a man she hardly knew?

Looking at the consequences of leaving with Patrick made her feel the same as when she'd glanced at the far-away ground from the conference room window—dizzy and terrified.

"No. I can't be that ungrateful to him. I do owe him everything."

"Then can I count on you not to give me away?"

"I will do what I can. And, Patrick, be careful."

He crushed her to him with a quick kiss, then disappeared.

After locking the door behind him, Louisa rearranged the remaining pillows on her bed and spread the blanket before hopping in and curling into a ball around her cold hands. Footsteps sounded above her and crossed the room as Patrick had done. Unfortunately whoever was above her discovered her pillows quickly, and someone walked over to and paused above her closet.

I'm asleep, I'm asleep, I'm asleep, she chanted in her head.

"Wake the master. The prisoner is gone."

"Where'd he go?"

"I don't know, but those are Misses' pillows. See the embroidery?"

Louisa cursed under her breath. *That stupid man.* She rose and put on her wrapper just before a heavy knock sounded at her door.

"What is it?" She tried to sound like she'd just woken.

"Louisa, answer the door." That was Cobb, and the gravel in

his voice said he'd been pulled from his bed and wasn't too happy about it.

"Just a minute."

"Now."

Louisa opened the door to the irate faces of her stepfather, Morlock, and the man whom she assumed had been guarding Patrick.

"Where is he?" Cobb asked. He held a lantern up to illuminate the room behind Louisa, and she squinted against the glare.

"Who?"

"Don't play coy with me. Was he in here? Did he—?" He pushed Louisa out of the way and knelt on the floor. There was still sawdust on the carpet. "Where did this come from?"

Louisa shrugged. "I'll talk to the maid about it in the morning."

Morlock stalked to the closet and looked up. "The trap door's been opened."

Cobb stood and said in a slow, even, terrifying tone, "I'm going to give you one more chance to answer me, Louisa. Where is the prisoner?"

"He's escaped." She glanced at the clock—ten 'til six. Would he have taken the escape pod early in hopes his friends would see him? But it was pitch black outside. They wouldn't be looking for him, and what if he crashed in the mountains?

"And did you help him?"

"No. He just came through my closet."

"Then how'd he have yer pillows, Miss?" Morlock asked. "He tried to make it look like he were sleeping in his bed."

"He must have taken them when I went to hide in the lavatory."

Cobb's bushy gray eyebrows met over the bridge of his nose. Louisa knew their conferring wouldn't be good for her.

"You're not telling the truth. Come here." He looked at her face, turning it to the right and left under the light. Then he let her go, but with a light slap across her face. It wasn't enough to leave a mark, but enough to sting her pride. "You've got beard marks around your mouth, girl. What were you doing in here?"

She pressed her lips together in humiliation.

"Search this level," Cobb told the men. "We would have seen him if he'd gone upstairs. I'll deal with you later, stepdaughter."

Louisa checked the clock—five 'til six. *Just go,* she thought toward Patrick. Parnaby's hand mark still stung on her cheek.

No, wait, I want to go.

She threw on a day dress over her shift—no time to put on a corset—and after tying it as quickly as she could and checking to see the men weren't outside her room, she ran toward the escape hatches. She opened one—it was empty. Then the second one—still nothing. She reached for the third, and a hairy hand grabbed her wrist.

"Are you looking for something?" Morlock asked with a sneer. "Hey, Mister, over here!" He threw the lever that would keep the escape hatch from being disconnected from the inside. The door was locked, but Morlock held Louisa, his fetid breath closer than was necessary, as his companion forced the compartment open with an axe and Cobb supervised. When there was a hole big enough for the man to peer in, a fist punched him and sent him reeling back.

Morlock tossed Louisa aside and jumped in.

"Don't hurt him," she cried and tried to follow Morlock, but Cobb held her back. The two men subdued Patrick and dragged him out. When he saw Louisa, he narrowed his eyes.

"You told them where to find me?" Betrayal coated his voice.

"Yep, led us right to you," Morlock said.

"No, I didn't mean to." Louisa reached for Patrick, but Cobb wheeled her around and put a hand over her mouth.

"This is for the best, dear daughter. He's beneath you. Whatever you feel for him, it's just a passing infatuation. There are better men for you out there."

By that time, the two guards had taken Patrick out of the corridor, and Cobb released Louisa.

"You had just better hope he didn't ruin you," Cobb snarled. "It'll be hard enough to marry you off without you being spoiled, you ungrateful chit."

Louisa pulled free, stalked to her room, and slammed the door behind her. As satisfying as the sound was, it didn't help her bruised heart.

A passing infatuation? It's been six years. She sat on the bed and hugged one of the remaining pillows to her. The other two dropped through the trap door, but she ignored them and turned her face toward the windows and the little table where her cylinder player stood.

She frowned. Patrick had left his message tube. She went to the table and picked it up, marveling at the scratches and pits on it that had produced the voice. What would his friends think? They were still in danger floating far below waiting for him. What if Cobb or one of the *Blooming Senator*'s sailors saw them?

She took out her quill sharpener and drew a big X on the waxy surface before popping it back into its wire cage. Then she opened her window, ignoring the frigid air, and dropped the cylinder out and away. Hopefully that would give the message to Patrick's erstwhile rescuers that they would have to find another opportunity.

CHAPTER FIVE

Somewhere over the Eastern seaboard, 11 March 1871

Iris squinted through the telescope at the *Blooming Senator*, willing the escape compartment at the end to detach and float down to them. Enough light came from the moon that she could make out the ship's air balloon, but she knew the only parts of the escape compartment she'd be able to see would be the parachutes. She fought back the panic that arose at the memory of her own harrowing escape from that very airship a mere nine months before. For Patrick's sake, she hoped Cobb had had the compartments inspected and their parachutes fixed.

"See anything yet?" Marie asked.

"No. The ship remains intact." Iris lowered the device and rubbed her eyes. "I don't know if I can watch anymore. Here." She handed the telescope to Marie and rotated her head to loosen her shoulder muscles.

Marie peered up and frowned. "I think something just fell from the ship." She yelled through the message tube to the bridge. "Nets out! He's sending something back."

"Are you sure it's from him?" Iris asked.

"We need to catch it and see." Marie grinned, and Iris couldn't help but smile back even though she was so tired her cheeks ached. Marie loved her adventures, and Iris knew that no matter where Marie landed, she'd be happy as long as she could continue to find challenges.

The *Skycatcher* tilted as it turned to intercept the tube, and Iris clutched the observation deck's railing with one hand and Marie with the other so her friend wouldn't tumble into the opposite bank of windows.

"I should've anticipated that," Marie said and grabbed the railing. "All that time lifting rocks out of the way gave you some good arm muscles."

"Thanks, I think," Iris said. She was happy to hold on with both arms.

The *Skycatcher* righted itself, and both women slumped to the floor and shook out their arms and shoulders.

"Are you two all right up there?" Johann asked through the tube. His voice sounded tinny.

"Yes, but give us some warning next time," Marie replied.

"Sorry, but we got it. Armand's landing now."

Iris looked at the glow that was the *Blooming Senator* until it disappeared behind the clouds. Still no parachutes.

"Something went wrong." Disappointment made Iris slump against the cool window.

"Don't worry, we'll rescue him somehow," Marie told her. "Can you manage the ladder?"

"Yes." Iris didn't allow her disappointment to show but knew her friend suspected her feelings. *What will it take to bring us all together again?*

A chill slithered between her shoulders at the thought, and she flexed them back to stop it. *My arms are fatigued from having to catch Marie, that's all.*

Marie preceded Iris down the ladder, and Edward supported Iris for the last few rungs. She felt disloyal for thinking it, but she was glad to be on solid ground again. The glass-enclosed gas lamps on the side of the airship flared to life to illuminate the nets, and Johann untangled the wire-encased wax tube.

"Did he put another message on it?" Iris asked.

"Not really, just this." Johann showed the rest of them the tube, which had a big X scratched on it.

"What does it mean?" Edward asked.

"That he doesn't want us to come after him, maybe?" Iris wasn't sure. "Is it too dangerous?"

The four of them exchanged stricken looks. The Irishman had been a great help to them, twice in Paris with Edward and then in the few weeks he and Chadwick Radcliffe had spent with them in the Ottoman Empire. More than his brawn and his genius way with devices, Iris missed his easy laugh and the way he found the humor in most situations. And if he got bored, he created conflict, which didn't always work out well, but still... She didn't trust Cobb not to harm him.

Marie frowned and took the cylinder from Johann's hand. She unwrapped a hair that had gotten tangled in the wires when the device was reassembled.

"Looks like yours," Johann said.

"It's not. It's too fine to be mine. Patrick may be in more trouble than we thought."

"How so?" Iris asked.

"This belongs to Louisa, Cobb's stepdaughter. I had to clean her hairbrushes often enough I recognize it. She's not as bad as Cobb is, but she's a spoiled young lady."

"Is Patrick in danger?" Iris frowned up at the sky like she could make the airship reappear and reassure her the Irishman was all right.

"Only if he loses his heart to her. She's been known to deceive men, take what she or her stepfather wants, and spit them out."

———

Claire sat at the table in the dining car and watched the scenery pass by. Well, as much of the scenery as she could see through the dark. Occasionally the train would go through a field, and she'd catch a glimpse of a farmhouse beyond, the light from the hearth glowing through the windows. Sometimes the fields had steam-tillers turning the early spring soil in anticipation of planting when the sun came up.

She stifled a yawn. She normally wouldn't be up so early for breakfast, especially after catching the train so late the night before, but the cook and steward were doing her and her fiancé a favor by allowing them to eat together before it opened for the regular patrons at seven. Otherwise, since they weren't yet married, she traveled in a private car and he with the colored passengers in a car at the back.

"Right this way, Doctor."

Claire looked up and smiled when she saw her breakfast companion. Her heart never failed to lift when he turned his gray eyes on her. A grin lit his face.

"You look beautiful," he said and kissed her on the cheek.

"Thank you." She felt beautiful when he looked at her even if she'd been lamenting the dark circles under her eyes that the window showed her when there wasn't anything to see beyond it. When she slept, she heard the screams of the soldiers who had died as a result of her and Patrick O'Connell's invention. Even though the aether weapon *La Reine* had ended the war and freed millions, she shuddered at the cost.

"How did you sleep?" she asked. She wanted to revel in this feeling of normalcy, manufactured though it may be by the kindness of the dining car staff.

"Fine. The negro car is more comfortable than the barracks, but someone in there snores even worse than Patrick."

Lawrence, the steward brought two menus and a steaming pot of coffee. He talked as he poured the fragrant liquid into their cups.

"Straight from New Orleans with a little chicory to get you going."

"Thank you so much for doing this," Claire said.

"It's my pleasure, Miss. Now what can I bring you to eat?"

Claire opened her mouth to order, but the door to the dining car banged open, and she heard a voice that had haunted her nightmares.

"What is *he* doing in here, dining like a regular person?"

The look on Chadwick's face confirmed it—not only was their intimate breakfast interrupted by a racist, the bigot in question was Claire's aunt, Eliza. Claire hunched her shoulders and hid her hands underneath the table. She wore her shorter gloves, and the ropy scars at her wrists were evident. If her aunt Eliza hadn't figured out who Chad was—and if she had, she surely would have said so—then maybe she wouldn't recognize Claire.

"Excuse me," Lawrence said and moved toward the disruption. "I'm sorry, ma'am, but the dining car isn't open for general service yet."

"I'm not here for general service. Do I *look* like the general public?"

Chad sipped his coffee and with a wink mouthed, "She's the same but fatter. Do you want me to say something to her?"

"I have no doubt, and no." Claire envied Chad's and Lawrence's composure. She also appreciated Chad taking her cue rather than being a typical male and confronting Eliza. There needed to be a conversation at some point, but not until Claire could talk to her mother. Now that she had all her memories back—including the ones of the evening when she'd been injured —Claire feared she would say something inappropriate to her aunt, and she didn't want a scene.

It seemed that Eliza didn't mind making one, however.

"I demand to be served," Eliza was saying. "This train is too slow. I have an important meeting in Boston for my niece's bridal shower, and I don't trust my sister to manage the details correctly. I'll be disembarking in Terminus to catch an airship, and I need breakfast beforehand. I can't handle takeoff on an empty stomach."

"If you like, I can have something sent to your car." Lawrence seemed determined to match Eliza's stubbornness. Claire fought the urge to cheer him on.

"How does she know?" Chad murmured.

"I telegraphed Aidan to tell Mother we're coming home. He must have given her some of the details but not all of them."

Eliza bowled over Lawrence's offer with, "I don't have room for a tray to eat in my compartment. My passage was booked at the last minute, so I only have a berth, not the car I'm used to, so I must eat here."

"We need to leave," Claire said. Eliza's familiar self-importance and irritability at anyone who dared contradict her grated against Claire's heart. Worse, it threatened to set off the blocks the Parisian neuroticists had hypnotized into her, which she thought had been healed. Her ears buzzed, and blackness appeared at the edges of her vision. Her face felt hot and cold simultaneously, and from Chad's concerned expression, she guessed she had gone even paler than her natural state.

"Can you stand?"

"I think so." She inhaled through her nose and exhaled out of her mouth. She hadn't felt like this since before her hypnotic blocks had been removed. She shouldn't have anything like that now, so why was she reacting?

It's probably just good, old-fashioned nervous hysteria at meeting my evil aunt unprepared.

But logic wasn't helping. She wanted to strip off her gloves to cool her hands but dared not.

Chad stood and said, "Lawrence, thank you, but my fiancée isn't feeling well. We're going to head back to her cabin."

"I'll send something along for you momentarily," the steward replied calmly, as if he wasn't engaged in a battle of wills.

"Good," Eliza said. "I'm glad somebody knows his place." She settled into the booth nearest her with an audible puff of air from her skirts.

Now Claire had a different problem, walking by Eliza

without being recognized. She hoped her aunt would be too engrossed in the menu, but she guessed not. Most people were fascinated, and many appalled, when they saw her and Chad together.

Chad helped Claire stand and held her while she accustomed herself to the motion of the train under her boots and the wobbliness that had come to her knees. He walked between her and Eliza, but the older woman said, "Stop! You look familiar, negro."

"I'm sorry, but I have to get my fiancée to her room."

Claire turned as if she was looking out of the window. *Come on, come on...*

"You're not allowed in that part of the train."

"I'll pretend to be her servant. Good day, Madam."

He and Claire rushed from the dining car and through the connection into the first coach compartment. They didn't stop until they reached her berth, one of the smaller ones but still big enough for two people comfortably.

"Guess I'm stuck here until Terminus," Chad said with a grin. "I'll slip off and back to my car when we stop."

"Don't." Claire took his hand. "Stay here with me. It's not right for you to have to ride back there. It's not right for anyone, and I won't see you again until we arrive."

"You know I agree with you," he said and took her in his arms. "But that's how it is for now. Just wait till we're in Boston and can use our influence to change things. We're war heroes, remember?"

She nodded but didn't tell him she didn't feel like much of a hero. He had enough to worry about.

"Since when are you such an optimist?" Claire teased instead.

"Since I have reason to be one." He leaned in for a kiss, and Claire closed her eyes, ready to lose herself in it.

Once again their romantic moment was interrupted by the arrival of her aunt, who flung the door open.

"I thought that was you, Claire McPhee. You should have

learned your lesson. You're getting off with me at Terminus so you can explain to the Ladies' Guild why you won't be having a wedding, after all."

Claire straightened but held Chad's hand. "No, Aunt Eliza, I will do no such thing. Doctor Chadwick Radcliffe and I are engaged." She narrowed her eyes and dared her aunt to contradict her.

"Is this her?" The conductor appeared behind Eliza.

"Yes, this is my poor niece." Eliza dabbed her eyes. "She's been under the influence of this negro charlatan and is convinced she's engaged to him. She's had hysteria before. We had to send her for treatment in Paris."

Claire fought the wave of heat that rose from her chest and threatened to close her throat. She kept her voice calm and, she hoped, professional. "I am Doctor Claire McPhee," she said, "and this is my fiancé, Doctor Chadwick Radcliffe. We're on our way from Fort Daniels in Tennessee back to Boston. Perhaps you've heard of the decisive Union victory there?"

"Yes, but the papers said that was an Irishman, not a negro or a girl." The conductor sniffed. "Look here, if this lady says you're not right in the head, I'm not going to argue with her. Now come along."

Two burly stewards came in, but instead of grabbing Claire, they took hold of Chad so he couldn't help her.

"I will do no such thing, and unhand my fiancé! Telegraph to Fort Daniels at the next stop and ask for Major Longchamp. He'll send word corroborating our story."

"Don't believe a word she says, poor dear." Eliza patted Claire on the arm and added in a stage whisper, "She spent time in an asylum. They hypnotized her so she'd seem normal."

Claire drew back as much as she could in the small space. "I am normal. I am a neuroticist, and *you're* suffering from delusions of grandeur."

"No, I'm simply your caring aunt, and they're not delusions." Eliza took Claire by the upper arm and pulled her from the room. "Now come along. You've kept me from having breakfast, and I'm going to be very cross with you."

"Now as for you," the conductor said to Chad, "I'm going to hand you over to the authorities at the next stop..."

With a sinking feeling, Claire realized what she should have since she first knew Eliza was on the train—her aunt had bribed the conductor. And now Claire was stuck and Chad would be ejected in Terminus, lucky if they waited for the train to slow first. She hoped she could get help for Chad once she arrived in Boston.

CHAPTER SIX

Boston International Airfield, 11 March 1871

Louisa tapped her toe as she waited for her trunk to be loaded on the carriage. She had never been so glad to have an airship ride behind her even if this was the one she'd felt the least ill during. It was amazing how well fury kept her stomach from trying to turn itself inside out. After she'd dropped the message cylinder out of the window, she'd found herself unable to sleep, so she'd had plenty of time to stew over the night's events.

She kept coming back to how she should have accompanied Patrick when he first asked, even if the thought of dropping away from her former life into a new one made her stomach flip worse than air travel did.

Could she make it on her own without Parnaby Cobb's patronage? She didn't know if she could trust Patrick to take care of her—she hardly knew him, after all, and he'd immediately assumed the worst about her when he was discovered—and she certainly didn't have any marketable skills with which to earn a living. She couldn't tell others about her talent. No one would believe her.

As for marrying... That seemed her best course of action, as she was still attractive and young enough to bear children. But she needed Cobb to approve of her finding a husband since he would provide the dowry.

Thankfully her stepfather had remained behind to attend to some business. She didn't know what kind, and she didn't care. Well, not for him. She craned her neck to peer behind her for a glimpse of Patrick's orange-red hair and beard as her carriage rolled away from the *Blooming Senator*.

It hardly seems fair that a capable woman like me should have to depend on a man for her fortune and keeping.

She watched the marshlands that surrounded the air field turn into the outskirts of the city. Steamcarts joined the horse-drawn vehicles on the rails laid into the cobblestone streets, and her carriage's progress slowed, especially as they reached the city center and the congested commercial areas. The trees were still bare, and patches of dirty snow gathered in corners and along curbs. A few shrubs showed signs of new budding life trying to come through. Louisa focused on those. She recalled something her mother had told her when she was a little girl, how fairies came in the spring and woke up the plants from their winter sleep.

Louisa needed a fairy godmother now. *And a prince would be nice.* She'd had disagreements with her stepfather before, but he'd never laid a hand on her. She shouldn't have allowed Patrick enough liberties for signs of their tryst to be evident on her face, which still flamed at the memory. But Patrick O'Connell's kisses had awakened something in her like her mother's fairies did with the plants. She had never attempted to defy Cobb before, and she knew from having observed him with his underlings that there would likely be hell to pay even beyond her hidden bruise. As was typical for him, he'd hurt her, and it stung, but she thought it wouldn't show. Or maybe she hoped it wouldn't.

When Louisa arrived at the townhouse on Beacon Hill, she exited the carriage and drew her shawl against the wind that didn't carry even a hint of the spring softness she'd briefly enjoyed in Tennessee. *Fine—the weather matches my mood.*

Louisa freshened up in her room and glanced at the bed. Now that she was in her familiar surroundings, the events on the airship retreated into the same realm of reality as vivid dreams. Could she go to sleep and wake up that morning in her own bed and in her old life, where her position with Cobb was secure and she didn't have to worry about an Irishman who kissed like an angel and made her want to do things that would shock her priest?

The little clock on her bedside table told her it was just past noon, time for lunch. She hadn't heard any of the noises that would indicate her stepfather had returned, which both delighted and annoyed her. She didn't care for his company and was happy he likely had gone to his offices, but she wanted to know what had become of Patrick. Where would he be staying? Working? And how could she make him understand she hadn't betrayed him?

When she reached the bottom of the front stairs, the butler met her with a telegram on a tray and said, "This just came. And there is a woman here to see you."

The tone of his voice when he said *woman* told Louisa a commoner visited her, so she took the telegram first. She smiled for the first time that day when she read it. Eliza Adams had sent it from a place called Terminus, which as Louisa recalled was somewhere in the Deep South, with her regrets that she wouldn't be able to host the tea to plan her niece's wedding that afternoon since she was detained on important business. Her final words—*shocking news, come for tea tomorrow*—piqued Louisa's curiosity. She had to attend a rally earlier in the day and play the dutiful daughter, but she could make an afternoon event.

Eliza must be in a state if she's inviting me through a telegram and not a hand-written invitation. I hope Bryce is all right.

Eliza's son was at the front, somewhere in Tennessee, but since the war was finally over, there shouldn't be any more fighting. Louisa hadn't paid much attention to the papers beyond the headlines.

And now on to the second surprise of the afternoon...

"Please send a note to the Adams' house that I will be delighted to attend tea tomorrow. As for the visitor, I'm not expecting anyone. Did the woman give you a card?" There wasn't anything on the tray besides the telegram, so she doubted it.

"No, Miss, but she said to give you this." He handed her a locket.

The chain and locket itself were tarnished but otherwise in good shape. Louisa opened it and saw the two photos were of handsome dark-haired people. One of them looked like her, but with an old-fashioned hairstyle and a neckline that was a score out of date. With a toe-to-head shiver, she realized it was her mother. The picture on the other side was of a young man who looked familiar, but only because Louisa saw his chin in the mirror every day.

It was her father, the man who had disappeared when she was a small child. The only memories she had of him were vague flashes of sense—the smell of his wool sailor's coat and tobacco, the feel of his coarse dark hair under her little hands and his whiskers on her cheek when he kissed her goodbye. She had tried so hard, especially after her mother died, to remember what he looked like, but she'd been unable to, and her mother in her grief had hidden all his pictures.

With great care not to allow the upwelling of gratitude and grief to show, she closed the locket with a snap. "Very well, I will see her."

"Very good, Miss. I had her wait in the library."

Louisa nodded. This visitor wasn't of high enough rank to show to the parlor. But when Louisa arrived at the library, it was empty. The visitor had left a piece of paper with an address scrawled on it under the one lit lamp. She didn't know exactly where the place was, only that it was in the poor part of town she and Cobb were to be in the next day.

It looks like I'll have an errand to run.

After one more look at the pictures, Louisa slipped the locket's chain over her head and tucked it beneath her blouse so her parents could rest close to her heart. It seemed a small miracle amid the turmoil of the day, and she allowed one tear to escape before she wiped it away.

After the moment of sentiment, her logic kicked back in. Even if she would end up near the address on the paper the following day, Cobb wouldn't let her go. Plus, with their current state of mutual mistrust, he would have his men watch her like one of those creepy steam ravens and hawks made by Paul Farrell, Cobb's pet inventor.

I need to find that woman today.

Cobb wouldn't expect Louisa to remain at home because he would think she was meeting with Eliza.

This may be the only free afternoon I have for months.

Louisa found the butler in the pantry. He gave her a surprised look—she hadn't ventured into the servants' areas since she had been a child and still learning the difference between her and them—but she ignored it.

"The woman who left this—what did she look like?"

He shrugged. "Ordinary, I suppose. Of the working class, but well-enough dressed."

She clenched her teeth against the frustration that rose in a wave from her middle. Of course he wouldn't have paid that much attention to someone he considered beneath him. She might not have, either, but she needed details.

"How old was she? What color was her hair? When she spoke, could you tell what part of town she came from?"

"I'm sorry, Miss, but I can't tell you." Now he at least had the courtesy to look embarrassed. "Ah, but she did drop something."

Louisa followed the butler back to the library, where he pulled a small piece of paper from the dustbin and handed it to her. She saw it was a ticket to the nearest trolley station.

"Thank you." She dashed upstairs to her rooms, donned her

gloves, shawl, and daytime bonnet, and paused at the front door. It would be unseemly for her to go unescorted anywhere, particularly to the trolley station, where those of lower classes might congregate.

But this was possibly her only chance to catch the woman and find out more about her father—her true father. She opened the front door and, after a glance in either direction to ensure no one she knew was out and about, she closed the door quietly and descended the steps to the street.

———

Patrick stood by the laboratory window and watched the airship being unloaded. Even if he dared risk a broken leg or worse by breaking the window and escaping through it, the guard who stood by the door with weapon in hand kept him from considering it. Patrick hadn't been alone since his botched escape attempt that morning. At least he had the memory of Louisa's kisses for company even if she had betrayed him after.

He understood why—or thought he did—but her actions still stung. She was dependent on Cobb and needed to stay in his good graces. Going with Patrick was too big a risk, although it smarted that she didn't trust he'd take care of her.

But why had she led the men right to him? Had she changed her mind and made a mistake, or was she trying to put herself in Cobb's good graces? Patrick knew Cobb had a ruthless streak, but he didn't think Louisa had inherited it.

Her carriage had rolled away two hours beforehand, and if he was the poetic type, he'd have said the day grew darker when she left. But no poetry was needed. The clouds gathered and hung heavy with the promise of snow. They only contributed to his bleak mood.

The door opened, and Cobb strode in.

"We're ready to go to the city," he said. "Are you going to come peacefully, or shall I have the guards knock you out for transport? I'm giving you one chance to act like a civilized human being."

"Just one?" Patrick eyed the monkey-faced guard, who looked all too pleased at the idea of coshing him over the head with the butt of his steam rifle, or whatever else he would use.

"Your humor is lost on Morlock," Cobb said. "I've never seen the man smile unless he's doing violence to someone. Or thinking about it."

The man in question lifted one corner of his mouth in a lopsided grin, and Patrick didn't want to know what he imagined. Patrick had confidence he could overpower Morlock if they were hand-to-hand, but the weapon put Patrick at too great a disadvantage.

"Fine, I'll come along peacefully."

"Good." Cobb nodded as if he had anticipated the answer. "Oh, and if you have any notion of escaping once we're close to the city, I just received this." He tossed a folded telegram on the table. Patrick picked it up and cursed under his breath as he read it.

"Have Claire in Terminus. Negro detained. Home this evening. E.A."

Patrick looked up from the telegram, which appeared official, to Cobb's gloating grin.

"As fortune would have it, I had already arranged for Eliza Adams to be on the same train as Doctors McPhee and Radcliffe, who attempted to sneak away from Danielsville in the middle of the night." Cobb shook his head. "Your attempt to escape last night indicated you didn't think I was serious about interfering with their plans."

"I trusted my friends could take care of themselves." *And then who sent the message tube? The clockwork looked like Edward's work. Have they not rendezvoused with Chad?*

"Ah, then you displayed an admirable amount of ruthlessness risking their freedom for yours. For that I commend you. Perhaps we have more in common than I thought."

Patrick cringed at Cobb's echo of the word ruthless and

fought the urge to clench his fists. He wouldn't show Cobb how the man was getting under his skin. "You and I are nothing alike."

"Oh, I disagree. We both have interest in Claire McPhee, and if you want to see her again, you will cooperate."

Patrick wanted to argue, but he wouldn't stoop to taking Cobb's bait. He only assumed what he hoped was a neutral expression and shrugged.

"Ah, very well," Cobb told him. "Morlock, take the prisoner down to the transport carriage and lock him inside. I have rooms for you in the space at the bottom of my offices, Mister O'Connell. I trust you'll find it comfortable."

"Not bloody likely," Patrick muttered.

"Hands where I can see 'em, Red," Morlock said and gestured for Patrick to precede him and Cobb from the room.

Patrick complied and placed his hands atop his head. Two more guards stood outside the door, and there was nothing within easy reach he could use as a weapon. Plus, if it was true that Claire was back in the clutches of her evil aunt, Patrick would have to cooperate to give her and Chad time to figure things out.

And where the hell was Davidson?

CHAPTER SEVEN

Terminus, 11 March 1871

Inspector Henry Davidson paced outside the train station in Terminus and looked at his pocket watch for the hundredth time. He checked his men's positions for the fiftieth, at least. Richard sat on a bench pretending to read a newspaper. Colin leaned against a wall in shadow. Lou smoked a cigarette on a balcony in a warehouse that was actually their headquarters, but no one but them knew that. Scratch that—Lou had run out. And Eric was inside the station ostensibly waiting on a train. He'd already sent a message out that two telegrams had gone out from an E.A. to Boston, one to Cobb at the airfield and one to his daughter at their residence.

Now that Henry had evidence that Eliza Adams had Claire McPhee, he knew the older woman should be bringing the girl out to one of the waiting carriages to take her to the airship field. They should have seen her by then. The same went for if Chadwick Radcliffe had been detained and escorted off the train. The train itself still stood at the station, but the noise from the engines said it was preparing to leave.

Rescuing Doctor Radcliffe was the top priority. It wouldn't do to have him languishing in a Southern prison. Every delay put the man's life in danger. Here they were waiting to intercept him and confirm Cobb's plans for Claire McPhee, so where was everyone?

Henry needed this to go well. He thought he'd planned ahead by having Claire and Chad take a midnight train from Danielsville, but Cobb had been ahead of him every step of the way. Somehow he'd gotten hold of the information about their tickets. Before that, Henry had contacted Iris Bailey and her crew and arranged for them to rescue Patrick O'Connell. He'd hated having to deliver O'Connell to him, but he needed someone on the inside to tell him exactly what Cobb planned, what kind of aether device he wanted and why. Henry doubted that Cobb's interest in the aether was limited to it as a power source, although whoever controlled a viable substitute for coal would be rich. No, Cobb was more subtle than that. At least he hadn't caught on—yet—that Henry was a double agent feeding information about Cobb to his organization.

One thing Henry knew of Cobb—the man liked to gloat, so he would have likely told Patrick what he wanted from him early on. With that information, Henry could catch the shady businessman red-handed in something nefarious. He only hoped Iris and the others had succeeded.

A dark shadow caught Henry's attention, and he spied a large bird swooping overhead. Hawks were native to the area, and this one flew directly over the station. It wasn't after prey, at least as far as Henry could tell. Nor was it circling looking.

There's something unnatural here. Henry coughed. Richard stood, folded his paper, and strolled toward him. Henry signaled to his other men to hold their positions and followed the bird with Richard a few steps behind him.

This could be a wild goose, er, hawk chase, he admonished himself. *I'd never let the others leave their posts like that.* But he'd learned to trust his instincts. They weren't as strong as the special abilities women enjoyed, but he'd found them reliable. So, if there was something unnatural about the bird, he would follow it.

The hawk led him and Richard around the side of the station and past the passenger area to the alley in the back that led to most of the warehouses. The expected carts and wagons were lined up, but there were also a hired carriage and a police cart.

Aha.

With hand signals, he told Richard to round up the other men and split up to watch the different places the cart and carriage could exit the station complex. His priority was to rescue Radcliffe, as Doctor McPhee would be easier to extract in Boston.

"Move it," someone growled. "Gotta get this uppity negro to the station, teach 'im a lesson to keep his filthy hands off a white woman."

Davidson ducked into the shadows and watched as Chadwick Radcliffe was handed none-too-gently into the police wagon. He ducked from the spittle and punches the men aimed at him.

Henry kept himself back with effort. He wanted to intervene, but he was also outnumbered. Terminus city officials' corruption was legendary, and he had no doubt Eliza Adams or Parnaby Cobb had paid good money for the Terminus police to send two, no three, officers to arrest a harmless man.

And two police wagons. Henry cursed under his breath. Of course Cobb had anticipated what Henry would do.

The alley was wide for cargo, so the police cart had plenty of room to maneuver. Henry pulled his cap low and followed the wagon that contained Radcliffe, but someone grabbed his arm. Henry looked up, surprised, into the toothy scowl of a foreman.

"Ain't got no use for lazy men. What team are you with? Get your freckled ass back to work unloading."

Henry twisted his arm out of the other man's grasp and ducked away between some crates. He tried to keep sight of the wagon, which gained speed as it cleared the stacked cargo, but someone tackled him. He spit the filth of the alley from his mouth and tasted blood.

"You won't get away from me so easily, rat," the foreman

said from above him and ground his crotch into Henry's backside. "I didn't get my chance at that nigger, but you'll do, especially since you found us a nice spot all private-like. And don't try to yell. It won't do you any good but might get me more excited."

Henry jerked his head back and felt a satisfying crunch under the back of his own skull. The foreman cursed and rolled off, and Henry staggered to his feet, almost blind with rage, shame, and the stars left from his head punch. A kick to the kidney made sure his would-be rapist wouldn't follow him. The police wagon was gone, and he limped from the alley, hopeful that the liquid running down his leg was puddle water, not blood, but he suspected not.

"Boss?" Colin came to support him. "What happened?"

Henry tried to wave him away, but he stumbled, and Colin caught him. "The wagon. Did you get Radcliffe?"

"It came out too fast for us to jump it, but Eric and Lou are chasing it on horseback."

Henry cursed under his breath and limped in the direction he thought it had taken, but Colin held him back.

"You'll not get far in the shape you're in. Trust them. They'll get the target."

Henry heard what Colin didn't say—that he should have sent his men in after the police wagon if he had a suspicion, not risked himself.

But when you're in the business of espionage, trust doesn't come easy. And I'm used to working on my own.

People stared at the two of them as Colin helped Henry into the alley behind the row of warehouses, but not for long. Injuries were common, the steam contraptions they used to unload the trains not well-maintained and therefore apt to break. There was an infirmary for union workers in the warehouse next to Henry's headquarters, and sometimes the sounds of moaning and screaming kept him awake at night.

Colin brought him through the back entrance to their warehouse and helped him settle on a wooden chair before grabbing the box of medical supplies.

"What happened to you?" Colin asked and rummaged through it.

Henry shrugged and swallowed the acid that tried to come to his throat when he saw the slick dark liquid staining his left pants leg. He could handle other people's blood, but his own... He hated the reminder he was human, a bag of flesh and bone like everyone else.

"I tried to follow the wagon with Radcliffe, and one of the foremen tried to teach me a lesson for shirking my duties."

"They're beasts."

"You're not kidding." Henry shoved the memory of the brute trying to pin him to the ground to the back of his mind. He'd escaped, but there had been a moment he'd been afraid he wouldn't.

"I'm going to need to see the wound." Colin brought out a pair of shears.

"Here, let me." Henry took them and cut the pants leg away. It was his leg, the reddish-brown hair flattened to the freckled skin by moisture. About six inches above the knee a nasty gash of about three inches bled freely now that the cloth that had pressed on it was gone.

"Sorry, Boss." Colin held up a bottle of medical-grade alcohol. "This is going to sting, but god only knows what's in that alley water."

Hoofbeats in the alley heralded the return of the other two men.

"Do whatever you need to do," Henry told him. "It sounds like I'm about to be distracted."

———

Claire looked for opportunities to escape from her evil aunt even before the train slowed, but Eliza seemed to anticipate her. She confiscated Claire's money and anything else Claire might have of value except for Claire's ruby engagement ring, which Claire refused to give her. And Eliza knew Claire wouldn't sell it. When the train stopped, the conductor and a burly officer came to escort them off the train, through the station and into an alley, and into a waiting steamcoach that locked from the outside. Padding covered all the surfaces inside, including the benches.

Claire alternated glaring at her aunt with refusing to look at her during the entire humiliating process. As a neuroticist, she knew what such coaches were for—to bring people to places where they would be processed and disappear. She suspected her fate, should she and Chad fail to get themselves out of their respective pickles, would be similar, but in nicer surroundings with a brute of a husband her aunt would pick for her.

She had no desire for a gilded cage, but she lacked opportunity for escape, as two officers from the airship met the coach at the airfield, which was situated in a flat field south of the town. They escorted her to a private room with a water closet in spite of their only being on the airship for a day. Eliza had stayed behind to supervise the loading of luggage, including Claire's battered trunk, but soon joined her along with a young man who carried a lunch tray. Claire took note of the dull utensils and lack of knife.

"Is that really necessary?" she asked, thankful she could muster a neutral tone in spite of the pressure that built in her chest and wanted her to explode with a mixture of tears, shouting, and shaking—not what she needed to convince the steward that she wasn't a hysteric. Instead, she drew on her professional training, which had taught her to stay calm in the face of strong emotions, even her own.

"I don't want you hurting yourself, dear niece," Eliza said and dabbed at her eyes with a handkerchief. "We've all been so worried about you, running off to the battlefront to be with that negro."

The steward's eyebrows raised, but he didn't say anything.

Claire bit the inside of her lip because she needed to do *something* to express her frustration, even if it was painful to only herself. How had her aunt managed to cut off any potential allies before Claire had a chance to recruit them?

Oh, right, because Eliza was an expert manipulator, as all the women in her set were. Claire didn't want to be dragged back to that world, but circumstances seemed to be conspiring to bring her there.

"You can indulge in all the delusions you want, dear Aunt," Claire said. "But that doesn't change the fact that I am of age, and you are bringing me along against my will."

Now the steward's eyes narrowed. *Good, let him doubt her word.*

Eliza turned to the young man. "She has delusions. Ignore her."

"I am well within my right mind and would like to speak to the captain," Claire told him. "Please arrange for me to do so immediately."

"He's busy with takeoff, ma'am," the boy said, his voice cracking. Claire hadn't realized how young he was until he spoke. Indeed, the ship lifted, and Claire's stomach dropped through her legs and stayed on the ground. Or maybe her heart stayed behind to be with her love, whom she didn't know if she would ever see again.

She sank to the bed, and an electric-feeling jolt made her clasp her hands, locking her fingers so they wouldn't tremble. Chadwick was down there in danger—why could he not be in a newly emancipated city where emotions, particularly resentment, ran high? Claire had no doubt her aunt had arranged for him to be shipped off to some prison, where he would be harshly treated. He wasn't good at playing humble, either, which would make things worse.

"All the more reason for me to speak with the captain," Claire said and tried to keep her voice from shaking.

The boy nodded. "I'll see what I can do, ma'am. Uh, do you want your lunch?"

"No, thank you." Claire didn't trust that the food wouldn't be laced with laudanum or something else that would put her to sleep. "Please let me know when someone is ready to escort me to the captain."

"If you insist on going along with this game, then I insist on being in attendance," Eliza said. "I am her aunt and I will not allow her to risk her reputation to bring others into her foolishness."

Claire shrugged as though she didn't care. She had no doubt Eliza would do everything in her power to besmirch Claire's credibility, but Claire could figure out how to handle the situation. She'd been dealing with neurotic people for years.

———

"This will be your laboratory." Cobb opened the door to a basement space with a key that looked like it belonged more to a Gothic tale than to a warehouse that had been converted to offices near the wharves. Patrick couldn't help but notice the expressions of the three men around him, the guard Cobb had designated from the airship field to town. The thugs' pugnaciousness had been replaced by caution, and two of them held back such that they stood closer to the nearest door than the one Cobb had just unlocked. Only Morlock stood near, tethered to Patrick by the rope that confined Patrick's wrists.

"So I'm to be the damsel in the basement?" Patrick asked. "What kind of monsters should I be worried about?"

Cobb laughed, but his men didn't. "Don't worry, no one's actually seen anything down there."

"Nay, there have just been noises, bumps, and equipment turned over," Morlock said with a gleeful tone. "I wouldn't sleep too soundly if I was you."

Patrick would have stroked his beard had his hands not been tied. Putting both of them to his face would have looked ridiculous, so he stuck with a sage nod. "Good thing I'm Irish, then. I'm well versed in supernatural beasties."

"Then you're just the man for the job." Cobb gestured for Patrick to precede him into the gloom. "Plus we men of science don't believe in such things, do we?"

Patrick decided not to contradict Cobb even though the man was holding him prisoner in order to chase the supernatural abilities of a strange substance. And he certainly wasn't going to agree. Patrick descended the narrow stairs and suppressed his wince when the echo of the door slamming behind him reverberated off the stone walls. The space was lit by gas lamps with what he'd come to recognize as the Cobb design, enclosed with extra tubes into the glass for gas and oxygen intake and exhaust, perfect for poorly ventilated spaces where carbon dioxide and monoxide may build to dangerous levels. He sniffed the air—mold, the acrid edge of coal dust, an overtone of street smell and just the barest hint of saltwater. He guessed there was a grate somewhere and that he wouldn't be able to fit through, but he would check once they left him alone. Holes could always be widened.

"What was this place?" Patrick asked. The feel of age told him it preceded the buildings atop it.

"Old Revolutionary gunpowder storage turned coal cellar." Cobb gestured to the rough-hewn walls. "None of that's here anymore, of course, but I find it useful for keeping precious things I don't want others to know I have."

"Ah, I didn't know you cared, but I can't say that I feel the same about you. Perhaps we should just call things off, then."

Patrick moved toward the stairs, but Morlock stepped in front of him.

"Nice try, Red," he growled. "I'm looking forward to not having to see your ugly mug on my ship anymore."

"Now that feeling I can say is mutual."

Morlock cut Patrick's bonds off none-too-gently, and Patrick flexed his fingers, relieved the thug had missed his skin with the knife. He thought about making a dash up the stairs, but the other two bruisers waited up there, and he didn't want to give Morlock the opportunity to shoot him in the back. Instead he flexed his fingers to get through the pins and needles faster so he could think.

"I'll have your equipment delivered later," Cobb said. "Meanwhile, make yourself comfortable."

"As comfortable as you can," Morlock added, his crooked-toothed grin frightening.

Cobb ascended the stairs followed by Morlock, who walked backwards up the steps, gun trained on Patrick, until he rounded the bend. Patrick continued to rub his hands, gritting his teeth against the stabbing return of sensation. When it had subsided to a merely uncomfortable buzz, he walked the perimeter of his prison, alert for any draft that might give him a direction for escape. As he suspected, there was a grate over the nook where a stone privy stood, but it was too narrow for him to fit through and too high for him to reach even if he were to stand on the toilet.

Patrick cursed under his breath. He hoped Cobb had been lying to him about Claire being in her Aunt Eliza's custody and Chad being gods only knew where. He paced back and forth in the space that made up his prison, about ten by twenty feet with the alcove for the privy. A straw mattress lay on the other side. He walked up the stairs and paused at the door. A narrow crack underneath let the light through, and he made out the shadow of a guard standing outside shifting his weight from foot to foot. Patrick remembered the guards' consternation and Morlock's glee and wondered what exactly they'd been afraid of.

And how he could use it against them.

When he descended into the former coal cellar again, the light flickered in spite of being enclosed so it shouldn't, and the sensation of cold mist on his exposed skin made his hair stand on end. When he ran a finger over the back of his other hand, he found it to be dry except for the sweat that had popped out.

"I see I'm not alone down here," he said. "Whoever you are, show yourself."

Nothing appeared, but the temperature rose, and the light returned to its normal steady illumination from its fixture.

So it seems the monster isn't accustomed to being addressed. However, he didn't know what it would do when he let his guard down. Was it a normal generally harmless ghost or something more sinister? If it could knock over equipment, he would have to befriend it if possible. If not, he would have to sleep with one eye open, as Morlock suggested.

Patrick shivered again, this time from a draft from the grate, and pulled his coat more tightly around himself. It seemed he would have to be on his guard no matter what.

CHAPTER EIGHT

Boston, 11 March 1871

Louisa followed the streets to where she thought she remembered the local trolley station being. Due to the coal shortage, the trolleys were running a half-schedule with twice the length of time between cars, so there was a chance she could catch the woman. She hoped that whoever it was would give her a sign of recognition since Louisa wouldn't be able to pick out anyone specific with the butler's vague description.

Crowds milled about the Charles Street stop, and scowls dominated the expressions of the laborers gathered there. Louisa thought she heard the grumbling of stomachs below that of the working classes, hungry for both food and fairness. She thought with some guilt about the rooms at the townhouse, which always had low fires burning even when they were unoccupied.

Someone jostled her, and her high-heeled boot slipped in something she didn't want to think about. A rough hand caught her arm before she fell.

"Careful, lass. If ye go down, they'll pick your pockets an' bag clean before they trample you."

The man's dark eyes crinkled at the corners, but his expression was serious below his round-lensed glasses. A trolley arrived, and he held Louisa steady against the crush of people who rushed toward the vehicle. The conductor had two guards with him, who brandished steam rifles at the crowd, first to allow passengers off and then after the vehicle was full almost to bursting and with men hanging on where they could. Louisa craned her neck to examine the women, but she could only see bonnets, not faces, of the ones in front of her, and none around and behind her would meet her eyes.

So much for that plan...

Once that vehicle had departed amid grumblings of how there was enough coal for the police weapons but not the trolleys, the press of the crowd eased, and the man released Louisa. He tipped his hat, and this time his smile reached from his eyes down into his salt-and-pepper bearded cheeks. He wore a well-cut suit under a cloak, and he seemed almost as out-of-place as she did among the rough crowd.

"Apologies for handling ye roughly, Miss, but I didn't want you to be the station's next fatality."

Louisa nodded and straightened her shawl. "Thank you, sir." Then she couldn't resist asking, "People have been killed here?"

"Aye. These busy stations are the most dangerous."

Then the woman who brought the locket must have really wanted to get it to me. Louisa clutched at it below her clothing and was relieved to find it was still there. However, her watch was missing, as were the few coins she'd had in her pocket. She sighed. So much for her plan to take a cab home. Even worse, the heavy clouds had come through with their ominous promise and had started spitting a mixture of snow and cold rain.

"It was stupid of me to come," she told the man. "Thank you for your assistance, and I apologize if I made you miss the trolley."

"Who are ye looking for?" he asked. "And ye did, so I may as well walk you back to where you belong."

"That's very kind of you, but I'm fine on my own."

"I doubt that. You look very much out of your element here. I'd hardly be a gentleman if I let you go back on your own."

She would have frowned at his impertinence, but he was right, and he couldn't lie to her anyway.

"So you're a gentleman?" she challenged.

"Of an academic sort, engineering specifically." He touched the brim of his hat again. "Professor Artemus Malloy at your service." He crooked an elbow, and she took it.

"I'm Louisa," she said and added to deflect him from asking her surname, "and it's funny your last name rhymes with alloy since you're an engineering professor." She didn't want to reveal her true identity, even once they left the station. She thought she'd heard Parnaby Cobb's name mentioned in the grumbling about the coal.

But the man fixed her with a shrewd gaze. "I know who you are, Miss C."

"What happened to your Irish accent?" she asked. She would have asked how he knew who she was, but most people of a certain class in Boston did.

"It's still there, but I exaggerate it when I'm among the laboring class to deflect attention. I was on my way home from Harvard when I saw you walking unaccompanied and thought I'd follow you to ensure your safety."

She tried to pull away in surprise, but he covered her hand with his. She should have felt panic, but instead, anger flashed through her.

"You presume too much, sir." She tugged harder, but he still wouldn't relinquish her hand. "I already have a father and don't need another."

"Indeed? It didn't seem so to me." His shoulders moved in a shrug under his suit, which the gap between her glove and sleeve told her was of a scratchy woolen material.

She had to admit he was correct. She had acted foolishly. Louisa would have questioned her safety with him had they not been in public, which brought up another quandary. What if someone who mattered saw her on his arm? He seemed to be about ten years older than she, and academics, particularly those at Harvard, were respectable, but she didn't want rumors to start. He had acted kindly, but there was something about his character she found unpleasant. Plus, she already dreaded what she would see when opening the gossip section of the newspaper on the morrow already. Although no one could possibly know what had transpired between her and O'Connell, she felt some part of it must be apparent to those with eyes shrewd enough to see. Would the papers be questioning her virtue?

With a shake of her head, she dismissed the irrational thought and the one behind it that perhaps she wanted her virtue to be questioned, but only by O'Connell, and only when she was in her night shift again.

Assuming he would ever speak to her. He still thought she had betrayed him.

They passed a newsboy, who held aloft a paper and called out, "Union hero's arrival delayed! Inventor of *La Reine* disappears under mysterious circumstances."

"Would you mind?" Professor Malloy asked. His expression had once again become somber.

"Not at all." She was grateful to release his arm and rubbed her fingertips free of the sensation that they had been touching the arm of a strange being.

He bought a paper, and they stepped out of the flow of traffic to read the information on the front page. Louisa pretended to be interested in spite of knowing what had happened to "talented tinkerer and engineer Patrick O'Connell." The reporter speculated he'd been kidnapped by a band of Confederates who wanted him to build a similar aether-powered weapon for them, but the former Confederate government denied any involvement. Most of the Confederate officials were in jail, anyway. Others wondered if the Union had orchestrated his disappearance in order to keep him out of the enemies' hands until the

Union had gotten full restitution from the Confederates for their insolence.

"That's unfortunate," Malloy said once they'd both scanned the article. "He was one of my best students. I hope he's not in serious trouble." He said the last sentence with his eyes on her face, not the paper.

He knows Patrick.

A strange combination of delight and anxiety spread through her middle. What did he know about Patrick? Could he help get her back in his good graces?

Or did Malloy suspect she or Cobb was involved in Patrick's disappearance?

"I'm sure he's fine." Louisa tried to keep her tone hopeful and neutral. "He seems a very clever sort. At least what I've read of him," she added quickly.

They joined the sidewalk traffic but Louisa couldn't force herself to take his arm again.

Malloy stroked his beard. "He is, but he's also good at getting into situations over his head. I only wish the article had mentioned what became of his friend, the doctor. From what I heard, they were stationed together at Fort Daniels."

A shrewd glance from him made her hope the heat in her cheeks would be attributed to redness from the wind, not a blush.

"Oh?" She blinked and shrugged.

"Yes, you met them. You were at Claire McPhee's birthday party the night of the accident, were you not?"

Louisa put together the pieces. *Of course.* Claire's father, Allan, had been a tinkerer, so he would likely have known Malloy, who would have been a young professor at the time.

Which meant Malloy was at the party. Which meant he knew Louisa knew all the players. But would he figure out Cobb's role in Patrick's disappearance? Or was he searching for evidence of a different sort that Louisa was upset as a lover rather than a concerned citizen?

"Here we are," Malloy said when they reached the townhouse. "It's been a pleasure. May I call on you sometime?"

"I'm not sure why you would," Louisa told him. "My stepfather is not currently allowing me to entertain suitors."

"I'm not interested in being your suitor, Miss Cobb." With that odd statement, he tipped his hat and walked away, leaving Louisa staring open-mouthed at him. She had no interest in him courting her—if she was to be with an Irish engineer, she'd prefer red to a black beard, and darn her betraying mind for making her remember O'Connell's kisses.

But what did he want?

He must know Cobb has Patrick. And he's not going to help me because he thinks I helped. She bit her lip. *But I did, even if it was accidental.*

One thing was certain—she had no interest in any further contact with Artemus Malloy.

Louisa once again regretted her rash decision to join O'Connell in the escape compartment of the *Blooming Senator*, not only because it caused him to be captured, but also because she knew she didn't have the gumption to go against Cobb. If someone were to confront her about O'Connell's whereabouts, she would lie to protect her stepfather, as bitter as the words would taste on her lips.

The sensation of a feather tickling her right temple made her look up, and she saw Cobb watching her from his study. He gestured for her to join him.

Her spirit deflated like a hot air balloon shot through with a shell, and she walked slowly up the stairs and into the house. Once she was out of sight of Cobb, her thoughts snapped back to their usual acuity. She just needed to come up with a plausible explanation for keeping company with a Harvard professor and keep her thoughts from fogging with panic when she was with her stepfather.

Or maybe Malloy would give her the perfect excuse for

having left the house, and she could keep the significance of the visit from the woman with the locket to herself.

Now the game felt familiar. Louisa smiled, thankful that Cobb didn't have her talent, and she had no difficulty lying to him, or at least not giving him half-truths. And maybe someday she would have the courage to ask the truth of him.

————

"This is the closest I can get you," Armand told Iris, Edward, Marie, and Johann, who had been chased into the Richmond airship station commissary to warm up while the *Skycatcher* refueled. "I know I promised Boston, but they're diverting all small traffic due to a late-season snowstorm. The tower just got the telegram and informed me when I landed."

Iris looked around the sunny airfield and sighed. "What are our options?" she asked.

"There's a passenger dirigible scheduled to stop here for fuel, and if their weight will allow, they can take you on. That will get you to your destination."

"We'll do that, then," Edward said.

"Yes," Iris agreed and reminded herself not to show surprise at her husband's making the decision for the group. "We need to get there while Patrick's trail is still fresh." She only hoped that with the combination of her and Marie's talents, they could find him. Iris knew the chances dwindled from slim to nonexistent the longer it took them to get to Boston, but they had to try.

Johann and Marie were in agreement with the plan. Armand unloaded the few belongings they'd brought with them, and as promised, the sky soon darkened with the shadow of the descending airship. While the coal stewards refilled the fuel stores, the captain confirmed there was room for them. They hugged Armand goodbye, and Iris said a little prayer for safe travels for him back to the Ottoman Empire.

"So that will be four first-class tickets?" the clerk asked.

"No, second class," Iris said.

"The captain says their only room is in the first-class lounge. I can take a little off since you're being inconvenienced by the weather, but the lowest I can go is…" He tapped on his adding machine and showed them the slip.

Iris's heart fell when she read the ticket price. "I don't think we have money for first-class fare," she said. Edward, the best among them with numbers, shook his head.

Johann stepped forward and put a hand on her shoulder. "I am renowned violinist Johann Bledsoe," he told the clerk. "If you allow me and my friends passage to Boston, I'll be happy to entertain the first-class passengers."

Iris and Marie clasped hands. It was risky for Johann to put himself forward like that, but what else could they do?

The clerk sent the message to the captain through the pneumatic message tube and soon received a reply.

"You're in luck," the clerk said. "The captain has been wanting to hear you play after the reviews of your performance in *Light Fantastique* in Paris leaked out. He's French," he offered as an explanation with what Iris considered to be a classic French shrug. "Here are your tickets."

"What were you thinking?" Marie asked Johann as they walked to the large airship followed by a porter with their bags. Her tone was no less intense for its low volume.

"We need to get to Boston," Johann told her.

"And you can't resist the stage for that long." Marie's lips tightened into a straight line, and her eyes dared him to retort.

"We are who we are, love," he said and squeezed her hand. "And Cobb doesn't know we're together. He won't even know about me performing on the airship. It's a good chance for me to work this out of my system."

"You are, as always, the gambler," Marie huffed, but the tension around her lips had disappeared.

Iris shook her head at them. She and Edward didn't quibble like her friends did, but at least Johann and Marie had passionate discussions, after which they became even closer. Sometimes Iris wondered if she was still suppressing her own emotional reactions for fear of setting off Edward's anxiety or the melancholia that had gripped and almost destroyed him in Paris.

A flash from the side of the field caught her eye, and she turned to see something brass-colored flit away. *A clockwork butterfly!* It hadn't been close enough to hear them, had it? Or was it just doing random reconnaissance in case it recorded something interesting? Neither Cobb nor the Clockwork Guild, the inventors of the creatures, did anything randomly. Did it know they were there?

"Hurry," she murmured to the others and made a fluttering motion with thumb-linked hands to indicate what she had seen.

Marie blanched, her hazel eyes wide, and she glanced around. "Where?"

Iris indicated the side of the field. "We'll have to watch out for them on the ship."

The entrance to the passenger dirigible welcomed them with relief from the sun, although the stuffy air made sweat break out on Iris's back and beneath her arms. A steward greeted them, looked at their tickets, and indicated that they should follow him. When they reached the airy first-class tearoom, Johann went to talk to the staff musicians, and the rest of them found a table. The porter gave Edward a claim ticket for their luggage.

"I'm going to explore a bit," Edward said with a delighted grin. "I'll find you back here."

"Be careful," Iris told him and kissed him on the cheek.

The steward who had given Edward the claim ticket had brought a ticket to another table nearby and walked over to them.

"If this is your first time on a commercial passenger ship, the captain may allow you to observe takeoff from the bridge."

"Oh, that would be grand." Edward waved at Iris and followed the man out.

Iris watched Edward go with an indulgent smile. He had

always been fascinated by airships, and his childish glee whenever he was on one never failed to warm Iris's heart. Then came the inevitable pang of regret—she wanted to imagine him sharing his delight in all things mechanical with a little boy or girl with his blue eyes and maybe her blonde curls, but she didn't know if that would ever happen.

There's no point dwelling in the past I can't change or a future I can't control. The long past is more comfortable.

With a shake of her head to dislodge the unhappy thoughts, Iris brought her attention back to the present. Large windows lined both sides of the huge room the width of the ship. The ones on the sunny side had blinds drawn, and gaslight supplemented the indirect sunlight with a soft glow that flattered every complexion. Iris noticed the light fixtures were the patented three-tube Cobb design.

"We just can't escape from his influence," Marie murmured. "And here we go into the lion's den."

"Remember Patrick," Iris urged her.

"I do," Marie snapped. "But you can't blame me for being anxious, can you? My talent will only get me so far."

Iris drew back, stung by Marie's irritable reply. "All we have to do is go to Boston and meet up with Chadwick, and then you can hide while we take care of things."

"But how?" Marie shook her head and wiped tears from her eyes with the back of her hands. "You don't understand how powerful Cobb is. I don't want to lose everything."

"And you won't. You have us this time if you need to face him."

"Thank you." Marie squeezed Iris's hand. "I know I do. I didn't expect to have this reaction, but being there in Boston with him was horrible." She looked up, and her eyes widened. "Oh, no."

"What?" Iris followed Marie's frightened glance to a large woman at a table by the window. She frowned at the musicians as if their warming up disturbed her. Marie rose.

"I have to get off this airship."

"Why?" Iris tugged her back down. "Don't draw attention to yourself by making a scene."

"That's Eliza Adams. She's a close friend of Cobb's. She may recognize me."

Before Marie could leave the room, an officer spoke to Eliza Adams, and they went to a small room off the lounge. Iris watched the woman from behind the tea menu a steward had brought and envied her confident carriage. *What would it be like to know one's place in the world so assuredly?*

The scenery outside dropped away, and a glance at the window along with the increased engine activity told Iris they were taking off.

"We'll just have to do the best we can," she told Marie. "It's too late to get off the ship."

CHAPTER NINE

Eastern Seaboard, 11 March 1871

Calla fixed Claire's hair in a becoming style. The day's trip felt like it had lasted weeks, and there hadn't been enough time between stops for her to meet with the captain. Not that she had much hope he would help her—her aunt and Cobb's influence reached all levels.

Finally, now on the last leg between Richmond and Boston, she would talk to him. He had requested she meet him in the officer's room off the first-class lounge. Of course her aunt would be there—there was no avoiding that.

"You'll be fine, Miss," Calla said. As usual, she had worked her magic with Claire's red-blonde tresses and put them in a style that appeared elegant but was simple enough not to fall easily. Claire wanted to do everything possible to appear the competent, sane doctor she was.

As soon as the airship reached its altitude where the captain could set the course and hand it over to the first mate for a while, an officer appeared, as promised, at the door. Claire smoothed her floral-print skirt and tan jacket—the one nice outfit she had gotten at Fort Daniels after the rest of her clothing had been destroyed by Confederate shelling—and took a deep breath.

This is it. My one chance to escape before my aunt finds some way to keep me confined in Boston with her lies. My only chance to leave so I may search for Chadwick.

With the ache in her chest crushing her breath, Claire followed the young man up the stairs from the first-class sleeper cabins, through the lounge, and to the officer's room.

———

A flash of red-gold caught Iris's eye, and the sight of a young woman with red-gold hair made her sag with relief. *Not a butterfly, then, just a lovely strawberry-blonde.* A ruby caught a sunbeam and winked on the woman's finger, and Iris frowned as the spark echoed in her memory.

Iris had picked up one of Chadwick Radcliffe's pens by mistake while they were in the Ottoman Empire and saw a flash of memory, a young woman who looked very similar to this one. Chadwick had confided in her—in all of them—about his broken engagement while they'd been in Rome. Then, a few months later, she'd seen him toying with a ruby ring one evening after they'd been drinking wine and talking about what they hoped the Eros Element would lead them to. He'd caught her curious gaze and told her it had been his engagement ring for Claire, the tiny stone in the simple gold setting all he'd been able to afford on his medical student salary several years before.

From what Chadwick had said about Claire, Iris could believe that she wouldn't want anything too fancy and would have been fine with the original simple ruby.

But then, what was she doing aboard an airship, and where was Chadwick?

Iris shook her head. Perhaps it was only a coincidence. The motion of her head rattled another memory loose—that Claire had an evil aunt named Eliza who had been instrumental in keeping Chadwick away from her.

But if Claire was traveling with Eliza...

"Oh, gods," Iris said and leaned forward. This time Marie kept her from rising.

"What?" Marie asked.

"That woman, Eliza Adams, does she have a niece?"

Marie frowned. "Maybe? I was only a maid in Cobb's employ, but I think I remember her mentioning a niece who was in treatment in Paris. It stuck out to me since I'm from—oh! That's Claire. Chad's Claire."

Iris nodded. "Yes, that must be her."

Iris watched Marie's thoughts take the same track hers had. "Then where's Chad? *Merde*."

"We have to talk to her, find out what happened to Chadwick," Iris said. "But how?"

Marie spread her hands. "If Eliza has her, it won't be easy."

The steward came to take their order and informed them that whatever they wanted was taken care of since they were with the famed Johann Bledsoe. Indeed, when he stood to play the opening chords of a famous Bach Concerto in G, the lounge hushed for a moment, and then there was a crescendo of whispers starting with the English patrons.

Iris ordered high tea for four and decided to take a chance. "I'd like to invite the young woman who just walked through here with the officer to join us."

"Oh, her?" The steward stood with his pen poised over the pad. "She's not allowed out of her room, Miss. Her guardian has informed us she's not right in the head."

"Then luckily I'm a trained nurse." Marie straightened her shoulders and assumed a confident air. "And I can tell you that if she is a neurotic, being in the company of others her own age and in a normal social setting can only be good for her."

Iris watched as Marie engaged her talent of making others believe she was who she pretended to be. The actress's features softened, and her clothing dulled, like she had pulled a blanket over herself that had changed her into a comfortable, nonthreatening person perfect for watching over a skittish neurotic.

Iris caught it because she'd observed it and knew what to watch for. The steward, on the other hand, nodded, his expression dreamy.

"I will inform the officer who escorted her." He walked away, and Marie's appearance snapped back to normal.

"It still amazes me every time you do that," Iris told her.

Marie bowed slightly. "*Fantastique* at your service, Madame. Hopefully it worked."

———

When Claire arrived at the captain's dining room, she found Eliza waited for her with two men, one of whom had more decoration on his uniform as well as gray mutton-chop sideburns and a thick mustache. She guessed he was the captain.

A closer look at the other one made her eyes widen slightly. It wasn't a young male officer with very short hair, but rather a female with her dark hair pulled back below her hat, and in trousers, of all things. Claire couldn't help but smile, and the young woman grinned back. Claire sensed her satisfaction at surprising others.

They all sat, and the man cleared his throat. Claire returned her gaze to him. His light blue eyes held the power of a hurricane paired with the deceptive peace of the eye—a dangerous combination. She opened her abilities and felt the young woman's curiosity, Eliza's irritation, and... Nothing from the captain. The lack of emotion from him made Claire immediately wary but also hopeful. The last man she had met who could block her perceptions had been of a nontraditional sort.

"I'm Captain Andrews," he said. "And this is my First Officer, Lieutenant Crow. My ensign tells me that you have a suit to press, young lady. I hope you recognize the seriousness of the situation. I don't have the time to deal with flighty girls."

Eliza leaned forward. "And that is precisely what I've been trying to tell you, Captain. My niece is a hysteric, and she's predisposed to delusions of grandeur and persecution. This is all a waste of your time, and I suggest—"

"Let the girl speak for herself," Captain Andrews snapped. He hadn't taken his eyes from Claire, not even when Eliza had broken in. "Go ahead, Miss McPhee."

Claire nodded. She knew everything rested on the next few seconds, assuming the captain hadn't made his decision already.

"My name is Doctor Claire McPhee. I am a neuroticist trained in Europe, and I was sent to Fort Daniels in Tennessee to help soldiers recover from their mental wounds. While I was there, I reconnected with some previous acquaintances and was traveling back to Boston with one of them, Doctor Chadwick Radcliffe, when my aunt bribed the conductor to allow her to take me from the train."

"And how was your aunt on the same train as you, Doctor McPhee?" the captain asked.

Claire didn't detect a sneer when he used her professional title, and the crush in her chest loosened slightly. "I don't know. Perhaps she had gone to Tennessee to see my cousin, who was stationed at Fort Daniels."

One of the captain's bushy gray eyebrows raised. "So let me see if I understand this—your former acquaintances and cousin *happened* to all end up at a quite active and dangerous fort that also *happened* to be the site of the final battle of this most un-Civil war, and your aunt *happened* to be on the same train as you traveling back to Boston? Then she intercepted you and forced you to join her on this airship?"

Claire looked to the first officer for support, but the woman studied her with pursed lips and a puzzled expression.

"I know it sounds farfetched," Claire said, "but if you were to contact the neurology department at the University of Pennsylvania or Major Longchamp at Fort Daniels, you would find my credentials are in order and my story true."

Eliza studied her nails and looked up with a coy glance. "Ask her about the ring."

Claire instinctively covered her left hand with her right, but the female officer held out her hand.

"Let me see," she said.

Claire allowed her to examine the small ruby piece of jewelry.

"It's lovely." Lieutenant Crow turned Claire's hand in the light so the ruby gave off red flashes. "A beautiful stone and simple but elegant setting. Where did you get it?"

"My fiancé gave it to me," Claire told her. She wouldn't lie.

"And your fiancé is...?" the Captain asked.

"Doctor Chadwick Radcliffe, the man I was traveling back to Boston with."

"Why didn't you mention that originally?"

"Because many people don't understand our relationship, and I didn't want you to judge me based on that. He's half-negro."

Now both the captain's eyebrows raised and were joined by several forehead wrinkles.

"You have an astonishing story, Miss McPhee. And where is your fiancé now?"

Claire didn't miss that he hadn't used her professional title, and she struggled not to allow her shoulders to slump around her squeezed heart. "I don't know. They took him away off the train in Terminus."

"Of course they did. So you have no one to corroborate your story? You do realize we have no way to communicate with the university or Major Longchamp while we're in the air."

"Yes, Captain. And no, I don't have anyone. It's my word against hers."

"Give us a moment to discuss," the captain told her. He and the first officer went to the far corner of the room and whispered with their backs turned to Claire and Eliza, who sat with a satisfied smile on her face. Claire wanted to wipe it off with a slap but knew that wouldn't help her case for being a sane person. Something blocked her from sensing the emotions of the captain and lieutenant.

The animated whispered conversation ended, and the captain and lieutenant returned to stand in front of Claire, who rose. Eliza struggled to her feet.

"Your story is too fantastic to be entirely true," Captain Andrews said. "But Lieutenant Crow doesn't feel you are any danger to the ship, so rather than confining you to your chamber as your aunt has insisted we do, you will be able to stay in the lounge and enjoy the entertainment if you wish. However, you will remain in Miss Adams's custody."

Eliza put a hand on Claire's arm. "Dear niece, this must have been trying for you. Why don't you go lie down? We'll have music for you in Boston."

Claire sent one more pleading glance to Lieutenant Crow, who wouldn't meet Claire's eyes.

"No, I shall stay here and enjoy the music." She curtsied to the captain. "Thank you for your time, Captain Andrews."

Claire opened the door to find a steward with his hand raised as though to knock. He stepped back, his mouth an *O* of surprise.

"I'm sorry, Miss. I was just coming to extend an invitation to you from that table over there, the one with the English women. The dark-haired one is a nurse, and she'll keep an eye on your niece for you, Mrs. Adams."

"Oh, do go, Claire." Eliza clapped her hands. "Obviously people can tell you need some extra help."

Claire was tempted to go back to her room to spare herself further humiliation, but the feeling she got from the table of young people who had invited her was a desire to help, not the rude curiosity she'd expected. Or perhaps they were idealistic do-gooders as she had once been.

"Very well." With a sigh, Claire went to face this new challenge.

———

Edward returned to the table, his hair windswept, and his deep blue eyes alight. He looked younger than his years, and Iris caught her breath again at how handsome her husband was.

He frowned when he mentally counted the number of chairs and found there were four.

"Are we expecting someone to join us? Or is Johann going to get away for tea? He seems to be enjoying himself."

Marie nodded and looked at her husband with an indulgent expression. "He feels the same way about the stage and his violin as you do about airships and aetherics, Edward."

"And we may have another person joining us." Iris patted the chair next to hers. "But there's always room for you."

Edward sat and related how he'd gotten a tour of the bridge and the engine room as well as a close-up look at the balloon itself, which required him to go outside on a tether. Iris listened with wonder—he would never have done anything remotely dangerous prior to their first journey to Paris and then Rome. Was he getting too brave to the point of recklessness? Or was she overly determined to anticipate the worst?

The young redheaded woman approached them with a wary expression.

"Thank you for your kind invitation," she said. "I appreciate the reprieve from my aunt, but I can assure you that I am not in need of any nursing care at the moment."

"Thank you for joining us." Marie held up the teapot. "Would you like some tea? And by the way, I can assure you I'm not a nurse."

The young woman stopped twisting the ruby ring around her finger. "What do you mean? The steward said you were. And yes, please, to the tea." She glanced at the table of tea sandwiches and pastries, then quickly away. Her stomach growled so loudly Iris could hear it.

Iris handed the girl—no, young woman—a plate. "Please,

help yourself. They brought more than we can possibly eat." The cucumber sandwiches she and Marie had already consumed had barely made a dent in the pile on the tiered plate, and she knew Edward was excited to see cream puffs on the top layer—his favorites. It seemed a feast since the *Skycatcher* had only basic provisions. She hoped that once they arrived in Boston, they could return to eating normal meals, but first they needed to determine whether this woman was, indeed, Chadwick's Claire. And if so, how they could help her.

Marie introduced herself, Edward, and Iris, and she pointed out Johann as "that handsome blond show-off violinist I happen to be married to."

"I'm Claire McPhee," the young woman said. "Originally from Boston."

Iris and Marie exchanged glances—the name fit.

"Edward, why don't you bring Johann a couple of the finger sandwiches for him to eat on his next break?" Iris asked.

"Yes, dear." He made a plate for his friend and left with a good number of the cream puffs.

"We didn't want you to feel uncomfortable," Iris told Claire. "I'm afraid we have questions of a rather personal nature for you."

Claire's tired expression returned to wary. "I'm not sure I have the kind of answers you need, as I am not myself married."

"Not that kind of question," Iris assured her. "But you may have news of a friend of ours, Chadwick Radcliffe."

Marie assisted the young woman by taking the plate from her trembling hands. Tears spilled from Claire'sblue-gray eyes.

"You're friends of Chadwick's?" she asked. "Do you know where he is? Is he all right?"

Iris took Claire's hands and willed her to be calm. With a couple of hiccupping breaths, Claire's weeping ceased.

"I'm sorry," she said. "But today has been an ordeal. The last I saw Chadwick, he was being taken away from me by the guards on a train in Terminus. My aunt..." She inhaled with a shudder.

"She arranged it, I'm sure of it. I just wish I knew how she found what train we were on."

"And what of Patrick O'Connell?" Marie asked. "Was he with you?"

Iris wasn't sure what she hoped Claire would answer. If he was in Terminus, then they were chasing the wrong airship. But if not...

"No," Claire said. "He went off with a man named Inspector Davidson in Danielsville, Tennessee."

Marie and Iris exchanged glances. "The telegram said as much," Iris murmured.

"Then how did he end up with Cobb? And who sent us the telegram about the airship?" Marie shook her head. "None of this makes sense."

Iris recalled how she'd felt when she found out Cobb had orchestrated all of them meeting in the north of France, that she was a helpless bug caught in a web too big for her to see all the pieces, and a large spider pulled the strings.

A young man in uniform approached. Iris blinked—not a young man, but a woman. She inclined her head in admiration, and the woman smiled.

"I apologize for interrupting y'all," she said. Her accent was American Southern. "I'm Lieutenant Crow."

Claire looked down at her cup. "Did my aunt send you over?"

"No. I just wanted to let you know that the captain and I are sympathetic to you, but we had orders not to allow you to leave your aunt's custody."

"What?" Claire looked up at her, and her freckled cheeks mottled pink. "Orders from who?"

Crow shrugged and leaned in, her voice lowered. "I can't say. That's what the captain told me. And I shouldn't be saying anything, but I could tell your story was true. Here." She handed Claire a piece of paper and whispered, "Read it and destroy it." With that, she turned and left.

Claire unfolded the paper and read it with her red brows

drawn together. "Do you know what this means?" she asked and handed the paper to Iris.

"Butterflies may not normally swarm, but when they do, find the chaos."

"That's cryptic," Iris said. "And creepy." The thought of butterflies made her own stomach flutter—did Crow have something to do with the Clockwork Guild?

"Perfect for you, then," Marie replied with a wink. "Iris is good at solving puzzles," she explained to the bewildered-looking Claire. "The more mysterious the better."

Iris smiled but couldn't suppress a shudder at the thought of what she'd discovered in a tomb far below the sands of the Ottoman Empire. She wished she'd left that particular puzzle buried even if it had given her an important clue as to the nature of her husband's beloved aether.

"Are you all right?" Claire asked. "You seem frightened by something."

"I'm fine." Iris took a sip of tea to bring herself back to the present. "I just remembered how careful we need to be when dealing with the strangeness around us. Let me ponder this message, and I'll let you know if I figure it out."

Claire nodded. "There definitely is something strange about all of this." She held out her cup, and Marie poured more tea. "And it started even before I left Fort Daniels." Claire sat up straight as if bracing herself for something.

Before she could explain further, her aunt blustered over. Iris wondered how Claire had known since Eliza came from behind her.

"Claire, darling, I know you're enjoying the company of your new friends, but you must go and rest."

Iris resisted the urge to tell Eliza to go away. Had the woman sensed they were talking about important things? But then she looked past the meddling woman and saw Lieutenant Crow standing by the window, ostensibly enjoying the music, but she nodded once when she caught Iris's gaze.

"Perhaps you should," Iris suggested as gently as she could.

Claire's eyes widened, but she acquiesced. "Perhaps you're right." She stood. "Thank you for allowing me to join you. I hope we'll encounter each other in Boston."

"I'll count on it," Iris said.

Marie kept her head bowed, but after Claire walked away, Eliza paused and studied Marie.

"You look familiar, Miss...?"

Marie shrugged but didn't look up. Her face looked more angular and tired. "You don't, lady," she said in a Cockney accent. "Now why don't you waddle off and leave us be?"

Iris choked on her tea, and Eliza walked off with a "Well, I never! Young people these days have no manners."

Marie grinned over the rim of her teacup. "How do you like them apples?"

Iris coughed the rest of the liquid out of her windpipe. "You could've waited for me to swallow."

"Sorry, it was the first thing that came to mind. I'd always wanted to say that to the old biddy when I worked for Cobb."

Iris looked at the message Claire had left behind, and a shiver crossed her shoulders. "I don't know what Lieutenant Crow is up to, but I hope she doesn't endanger everyone in her attempt to help us."

CHAPTER TEN

Terminus, 11 March 1871

Henry Davidson hadn't thought his day could get any worse, but his men returned empty-handed. He didn't want to admit it, but he'd doubted they would rescue Radcliffe.

"Another police coach joined the first, and once they reached the open road, they managed to weave around each other. Then one of them disappeared," Lou explained. His hands shook, and Henry guessed he was craving another cigarette.

"How do two clunky police carriages weave around each other?" Henry asked. "Those things are designed to carry people securely, not for maneuverability."

"There was something odd about those two," Richard told him. "I've never seen one move like that."

"And the one that vanished. That was just weird." Lou spread his hands. "Just like that."

"Where was it?"

"Close to the old Heron plantation," Richard said. "I followed the other one, but when I caught up to it at a railroad crossing, I made the driver open the door, and it was empty, so Lou must've been following the one with our man."

"Of course." Henry put his head in his hands. The old

Heron plantation was a shell of a mansion north of the city. Rumor had it that a Yankee spy had burned it in the mid-sixties, and then the Confederates had turned the storage tunnels into prisons.

He could guess where Chadwick Radcliffe would end up—somewhere Cobb could easily get to him in order to use him to manipulate O'Connell. And to keep Patrick working on the aether, which the British government, the one that had Henry's closest allegiance, was very interested in. It seemed that Henry had once again underestimated his foe, and now he'd lost O'Connell, Radcliffe, and Claire McPhee. He should have focused his efforts on saving her from her aunt, if only to keep yet another pawn off of Cobb's board.

"Sir?" Lou asked, his tone tinged with desperation. "We need to see to the horses."

And to your addiction.

"Go." Henry waved one hand. "All of you. I need to think."

They left the space that had been the dining room in the townhouse's former life and now served as their operations room. Diagrams of the area covered the large table along with the plan for how Henry and his team would handle the train and its passengers when they came in.

How had it gone wrong? It seemed that Cobb had known exactly what he would plan and how to thwart him.

Do I have a traitor on my team? My bosses swore they'd checked out every one of them. Henry flipped the map closest to him, and it slid across the table with a less-than-satisfying hiss. *I told them I work best by myself.* He couldn't do much more with his aching leg propped up and stiff. That irked him even more. If his leg hadn't been injured, he would ride to where the coach had disappeared and find out where the hell it had gone. But a glance out the window showed him the light already waned.

A knock on the door disturbed his frustration, and the ache in his fingertips told him he'd been drumming them on the table.

"What?"

Colin poked his head around the door. "Sir, a message just came for you."

"From whom?" Henry tried to stand, but his leg wouldn't allow it. "Bring it here."

Colin entered holding an ivory-colored envelope in his right hand. Henry recognized it as being from the people he least wanted to hear from after a failure—his bosses. Colin handed him the envelope and stood back while Henry opened the missive.

"Dear Inspector Davidson," the looping handwriting of a confident female read. "Need an update on the situation regarding Doctors Chadwick Radcliffe and Claire McPhee. Join us at Mary MacGovern's Tea Room promptly at four o'clock tomorrow afternoon. Sincerely, Hobbes and Violet."

"Great, just great," Henry sighed. He struggled to his feet.

"You shouldn't—" Colin started to say, but stopped when he saw Henry's expression.

"I shouldn't, but I am. I need to get cleaned up and then rest so I can think and prepare. Tell the men to stand by in case I need them. No, even better, I need you to go check out the place where the coach carrying Radcliffe disappeared. I need something to report."

"Violet and Hobbes?" Colin asked.

Henry nodded. "The very same. You're my second in command here. You may need to assume my position if they can me."

"They wouldn't do that. You're too valuable."

Henry leaned on Colin when his leg wobbled. "And I know too much. It's just as likely that my tea will be poisoned. Please make sure there's a pretty girl waiting for me when I return in case tomorrow is my last night on earth."

Colin shook his head at Henry's attempted joke. They all knew he didn't drink or engage in debauchery.

The problem was that he wasn't joking about the possibility of being terminated the literal way. Due to the utmost secrecy of their organization, there was no retirement, only disappearance. They all understood that when they signed on.

Colin left, and Henry hobbled into his washroom, which thankfully had running hot and cold water. He filled the sink with warm water and closed his eyes as he leaned on the porcelain, trying to anchor himself with the feel of its cold biting into his palms and warming with the water. Even that small effort had exhausted him.

When he opened his eyes, he found a scrawled message that emerged when the mirror steamed—*"If you value your life and that of the good doctor, talk to the cloaked figure in the alley tomorrow at eleven o'clock."*

———

When Louisa arrived in Parnaby Cobb's study, she avoided looking at the artifacts on the walls and shelves. The various statues, masks, and pictures leered at her or at the very least stared rudely. When she'd asked him once why he'd chosen those particular items to display out of his vast collection, he'd said they protected the study from prying eyes and ears. His own facial expression when he answered hadn't leered or mocked, but had a deadly earnestness that kept Louisa from inquiring further. She'd avoided the study since that time, and today a new addition glared at her from the corner, a large metal man. While its metal eyes lacked irises or expression, it still emanated a menacing air.

"Is that a present from your pet inventor?" she asked and gestured to it.

"From Paul? Oh, that. Don't worry about it, and close the door." Cobb didn't look up from his new toy, a wax cylinder player that produced music of such a fine quality that if Louisa stood in front of it and closed her eyes, she could imagine she was at the symphony.

Louisa complied with his request and stood in front of his desk.

"I just got a new shipment of cylinders," he said. "What would you like to hear?"

"Do you have anything French?" she asked.

"Not anymore," he muttered, but then added, "No, but there's a German gentleman who's taking the world by storm. Or *sturm*, if you will."

"That's fine." She wondered at his aside and wished she hadn't reminded him about Marie that morning. They both missed her in their own ways, but as Louisa grew older, she wanted less and less to think about what had happened between the maid and her stepfather. She'd never asked Cobb about it, all part of their careful dance. He never told her things that would make her enquire further about what he did or thought, and she never asked questions that may start such conversations.

"Sit," he waved his hand. "This will only take a moment."

She perched on the red velvet-upholstered Louis XIV chair he kept on the far side of the desk and watched him. He removed a cylinder from its casing and, careful only to touch the areas that lacked etchings for the music, inserted it in the open player and closed the lid. Louisa's eyelids drifted closed as the opening violin strains evoked the image of a forest at twilight, when the dark creatures that lurked in daytime shadows emerge to snare the unwary traveler. The sound of Cobb settling into his chair across from hers made her open her eyes.

"It's lovely, isn't it?" he asked.

"Yes, quite."

"It's important to be careful with beautiful things like that," he said. "One stray print from a too-warm finger could ruin the whole experience."

Louisa stiffened and decided not to play Cobb's favorite game, at least with her, of indirect communication. "If you're talking about this morning, I can assure you, nothing of import happened between me and Mister O'Connell."

"I had thought so, and I had moved on from the incident." He steepled his fingers. "However, I just observed you in the company of a strange man returning from gods know where. What were you doing?"

"Trying to help you," Louisa said with her most charming smile. She tried to put together half-truths to sound convincing. "That was a Harvard engineering professor. We just took a walk, and he told me about his ideas."

"Ideas of...?"

"He didn't give me any details, but he taught O'Connell. I thought he might be able to fill in the blanks of what O'Connell doesn't know."

Cobb drew his gray eyebrows, thin for a man's, together. They gave him a sinister rather than grandfatherly appearance like some older men's expressions. Not that it mattered—Louisa didn't trust any of them, and she could tell Cobb didn't believe her.

He finally sighed and said, "As much as I appreciate your efforts to help, I would prefer that you don't endanger your reputation. You're well beyond the age that most girls of your station marry, and I've perhaps given you the wrong idea of my expectations for your future by keeping you by my side for so long."

Louisa clasped her hands tighter. "What do you mean?"

"If you're going to be reckless with others' impressions of you, then it's time for me to find you a suitable husband before you damage others' regard irreparably and I have to send you to a convent."

"I'm not Catholic." Louisa tried to sound calm, but her heart had picked up the tympani line of the music with its frenzied march.

"No, but with a large enough donation, most convents would take you. It would be interesting to put you in the middle of a nest of women, especially with your abilities. I imagine you would be isolated fairly quickly."

Louisa, as much as she had lamented the games other women

played and had been grateful to be spared from them, didn't want to be stuck in a place where others would be brutally honest with her. But wouldn't that be a marriage, too? She'd watched her few friends in their relationships and observed the careful balance between husband and wife and how they sometimes gave each other half-truths in order to keep harmony.

Will harmony and honesty never coexist? It certainly isn't the case now.

"I would not like a convent." She lifted her chin. "Very well, I will consider a husband."

Cobb chuckled. "It's not up to you, girl. Remember—you're dependent on me. And this conversation comes at a less than ideal time since I do need your help with something."

"Oh?" A match-flame of hope appeared in Louisa's chest. If she could remain useful to him, perhaps he wouldn't marry her off quite yet.

"Yes, I deposited O'Connell in his dungeon this afternoon, and I can tell he is not going to be cooperative. Since he has an affinity for you, I need for you to tell me what I need to do to convince him to continue working on the aether project."

The feather-touch of someone looking at her made Louisa smooth the hair under her swept-up curls, and she glanced behind her to see the only eyes that could have produced such a sensation belonged to the metal man in the corner to the left of the door. It stared at her with its blank glass orbs, but a flash of light from outside gave them momentary life.

"Why do you look at my automaton?" Cobb asked.

"Because it looked at me."

"That's not possible. Don't let your feminine nerves get in the way of what I need you to consider. Can you tell me anything of use about O'Connell and not let your own feelings get in the way?"

"I don't have any feelings for him." The lie tasted of unripe blueberries, but Louisa ignored the unpleasant sensation. *It's all part of the game.*

"Then you should be able to offer me objective observation. What motivates him, beyond the usual wiles of a beautiful woman?"

"He is a man of integrity. He loves his friends—but you knew that. What more do you need?"

"More information. Very well, I shall have to observe him myself, and you shall assist me in manipulating the situation so he reveals what I need—his core weakness."

Louisa nodded, and the downward shift of her chin made her feel her pulse at her throat. Was Cobb offering what she thought he was? And would she have to betray Patrick again—this time intentionally—to stay in her stepfather's good graces?

But what was the alternative? A convent? She wouldn't put it beyond Cobb to punish her like that.

"Good." Cobb stood. "I shall invite him to dinner this weekend as a show of goodwill and let you work your womanly charms on him. Carefully, Louisa."

She played with the lace at one wrist. "Of course. I will do what I can within reason."

"Very well, now go and rest before supper. I imagine you must be exhausted, and I need you fresh for the rally tomorrow."

"So I'm still going?" The station where the woman had bought the ticket was located near the rally site. Could Louisa get away to find the address?

"Yes, nothing gains a crowd's sympathy like a young woman who cares about their cause and is able to manipulate a grumpy old man to help them." He put a hand to his breast and sighed as though he was helpless against her. She wished his gesture wasn't an act.

"I'll do my best, then." She stood. "And I am tired. I'll take my supper in my room."

"Fine, tell the housekeeper." With a wave of his hand, he dismissed her.

His motion, again like that of a master to his dog, would have freshly offended Louisa, but her mind buzzed with what to do with the opportunities he was giving her, both intentionally and inadvertently.

She gave the metal figure one more glance before she left the room. With a chill, she noticed it seemed to have tilted its head slightly as though to follow her progress when she rose from the chair.

CHAPTER ELEVEN

Boston, 11 March 1871

Patrick caught a shadow in his peripheral vision, but when he turned toward it, it disappeared. He rubbed his eyes. The blasted thing had been doing that to him all day.

Chadwick would tell me to use logic, not my fears, to guide my actions, he reminded himself. He said a prayer that his friend was safe. Except he hadn't prayed in so long and he had seen so many strange things he wasn't sure he directed his thoughts to the correct deity. When he closed his eyes, finally exhausted, a memory floated into his mind, of his grandmother with her church shawl on and her rosary beads clinking through her fingers as her lips murmured through the prayers. He'd never had much use for religion or a god that would allow someone like his father to live while his mother had died in childbirth with his younger sister, who became the next angel within an hour. Then his father's drinking and whoring had really taken off, and Patrick had left as soon as he could so he wouldn't be a burden on his oldest sister.

The sound of the door at the top of the stairs scraping open made him open his eyes and wake from the half-dream, half-memory. He suppressed the urge to run for it and barrel through whoever was up there whether they had a weapon or not. Anything was better than the tricks his mind was playing on him.

He refused to believe in a ghost, and he had no use for memories.

The man who descended in the company of an armed guard —not Morlock, thankfully—had a shock of salt-and-pepper hair and wore a purple suit. His lack of beard showed the hollows in his cheeks, and he stared at Patrick from behind a monocle.

A monocle? Patrick blinked. *Now I know I'm seeing things.* Of all the oddities he'd seen that day, the man's eyepiece made him want to giggle madly, but he held himself in check.

"So you're the famous inventor they've brought in," the man said with a sniff and a glance around. "I can't say I'm impressed with your accommodations. You should insist on better."

The man's voice sounded familiar, but remembering made Patrick question his sanity even more. He and the others had been in Paris at the Théâtre Bohème, and a voice behind the wall had been saying something in French. Patrick hadn't been able to make the words out, but the tone and the fact that nothing should have been back there had made his hair stand on end. Still, he wouldn't give the man an advantage.

"Are you bringing my dinner?" Patrick asked. "Because if you're not, I'm not interested in speaking with you."

The man made a rude noise. "No, I don't have your supper." He gestured to the armed guard. "Go. I'll be fine here."

"The boss said not to let anyone come in here by themselves with him." The jerk of his head and the man's tone told Patrick he'd been relegated to the role of monster in the dungeon.

"I'm armed, don't worry." The man in the purple suit made a shooing motion. "Now go. We have important things to discuss."

The guard looked hesitant for a moment, then shrugged his shoulders and muttered, "They don't pay me enough to deal with them weird tinker types." He ascended the stairs and called over his shoulder before rounding the curve, "Yell if you need something." The sound of the door closing echoed through the stairwell.

"Ah, so we're finally alone," the stranger said and adjusted his sleeves.

"As I said, unless you have food, I'm not interested." Patrick pondered pouncing on the man and overpowering him for his weapon, but there was something about the stranger that made him hesitate. He seemed too confident. Was it an act? Patrick wasn't sure he was equipped to call the bluff with his senses muddled by hunger and lack of sleep.

The monocled man brushed some imaginary piece of dirt from the elbow of his garish suit and, apparently satisfied, looked at Patrick with both eyes. "You may be interested in what I have to tell you, and whether you listen or not, at least I can say I've done my part."

"Which is...?" Patrick asked in spite of himself.

"To warn you. This imprisonment wasn't part of Davidson's plan for you."

"No shite." Patrick crossed his arms. "I'm not thinking he had any sort of plan for me." He added Davidson to the growing list of people he wanted to punch.

"Right. So you may as well just share what you were going to do and let me finish it for you. Then you can be free." The monocle distorted the man's satisfied blink into that of an unbalanced owl.

Patrick remembered hearing the name of the inventor Cobb had stolen automaton plans from and then had escaped from Paris with. "You're Paul Farrell."

The stranger bowed. "I would say, 'At your service,' but I'm really not."

"No, you're looking out for your own interests. Why the warning?"

Farrell shrugged. "Professional courtesy."

"Or you want me out of the way." Patrick sighed. "No dice."

Farrell glowered with his monocled eye. "Look, you want out

of here. Your only chances are to do what Cobb wants you to or to let me do it. Either way, you're a dead man once he gets sufficient control of the aether."

Patrick matched the glare. "So what are you proposing?"

"That you tell me your secrets and let me take the glory. Then I'll free you."

"And why should I trust you?" Patrick asked. "You could take the credit and leave me to rot."

Farrell pulled up one sleeve, and Patrick saw the tattoo—a circle inside a square. "Or I could stall the project and free you for your trouble."

The inked symbol, fresh enough to still show redness around the lines, chilled Patrick more than any supposed ghost could have.

"You've joined the neo-Pythagoreans. What, did they offer you more money than Cobb?"

Rather than being offended, Farrell rolled his sleeve down and gave Patrick a measuring look. "Let's just say I've been convinced that Cobb's mission is foolhardy for both him and the world."

Patrick leaned against the wall and ignored the damp that soaked into the shoulder of his coat. "Oh, do tell?"

"You're playing with forces beyond what you could ever imagine." Farrell wiped his face with a handkerchief. "You're not only dealing with the power of Eros but the god himself."

"And there's your mistake." Patrick shoved himself away from the wall. "I don't believe in ghosts, and I don't believe in gods." Some good his prayers had done him to this point.

Farrell backed up, but Patrick had him cornered against the wall by the stairs.

"And now, what sort of weapon do you have?" Patrick asked.

Farrell clasped Patrick's wrists, and too late, Patrick felt the prick of wires. An electric jolt knocked him backwards. Farrell hadn't been cornered, only bracing himself.

"Consider my words, Mister O'Connell. There are forces at play beyond your control."

The electricity running through Patrick's nerves made him shiver and convulse on the floor. Farrell ascended the stairs and knocked at the door. His voice floated down the stairs.

"I'm quite done in here. You might want to check on him. He seems to have had quite a shock."

Bastard, Patrick thought, but he couldn't focus on the words his mind tried to make—most of them of the unsavory sort. A mist formed over him, and he found himself looking into the face of a woman who resembled Louisa, but older and with darker, sadder eyes.

———

Iris watched Claire leave the lounge and wanted to follow her, but Marie put a hand on Iris's arm.

"Wait. Eliza is going after her. We can find her later."

"I don't know if we'll have time." Iris pulled away. Her suspicions were confirmed when she looked out the window to see a glittering gold cloud heading their way.

Marie's grip tightened. "Are those...?" she asked.

"I believe so." Iris spoke around the panic knotting her windpipe and tried to push away memories of their terrifying fall from the sky the year before. "The Clockwork Guild must have found us somehow. Get the guys—we need to head..." She forced an inhale through her too-tight throat, and her next words squeaked out, "for an escape hatch now."

Marie nodded. Iris liked how her friend didn't protest about their luggage or any of the other worries a typical female would have. Things were just things. Their lives, however...

Will always be in danger no matter what we do. The thought was almost enough to deflate Iris's resolve. Would they always be running? She wished they hadn't had to send Armand and the *Skycatcher* away.

"Come with me," a voice at Iris's elbow said. Iris turned to see Lieutenant Crow.

"Why should I trust you?" Iris asked. "You betrayed Claire."

Crow didn't look offended. "I need to get her away from her aunt, but that wasn't going to happen here. This will be the perfect chance."

"If the ship is under attack, Claire's aunt will stick with her even closer." Iris gestured to the lounge, where a worried murmur had erupted among the patrons. "Do you think she doesn't know yet?"

Marie held a frantic whispered conversation with Edward. Johann had noticed them and was hurrying his piece, dragging the rest of the chamber ensemble along with him. If Iris's brain hadn't been whirling with escape scenarios, she would have sent an apology to poor J.S. Bach's ghost.

Lieutenant Crow's full lips drew to the side in a disapproving expression that made Iris's memory flicker. "Eliza Adams is the type of woman who will be most concerned with her own affairs. I'll take care of her. Just come with me so you can take care of Doctor McPhee."

The music stopped with the grace of a railway car slamming into a brick wall, and the musicians threw instruments into cases. Johann, Edward, and Marie joined Iris at their table. Iris explained what Crow was proposing.

"I'm not sure about this," Marie said.

"Please, you have to trust me." Crow made a hand gesture as though to tuck her hair behind her ear, and Iris caught a glimpse of something on the woman's wrist. She grabbed it, and her fingers met the cold metal of a watch Crow wore strapped to her wrist rather than on a chain. Iris barely had time to think, *A wristlet watch? How curious,* when the impressions she got from the object slammed into her brain.

Crow spoke through a tube to someone scheduling the attack while the captain looked the other way. Then a flash of the scene with Claire and Eliza in the officers' room followed by an image of Iris, Claire, and Marie talking, and finally a stab of satisfaction. Over it all was the sense of following orders beyond the captain's.

Iris turned over Crow's wrist, pushed her sleeve up, and found the tattoo of a square inside a circle.

"You planned this. You're a neo-Pythagorean."

"I need Doctor McPhee away from Parnaby Cobb's influence," the lieutenant said. "I didn't know you would be on the airship when I planned for this, but you're the perfect ones to hide her away."

"And what about Chadwick and Patrick?" Marie asked.

"Their rescues are being secured," Crow assured them. "Now hurry, I've gained Adams's trust, but I'm not sure how long that will last."

"Do we believe her?" Marie asked.

Iris wondered when she'd become the leader of their little troupe, but what else could she do? "Yes. I believe we have no choice. If we resist she'll arrest us."

"Smart woman. Good, follow me," Crow told them. "Your luggage has been stowed in Escape Hatch three. Head that way once we extract Doctor McPhee from her aunt."

———

Claire lay on the bed and pretended to sleep. Her aunt had taken advantage of the private bedroom to spend an inordinately long time in the bathing chamber, and Claire wondered if the rooms would be habitable after Eliza was done. Claire had spent enough time on military bases and around hospitals to have a high tolerance for certain smells, but she'd always had the opportunity to escape if she needed it.

Once she was sure Eliza was fully involved in what she was doing—one minor advantage of the many layers of skirts women had to wear was that lavatory trips were never short—Claire rose from the bed and tiptoed to the door. It was locked, of course, but she pulled a hairpin from her coiled tresses and inserted it into the lock as Patrick O'Connell had once shown her. Not that she had anywhere to go where she wouldn't be found, aside from the escape compartments. She only hoped they didn't require some central control to be loosed.

A knock startled Claire and nearly made her fall backwards on her bustle.

"Who is that?" Eliza called.

A flurry of activity from inside the lavatory made Claire reply to keep her aunt from coming out, "Nothing to worry about, Auntie." To the door, she said, "What is it?"

The voice that answered was Lieutenant Crow. "Doctor McPhee, is your aunt in there with you?"

Oh, now she calls me Doctor. Waves of urgency came through the door, however, so Claire merely answered, "Yes."

"In the room or in the lavatory?" Crow asked.

A hot flush crept up Claire's neck. It was one thing to discuss such matters in a medical setting, but her old society training kicked in, and she couldn't speak for a moment.

"Doctor McPhee, it's all right." This was the voice of the dusky-skinned woman Marie. "We just need to know if you're truly alone, or as much as you can be."

"In the lavatory," Claire whispered.

"Good," Crow said so quietly Claire strained to hear her. "The powder I put in her tea is working. Now go and lock the door—the lavatory chamber in your room locks from the outside."

Claire did as she was bid, and when the lock clicked into place, Aunt Eliza made a satisfying sound resembling an indignant chicken's squawk.

"Claire Alice McPhee, you open that door right this second." The demand was punctuated by a long, emphatic fart.

Claire put her hand over her mouth to suppress a giggle. "Sorry, auntie. It sounds like that's the best place for you right now." She opened the door.

"Quick, grab your valise, and let's go."

Claire shoved the few things she'd taken out into her luggage, then whirled around. "Calla. I can't leave without her. I promised her I'd find her a position in Boston."

Crow frowned. "I wasn't aware you traveled with a maid. You didn't board with one."

Claire sighed through her teeth. Did no one understand how things worked, fair or not? "She had to board through the back. She's negro."

"I'm really sorry, but we don't have time," Crow said. "An attack is imminent."

"Then we need to go by the servants' floor first," Claire insisted. "I'm not leaving without her."

"We can't." Crow tugged so hard it felt like she wanted to pull Claire's arm off, but she gritted her teeth and held on. She looked at Iris and Marie, who whispered together. Marie nodded and took off down the hall.

"Oh, Clai-ire." Eliza's singsong voice was interrupted by another flatulent outburst. "Don't forget, only Parnaby and I know where your beloved is."

"That's not true." Crow grabbed the handle of Claire's valise, but Claire held on to it. "We know where they're keeping him, and help is on the way."

"And why should I trust you, any of you?" Claire asked. "I appreciate you wanting to rescue me, Lieutenant, but I can't leave Calla to die." She also felt the deceit in Crow's words, although she couldn't tell which part—the attack, them not having time to fetch Calla, or her knowing where they held Chadwick. And there was the desire to take Claire into her influence. A glance at Iris's face told Claire she was wary, and her own mixed feelings swirled.

"Marie is going to fetch Calla." Iris toyed with the buttons on the gloves at her wrist. "We can all meet at the designated escape hatch."

"You can go," Eliza said, "but then I'll send the order for your precious Chadwick to be executed."

Claire didn't need her talent to tell how gleeful Eliza felt about ordering what she felt should have been done long ago—the ultimate punishment for a half-negro who dared to love her precious niece.

"It doesn't matter," Crow said. "She'll die when this airship crashes."

"Wait," Iris and Claire said, then Iris followed with, "You didn't say anything about a crash."

"All these innocent people," Claire added. "We can't..." The thought made her stomach and heart quiver together with horror. "No, I'll stay. Call off the attack."

"This would be a small sacrifice compared to the damage Cobb will do if he gains control of the Eros Element. Plus, I can't call it off," Crow said, but Claire and Iris exchanged glances. They both knew she lied.

"Yes, you can," Iris insisted. "I've been through a Clockwork attack. They do so swiftly, not as a cloud waiting for someone's order."

"I can't risk Chadwick." Claire's anxiety overflowed into tears. "You're going to have to figure out something else." She used Crow's surprise to grab her valise back and slam the door in the lieutenant's face.

"Are you going to unlock the door?" Eliza asked.

"Maybe when you're done with whatever needs to happen in there," Claire replied. "I need some quiet to think."

Footsteps in the hall told her that the others left, but then more arrived, and there was a knock at the door.

"Miss?" Calla's soft, hesitant voice carried through the wood along with her anxiety at being betrayed.

Claire opened the door, and Calla fell into her arms. "I was afraid you'd leave me."

"Never," Claire promised and held the girl tightly. "We're in this together."

CHAPTER TWELVE

Somewhere over New England, 11 March 1871

Iris followed Lieutenant Crow through the hallways and narrow passages that led from the passenger areas to the bridge. Trotted to keep up with the taller woman's heel-sparked stalking would be a better description.

"Stupid girl," Crow muttered. "We'll have her precious negro lover soon."

"But you don't have him yet," Iris pointed out. "And you can't blame her for not trusting you. Plus you can't expect us to condone the killing of hundreds of innocent people to get rid of one horrible woman."

"You don't know what's at stake." Crow whirled around, forcing Iris to dart to the side so she wouldn't run into the lieutenant. "Why are you still here?" Crow demanded. "Shouldn't you go and join your aetherist husband in Escape Hatch Three?"

Iris straightened to her full, albeit not so intimidating, height. "Marie's gone to fetch him and Maestro Bledsoe. We're going to make sure you don't crash the airship." Not that she had any idea how they would prevent it, but they'd do their best.

Crow looked down at her with a half-grin. "I admire your

feistiness. I'd heard about you, but I'm glad to see our dossier wasn't exaggerating."

Iris recalled Crow's tattoo, but she didn't move in spite of the shudder that made her back muscles dance. What else did the neo-Pythagoreans have in her file? Were they the ones who spread rumors about her involvement in Jeremy Scott's death?

And did they know about the Eros Element's evil side? They wanted to stop its use, that much Iris knew.

"What you have on me doesn't matter," Iris said. "Stop the attack. Now."

"As you wish. Madame." Crow bowed mockingly, then turned down a corridor that didn't seem to lead anywhere.

"Look, we want the same thing," Iris said, somewhat breathlessly as she had to hold her skirts and almost run to keep Crow in sight. Had the woman's legs gotten longer?

"And what is that?" Lieutenant Crow made another sharp turn, and Iris would have skidded had the metal grate not prevented her.

"For the Eros Element not to fall into the wrong hands, to keep it from being used for evil things."

Crow stopped suddenly again, but this time Iris executed a graceful half-spin and stood beside Crow. Iris couldn't help but raise her chin. *So there.*

"How do I know I can trust *you*?" Crow asked. "You could turn me in as soon as we arrive in Boston. You know your friend Henry Davidson wants us all jailed or worse."

"He's not my friend. He appears when he's least wanted and makes things unnecessarily complicated." Iris couldn't help the bitterness in her tone. Yes, he'd been somewhat of a help in Paris, but only after making them all feel threatened and under suspicion. And he hadn't given them enough help with rescuing Patrick.

Crow's half-smirk reappeared. "That sounds about right. Fine, we'll declare a truce for now." She unlocked the door, and Iris followed her into a room with a small window. The rhythm of the engine throbbed in Iris's ears, and the stink of hot metal and coal made her nose run and eyes water.

Lieutenant Crow took a deep breath. "It doesn't always smell pleasant in the belly of the beast." She went to a trunk shoved in the corner and removed one of the clockwork butterfly mechanisms. She wound it up, and as it unspooled, she said, "Stand down. Truce achieved." Then she opened the window and let it out.

"There, are you happy?" she asked.

Iris's heart thumped in time with the engine. Would the device reach the right person? Would the message be understood? It seemed silly to rely on such a delicate means of communication, but she said, "I suppose."

"You'll have to trust me," Crow put out a hand. "Do you agree to the truce?"

Iris again wondered how she got to be the spokesperson for their group, but she nodded and took the other woman's hand. "I agree."

"Good, then we'll figure out how to stop Cobb together."

"While I can agree to a truce, I cannot do anything further without talking to my colleagues," Iris told her. "All of them."

"Very well. But don't think you can give me the slip. I will find you again once you're on the ground."

Iris shrugged. She didn't even know what their plans were in Boston beyond rescuing Patrick, so she couldn't imagine how Crow could find them once they disappeared into the city. But the neo-Pythagoreans did have spies all over.

In spite of the warmth seeping into the room from the engines, Iris shivered. What had she just done?

By the time Patrick regained consciousness, he was surrounded by crates. He unpacked the boxes without much organization, seeking anything that would allow him to fashion a lock pick or other means of escape. His concentration on his goal allowed Patrick to distract himself from the vision of the woman who looked like but unlike Louisa. Had he been in his right mind, he would have guessed the ghost of Louisa's mother had come to check him out. However, he knew that an influx of electricity to the brain could cause people to sense things that weren't there. Chadwick had mentioned something like that when he'd taken his nervous system class and talked about frog legs that jumped of their own accord.

Cobb had been too canny in his order. There was nothing Patrick, even at his cleverest, could use to escape. Any metal implements were too frail or too thick for the lock, and there were no tools he could use to widen the hole over his privy, even if he could stack the crates to reach it. As for those, whoever had dropped them off had pulled the nails out, so they would collapse under any weight.

"I shouldn't be surprised," Patrick muttered. "That rich bastard. And I doonna know what happened to Chadwick." He collapsed on to one of the crates when the horrible possibilities for his friend's fate slammed into his mind.

The crate, of course, crashed to the floor.

I better not have splinters in my arse. He stumbled to his feet and leaned over with his hands on his knees, trying to calm his whirling thoughts. He'd managed to push them aside while looking for his own escape because he knew the first thing he'd do would be to go looking for Chad. As for Claire, whom they both had great affection for, although Patrick's feelings for her resembled those of a brother for his younger sister, she would be next.

Patrick knew Chad was clever and could possibly figure his own way out of the mess he was in. But Patrick had protected Chadwick since the day on the quad when some of the white students in Chad's medical school class had tried to make an example of him for doing better on the first test than they had. Patrick had been delivering something and had dropped it to jump into the fray and even out what he'd thought was an unfair fight. Since then, Patrick had served as a bodyguard, advisor, and friend, and Chad had returned the friendship and encouraged Patrick to be his best self. Chad had convinced Patrick to get his master's degree in engineering.

Then they'd met Cobb and gotten dragged into this mess. Patrick straightened up as much as possible. He couldn't stand a cluttered workspace, although that was all he'd had at Fort Daniels. More evidence of Chadwick's influence—his being in the military had instilled in him an obsession with neatness, and at some point, his tendencies had tempered Patrick's external chaos as much as Chad's calm rationality had influenced Patrick's tendencies to get into trouble.

Yes, Patrick had to escape. Whether he needed more to rescue Chad or to keep his own worst characteristics from emerging, he didn't know.

"Well, let's see if you can help me out here, Eros you trickster."

He assembled the aether isolating device—glass and copper spheres connected by a rubber stopper that could be closed—on a work table too rickety to support him but sturdy enough for his work, then cursed under his breath. He would need the ice water to cool the copper globe to make a vacuum, so he couldn't progress until someone brought him some. Or maybe it was chilly enough—he could see his breath, and he put his coat on.

It wasn't this cold in here a minute ago, was it? Rats, whoever is in here is curious. Just what I need—a nosy spirit. Or perhaps a useful one. He closed his eyes. He'd sworn after Paris that he didn't want any more contact with the supernatural. But sometimes oaths didn't work out.

"Whoever you are, could you concentrate your cold over this sphere when I ask you to?" He waited and didn't get a reply, but the temperature seemed to warm slightly. *Thank you.*

Patrick warmed a little bit of room-temperature water from

the glass bottle that had come with the supplies until it steamed in the two globes. Then he said, "Now, please, chill this one."

He snatched his hand away from the copper globe before a finger froze off. Ice crystals formed on the globe, and once the steam condensed into water again, but this time only inside the copper, he shut the stopper between the two spheres.

"Thank you," he said. "Now I just need a tad more light."

The lamp above the table flared brighter, and Patrick selected two tuning forks and placed the ends on the globe after striking them. An undulating mass appeared in the middle of the glass like an opalescent snake eating its own tail. He picked up two more, did the same procedure, and the aether stabilized into something that looked almost solid.

"Thanks again." The light dimmed to normal. Patrick put the tuning forks on the table and, leaning on his hands, studied the aether cloud he'd isolated. Most aetherists and other scientists thought of aether as the substance light passed through, but he, Edward Bailey, and the others knew it could be and do much more.

"That's fascinating," a soft female voice said from just behind Patrick's left shoulder, "but what do you do with it?"

Patrick turned slowly to see a misty woman standing behind him. It was the same one he'd seen when Paul Farrell had shocked him, but this time she shimmered along with the aether, and her features were so clear he could see the small mole on her left cheekbone under her eye. His thumb had found a similar one on Louisa's cheek, but hers was flesh-colored, not darker like the ghost's.

"Who are you?" he whispered and tried to back away, but he was trapped by the table.

"Oh, you can scoot around all you want," she said with a laugh, "but you're stuck down here with me and my bones. Now please tell me, do you have news of my daughter Louisa?"

———

Louisa should have been exhausted, but after the light dinner she'd taken in her sitting room, she couldn't settle. She wondered again whether the events of the previous night had been a dream, but when she touched her left cheekbone, where a tiny mole just like her mother's sat, she felt the tenderness left from Cobb's slap. She regretted again that she hadn't taken Patrick's invitation to run away with him, and then she wished harder that she hadn't inadvertently led Morlock right to him. Above all, she regretted that Patrick thought she betrayed him.

Frost edged the windowpanes, and Louisa looked out into the dark cold, where streetlights became stage lamps for dancing snowflakes. She shivered. Where had her father stashed Patrick? Was he warm enough? Was this weather a shock for him after being in the warmer southern states?

And why did she care so much? Even if she could manage to somehow rescue him, she couldn't ever be with him. Being Parnaby Cobb's stepdaughter and only heir made her a valuable commodity to be traded for the biggest payoff possible.

The crack of something near her face startled her into drawing back from the window. Then another sharp tap made her douse her light and pause, her heartbeat replaying the timpani line from the symphony she'd heard earlier. Girlish fantasies of Patrick standing underneath her window and throwing rocks to get her attention battled with the practical knowledge that it couldn't be him—Cobb wouldn't have put him in a situation easy to escape from.

Then who dared disturb her by aiming pebbles at her window?

Now that she'd turned the lamp off and her eyes adjusted, Louisa could see more outside. A shadowy figure stood in the winter-dormant garden two floors below her window, its face turned upward. For a moment, she thought the automaton lurked below waiting for its opportunity to lure her out, but she knew it couldn't act of its own accord, could it?

Another tick at the window infuriated her. The stepdaughter

of the city's most powerful businessman, she didn't have time to trifle with some worthless suitor, although she admired the gumption of whoever had scaled the spiked garden wall. Still, she decided this pointless exercise needed to end lest she be accused of encouraging strange men to rendezvous at late hours. She'd gotten in enough trouble that day.

Louisa threw open the sash and whisper-snapped into the darkness, "Whoever that is, cease at once. I have no desire to meet with you, and if you continue hurling stones at my window, I'll let the dogs out." They didn't have dogs, but she gambled the person below didn't know that.

"Miss Cobb, you don't have dogs," came the reply in a voice that sounded familiar, but she couldn't place it.

Well, merde, she thought, borrowing a phrase Marie had uttered when the maid didn't think anyone could hear her. "Fine, but I still want you to leave."

"It's about Patrick O'Connell. You need to speak with him, deter him from his current course."

Louisa couldn't keep her cheeks from lifting, but she stifled a mocking laugh. "You've obviously never met the man. Nothing keeps him from what he wants." *Except his own honor.* He had pulled away before ruining her although they'd both craved it in the moment.

"Please, you have to come. You're the only one he'll listen to. Plus, I can show you where he is and how to get him out."

Louisa's left eyebrow escaped from her control and raised in an arc of interest. "Oh?"

"Yes, but you have to come quickly."

Now she recognized the man—Paul Farrell, Cobb's pet inventor who was good with automatons and creepy steam-powered animals, but not much else.

"Why should I trust you?" she asked.

"Because..." A huff that could be a sigh produced a cloud of vapor. "Because you should."

"Or it could be a trap set by my father to show how unreliable I am. Go home, Mister Farrell. I'm not interested in playing his games tonight."

She closed the sash with a satisfying *click*. Who did he think he was, or how gullible did he think *she* was? She'd confront Parnaby in the morning.

But when she dreamed that night, it was of streams of shining light emanating from her father's new street lamps in the poorest part of town. Instead of illuminating, they captured and devoured anyone who came near.

At one point, when Louisa woke, she found the automaton staring at her from the foot of the bed, but she was paralyzed and couldn't scream. It reached for her, its blank eyes flashed golden, and a faint took her away.

The passenger airship landed in Boston at around ten o'clock after having been diverted around New York due to the snowstorm that produced a lovely intermittent flurry in Boston but had caused a snarl in air traffic around other large Northern cities. Plus the captain had had to slow their speed to give himself as much time to maneuver should another airship come at them from out of the clouds.

Finally they touched down. Iris, who'd thought she had gotten her air legs, found herself glad to be on solid ground, where gusts of wind wouldn't make the entire world lurch.

The passengers had talked of not much but the mysterious golden cloud, and the few who had speculated that the Clockwork Guild—a notorious international organization—had appeared were quickly silenced by the officers. Then the captain had bought the entire first class lounge alcoholic beverages, and talk had turned to other, more lively topics with the help of some of the officers who appeared to imbibe but actually nursed their drink for hours.

Lieutenant Crow had brought Iris back to the first-class

lounge and disappeared. Iris was disappointed not to see Claire again, but she understood and hoped that she would be able to call on Claire at some point so they could plot the girl's next move.

While Iris waited with Marie and Edward for Johann to find a cab, a boy approached them with a telegram. He studied each of them in turn, and when he saw Iris, a large grin showed off his missing front top teeth.

"I'm to give this to the lady who looks like a fairy," he said. "You've got white hair and purple eyes, so it must be you."

He shoved the folded paper at Iris and scampered off so quickly she didn't have time to get a coin from the swiftly dwindling supply in her reticule to tip him. She opened the telegram, which had come from Terminus.

"Regards McT. Have you fetched red yet. Working on CR. Rooms for you at Oasis, my compliments. Wait for contact in a.m. LFATB."

The ending, which stood for *Light Fantastique at the Théâtre Bohème*, was Davidson's coded signature. Iris wanted to be annoyed at him—as if "fetching" Patrick were as easy as going to the Irish tinkerer section at a grocer and saying, "I'll take that one, please." But as she and Edward had talked and discovered that they only had enough funds for the cheapest of accommodations for the four of them, she decided to be grateful instead for his help.

"What does it say?" Marie asked. "I'm guessing it's from H?"

Iris nodded and told her the gist of it. "So we'll figure out things in the morning."

Lieutenant Crow appeared with a very unhappy-looking Johann.

"My carriage will be here at any moment," she said. "I can give you a ride to your hotel."

"No, thank you," Iris told her. "We're fine."

"She chased off the last cab," Johann grumbled. "We're stuck."

Iris, Edward, and Marie exchanged glances. If they accepted transportation from Crow, she would know where they stayed, and they'd all four agreed they wanted nothing to do with the ruthless neo-Pythagoreans.

"So I'm afraid you'll have to take me up on my offer." Crow hefted Iris's valise. "Come with me."

Iris had to follow, if only to make sure her valise didn't disappear. Not that she had much of ordinary value in there, but she had brought what few items she had from her father. Edward and Johann grabbed the rest of the bags, and they all trotted after Crow into the darkness.

"By the way," Crow said over her shoulder without slowing her stride. "I have a contact at the Boston Museum of Ancient Cultures who knew your father. He's looking forward to meeting you."

Iris almost tripped as her mind whirled from excitement at the prospect of meeting a fellow archaeologist who could potentially help her figure out what to do job-wise to dismay that Crow had beaten her to that avenue. Plus she didn't need the distraction.

"Thank you, but my time here is spoken for," she said. Marie squeezed her hand.

"It's all right," Marie whispered. "There are more museums here than you would believe."

"Nonsense." Crow tossed Iris's valise on to the rear of a steamcart. "You wanted me to prove to you that you can trust me. I'm trying to help."

"I don't want your help." Iris knew she sounded like a petulant child, but she had no patience for others telling her what she should and should not do. "I want you to leave me alone."

"Not here," Marie clarified. "Since we need a ride into town."

Iris shot her friend a look, but Marie squeezed Iris's shoulder. Iris couldn't help her rueful grin at the reversal of roles—typically Iris played the part of the logical one.

"We can figure it out tomorrow," Marie said. "We're all very tired."

Edward and Johann caught up and helped Crow to load the rest of the baggage on to the cart. Then Edward handed Marie and Iris into the passenger compartment.

"If you like, you can keep the door cracked so you know I'm not locking you in," Crow announced. "But I do recommend you use the safety braces."

"That's quite all right," Iris replied stiffly. The wind had picked up, and she didn't want to add the breeze from the moving air.

Crow climbed into the front seat, and Johann took the front passenger spot.

"It's a bit crowded on the back bench," he said with a grin. "Besides, I've been looking forward to seeing Boston. I've heard so much about it."

Crow didn't say anything, only nodded, and Iris wondered if Johann was using his own talent. She and Marie had discussed it, how he could charm anyone, and sometimes it seemed that he had an extra push similar to Marie's ability to make anyone believe she was what she portrayed, but weaker. She appreciated his stepping in to help. Meanwhile, Edward held her hand, and although two layers of glove separated their skin, she felt his love and support. Not for the first time, she sent a mental prayer of gratitude to whoever had put them all together.

"Now where are you staying?" Crow asked once she'd driven out of the airfield.

"The Oasis," Iris said. She blinked away the disorientation of the steamcart driving on what seemed to be the wrong side of the road. No matter how many places she'd been, driving on the right side always seemed backwards until she was accustomed to it.

Crow shouted, and something clanged against the steamcart, causing it to shudder. It rolled to a stop.

"Johann?" Marie called. "Are you all right?" She unclipped her safety brace.

"We're fine," he said. "Stay back there." The vehicle moved forward again. Iris peered through the window but couldn't see anything in the shadows outside.

"What was it?" Iris asked loud enough for Crow and Johann to hear.

"I don't know." Crow sounded shaken. "Just sit tight. I'm getting us out of here as quick as I can."

CHAPTER THIRTEEN

Cobb Townhouse, 12 March 1871

When Louisa arrived in the breakfast room, she found her stepfather already seated at the head of the table with a cup of coffee in front of him and his nose buried in the paper. Without looking up, he said, "Good morning, Louisa. How did you sleep?"

She analyzed his tone and what she could see of him—he didn't look tense, but then, he rarely did. She wanted to gloat that she hadn't fallen for the trap he and Paul Farrell had set for her, but between the odd visit from the automaton—which she wasn't sure had happened or if she'd dreamt it—and the other strange dreams she'd had, she didn't have the energy for gloating. Especially if she needed to play the part of dutiful daughter at the rally.

So she only said, "Fine," and helped herself to a soft-boiled egg and some toast. She sat at the foot of the table, which had been set for her, and a maid appeared to pour her some coffee.

Unlike many women, Louisa drank her coffee black, but she couldn't say why. Had her mother done so? She'd often wondered, but when she tried to reach back into memory, she recalled her mother drinking coffee, but not how she took it.

"Parnaby, may I ask you a question?"

He looked up. "Maybe. I'm busy right now. Is it a short one?"

"Yes." She watched his eyebrows for signs that they would draw together in disapproval, which would bleed into the rest of the day. "It's about my mother."

"A short one, then."

"How did she take her coffee?"

One of his eyebrows went down, but the other one raised, and he looked up as if searching his own memory. "Black, I think. Like you."

"Do you know why?"

"Yes. You were poor before I married her, and she couldn't afford cream and sugar. Now can I get back to my reading? This blasted weather may interfere with our plans. Can't get people excited about light if they don't have heat."

"Yes, thank you." Louisa frowned at her egg. Why couldn't she remember more of life with her mother before Cobb? Sure, he'd married her mother when Louisa was seven, but most people had memories from childhood, didn't they? She dared not ask another question, at least not that morning, but she wondered why she hadn't been more curious.

She took a deep breath and felt the locket press between her breasts, almost like the anchor on one of her father's ships. Perhaps she hadn't thought about the past because she didn't have anything to prompt her to do so. Or had she lied to herself that it wasn't important because this was her life, and she was comfortable.

"Hurry up, Louisa," Cobb told her. "Stop daydreaming and eat. We have a busy day."

Beforehand, she would have meekly done what he asked right away, but this time she lifted her chin and looked directly at him. He studied her with a quizzical expression.

"Is something wrong?" she asked.

"I was going to ask you the same." He lowered the paper.

"Remember our conversation yesterday. As long as you're useful, I won't ship you off to a convent or marry you off right away. Need I remind you? You owe everything you are to me."

"I am well aware of that." Louisa lowered her eyes. "I will be finished in ten minutes."

"Make it five." He stood, dropped the paper on the table, and left.

Louisa's hands shook so badly she couldn't crack the eggshell on the first try. Or the second. Every tap of her spoon made her want to hit the egg harder until she reduced it to crushed pieces, but she contained herself. She was Louisa Cobb now, but she had once been someone else, and she meant to find out who.

———

When Claire opened her eyes to the room she'd slept in as a girl and young woman, she thought she dreamed. She often came back here in her mind's nocturnal wanderings, and at first she felt relief because it meant she wouldn't have a true nightmare—those always occurred in the asylum in Paris. Then the events of the previous day came back to her, and she bit back a scream of frustration. How could she be back here, back in the power of her Aunt Eliza?

The clock on the fireplace mantel showed it was seven o'clock, and she pulled the blanket over her head. She'd fallen right back into the pattern of the household—rise at seven, breakfast at eight. She twisted the ring around her finger and hoped Chadwick was all right. She played back through the scene on the train in her mind, wondering if she could have done something different to save them both. But she knew that if she and Chadwick had stayed apart on the train, Eliza would still have figured out a way to capture Claire and send Chadwick away. Her aunt hadn't been at the fort visiting Bryce, so Claire knew Eliza's objective had been her. But for what purpose?

A soft tap on the door made Claire emerge.

"Come in?"

Calla poked her head around the door. In spite of the very late hour they'd arrived, the girl's eyes sparkled and lacked the dark circles of exhaustion Claire knew she sported.

"Are you ready for me to help you dress, Miss?"

"Yes, thank you." Claire peeled herself from the bed, and Calla helped her to put on undergarments and then a dress from her previous life that fit loosely—life at Fort Daniels had provided Claire with more fresh air, exercise, and excitement than she'd realized. She probably could have gone without the corset, which Calla had to lace tightly. After Calla had fixed her hair in a simple but elegant updo, Claire looked at herself in the mirror. Even with her glasses, she looked more like Claire McPhee, daughter of Melanie and Allen McPhee, than Doctor Claire McPhee, neuroticist and war hero. The light blue day dress set off her eyes, and she fingered the lace at the collar. She hadn't worn lace since leaving Boston the last time, and it felt like shackles, not a luxury.

*It's not real, it's not real, it's not real...*Claire chanted the three words in her head until they lost their meaning and became a collection of nonsense syllables. Then she switched to *Wake up, wake up, wake up...*But that, too disintegrated under the reality of walking through the upper hall of her childhood home, then down the stairs and into the kitchen, where her mother stood at the counter.

"Mama?" Claire asked. Could this thin, pale woman be all that was left of the robust Melanie McPhee, who had defied her own family to marry a tinkerer?

Melanie turned from the steaming coffee-making device with a smile.

"Oh, Claire, is that you?" She stepped toward Claire but stumbled and caught herself on the back of a chair with hands that looked more like claws. She blinked, her mouth and cheeks a vague echo of the dazzling smile that had won Allan McPhee all those years previously, and which Claire missed most of all about her mother.

"Forgive me," Melanie said. "I'm clumsy these days." She balled one hand into a fist and pressed it to the base of her spine.

"Is it your back still?" Claire asked. She joined her mother behind the kitchen table and noticed that Melanie's pupils didn't change size. In fact, they were such tiny pinpricks, they gave her mother the appearance of a strange being.

"Yes. I wanted to be awake when you came down." Melanie massaged her back with one hand and took Claire's arm with the other.

"How much of that stuff are you taking?" Claire gestured to a bottle labeled as "Doctor Lewis's Tonic" on the shelf. She guessed it had a fair amount of opium in it.

"A teaspoon here and there when the pain gets too bad." Melanie's thin shoulders barely moved her dress when she shrugged. She took mincing steps like an old woman. Well, an older woman than she was, Claire amended. Eliza, who was Melanie's senior by a good ten years, seemed younger.

"You need to be careful. No one knows what's in those things, and their 'proprietary blends' could contain ingredients that are harmful."

Melanie waved away Claire's concerns. "How was your trip, dear?"

Claire wanted to say something like, "Fine except for my fiancé being ripped from my side and my being kidnapped," but she knew Melanie had to live with Eliza due to Melanie's frail health. Would her mother even remember this conversation? Still, Claire didn't want to upset her.

"Rough," was all Claire would say. The journey between kitchen and dining room felt like an expedition, but finally they arrived, and she sat her mother at the table. "Here, let me fix you a plate."

"I always worry about you traveling after that horrible accident." Melanie twisted her napkin in her hands. "You never know when someone walks out the door if it will be their last time."

Claire nodded, biting back the tears that stung the back of her throat at the painful reminder of Chad's uncertain fate. She couldn't help but glance at her parents' wedding picture, which a friend had painted for them, over the mantle. They sat stern-faced like most portraits of the day, but the artist had captured her father's twinkling eyes and her mother's serenity. Claire knew her father was dead, although Melanie and Eliza had tried to hide the fact when Claire returned from Europe due to her "fragile state of mind," or so Eliza had said. It was hard to believe someone was "off on some diplomatic matter" when one had seen and spoken with his spirit, but she wasn't going to mention that, either, although she wished she could.

As a neuroticist, Claire understood how the mind could play cruel tricks on the body. She wondered if Melanie's back pain could be a result of the rumors of Allen having killed himself due to self-blame for the accident that had caused Claire's hysteria and the physical scars that still wound over her hands.

"Claire?" Melanie's soft voice brought Claire back to the present.

"Not awake yet, I suppose," Claire said and turned from the sideboard. She almost dropped her plate when she saw the shadowy form of her father standing beside her mother, his hand on her shoulder.

"Is something wrong?" Melanie asked. "You've gone pale."

"N-no, not at all." Another lie, but Claire had to say something so she wouldn't blurt out something unladylike at the ghost who had appeared and then abandoned her at Fort Daniels. He vanished, and Claire asked, "Eggs?"

"Just toast. If I have too much in my stomach, the tonic won't work."

"But if you don't eat, you won't heal," Claire argued. "And you can't survive on just bread and butter."

"I'll add jam, don't worry. Don't argue with me, Claire." Melanie put her hands under the table, but not before Claire noticed them shaking.

Claire would have continued to protest, but Eliza swept into the room. Claire sent a cross look in her direction before turning back to the food. *Does the woman never enter a room normally?*

"Good morning, lovelies," Eliza chirped. "Claire, I trust you're well-rested."

"As much as one could expect." Claire turned and handed Melanie her toast across the table, then fixed herself a plate as quickly as she could. "I'll be eating breakfast in my rooms. I feel a sudden headache coming on."

"Right, and we mustn't strain you, dear. We wouldn't want a recurrence of your hysteria," Eliza replied without missing a moment.

"Oh, yes. Do go lie down, Claire," Melanie said. "I don't want you to become ill again."

"That is highly unlikely." But Claire paused. Was there some advantage to her playing up a possible relapse? She mentally gave herself a shake—she didn't need to risk ending up in another asylum, and she needed to make herself as credible as possible. Surely there was someone in Boston who would believe her.

"Yes, you need to rest up," Eliza told her. "Louisa Cobb is coming for tea. I thought it would be good for you to have someone your own age to talk to."

Meaning someone you approve of and who already thinks me insane.

"Very well." Claire left, but as she walked into the hall, she overheard Eliza say, "Melanie, dear, you're shaking. Have you had your medicine yet this morning? I'll fetch it for you."

Claire almost turned to challenge her aunt but decided to wait, as much as it concerned her. Encountering the ghost of Allen McPhee in the hall looking anxiously toward the dining room didn't help, but Claire brushed past him and ignored the chill when he reached for her.

"If you really want to help," she whispered at him over her shoulder, "figure out some way to rescue Chad, then Patrick, and then me. Otherwise, just leave me the hell alone."

———

Louisa stood in the front hall and waited for the driver to bring the steamcoach around and for her stepfather to appear. Dressed warmly in anticipation of being outside, she would have perspired had she not had the sensation of being watched from the upper hallway. But every time she glanced over her shoulder, she found the space above to be empty, at least what she could see of it.

Heavy footsteps startled her, and she whirled around to see Paul Farrell descending the stairs. He looked as disheveled as she felt, his normally smart appearance rumpled and wrinkled. He carried his hat in one hand, and his beard badly needed a trim.

"What are you doing here?" she asked. "I thought I told you to go away."

"Trying to get your father to stop this madness." He straightened his monocle, but it immediately skewed again, making him look even more ridiculous.

"What madness? He's bringing gaslight to an area that needs it."

Farrell had reached the bottom step and looked down on her pityingly. "Silly child, is that what you think he wants to do?"

"Of course. I know his reasons are not likely entirely altruistic, and this will help his business ventures, but I feel it's best to do what we can for the poor and destitute."

"And what about you? What are you getting out of this?"

Before Louisa could answer, her stepfather's voice boomed from upstairs, "Begone, Farrell, until you return to your senses."

Louisa looked up to see Cobb standing at the top of the

stairs, his face red and his eyebrows dipped into the position of most displeasure.

"I know what you're up to," Farrell said and pointed with one trembling finger. "*We* know what you're doing. Don't think you'll get far with these plans."

"You've gone aether-mad." Cobb descended one step. "Now leave before I have my guards remove you."

The inventor glanced at Louisa, and she moved out of his reach lest he do something desperate. He turned on his heel and walked out of the front door, which he slammed behind him.

She winced at the noise and accompanying blast of cold air. Had the temperature dropped even more? The light through the diamond panes flanking the door showed gray, and the shadows outside them danced with the wind.

"Smart girl, moving out of his way," Cobb said when he reached the bottom of the stairs. "I suspect he carried a knife with him."

"What did he mean?"

Cobb shrugged. "I need to speak with the men before we go. Wait here." He walked into the back hallway, presumably to find the men in the back kitchen, where they would be having breakfast before they brought the carriage around.

While she waited, drumming her gloved fingers on the end of the banister, Louisa pondered Farrell's question as to how Parnaby's plan benefitted her. She knew the obvious answer, the one she counted on everyone thinking—to still appear to be a dutiful daughter. But then there was the other possibility, that she would have the chance to discover more about her family, the one that had receded into the fog of memory.

It was the opposite of a fairy tale. Instead of a commoner finding out she was a princess, she was an American princess finding out she had common blood, which would allow her to be with her prince. Or the tinkerer. If he would still have her.

Now she wished she had gone with Farrell the night before. If he and Cobb disagreed on something to the point Cobb would fire him, then the inventor likely wouldn't have cooperated in trying to trap Louisa in a situation that would send her to the convent.

That's it. After the rally, I'm going to see Patrick. Well, after I find the woman who left the address for me.

With that decided, she walked to the front door to listen for the sound of the steamcoach's arrival.

CHAPTER FOURTEEN

Wharfside Dungeon, 12 March 1871

Patrick had filled in the ghost of Louisa's mother as much as he could, leaving out the parts about his and Louisa's interlude on the airship, of course. The ghostly Maureen had nodded and gave him a look he remembered from his own mother, that she could tell he left out some details, but she didn't pry.

"You need to sleep," she'd told him. "I'll watch over you. Then tomorrow, once you're rested, we shall discuss your escape."

Patrick had wanted to argue, then ask more, but exhaustion overtook him. He woke the next morning with a start at the first lightening of the room. The lamps had been turned off, but as soon as he sat, they flamed to flickering life. He looked over to see Maureen standing and watching the aether, which hadn't changed. Neither had she except to become slightly more solid-looking, but when she moved away from the aether, she returned to her wispy state.

"How did you sleep?" she asked.

Patrick answered "Fine, you?" before his brain caught up with the situation.

Maureen laughed, and it sounded like Louisa's except with

more hollowness than mirth. "I haven't slept in a decade, and even then, it was fitful." She twisted her skirt. "I haven't slept well since my husband was lost at sea."

"Wouldn't moving on help you find him?" Patrick asked, then added, "Sorry, I'm a daft twit in the morning. That wasn't tactful of me."

She looked at him from underneath furrowed brows but didn't say anything. Patrick knew what that meant—he had better say the right thing, and fast.

"What I mean is that obviously you have a reason for staying —Louisa."

Maureen nodded. "It was stupid of me to think I could secure her future by marrying Parnaby. I didn't see until it was too late that he'd married me because of her ability. And then he got me out of the way once I recognized his deception."

"Wait." Patrick rubbed his eyes. "Parnaby killed you?"

"Yes, and I was so shocked it knocked me back here to the space that used to be my laboratory." She gestured around them.

"This isn't a nice place to work," Patrick said.

"Yes, but it's secure and secret." She sighed. "After Arthur was lost at sea, I worked first as a housekeeper and then as an apothecary for Parnaby. I had some knowledge of herbs and such from my people, and he caught me one day treating Louisa for her sensitive stomach."

"What did he want with an apothecary?"

Fear flickered over the ghost's face so quickly Patrick thought it must be a trick of the lighting or the aether, but she then replied, "He was interested in ways to make people do and say things they wouldn't otherwise. That's what attracted him to Paul Farrell, who took over after me. He has a special truth smoke he uses, but once Parnaby found out about Louisa, he set Paul up to do other things. He worked down here, too, or tried to."

Patrick could only imagine what she had done to her replacement. He knew it was rude to ask, but he had to know the answer to one more question in order to gauge the danger he might be in.

"And then how did you die?"

Once again, Maureen surprised him by her lack of emotion. "A sudden illness that wasn't treated properly, or perhaps my own herbs being turned against me. I don't know."

Patrick looked at the empty dishes from the previous evening's dinner, and his own stomach jumped. Would he be subject to the same? Any illness he would develop would likely be attributed to the conditions he was being kept in.

"And what was that about helping me to get out of here?"

"Now that I have seen and felt the aether, I need time to think about what will be best for both of us."

The scrape of the door opening echoed down the stairwell, and Maureen disappeared.

"Wait." Patrick reached toward where she had stood, but his fingertips met only regular air without a trace of chill or anything that would indicate a ghost had stood there. He'd met otherworldly beings before, and they all had their own agendas, but this one stymied him.

Morlock accompanied another guard, and they both glanced at the aether but not long enough for Patrick to take advantage of the distraction.

"Glad to see you've given up and are getting to work," Morlock said and kept his pistol aimed at Patrick. The other guard set the tray he carried on the table beside the dinner dishes and traded them out with efficient gestures, leaving Patrick with some rashers and eggs he would have to eat with his fingers and the toast provided. At least there was a cup of coffee. Patrick guessed it was lukewarm, but he would take it.

"We'll be back to check on you tonight," Morlock said. "Work well, and maybe the boss will reward you."

"And what about lunch?" Patrick asked. "You can't expect a man to work for twelve hours straight without sustenance."

"Save some of yer breakfast if yer that worried," Morlock

growled. He kept the gun on Patrick until the other guard had reached the top of the stairs and yelled, "Made it, come on."

"No funny business, you hear?" Morlock backed up the stairs, and Patrick forced himself to approach the food slowly, testing each smell as it reached his nostrils for aspects too bitter or strange. The eggs had flecks of green in them, but when he isolated one on his tongue, he found it to be a chive. Eventually his stomach wouldn't let him dally any longer, and he wolfed down all but a piece of the toast and a rasher, which he saved for his lunch. He turned from his meal to find Maureen watching him.

"I remember food," she said. "I miss it almost as much as I do Louisa. What does Parnaby want with you?"

Patrick sighed. "Other than a more efficient aether device that combines the therapeutic one with a system like we made in Paris? I wish I knew what his real intentions are." He studied the ghost. "Do you think Louisa does?"

"She likely doesn't, but more because she's afraid to ask. I'm afraid I did too well with raising her to appreciate the comforts she has with him. I've also wondered why she doesn't question more to herself."

"Aye, she's too comfortable." Patrick moved to the work-bench and picked up a length of rubber hose. "Now if you'll pardon me, I have work to do. Unless you're going to help me escape."

She disappeared again, and Patrick knew he had his answer.

"Fecking ghost," he muttered and got to work.

———

Louisa thought she had never been to the industrial area of town before, but once they passed the river, the ball of determination in the middle of her chest expanded into a glow of nostalgia. She couldn't explain how, but the buildings they passed had an air of familiarity, although shabbier and older like a beloved relative returned from a long, exhausting journey.

The pang of loss at seeing the burned-out shell of one store made her avert her gaze from the steamcoach window, and she noticed Parnaby watching her.

"What are you thinking?" he asked. It was an open enough question, but Louisa knew there was a right and wrong answer.

"There are surprisingly few steam vehicles here," she said. Not a lie exactly—she had noticed their absence.

Parnaby nodded. "It's the coal shortage. When it's cheaper to have a mule or horse than a steam engine, you know things are dire."

"And yet you're bringing gaslight here." She hadn't really talked to him about it much, what they were doing there.

"Sometimes you have to distract people from what they don't have with what they want more, in this case light for safety, although there has been some resistance."

"I can't imagine from whom." Louisa gestured to the window, through which she saw a man lying on the sidewalk. She hoped he was asleep. "It's too easy to become a victim in the dark."

"One would think." Cobb stuck his unlit pipe in his mouth. He said he didn't smoke in the coach out of courtesy for her since she had a delicate stomach. His "courtesy" served as a strategy to minimize the chance of her vomiting in his nice steamcoach and give him the continued appearance of being a good stepfather, but Louisa appreciated it nonetheless.

She would ask who resisted, but she had already annoyed him earlier with her questions, so she decided to find out through other means. How, she wasn't sure, but she did have tea at Eliza Adams' house. The woman had her pulse on anything in the city —country, really—that could be scandalous. And Eliza loved to talk about all of it.

The coach slowed as they approached the square where the rally to stir up excitement about the project was to be held once the people returned from church. Louisa looked out of the window at the gathering crowd. In spite of the drab weather and predominance of black outerwear, a few spots of color showed through. A blue feather on a hat, the flash of a crimson skirt—likely a lady of ill-repute—the green sleeve of a dress under a too-short cloak...

Finding the colors was like a treasure hunt, and Louisa gave herself a point for each find, double for purple, her favorite color. So engrossed was she in the hunt that she almost missed the flash of a face she had to search her memory for—Harvard professor Artemus Malloy.

What is he doing all the way down here? But she'd encountered him at the trolley station, and she'd been searching for the woman from this area who had brought Louisa the locket.

Perhaps he lived here among the laborers and day-hires?

An odd place for an engineering professor to live. But then, I don't know how much money they make. Perhaps I should look into that if he tries to pursue his suit with me.

He disappeared into the crowd, but not before tipping his hat at Louisa. The steamcoach pulled up to the bunting-wrapped fence around the stage, and one of the policemen opened a section for them to pull through. He, too, tipped his hat.

The vehicle stopped beside a small tent behind the stage, and a guard opened the door and held a curtain aside.

"No sense in freezing while we wait for the festivities to start," Cobb said.

Some of the spectators nearby booed, and a piece of sleet landed on Louisa's neck, causing her to shiver, but when she looked up, nothing else fell from the sky.

"I'm going to walk around to settle my stomach," she said and sidestepped the open curtain. "Hiding from the cold isn't going to help you win over the crowd."

"I've done enough for them." Parnaby dismissed them with a shrug. "As for you, clear your head if you need to, but don't get too close to the barriers. They're there for a reason."

Parnaby told the guard to stay with her and then ducked into the tent, leaving Louisa and the man outside. He didn't meet her eyes, and Louisa sighed.

"Are you cold?" she asked.

He nodded, still not looking at her, and his teeth chattered beneath his clenched lips.

"Go stand where it's warmest, and you can keep an eye on me."

"Thank you, Miss. Some of the others have a fire going in a bucket beside the stage. Come warm up if you need to."

"I will, thank you. And what is your name?"

"Greely, Miss. Arvind Greely."

"Arvind Greely," she repeated to make sure she would remember it.

"Aye. And make sure you stay away from the fence. Wouldn't take a second for a pretty bag like yours to disappear in this part of town."

"I'll keep that in mind." She paced through the small space they'd fenced off beside and behind the stage, always keeping Greely in sight or making sure he could see her.

She'd just passed the corner when someone in the crowd hissed, "Pssst."

Louisa wheeled around to see Artemus Malloy standing just out of sight of the guards. She ambled over, ostensibly to check a corner of the bunting.

"Why, Professor Malloy, what a pleasant surprise." She batted her eyelashes.

He leaned over the fence and glanced right and left before saying, "I can't linger, but I wanted to tell you to get back in your steamcoach and get out of here. What was Cobb thinking, bringing that coal-burner here? The people are angry enough. They haven't been able to heat their houses in weeks."

"He's giving them something they want—gaslight—to distract them from what they don't have." She tried to put as much conviction behind the words as Cobb had.

"That's a poor excuse. Trust me—you need to leave. This is no place for a girl like you."

"I'm from this part of town," she snapped, and she knew it was true. "My mother and I lived here before she married Parnaby."

"I'm well aware of that, but are you? Do you even remember living here?"

"Vaguely." She imitated one of Cobb's hand waves.

"That's what I thought."

Shouts behind Louisa made her turn around, and she gasped. The bucket the guards had been using for their fire had tipped over, and flames flowed through the bunting and over the corner of the wooden stage. A gust of wind blew the smoke in her direction, and Louisa coughed.

With a shout, the crowd surged toward the fence and the stage.

———

Henry Davidson opened his eyes to dim light outside his window that told him the day would be gloomy.

Fitting for my last day on earth.

He preferred the clouds to sun, particularly if they spit a fine mist, as they seemed to do when he rose and looked out the window.

Something fell on his left foot, and he looked down to see the dried remains of the poultice Colin had put on his wound the night before sitting atop his toes. It had stung and smelled horrible, but the Irish medicine seemed to have done the trick. The gash on his leg still had angry red lips, and the muscles moved stiffly but without pain. For that he was thankful.

A shadow moved in his peripheral vision, and he turned to see an apparition he'd come to call the Green Lady standing by his washstand.

"Perhaps we'll be able to talk tonight," he said.

She cocked her head, showing the gash at her neck, but he ignored the grisly wound. The girl had been beautiful in life, he was sure, with black hair and eyes of a green so dark he had thought them brown at first. He'd been frightened of her when she'd initially appeared, but when she proved merely curious, not harmful, he came to welcome her, the only woman he could speak whatever came to his mind with. She never stayed long or spoke to him, but she'd become a familiar presence.

"I fear I shall be a ghost like you before the sun sets," he told her.

She straightened her head and shook it with a bemused expression as if to say, *You living ones are too anxious.*

"No, I'm serious." He sat on his bed. "I and my men have failed, and my bosses will be unhappy with me. They're already angry I haven't managed to gather enough evidence against Parnaby Cobb."

The apparition shrugged and faded away. *Perhaps she didn't understand.* But he felt she did, that she thought he was overreacting. *And that's why I don't have a real wife or anyone else, even beyond the restrictions of my work.* He'd never felt understood by women, who didn't typically have patience for his seriousness. The only one he'd met that he felt he could have come to an understanding with was already betrothed when he'd met her and now was married, a much better arrangement for her.

Henry shook his head. Lamenting over something that never could be almost sat worse with him than facing his doom, although he guessed taking stock of his life was to be expected. He dressed without help and limped downstairs, sinking into a chair at the table with an exhale of relief. His leg gave a warning throb. The clock on the kitchen mantle said it was nine o'clock, two hours before he was to meet the mysterious person in the alley.

"How are you feeling?" Colin asked. He set a plate of eggs, rashers, and toast in front of Henry.

"Better, thanks. Your poultice worked wonders."

"Good. You should take it easy today, rest the muscles."

Henry snorted. "Right. I'll do the best I can, but there are no guarantees."

"There never are, are there?"

"That's the truth."

"Oh, and this arrived early this morning." Colin handed him a telegram.

Henry's shoulders slumped when he read it. Of course Iris and the others hadn't managed to retrieve O'Connell. Rescuing Radcliffe now assumed double importance—if he didn't, Cobb would be all too able to force O'Connell to do what he wanted by threatening his friend.

Henry ate but didn't pay much attention to the food, although Colin had once again proved to be an excellent cook. *He's wasted in this organization. Some unlucky woman is missing out on a great husband.*

That was one thing Henry had no delusions about—he would have no idea what to do as someone's mate. He had basic skills and could take care of himself, but as for others... He barely knew what to do as a leader of his merry little band and much preferred to work solo.

He spent the next two hours organizing the strategy room so that if he never returned, Colin would have an easy time continuing. The men came in and spoke with him briefly before heading out to continue the search for Chadwick Radcliffe. Henry reviewed the plans with them and hoped someone would have something to tell him before it was time to meet with Violet and Hobbes that afternoon.

But first... Henry limped back to the kitchen and through the back room, where he grabbed one of the large cloaks the men used during inclement weather and at night to conceal their body shapes and faces. He was doubly grateful for the gray day and mist, which justified his apparel. He walked down the alley behind the buildings, and when he turned a corner, he found himself cloaked face to cloaked face with a mysterious figure.

"Henry Davidson, I presume?" the other man asked the question in a gravelly voice.

"You are correct." Henry wanted to lean against the wall but held himself upright.

"You came alone?"

"Yes. I can only fit one of me in this cloak."

A harsh laugh. "As expected. And what if I were to ambush you with some of my colleagues and make you disappear?"

Henry shrugged. "My day is likely not to end well. You would only be advancing the inevitable."

"Ah, a fatalist, I see."

"I didn't come here to be analyzed." Henry's leg throbbed. "What do you want? How did you get in my bathing room?"

"You know as well as I that the alley is narrow and the roofs connected. You should be more careful about locking your windows even if you are on the fourth floor."

"Ah, right." *Not that it will matter to me, but I'll mention it to Colin.*

"We want to help you, Inspector. You have the power to do something we want, and we have the ability to retrieve your Doctor Radcliffe."

The only thing Henry was certain of was that the man knew too much, and he fingered the revolver at his belt.

"I wouldn't do that if I were you, Inspector. I do have others here, and they will not hesitate to eliminate you should you draw a weapon on me."

"So this is an ambush."

"No, it's a discussion."

Henry pivoted a quarter-turn to check behind him. He couldn't see anyone, but he was also conscious of the space above him and the dead eyes of windows that gave no light but could conceal someone.

"I need proof you can help me."

"We will deliver Doctor Radcliffe to your headquarters at three o'clock this afternoon. In return, you will allow Paul

Farrell to go free when you have the chance to apprehend him."

"Cobb's favorite inventor?" Henry scoffed. "Never. He knows too much that can help me finally get Cobb."

"Then you will never see Radcliffe alive, and your own life continues to be in peril."

Henry mentally calculated the costs of cooperating. His men were excellent trackers. If anyone could find Radcliffe, they could. And if they couldn't, it was unlikely anyone else would succeed.

"Fine," he said and put a hand out for the other man to shake. "If you deliver Radcliffe to me, I will let Paul Farrell go if I have the chance to catch him."

They shook hands, and the other man stepped back into the shadows, which wrapped him in their gloom. Henry allowed himself a brief lean against the wall.

CHAPTER FIFTEEN

Rally Site, 12 March 1871

"Run," Malloy said and grabbed her hand.

"What are they doing?" Louisa held on to him with both hands to keep from being swept toward the fire.

"Grabbing pieces of the stage to use as fuel at home."

"But they'll burn."

"They don't care."

"Louisa!" Someone called her name, and she turned, but Artemus held on to her. Something hissed behind her, and gray smoke billowed around them and kept her from seeing what happened by the stage.

"Oh, thank goodness, they've got water." She coughed, almost doubling over as the smoke thickened.

"Come with me." Artemus spoke into the shoulder of his coat, but she could still hear him. She thought he then said, "I'll get you to safety and then bring you home. You can't stay here."

She nodded, and holding on to each other, they made their way through the crowd. While many of the people fought to get to the stage, the others moved away from the smoke, and Louisa and Artemus joined one of those streams. As soon as they could break away, she reached into her reticule and pulled out the piece of paper with the address.

"Let's go here," she said and showed it to him. "That's near here, isn't it?"

He read the address, but he didn't react beyond a nod. He led her to a small store tucked between two shabby building entrances. Chipped stenciling on the window read, "Benandanti Charms, Oils, and Remedies."

The smell of the smoke that clung to Louisa's clothes and the watery sunlight brought upon her a sense that she'd been to this place before, and her mind filled in the chips in the letters and brightened up the facade of the building, simultaneously making both bigger.

"Come on, Louisa. Don't dawdle. We need to get this over with."

"Can I have one of the pretty rocks?"

"Once I marry Mister Cobb, you can have all the pretty rocks you want. And they'll be cut and polished, and they'll sparkle like magic."

"Like magic?"

"Like magic," Louisa murmured and flexed her fingers. It seemed that if she looked hard enough, she would see her own small hand tightly gripped in her mother's bigger one, the wrinkles in the too-large hand-me-down gloves pinching her palm.

"Like what?" Artemus asked with a grin.

"Nothing."

"Well, the Benandanti were supposedly the good walkers, Italian witches, and in some legends, werewolves." He held the door open.

Louisa hesitated. She only saw blackness beyond. "Are you sure this is it?"

"This is the address."

Louisa descended into the gloom of the shop. It smelled clean, and the shelves sparkled. As her eyes adjusted, she saw it wasn't the shelves themselves, but what they held—different metal charms and rocks. Artemus rubbed his hands, and Louisa guessed she'd been squeezing them hard.

"I'm sorry," she said. "Did I hurt you?"

"No, not at all. Although you do have a strong grip for a woman."

"Women have many surprising strengths, Tinkerer." The voice from the back of the shop made Louisa whirl around. She hadn't noticed the older woman with gray-streaked black hair pulled into a severe bun and dark eyes that glittered like the jet beads at her throat.

Artemus swept his hat off. "Madame, I didn't see you there."

"You made enough noise coming into my shop. And who is this young lady who shouldn't be out and about without a chaperone?"

She walked toward Louisa, who fought the urge to run. Although the strange woman only came up to Louisa's shoulder, she radiated something—power, maybe? Yes, some force surrounded her.

"What is your name, girl?"

Louisa wanted to give a pseudonym to protect her identity—Cobb wasn't a popular figure in the area, and there was a chance she hadn't been recognized—but her tongue moved of its own accord."Louisa Cobb."

She clapped a hand over her mouth, but a frisson of delight made the corners of her lips lift. *Who is this person with the same talent as mine? Are we related?*

"Ah, good. I knew you would come once you got the locket. Let me see it."

Again, Louisa felt compelled to obey, but this time by her own curiosity.

"Who are you?" Louisa asked as she unbuttoned her collar, thankful that Artemus turned away. She pulled the locket out from her bosom, and it felt warm on her fingers.

"Don't you remember, child?" The older woman caressed Louisa's face with fingers that smelled of a strange combination of metal and vanilla before touching the locket. Louisa made to lift the chain over her head, but the woman stopped her. "It's yours. Don't you know who these people are?"

"I know who the woman is, my mother. Is the man my father?"

"Yes, my handsome Arturo." With shaking hands, the woman released the locket and patted it where it came to rest on Louisa's chest. "He was lost at sea."

Louisa clutched the locket. Could this woman be her grandmother? But how had she not known?

Then her mother's cautions that many would be jealous of Louisa's good fortune to have Parnaby Cobb as a stepfather and would want to have a piece of that luck came to mind.

Louisa spoke cautiously, both to control her own hope and so as not to offend the woman. "I'm aware of that, and I'm sorry for your loss. I wish I could remember him more. All I have is vague flashes that may be dreams or recollections—I can't tell which." Louisa tucked the locket back under her dress and rebuttoned her collar before anyone could see her neck. The memory of the paintbrush feel of Patrick marking it with kisses made her cheeks heat.

"And did your mother ever tell you who owned the ship that took your father's life?" Now her lips disappeared into a compressed line.

"No." Louisa wasn't sure what to make of the woman's sudden change in demeanor.

"You live with him now, *mia passerota*."

Louisa huffed, her suspicions aroused. "Look, I know that my stepfather isn't popular in this part of town, but he has taken good care of me. And what did you just call me?"

"*Passerota* is little sparrow because you are trying to find your wings to fly away from him. You know the truth of what's happening, but you lack the courage to move against him."

Louisa closed her eyes against the regret of refusing and then accidentally betraying Patrick. "Sometimes flying feels like falling." She opened them to find the woman looking at her with a bemused expression.

"Parnaby Cobb takes what he can from people, and he only gives falsely in return. I can see in your eyes that you begin to see the truth. I only pray that you will have the courage to move against him before it's too late."

"It may already be. He's threatening me with marriage or the convent."

"Then you must do what you can to follow your heart." She tapped the place where the locket was, this time through Louisa's dress. "Even if it takes you to places that frighten you."

Artemus cleared his throat. Louisa had forgotten he stood by the door. "I should get you home. I'm sure your people will be looking for you."

Louisa turned back to her grandmother, unwilling to let go completely in case there was a chance she was genuine. "These are my people. May I return to talk to you, learn more about my father?"

"You may, but only after you are free. Otherwise it is too dangerous." She squeezed Louisa's hand, which took some of the sting away, but not all of it. "Thank you for bringing her, Tinkerer."

"Wait..." Louisa looked between the two of them. "You asked him to bring me here?"

"I asked him to find a way for me to warn you myself." She took Louisa's other hand so she held both of them, and pulling Louisa down into a bent position, kissed both of her cheeks. "Go and fly, *Mia Passerota*."

Louisa nodded, and the tears that stung her eyes burned more because of the smoke. Artemus led her out on to the sidewalk and to a waiting cab with a pair of dingy brown horses tied to it. The driver was so bundled up it was difficult to see whether he had the same dark-eyed, dark-haired appearance of the others in the neighborhood or if he was an outsider.

Louisa felt a little thrill at the realization she might belong somewhere, and if there was a grandmother, she likely had aunts and uncles and cousins. More memories teased the corners of her mind, of playing with other children her age. Had they played something called the Lie Game to see who had the family talent?

Impossible. I must be making that up.

"Let's get you home."

Louisa wanted to say this place had been her home. "Wait, first I need to make a stop. There's someone I need to apologize to, and I may need your help."

He scowled at her from the facing seat of the thankfully closed carriage. "I'm not your errand boy, Miss Cobb."

"But this will give you the answer to the question you asked me the first time we met."

He leaned forward. "Are you telling me, Miss Cobb, that you are bringing me to see Patrick O'Connell?"

Excitement welled up from Louisa's stomach at her defiance of Cobb in so many ways with this one action. "Yes. Because I really need to see him, too."

———

Iris waited for a response to her telegram to Davidson all morning. She couldn't seem to sit still, unlike Marie, who repaired a tear in one of her favorite skirts, Johann, who polished his violin and replaced one of the strings, and Edward, who lost himself in a book.

When eleven o'clock rolled around and she hadn't heard anything, she decided to take matters into her own hands. She had work to do, and she couldn't sit idle at the hotel waiting for orders.

"Where are you going?" Marie looked up from her needle and thread with a frown. "Have you heard something?"

"No. I just need to get out and breathe." Iris gestured to the window. "I'm going to jump out of my skin if I have to wait any longer."

"Do you want me to come with you?" Edward asked. "Are you going to the museum?"

"I don't know yet. I'm going to see if something came, and maybe the front desk missed it. I'll be right back." As soon as the words left her mouth, Iris knew how ridiculous she sounded. She wondered if she was the only one who felt the lack of adventure after having spent a few days in the smaller airship. The world had returned to its usual quiet, which likely relieved Edward, and Johann and Marie were happy wherever the other was.

So what's wrong with me?

When she walked down to the lobby, she found Lieutenant Crow sitting and having tea with a couple of rough gentlemen who appeared as though they would rather be drinking something of a different stimulating quality. Today she wore a narrow day dress with minimum decoration that ensured she would disappear from someone's attention after a cursory glance.

"Ah, Mrs. Bailey," she said and stood. "I was just about to come up and find you. Something arrived here for you just a few moments ago. I took the liberty of procuring it for you."

"Oh?" Iris stretched a smile over her clenched teeth. "Then please do give it over. As you must know, my situation is rather urgent."

"I will, but I have a favor to ask of you first. My colleague at the museum is quite keen on meeting you."

Iris cocked her head. "Is it a favor if it's coerced, Lieutenant?"

"Does it matter if I have something you want? Go fetch your hat and cloak, and let's be off."

Having had previous experience with hostage telegrams —*bugger, not again*—Iris raised a hand. "Show it to me first. Else how do I know you're not leading me on a wild chase?"

Crow held her hand out to one of the men, who put a

telegram envelope in it. She unsealed it and nudged the paper up so Iris could see the first line and know it was genuine: *Greetings from LFATB.*

"Fine," Iris said. "But I'm not coming with you alone."

"Oh, by all means bring your husband. I would love to pick his brains, too." Somehow a toothpick had appeared in her mouth, giving Lieutenant Crow a sinister appearance.

Iris didn't want to put herself in harm's way, but she especially didn't want to endanger her friends or husband. When she reached the room, she found Marie sitting alone.

"Where did Johann and Edward go?" Iris asked as she gathered her cloak and hat.

Marie sighed. "One of those infernal steam raven spy devices flew past, and they decided to follow it."

Iris's stomach dropped like a deflated dirigible. "Cobb knows we're here?"

Marie nodded, the corners of her mouth tucked in concern, but her chest lifted with a sigh, and her expression brightened slightly. "Whatever it's after, it seemed more interested in the building across the street, so Edward and Johann have gone up to the roof. Where are you going?"

"To the museum."

"Oh?" Marie stood and folded the skirt she'd been mending.

"Yes."

"But what about the telegram?"

"That's why I have to go to the museum." Iris sighed. "Lieutenant Crow from the airship got it first, and she's holding it hostage until I do something for her at the museum."

Now Marie frowned. "That sounds potentially dangerous." She glanced outside. "But is it more dangerous than here, I wonder?"

Iris knew Marie was right. But she was tired of waiting around for things to happen, and getting her friend away from the mechanical raven seemed a good plan. She knew Marie wouldn't be able to sit still in the room for long.

"On the other hand," Marie mused, "I haven't had the chance to practice my fighting skills in a while. Would you like me to come? I would like to know what she's up to."

"I would, too, and I would love your company." Iris rolled the edge of her cloak between two fingers. "Could she be interested in Patrick, too? She did mention she wanted Claire away from her aunt, so it would make sense for her to want to rescue him, too."

Marie removed her own outdoor coverings from the closet. "There's only one way to find out."

Iris helped Marie with her cloak and hat. She couldn't help but remember when Marie was posing as a maid and had done the same for Iris.

This is much more comfortable, Iris mused. *I much prefer having friends to servants.*

After a final pat of the hat's feathers, Marie nodded. "Shall we?"

"Yes, let's. We have a crow to catch."

CHAPTER SIXTEEN

When the door at the top of the stairs opened, Patrick expected the person who descended to be one of his captors or perhaps Parnaby Cobb himself. He didn't anticipate Louisa to appear with Patrick's old professor, Artemus Malloy. The professor's presence kept Patrick from saying what he wanted to Louisa, something about how she wasn't any better than her stepfather, and he'd never forget how she betrayed him and led the guards right to the escape compartment he had been only moments away from launching.

Or how he'd hoped the rap on the door was her wanting to come with him, and he'd kicked himself for a fool ever since.

Or how he would never be able to forget the feel of her body under his hands and lips.

No, he'd learned to just stay the hell away from people with the last name of Cobb, even if he was being haunted by one.

"What are you doing here?" Patrick asked, although not as harshly as he would have. Then his tinkerer's curiosity got the best of him. "And how did you get past the guard?"

Louisa shrugged with a smile, and Artemus looked away.

"You still have the mechanical flower that spits swoon spray, don't you?" Patrick asked Artemus. The man had been employed by various governments for a while until he'd realized his inventions were being used for nefarious purposes, such as rendering ladies helpless and fainting in the arms of government clerks who were more interested in matters of stealing virginity than of national security. Artemus had left Washington and taken his inventions with him, feeling academia at least provided some protection for his genius. He'd never liked some of what he'd invented, but his practicality allowed him to make use of them.

"I work for a greater good, Patrick. You know that. I haven't used the stuff in years."

"And there's nothing like a little bribery," Louisa added. "He said we have ten minutes."

His former—not old, Patrick recalled, Artemus being barely older than he—teacher's voice brought Patrick back to a less complicated time, when the lasses who'd caught his eye were servant girls who only wanted a momentary reprieve from their daytime drudgery, not spoiled capitalist princesses who used him for a lark and then went back to their papas.

"Then what are you doing with this one?" Patrick jerked a thumb at Louisa, then turned away to his aether device. "I'm busy."

The left side of his body grew cold, and he knew Louisa's mother stood beside him. "She's such a grown young woman now." Her voice made for a chill-tongued whisper in his ear. "So beautiful, but look, so sad."

"Not my problem," Patrick muttered.

"But she looks at you with such hunger."

Now that piqued his curiosity. He tried to rub the cold from his ear and turned to see Louisa and Artemus conferring with low voices. The color in her cheeks told Patrick Artemus had asked about their history, and every time she cut her eyes at him, her blush deepened.

Aye, let her try to explain her innocence to that one.

"What do you want, Miss Cobb?" Patrick asked. "Unless

you're here to help me escape, I'm not interested in talking with you."

Her chest heaved with her sigh, and he couldn't help but wish she'd do so again.

Don't be a fool, O'Connell. That's how she pulled you in the last time.

"I wanted to apologize and explain. I didn't lead Morlock to your escape hatch. I was trying to join you, to escape with you."

He crossed his arms and arched an eyebrow. "Were you, now? I'd given you the chance beforehand, and you refused."

She straightened her spine more, somehow, as if that were possible. He couldn't help but picture them as two opponents in a contest to convince him of her innocence.

"I was frightened." Her simple statement could only be true, but Patrick recalled how Cobb said she couldn't be lied to. That didn't mean she couldn't give falsehood.

"And then...?"

"And then my father came in, confronted me about what we'd been doing, and slapped me."

Patrick's lungs sucked in air of their own accord, and his fists tightened. "Where?" he asked.

"My face." She walked to stand by one of the three-tubed lights, and Patrick saw the bruise, cleverly concealed by cosmetics but evident when he looked closely. She flinched, and he suspected her mother's ghost—whom Patrick couldn't see but knew was there due to the temperature—had caressed her daughter's cheek.

"The bastard," Patrick growled. Artemus's jaw had also tensed.

"So I decided I couldn't stay there anymore. I looked to make sure it was clear, I swear I did." The sky blue of her eyes splintered into tears, bright like rain on a sunny day. "But then Morlock appeared from one of the other rooms and caught me. I'm sorry I wasn't careful enough."

Patrick wanted to pull her into his arms and kiss away the tears, but as pretty as her story was, she was still free—in a sense

—and he was still stuck in the dungeon. "How do I know you're telling me the truth, lass?"

"Isn't the bruise on my face enough?"

"Yes." Her special ability pulled the statement from him.

She closed her eyes and rubbed her temples. "I'm sorry. I didn't mean to force you. I have less control when I'm upset. What else do I need to do to convince you I'm trustworthy?"

There was less of a pull on his mind that time, and Patrick appreciated how she tried to give him some freedom, but it wasn't the kind he wanted. "Help me escape."

"How?" She looked up, her eyes wide. "I don't have enough money to bribe the guard that much, and even if I did, I can't get you past all the guards on the main floor. And there are a lot."

"Then figure something out." He'd almost asked for a kiss, and the honorable part of him chided the rest of him for using her. "Artemus, can you help me?"

Artemus stopped edging closer to the aether isolator. "I've had some of my lads working on an escape plan for you, but no luck so far. Cobb knows what he's doing."

Patrick didn't blame his former mentor for his curiosity. "Aye, he does. And even if I escape, there's the problem of Chad and Claire." He rubbed his upper arms. "They'll be punished."

Artemus's glasses moved with his smile. "Chadwick Radcliffe, your doctor friend?"

"Aye, the one languishing in a Southern prison in Terminus, and his bride-to-be stuck with her evil aunt here. Cobb made sure to guarantee my cooperation."

Louisa clapped her hands. "Claire's back? Ah, right, I'm to have tea with her this afternoon." She put a gloved finger to her lip. "I can speak with her. And my father is going to be hosting a dinner party on Saturday night, and he said you are to come and demonstrate your aether work." She walked to the table on which the aether isolating device stood. "Is this it?"

Patrick caught his breath. What if it responded to her like it had to Claire? Worse, what if strange golden creatures started appearing to Louisa and generally wreaking havoc again?

"Don't worry about Chadwick," Artemus told him. "I've got friends down there, and you have more friends than you realize here. We can stage a grand rescue of both you and Claire from the party. With Miss Cobb's cooperation, of course."

The fond look he gave Louisa made Patrick want to punch him.

"Then Saturday," Patrick said. "Or before if you have word that my friends are safe."

"Do you know what my father wants you to do?" Louisa asked. She put a finger on the globe. The aether flashed but otherwise did nothing.

"He wants me to do something with the aether. You heard him."

"Right. I suggest you do just enough to be convincing but not enough to be effective."

Patrick nodded. "I'd been thinking of that, but it's not that simple." He took Louisa's arm and guided her to the other end of the dungeon, away from the pulsating aether biscuit. "It sometimes has a mind of its own," he whispered.

"What? How?"

"We don't know yet. But I saw some strange things at Fort Daniels. Yer stepfather doesn't know what he's toying with."

"Then you need to convince it to help you."

Patrick couldn't determine whether she was serious or not, but her words gave him an idea. "I'll see what I can do." He glanced at Artemus, who now studied the aether, enthralled as all were upon their first meeting. Except Louisa, but Patrick hoped she was as fascinated by him as he was of her. He leaned toward her, and she didn't move away. At first he just brushed her lips.

The smell of smoke reminded him of home, of easier times before life became complicated with problems beyond most peoples' nightmares. She pressed into him, and he was so startled he almost broke the contact, but his hands found her waist, where they belonged, he reminded himself, not higher or lower. The dance of their tongues made him wish she wore as little as she had the last time they'd been in this position.

He moved his hand to the back of her head to tangle his fingers in her hair, and one of her hairpins plinked on the ground. Then a cold hand on his ear made him break from her. The ghost's fingers were almost solid enough to drag his face away from Louisa's, but he got the message if not the motion.

"That will be quite enough, young man."

Patrick looked over to see Louisa's mother, more solid than he'd seen her yet, scowling at him with hands on hips.

"Mama?" Louisa asked. Now embarrassed pink joined the blush already in her cheeks.

"Yes, and I raised you better than this. What do you think you're doing, kissing him? Do you know him?"

"Yes, I do." Louisa took Patrick's hand in hers. "And he's going to help me escape from Parnaby Cobb."

"Then you should wait until you can see if he follows through on his promise before you give way your virtue."

"Mama!"

Patrick hid a laugh by coughing to the side. He caught Artemus leaving a wire on the workbench by the tuning forks and nodded thanks. Artemus tipped his hat.

"You should go," Patrick told Louisa with regret. "I don't want you getting in trouble. At least not yet," he added with a wink. He clasped her to him for one last kiss and heard a hairpin hit the floor.

"Be careful," she said when they came up for air.

"I've got nowhere to go but here."

"We'll see about that."

———

When Iris and Marie arrived in the lobby, Lieutenant Crow smiled and reached out to shake Marie's hand like a man would.

"Madame Bledsoe, it's a pleasure to see you again."

Marie, taking on the air of a French noblewoman, limply offered her own hand. "I would say likewise, but we both know this is merely a business transaction. Our attendance for the telegram you've stolen from us."

Crow's smile held but a hint of regret. "I'm sure Mrs. Bailey will find our trip to the museum most enlightening. I don't expect you to trust me, but I am trying to help." With that she turned, and Marie and Iris followed flanked by the two guards. Before they left, Iris insisted upon stopping by the front desk to leave a note for Edward and Johann that she and Marie had gone to the Museum of Ancient Cultures and would be back by mid-afternoon.

The snow of the previous day had given way to a bitter cold, and Iris pulled her cloak more tightly around her. She glanced up at Marie, who seemed only to walk along with a disdainful air and not feel the wind that scraped across Iris's cheeks.

"My carriage is at the corner," Crow said. "These old streets are too narrow for it."

Or you prefer to have more maneuverability for a quick getaway. Iris didn't say the words out loud but used the thought as a reminder to be cautious. She wanted to find something of Crow's to hold so she could delve more into the woman's emotions and motivation, but there wasn't anything on the outside of the carriage, obviously. Before she got in, Iris noted the scrape on the front passenger side.

"Any more word on what that dwas last night?"

Crow shook her head. "I've put out feelers—the government here has a rule that one must register their automatons and keep them under control at all times—but you know as well as I that government agencies move slowly."

Iris nodded and wished she could talk to Marie's Uncle

Zokar, an expert inventor. It wasn't common for automatons to move about independently, was it?

If it was, well, that was a chilling thought.

The inside of the carriage was as spare as it had been the previous night. One of the burly men handed Lieutenant Crow up, and her hand lingered too long in his. Iris more closely examined the youth, or tried to as her eyes adjusted to the gloom of the carriage. The person whom she'd assumed was an unshaven young man lacked the prominent brow line of men, and there was a softness to the jaw. Iris couldn't get an idea of body shape under the person's overcoat, but she suspected that without a corset to narrow the waist and flare the bosom, many women could pass as men, especially if they used bandages or something else to bind their breasts.

Could Lieutenant Crow be an invert? She made a mental note to ask Marie her opinion later.

The person who had handed Lieutenant Crow in closed the door, and the steamcart moved as he/she mounted the driver's seat. One of the other guards sat up front as well, leaving Crow and the third in the back facing Iris and Marie.

"It's not that long of a ride," Crow told them. "I'm taking you to meet Bernard Langlois, one of your countrymen, Madame Bledsoe. He studied with Monsieur Firmin in Paris, but they had a falling out, so he came here to start the museum."

"Imagine that," Iris murmured. She shifted in her seat to dispel the panic that had made her spine straighten at the mention of Firmin. He'd been yet another man who wanted to use her father's reputation as a great archaeologist to his own advantage and take credit for Iris's discoveries. She didn't know what had happened to him during the Prussian siege of Paris, and she was glad she'd escaped with the ancient manuscript that had given her the clues to how the ancients had perceived and worked with the mysterious element of aether. Firmin didn't deserve her knowledge, and she had so much more now that she'd excavated. The question was, did Langlois?

"And is he part of your organization?" Iris asked. She didn't want to say *neo-Pythagoreans* out loud.

"No, but he is friendly to it. He, too, believes that some secrets are best left buried. But he is an academic and cannot contain his curiosity, so he is more moderate."

"And what is the purpose of my meeting him, then?"

"He may surprise you, Mrs. Bailey. As I've said before, we are working toward the same aim—keeping dangerous knowledge and power out of the hands of a madman."

"Cobb doesn't strike me as mad," Marie said. She'd been playing the bored aristocrat's wife to that point, a strategy Iris applauded because it would make the others underestimate Marie's vast and potentially dangerous abilities. Or did they have a dossier on her, too?

"He's mad to the point of wanting to concentrate power in his hands."

"As most men do." Marie inclined her head. "And women, if the truth is to be told."

"All right," Crow conceded. "His motivations are not uncommon. But his ambitions, as I've been informed by someone who was until recently in his employ, extend beyond what any sane person would tolerate."

"Oh?" Now Iris's curiosity really was piqued. "What are his ambitions? And who gave you this information?"

"Parnaby Cobb wants to control the other men of his stature, but not through the typical machinations of industry. He wants to hold power over their minds. He also wishes to have automatons with enough will to do his bidding without direct supervision. To that end, he is engaged in some experiments you ladies would find horrifying."

"Oh, do tell," Marie said. "We've seen and heard more than you realize."

Crow shook her head. "Not now. Let's just say that what he's seen and has been forced to do has driven Paul Farrell from a little mad to truly insane. I expect him to kill himself any day."

CHAPTER SEVENTEEN

Cobb Townhouse, 12 March 1871

Louisa walked into the townhouse with her mind half on what she would say to Cobb and the other half on the ghost of her mother.

Louisa had thought Maureen had died of one of the many illnesses that occasionally visited the city and didn't leave without taking a good portion of the populace with it. In Louisa's mother's case, it had been typhoid. Or so she'd thought. Not that Louisa had any expertise on ghosts and why they happened, but she'd thought they formed after violent deaths, often self-inflicted. She would have to ask someone. Perhaps Patrick. Irish people knew more about the mystical side of things than Americans, didn't they?

The thought made her smile, and she dispelled the coldness that came to her fingers and toes with the memory of the ghost by remembering her most recent kiss. Less shocking than the previous one, therefore more appropriate to imagine.

Not that her mother had approved. It seemed that even after death, Maureen Cobb had high marital ambitions for her daughter. *Not that marrying up worked out well for her.*

Something about the townhouse's energy told Louisa Parnaby Cobb was home, and she breathed into the feel of the gathering storm. Would he be angry at her for disappearing? Or relieved to see her? Formerly she would have guessed the latter, but after recent events... She decided to face the ogre and ascended the stairs to the second floor and his office.

This time when Louisa entered Cobb's office, she waited and peeked through the crack in the door to see if she could gauge his mood. He sat at the desk, writing furiously, but he looked up, and she knocked.

"Oh, thank god!" He stood and held out his hands. "I was afraid I was going to get a ransom note for you at any time."

Louisa stopped just short of the desk. She crossed her arms to contain her anger, but the words slipped out. "You were more concerned about your money than my welfare?"

He gestured for her to sit and did so himself. "No, of course I was worried for you. It wasn't considerate of you to disappear like that."

"I had no choice. I couldn't see with all the smoke, not to mention breathe."

"Where did you go, then? I had the men look for you, but you had vanished."

She decided not to mention Artemus and to give Cobb a partial-truth. "I was swept into the crowd and finally extracted myself and hid in a shop until the chaos was over. Then I caught a cab home."

"Is that all?"

"I might have made a stop."

He held up a folded piece of paper note. "One of the men who works in the old tannery building said he saw you and another man go in, and then a few minutes later, out. The man matched the description of the one who accompanied you home from the train station yesterday. So I'll ask you again, and I want the truth, Louisa. Where did you go?"

Louisa kept her hands folded in front of her so she wouldn't squish the butterfly of nervousness in her abdomen. Her grandmother had said to pursue her destiny, or something like that, so she decided to fling off fear. "I went to see Patrick O'Connell."

There went the eyebrows, swooping to meet over his nose. "With whom? And how did you get past the guard?"

With her admission, Louisa's heart had joined in the annoying fluttering, located in her throat now, and she tried to quash it with a swallow. This was familiar territory, and she wouldn't give more information than needed. "I have no doubt you've circulated his description among your contacts and will find out soon enough. But," she couldn't resist adding, "my friend is terribly clever." Was he her friend? She still didn't know, but the term worked for now.

"If he's a more suitable match for you than an Irish tinkerer of no fortune whatsoever, he can be a dunce for all I care." A muscle in his cheek jumped, showing he considered it, but then he dismissed the idea with a shake. "But I doubt he is in any way suitable. He looks like an academic, and while they have stable income, and I would like to take advantage of whatever inventions he may have used to circumvent my guard, I have higher ambition for you. You are showing remarkably poor taste these days."

Louisa lifted one shoulder and dropped it. "I am merely trying different things, as young ladies do." She wanted to say that O'Connell meant nothing to her, but the words wouldn't come out.

Cobb wrote something on a card, which he folded, put in an envelope, and sealed as he spoke. "I understand you are to have tea with Claire McPhee this afternoon. Eliza Adams will be there, I'm sure, gloating over saving her own niece from making a disastrous match. I'm going to ask her to seek a husband for you while she looks for one for her niece. She knows the eligible bachelors of our circle better than I."

Louisa doubted that. Cobb knew people like chess players knew the pieces on the board, and he maneuvered them like a master. Formerly she'd thought she meant something more to him, that he felt as a stepfather would to a beloved child, but the events of the past few days had demonstrated she had as much value to him as a lifeless piece of ivory, to be moved on his whim. She also knew Eliza Adams thrived on recognition through any means, positive or negative.

I hope Artemus was right, that there are machinations in place to help us all. The question is, do I agree with his version of "help"?

Cobb must have interpreted her silence as sulkiness. "Don't pout, Louisa. I'm sure there are plenty of handsome gentlemen who would be happy to make you their wife, at least until they find they can't lie to you. I'll have Eliza give me a list, and I'll narrow it down to three for you to choose from. In fact, perhaps I'll invite them for a dance and supper on Saturday. No, let's make it Friday—St. Patrick's Day." He smirked at his own joke. "The sooner the better. You can see how that Irish brute you're so fascinated by fares in contrast."

Louisa didn't mention that she'd seen Patrick in polite company the first time they met, and he'd stood out because of his size and hair but otherwise had managed fine. Well, aside from kissing her, but she'd freely given it.

Cobb pulled a cord, and one of the maids appeared at the door. Louisa studied her. Either she was close enough in the hall to hear the bell, or she'd been eavesdropping. The girl looked at Louisa, wide-eyed, so Louisa suspected the latter.

"Give this to James and tell him I want it sent to Eliza Adams immediately."

The maid took the envelope, bobbed a curtsey, and dashed out. When she turned, her eyebrows lifted for a moment, and Louisa followed the glance. She saw the automaton still stood in the corner, but it was slightly turned from the day before and sported a dent with scraped black paint.

"What are you going to do with that now that you've canned Farrell?" she asked.

Cobb smiled, but without pleasantness. "I have plans. Farrell has served his purpose. But you shouldn't worry—you might find your future husband more malleable than you think he'll be." He chuckled as though he'd just made a joke, and the anxiety in Louisa's stomach and chest coalesced into dread. Now she knew he was up to something. But what?

———

When Iris, Marie, and Crow arrived at the Museum of Ancient Art and Artifacts, the carriage brought them around the side of the building and into a back alley that concentrated the wind into an icy wall. They dashed into a door, which opened to reveal a workroom. Bernard Langlois, a compact whirlwind of a man with sandy brown hair and trimmed beard, suspenders, and gold wire-rimmed glasses, seemed to know who she was and greeted her enthusiastically. But he practically exploded with joy when Lieutenant Crow introduced Marie. She named her as Madame Bledsoe, but it didn't fool him.

"Fantastique!" He clapped his hands. "Oh, to be in the presence of the greatest actress of our time. I can die a happy man now."

Iris and Marie exchanged concerned looks. If he recognized Marie...

Langlois didn't allow their hesitation to deter his delight. "I can see you are in disguise. But please tell me that your marriage will not stop you from pursuing your art. The rest of the world could not bear the deprivation." He put one hand on his chest. "My own heart breaks at the thought."

Marie cocked her head. "You are aware that once a woman is married, she is to act respectably."

He vanquished respectability with a wave of his hand. "That

is only for ordinary women. For someone like you or Madame Bailey here, your talent overrides such silly social rules.”

Well, at least he's somewhat progressive. Iris touched him on the arm. “If you'll forgive me, Monsieur Langlois, my time is limited, and I am eager to see what you have in your museum that may apply to my own work.”

The joy vanished from his face with the speed and light-dampening of a snuffed candle flame. “You have been excavating at Smithneus, yes?”

Iris nodded. She wished she could bring back his former warmth to replace the dread on his face.

“Come with me. I have some documents and artifacts from an earlier attempt.”

Now Iris's heart leapt. When she'd first opened the temple site, she'd found signs that someone had been there before, but it was impossible to tell what had been taken. She only knew that there were pieces missing to her puzzle, and although she had enough for a general idea of the disturbing picture, she lacked important details.

“Shall we walk through the rest of the museum while they speak?” Crow asked Marie. It wasn't a request as much as it was a command.

“Is that all right with you, Iris?”

Iris appreciated Marie's caution, but she also sensed that Langlois wouldn't reveal what he knew to someone outside the field. “Yes, quite. Check back in thirty minutes?”

Marie nodded and followed Crow and the guards out of the workroom.

“Do you mind if I remove my gloves?” Iris asked. “Your furnace is quite effective.”

“Not at all. *Bien,* it can be helpful to handle objects without interference.”

Iris slid a look at him as she removed her gloves. Did he know she could discover things about people from touching their objects? Or did he have a similar ability? As far as she knew, aside from Johann Bledsoe, who had the minor talent to be extra charming, and her own father, who had the same ability as she, such powers only belonged to women. She'd guessed, although she didn't have proof, that they had developed to make up for the disadvantage females had in their modern society, sort of a natural selection.

"Well, shall we?" she asked. "I noticed some things had been taken and the site re-sealed. Do you know anything about that?"

He gestured for her to follow him into a side room. "When I came, many of the objects were already here and in a state of disarray. But there was one box that the workmen had not unpacked, and so it had its customs and provenance papers still with it. I recognized it came from the Ottoman Empire, but not like any of the shipments I had seen before. Then Lieutenant Crow came and told me she needed my help finding what it all meant but to wait to open it until she could find someone who had studied the mysteries of her beloved Pythagoras."

"And you know what she is part of?"

His regretful sigh made her like him more. "I am aware that there are some organizations who take their good intentions to extremes. I can assure you, Madame, I am a mere academic and archaeologist. I do not hold with extreme views that could result in the deaths of many."

Now they'd reached the door to the small room, and Iris stopped. Nothing visible stood in her way, but some force repelled her, and she found herself leaning on her toes so as not to topple backwards.

"What is it?" Langlois asked. "What do you feel?"

Iris reached out a hand, and her fingers only met air, but her arm felt as though it moved through thick mud. She had to step back when she recognized she couldn't breathe, and spots appeared in her periphery. Langlois guided her to a chair, and the air thinned to normal. She'd only felt an object affect the space around it once, but it hadn't emanated such a degree of resistance to discovery. In fact, the previous object had wanted to be found.

"What sort of sorcery is this?" Iris murmured after taking a couple of breaths as large as her corset would permit. She drew her brows together, fixing Langlois with a look she'd learned from Marie's mother, an intimidating woman in spite of her size. "You're not telling me everything. What do *you* feel when you're near it?"

"Probably something similar, but not as strong. At the very least like I should stay away from it." He looked at her with intensity she suspected he used on the objects in his study. "You are not surprised."

"No, but I don't know what it means." For the first time, Iris wished she'd brought the codex, or copies of parts of it, from the Ottoman Empire with her. She'd left the papers with her contact at the museum, feeling that ancient objects should be treated as the national treasures they were and not plundered by foreign scholars. Plus, she'd been disgusted by the implications of parts of it. She still saw the bodies emerging from the flames that a vision had shown her, an attempt to burn the temple that housed it before the knowledge it contained could be perverted. Perhaps if she could see what whoever had packed the box intended, she could find the clue to unlocking the spell.

A movement of Langlois's foot made Iris recognize he was trying to be patient with her, so she struggled to give him some sort of explanation.

"In the Archaic age, tyrants ruled as the hand of Persia in what's now the Ottoman Empire, and they often made elaborate burial chambers for themselves and their families. I had a book that had come from there, from a temple burning during the revolt against the Persians. It looked like records from the temple granary, but it was actually a code for something. My husband, who is talented with science and mathematics, helped me decipher it, and a scholar there aided me in translating the words from an old Hittite language."

"Fascinating. This sounds like a worthy story. Would you like some tea?"

Iris's tongue moved across teeth parched by the struggle to regain her breath, so she said, "Yes, please."

He pulled a rope, and a clerk appeared. Once he'd ordered the tea and a snack—it was lunchtime, after all—and the clerk had bowed out, he gestured for her to continue.

"The language gave the location of an old tyrant's tomb near the temple of Apollo Smithneus. But it turned out not to be a tomb, but a secret chapel, somewhat like that under the Porta Maggiore, but much, much older." She shivered at the thought of the power she'd felt once she'd opened the tomb and descended.

"Yes, I was aware of the Roman discovery." Langlois spread out a cloth on the table Iris sat beside with efficient motions. "But I thought it was your father's doing."

He must eat many of his meals here. She didn't blame him—she would, too, if given the opportunity to immerse herself in the past, although she preferred field work. Then his last comment registered.

"My father's discovery? No, he died before my team and I found it." Her team that was now torn apart and under threat. The thought of Patrick and Chadwick in trouble hurt almost as much as her grief over her father, who had been murdered to keep secrets like those she'd found protected.

"Ah, so you are the *I. McTavish* credited with the discovery? Bravo. But back to the tomb under the sands."

"Right. It had been opened before, and objects taken from the entrance room, but there were no signs of intrusion farther in. I suspect that whoever went in had felt something like I did here."

So what was the difference? Who was with me? Edward, Marie, Johann, Amelie Lafitte, and Salmah...

And Salmah did some sort of ritual for protection before we went in.

"And what did you find?"

Their tea and lunch arrived. Iris hoped Marie had found something to eat, although she could go longer without food than Iris. They joked that Iris was like a bird, small but needing to eat frequently to maintain her energy.

Iris stalled by pouring the tea and serving herself. The first bite of the sandwich calmed her growling stomach, and the tea soothed her dry mouth.

"Delicious, like from a hotel," she said.

Langlois smiled without opening his mouth, swallowed, and said, "It's from the Parisienne next door. In spite of the name, they cater mostly to English guests."

"I can tell. Thank you."

"Madame, I am sorry and don't mean to rush you, but you did say you had limited time. Did you find anything that could possibly be helpful for us to open that box?"

"One of my colleagues, a native Ottoman, did some sort of ritual before we entered the tomb there."

Instead of dismissing the ritual as superstitious, he asked, "Can you duplicate it?"

"I don't know. It was in her native tongue, which I don't speak, so I didn't understand the words."

He nodded. "I will do some research, then. Do you know what spiritual path she followed? Or was she a spiritual tinkerer like so many here?"

"I believe her path was more Greek than Arabic."

"And what god was she particularly devoted to?"

Iris closed her eyes and tried to remember. "Hera, I believe. Salmah was always talking about visiting the temple at Samos before she married."

Iris didn't give the context of those conversations, how she'd suffered a miscarriage a month after she and Edward had married and how Salmah had helped her through it. She wondered if Salmah had made her pilgrimage and had offered something to intercede for Iris.

"There was also a large cult to Diana there. And of course

the Mother of All, whom the Greeks adopted." He slapped the table with one hand, and the other curled. "I had hoped you could help me today, but I understand you were here under duress, and for that I am truly sorry."

"You were party to that? You do realize that two men's lives are in danger."

He placed his teacup on its saucer, and it rattled with the shaking of his hands. "No, I was not aware of such dire circumstances. Please forgive me, Madame."

His reaction seemed genuine, so she smiled. "I believe you. If my schedule permits, I can come back tomorrow," she said, then added, "I really do want to see what's in your mysterious box. It could end up helping us in our larger quest."

"Very well, then. I will see you tomorrow, and perhaps I will have Gil fetch some of the Parisienne's shepherd's pie for you."

"Thank you."

Female voices echoed down the hallway, and Iris stood. An irate Marie led Lieutenant Crow and her favorite guard, and Marie had the telegram clutched in her hands. Crow's cheeks burned, and she held the arm of the guard, whose lips had disappeared into an angry line.

"She picks pockets." Crow pointed at Marie. "I didn't realize it until I reached into my trousers to check for the telegram."

"What does it say?" Iris asked. Marie handed it to her. Iris scanned it and looked up. "Is that all?"

"'Fraid so." Marie jerked her chin at Crow. "It was all a trick to get us here. I at least hope your time was worth it."

A classically French sigh brought their attention to Langlois. "*Non*, I am afraid it was not. She cannot even get close to it. Although..." He frowned. "Mademoiselle, do you think an initiate of the Pythagorean mysteries could open the box?"

"Perhaps someone like that would know a ritual or two," Iris mused. She tossed the telegram on the table, and the typed letters lay flat under the light: *"No word yet. Will contact soon."*

"Is there a curse on it? And is it dangerous?" Marie grinned at Crow, who looked younger without her typical smug expression.

"You were supposed to get her to open it." Crow glared at Langlois, who shrugged in a very French manner. Marie snorted.

"And I couldn't. So now it's your turn." Iris put her hands on her hips. "Unless you're willing to let an old protection spell get in the way."

CHAPTER EIGHTEEN

McPhee Townhouse, 12 March 1871

When the household took its daily afternoon rest, Claire snuck into the basement and what had been her father's workshop. It still smelled of leather straps and brass mountings. She thought she caught a whiff of smoke from the furnace in the corner, which he'd modified to burn at high enough temperatures to mold the glass and other materials for his lenses. It hadn't burned since his death, so she wondered if his ghost was around. She hoped so.

"I thought you had gone to Heaven or wherever you were going after you left me at Fort Daniels," she said in case he was there. "I'm sorry I snapped at you on the stairs." A few hours alone in her own room with reminders of her former life had cooled her temper. Of her entire family, he'd understood her best, had encouraged her in her academic pursuits even though it wasn't considered ladylike to put on a leather apron and make things. Or—heaven forbid!—study men's subjects like mathematics and chemistry.

Claire shook her head. When she'd become a neuroticist, proving that it was possible to go from being a patient in an asylum to someone who helps others avoid such horrible places, she knew he'd be thrilled and had hoped her mother would be proud. But when Claire had returned from Europe to find her father dead and her mother in the clutches of her evil aunt, she had given up hope of being accepted by her family. And now the two friends who had supported her and who had admired her for her brain were both imprisoned. She was, too, but with fine china and plenty of substances available to numb her. Not that she would do that to her brain. She wouldn't take the coward's way out as her mother had.

"And now I get to pretend I'm a good girl and have a nice little tea with Louisa Cobb," she muttered and sat on one of the benches by the long wooden table. Someone had cleared it off, and a fine dust filmed it, but Claire remembered when it had been piled high with the clutter of invention. The whole had been chaotic but the individual pieces fascinating. She'd taken what she'd learned at her father's bench and had helped Patrick O'Connell make the aether weapon that ended the War Between the States.

She didn't want to claim the words out loud, but they raced through her mind anyway: *Is this my penance, the price for helping to build the weapon that took all those lives, fried those boys where they stood?*

She touched the small ruby ring she refused to remove. "If it is, I accept it and can only pray for their souls." Then she remembered the aftermath of the battle, how she and Patrick had been kidnapped by the rebels and had been imprisoned by them until Chadwick snuck on to the base and rescued them. Both of them had been so brave, but what had it gotten them in the end?

A sob erupted from her stomach, breaking through the cool, professional neuroticist persona she'd clung to in order to continue to seem sane around her family. She covered her mouth, but they kept coming, the sobs of the rage and frustration and despair she'd felt at the core of her soul. Claire wouldn't give Eliza the satisfaction of expressing her misery in front of her, to let on that she'd won.

It seemed an unfair penance, but she could accept there were young women who'd cried when they'd heard what happened to their brothers and lovers on the field.

"But if we must be apart, please at least let them be safe," she murmured.

A gust of cold air caused the dust to swirl off the table, and Claire coughed and choked as she stood and backed away from it. Ash flecked and flew to join the shape, which was of a young man in a rebel uniform.

"Who are you?" Claire asked through a series of coughs and sneezes as her nose and throat tried to clear the mucous from her crying and the disturbed dust.

The young man spread his hands and put them together, bowing to her. He didn't speak so much as whispered in her mind, *"Patience."* And then he was gone.

Eliza's voice scraped Claire's ears from upstairs. "Claire? Where are you? It's almost time for tea, and your mother and I want to speak with you."

Claire sighed and ascended the stairs. She found her aunt and mother in the dining room, where tea was staged to be served in the parlor. Someone had fixed her favorite cucumber and water-cress sandwiches, but the sight of them turned her stomach. Eliza shooed her back from the table.

"Ugh, where were you? Your dress is filthy, and you're covered in dust."

"I was in Father's workshop." She shrugged. "You should really have someone dust down there. It's not healthy even if no one goes in it."

Claire's mother looked away and dabbed at her eyes with a handkerchief. "It's been so difficult to manage the house since Allan died."

"Now see what you've done?" Eliza sighed with an exaggerated exhale. "You claim to be a doctor of the mind, but you keep upsetting your mother."

Claire wanted to upend the chicken salad sandwich plate and have the satisfaction of seeing the slimy filling dripping from Eliza's skirts, but she refrained. As long as Chadwick was alive, there was a chance they'd find each other again. They had before, even against all probability, but it wouldn't happen if she was locked in an asylum. Eliza didn't know that Claire could sense what she felt, and if there was any concern for Melanie, it was overshadowed by Eliza's need to look and feel important.

Claire folded her hands in front of her and with her most demure expression, asked, "Did you have something to say to me? I need to get cleaned up before Miss Cobb arrives."

"Yes, have a seat, but not too near the food." Eliza reached for a plate, then drew her hands back. She pursed her lips and rang for a maid. "Take the plates back into the kitchen for now. We'll serve from there." The girl did as she was asked without looking at Claire, but Claire felt her curiosity and a pang of satisfaction at Claire standing up to Eliza.

Eliza, on the other hand, inhaled, and Claire sensed the weight of something ominous about to happen.

"We've discussed your current situation, my dear," Melanie said.

Claire guessed the discussion had actually consisted of Eliza commanding and Melanie drinking laudanum-laced tea and nodding, but she resisted the urge to point that out.

"We just wanted you to know what you're getting into, to help you proceed with your eyes open."

Now Claire's hands balled into fists, and she covered her right hand with her left so they wouldn't shake. Her heart raced, and a little cloud of pain gathered at her right temple. She breathed against the building anxiety, a reminder of when she struggled with hypnotic blocks that caused physical pain whenever she was reminded of the past and events around her accident.

This feels like the conversation Mama and Father had with me the night Chadwick proposed the first time.

"What do you mean?" Claire asked, an echo of her younger self, but less hopeful.

"I received a note earlier today from Parnaby Cobb asking my assistance. He wants me to use my connections to find a suitable husband for Louisa." Eliza's self-satisfied grin made Claire look down, the sense of doom gathering like a thundercloud in her stomach. "I am very well-connected," Eliza continued, "and I feel I have several prospects for Miss Cobb. Then it occurred to me, assuming I can find someone who will overlook that you've been engaged to a negro, I could do the same for you."

Claire looked up. She had no doubt her aunt had had plans for her before Cobb's request. "I'm still engaged, Aunt. I'm not looking for another husband. Bigamy is illegal. Mother? You gave me permission to marry Chadwick all those years ago."

Melanie looked up from the handkerchief she twisted in her fingers. "That was a different time, Claire. We both agree it would be best for you to give up those girlish dreams and settle for someone with a good name who can take care of you should your hysteria return."

"And don't forget it's illegal for a white woman to marry a negro," Eliza said. "The fact that you still speak of it means you're delusional. Back when Radcliffe was an army doctor and needed in the war, that was one thing. The governor was more open to granting exceptions then. Now that the war is over, it's important for society to return to normal."

"Normal ain't right," Claire said, and she couldn't help the imitation of some of the rebel prisoners she'd worked with. "And Chadwick and I are war heroes."

"Patrick O'Connell is the war hero." Eliza stamped the statement as true with a jerk of her chin. "He's the one who managed the device that won the war. You merely gave him your father's knowledge, which he turned into something usable, and Chadwick stayed out of your way. It's the only intelligent thing he's done."

"He risked everything to rescue me and Patrick." But Claire knew protest was futile. The press, not wanting to grant the title of hero to a negro, had ignored that story, and she suspected Eliza would have twisted it to her advantage even if it had gotten out. And she hadn't missed Melanie's wince at Eliza's dismissal of Allen McPhee's knowledge of lenses and what materials make the best ones for different kinds of light.

Eliza hadn't approved of Melanie's choice of husband, either. That made Claire doubly frustrated.

"It doesn't matter what he did or didn't do." Eliza's tone had been dripped in condescension and rolled in contempt, and Claire struggled not to react. "What matters is that he is a negro, and you are a young woman from a good family who can make an advantageous match and be well-cared for into your old age." She cut her eyes at Melanie, who sipped her tea, her eyes already taking on a glazed look. Claire wanted her mother to stand up to her aunt, to tell her she didn't regret her love match to the poor tinkerer.

"And what about Patrick?" Claire asked, and she didn't try to hide her bitterness. "Is he suitable?" If she could manage to meet with him, she could possibly get him to give a message to Radcliffe. Or even escape.

"Good heavens, no!" Eliza waved her hand in front of her face as if she smelled something offensive. "He's *Irish*, Claire. And poor. Now go get cleaned up. Louisa will be here at any moment. Perhaps she can talk some sense into you."

Once again, Claire encountered her father's ghost in the hall-way, and he frowned toward the dining room.

"If you'd like to do some real haunting, I have a good candidate for you," she muttered. "You could drive her mad, you know. I'm sure she has sufficient guilt."

He shook his head with the *"you know better than that"* look she remembered so well, and her cheeks burned. She shouldn't use her knowledge of minds and what breaks them to harm anyone, but if she were ever to cross that line, she knew who'd be her first target.

Chadwick, wherever you are, be safe and come back to me.

———

"You want to do what?" Colin looked at Henry with an expression that could go either into a smile at Henry's jesting or shock at what he proposed.

"I want to ride out to where the others lost track of the carriage carrying Radcliffe." Henry sat at the table with a cup of strong tea that might have been laced with a little laudanum to take the edge off the throbbing in his leg. It hadn't reacted well to his jaunt in the alley.

"You can't ride with that leg. You'll open the wound again."

"Then it's time to bring out the wearable automaton, let it do the work." Henry thought he sounded reasonable, but Colin shook his head.

"It's not ready yet. It'll tear you apart if something goes wrong. Lou's still figuring out the balance."

Of course Henry knew Colin was right, but he would have to leave in a couple of hours to meet Violet and Hobbes, and he wanted—needed—to have good news to report. Otherwise he was sure he'd be given a scone laced with something that would kill him that night in his sleep. Or perhaps the Americans weren't so subtle. This was the Deep South, after all, and no one would think anything of a man getting shot or trampled on a deserted road.

"I don't care if it tears me apart." Henry tried to sound as patient as possible to keep his rising panic under control. Control, that was the problem. Since he'd arrived in Terminus and met this crew, he'd felt like he was barely in charge of events, especially once he'd gotten word of Radcliffe's and McPhee's kidnappings. Even in Paris with the threat of Prussian bombs at any moment, he'd had the calm of only being in charge of himself. And he'd accomplished what he'd set out to do—almost, until Paul Farrell had slipped through his fingers when the theatre lights had gone out.

Paul had been shot, and Parnaby Cobb had whisked him away and escaped.

"Look, I made a mistake. I should never have agreed to allow Paul Farrell to go free in exchange for Chadwick Radcliffe. That's why I need to go rescue Radcliffe myself. Then I won't be beholden to the Pythagoreans."

"And I'm telling you that you can't, not hurt like you are. Lou and Richard are back out there looking for where he's being kept. You need to trust them."

Henry slumped back and drummed his fingers on the table, ignoring Colin's exasperated sigh. Yes, he was acting like a child. He could go out on his own, risk further injury, but there was a lot of countryside around the city, and he only had the barest of directions. If Colin knew more detail, he wasn't telling.

With the wearable automaton, Henry could cover a lot of ground and break into any prison. He knew where they kept the device—in a warehouse next to the building they resided in. He stood, and Colin covered the kitchen in two strides to help him when his leg gave a piercing throb and Henry sank to the chair, his teeth locked so he wouldn't scream in agony.

"You need another poultice and then to lie down. Stop being a daft stubborn idiot. I'm going to have to get a doctor if your leg gets any worse."

Henry wanted to say something rude, but a soft knock on the kitchen door interrupted him.

"What?" he snapped, his voice raw with the pain.

"I'm sorry to interrupt you, gentleman." A dark man with tired gray eyes entered. "But did I hear that someone needs a doctor?"

CHAPTER NINETEEN

Harbor Building, 12 March 1871

After Louisa left, Patrick turned to the aether. He hadn't experimented any more with it, reluctant to give Cobb more power over him and it. But he also recalled Claire's experience, how she had managed to communicate with it.

And then the creature that had been released when the laboratory had been bombed... What was it? Before they'd stabilized it, the aether would disappear back to its usual state of being the substance light passed through. Did giving it form allow it to have will? Was the aether biscuit examining him as it slowly undulated in its glass globe just as he studied it?

Patrick shook his head and massaged his temples. Yes, they had seen some strange things at Fort Daniels, but perhaps there were other explanations.

Like ghosts or something. Because that's much less frightening.

At least Louisa's mother wasn't talking to him now that he'd kissed her daughter, and he had no desire for her company since she'd deemed him unworthy. He thought he'd gotten over worrying about other people's opinions. Plus Louisa hadn't come from high class stock if what he'd managed to piece together about her past held. Just his luck, her mother's prejudices had accompanied her beyond the grave.

Back to work.

He needed to do something to make the aether functional in a benign capacity that couldn't be twisted by Cobb. Radcliffe had used it to heal Claire's mind of the blocks that the hypnotists in Paris had installed, but he understood the brain and nervous disorders better than Patrick.

I'm better at destroying things.

He focused on the red hairs on the backs of his hands so he wouldn't recall what he'd done with the aether weapon on the battlefield—the flash of light, then smoke. The smells of charred clothing and flesh and young men shitting themselves in terror— on both sides. The sounds of screams, agony turning to deathly silence. And almost worst of all—almost—the triumphant cry of the Union forces as they watched their enemies, mere boys like themselves, annihilated by a ray of concentrated aether light.

What had that done to the creature inside the weapon? Had it been influenced?

They hadn't had time to ponder the ramifications should the aether actually have life and will of its own. As far as Patrick knew, the weapon was on its way to Washington for a demonstration for the president and the stabilized aether trapped inside still. He hoped it had been imbued with the noble intentions of the Union soldiers and the joy of the war being over, not the terror it caused or power it possessed.

As for the aether in front of Patrick, he needed to invent a device that would allow him to use the glowing substance to its best capacity. In Paris, he had observed it augmenting negative emotions. What if he could get it to give positive ones? Was something that conferred happiness any less dangerous than something that destroyed?

But wouldn't it be better to create an angel than a devil?

The thought of angels brought the image of Louisa to mind and the kisses they'd shared. There had been three—one at

Claire's party, one in the airship, and the one in Patrick's dungeon. In each case, he'd been at her mercy, and each time he'd been left wanting more. Not just physically, although he definitely had *those* feelings about her, too. He wanted to know her intellectually and emotionally as well, to talk to her, find out her opinions. If he'd discovered anything about her, it was that she sold herself short intellectually. She'd been taught her womanly assets would serve her best, but he'd seen her curiosity. What would she become if she had intelligent friends like Iris, Marie, and Claire to challenge her?

Oh, you poor fool. You've got it bad.

He'd watched his friends fall under the influence of women's charms over the past several months. While he conceded they were all worthy women, he'd thanked any god that might be listening that he'd been spared a similar fate. But perhaps he hadn't. No matter what happened with him and Louisa, he needed to create his ticket out of that dungeon.

He laid out the tuning forks and pulled the four that, in combination, produced the frequency that stabilized the aether and placed them in a row above the others, their spots empty. His mind made note of the mathematics of the things—the sizes of the tuning forks and their corresponding frequencies were parts of Pythagorian triples, the two sides of the triangle. He guessed the resulting frequency in the aether might be numerically related to what that hypotenuses would be. He'd had a motor in Paris that produced the different frequencies and adjusted them, but he would have to do so by hand here.

First he had to recreate what he'd done and eliminate the frequency combinations that had augmented the negative emotions, pulling out even the barest hint of darkness in the psyches of those exposed to it even as the resulting light had given those around it a rosy, youthful glow. Thankfully Cobb's men hadn't taken the leather-bound notebook he'd written his notes in and given it to Paul Farrell to continue Patrick's work.

Patrick frowned—why hadn't Cobb handed everything over

to Farrell? The man, from what Patrick had seen in the man's workshop beneath the Théâtre Bohème, certainly possessed a genius for devices.

Focus on your own work.

Patrick studied the tuning forks that remained and moved the ones that would produce frequencies close to the dangerous ones into the top row. That left him with a few possibilities. He cleared a space for his notebook on the crowded bench so he could work out the mathematics behind what he was trying to do. He wanted to promote harmony, so what would be the most harmonious of combinations?

When he sat, he knocked one of the remaining tuning forks to the ground. A large one, it hit with a low bell-like tone that reverberated through the room. Patrick grabbed it and silenced it, but the vibration continued through the air. Every hair stood on end, even the ones no one mentioned in polite company, and he resisted the urge to rub himself in case Louisa's mother's ghost still lurked around.

The back of his neck tightened with an electric tingle, and he turned to see Paul Farrell watching him.

"What do you want?" Patrick asked. Perhaps Cobb knew that Patrick still had something to work out and had sent Farrell to *help* him and then steal his work.

Farrell mouthed something, but Patrick couldn't tell what he said, only that Farrell didn't completely block the view of the stairs behind him.

"Are you a ghost?" Patrick asked. The air stilled, and Farrell's image disappeared, leaving Patrick covered in a cold sweat. *What just happened?* He realized he tapped the tuning fork against his palm and stopped lest he cause something else to occur. Then he set it above the line of others—no reason to risk that happening again, although he was curious.

I can experiment to my heart's content when I get out of here. He wished he could do something to allow himself to escape.

"First you kiss my daughter, and then you bring *that* in here?" A golden glow to Patrick's left revealed that Louisa's mother stood there, and she had the same furious expression from earlier.

"How did I bring him in here?" Patrick sat, his pencil poised over his notebook. "And why do you object to him?"

The ghost crossed her arms. Patrick wondered if she felt the same chill he did.

"You stupid man. Don't you recognize that every time you introduce a vibration into the air, it doesn't dissipate for several hours? You're pulling at the fabric that holds all this together." She gestured to their surroundings. "As for that creature, he is now the discarded refuse of Parnaby Cobb's machinations. He would be better off dead."

Patrick scribbled furiously, making note of the tuning forks he'd tried to this point and trying to determine which one would add to the vibration in the air in the most harmonious way. When he finished, he found the implement, one of the smaller ones, and struck it. The very air picked up the bell-like tone, and Patrick found himself grinning and feeling that the dungeon wasn't so bad, after all. The ghost disappeared with an emphatic huff for a being that didn't have lungs.

I've done it.

He finished his notes and without thinking, straightened up his workspace, lining the tuning forks back up and putting his notebook in a spot on the desk that created the most visual harmony. His logical self noticed how that euphoric feeling made him want to make the rest of the place more orderly.

Could that effect have reached the guard outside? He crept up the stairs to see. Perhaps if the guard was in a state of euphoria, Patrick could convince him to let him free. A small chance, but he had to see.

Patrick saw a long shadow under the door rather than the two that would have been there if the guard had been standing. Of course the door handle didn't budge when Patrick tried it, so he knew the guard lay in front of it. At least Patrick had the hairpin Louisa had dropped and the wire Artemus had left.

He glanced over his shoulder—should he free the aether? There wasn't time—there was no telling how long the guard had been out. Was the man's unconscious state due to something Patrick had done?

He used the hairpin and wire to pick the lock, nudged the eerily still guard out of the way, grabbed the man's weapon, and crept down the hall.

———

When Henry had met Doctor Chadwick Radcliffe in Paris, he'd been struck at the man's inner strength and composure. Nothing seemed to ruffle him, and now was no exception. Henry guessed Chadwick hadn't eaten since the previous day, at least nothing substantial, and the stiff way he moved told Henry he'd been beaten. Indeed, bruises showed on his dark cheeks, and one eye was almost swollen shut.

"It looks like you need a doctor more than I," Henry said. He gestured for Radcliffe to sit across from him, but the doctor shook his head.

"Not likely. I'm just bruised. You've got a nasty gash." He took the seat beside Henry and leaned over to examine the wound. "Looks like you cleaned it pretty well, but you're not resting it. You do know that overuse can lead to more inflammation and make it harder to fight off infection, right?" Even with his own injuries, he managed to give Henry a classic medical admonishment.

"Sometimes life doesn't give you the luxury of taking a rest. How did you escape?"

Colin set a mug of tea and a plate of eggs, sausage, and toast in front of the doctor. Radcliffe blew across the top of the tea, and his eyes flicked between Henry's wound and the food.

"Eat," Henry said. "Then you can tell us how you escaped. And what I need to do for my leg."

Radcliffe managed to talk and eat at the same time. "I'm not sure how exactly I escaped, only that a cloaked figure came into the prison, unlocked my cell, and let me out. The guards lay about like they'd been drugged. There was a horse waiting for me, and this address was in the saddle bag."

Henry looked at Colin. "We've been compromised. Go find the others and tell them to return. We'll be leaving for Boston on the next airship."

"The trains and airships don't run on Sunday, Boss. And you have your meeting."

"Bother." Henry drummed his fingers on the table. "Once the others get back, we'll go to the backup headquarters. Then we'll leave for Boston first thing in the morning. Double guard duty until then. Oh, and send a telegram to Mrs. Bailey that we have the doctor."

"How is everyone?" Radcliffe asked. Ever the gentleman doctor, he didn't speak with food in his mouth, although Henry was sure he must want to inhale the meal. "And where is Patrick? I thought he left Fort Daniels with you."

Henry shifted in his chair. "I had to let Cobb borrow him so I could have a man on the inside, but I miscalculated. I didn't count on Cobb treating him as a prisoner, and I lost track of him once he left Cobb's airship. I do know he's somewhere in Boston."

"You did what?" The coldness in Radcliffe's gray eyes matched the damp chill Henry still felt from outside. And inside, if he were to be truthful. This whole mission had been one mistake after the other. He suspected his superiors had wanted Patrick to go to Cobb so he could sabotage whatever Cobb's plans were for the aether.

"We had to ensure Cobb and Paul Farrell wouldn't take what Mister O'Connell and Professor Bailey had discovered about the aether—you as well with your therapeutic device—and do something nefarious with it."

He expected Radcliffe to become angry, so the man's calm concerned him. Or perhaps exhaustion overtook him now that he ate and was safe.

As safe as one can be in a nest of spies.

"I can see that. The combination of the aether, which we don't entirely understand, and Farrell's genius with devices could be very dangerous." His shoulders slumped. "And what of Doctor Claire McPhee?"

Henry would have preferred for Radcliffe to be focused on his wound. "She is with her mother and aunt in Boston."

Radcliffe slumped in his chair and put his head in his hands. "I had hoped that you had at least managed to rescue her."

"We were focused on you."

Radcliffe stood so quickly his chair toppled with a bang. "I am not important. You should have let me rot in that prison."

"Or be sold so far South you'd never be heard from again?" Henry tried to rise, but his wound sent a spike of pain into his groin, and he flopped back into his chair, which scraped back a couple of inches with a shriek.

"If Claire's aunt has her, I will never see her again." Radcliffe rubbed his eyes. "This is a nightmare. I need sleep to be able to think this through, find a solution, but I don't know if I'll be able to." But he swayed and had to grab the edge of the table.

"I suspect Colin made sure you'd sleep this afternoon."

Radcliffe blinked, and his eyes took on a faraway look. Henry rose, and leaning on each other, the two of them made it to the second floor, where Henry allowed Radcliffe to collapse on to an appropriately named fainting couch in the office.

"When you wake, you can have a bath," Henry promised. "Then we'll figure out what to do about Doctor McPhee and Mister O'Connell."

He made his way back down the stairs and straightened up the kitchen—he couldn't stand a dirty kitchen—and was headed toward the stairs when he heard the others come in. He glanced at the clock—Colin had barely been gone twenty minutes. The area where they'd lost track of the police coach was twenty minutes' hard ride outside of the city, and he suspected the roads were clogged with Sunday traffic.

"What are you doing back so early?" he asked Richard, who was the first to appear.

"You're looking rough there, Boss." The dark-haired man shook his head. "And I wish I had better news for you, but something strange just happened."

Henry sat on the steps. "Oh, do tell."

Colin entered next. No Lou, but Henry suspected he was having a cigarette. The grim look on Richard's face made Henry say, "Out with it."

"We were riding down the road where we lost the coach yesterday, and we saw this large dust cloud coming up just over the next hill." Richard moved his hands to indicate the size of it. "There were ten riders, all in black. They had the Pythagorean symbol on their cloaks, and all of them wore hats pulled low over their faces. Lou and I skedaddled to the side of the road and hid in the trees, but they saw our tracks and followed us. There was something odd about them, but I don't know how to describe it."

Henry looked up at him. "Try."

"They, I don't know, it wasn't smell... They felt funny. Like the air around them prickled. Like when you go to the fair, and you get close to the Faraday ball."

"They had electricity?" Henry frowned. "How?"

"I don't know. But that's not the weirdest thing. We had to calm our horses, of course. They acted like the men and their horses were ghosts or something."

"Right." He wished O'Connell had been there. Perhaps he would know what could produce that effect. "Did any of them speak to you?"

"The leader said that they had Chadwick Radcliffe and to go

back where we came from. Then they turned and rode off, but they disappeared."

"Because you lost sight of them?" Henry wanted to put his head in his hands—now he definitely owed the Pythagoreans for the rescue.

"No, they just vanished. Like they went over one hill but not the next one."

The implications tugged the corners of Henry's mouth downward. "That was a show of power." The thought chilled him further.

What had he done, bargaining for Chadwick Radcliffe's release?

CHAPTER TWENTY

Boston, 12 March 1871

When Eliza Adams had originally invited Louisa for Claire's bridal tea, Louisa had imagined a polite affair of old friends meeting. Claire would tell the others about her beau, and they would *ooh* and *ahh* at the appropriate places, pretending they were interested but in truth paying their social dues to a woman who held power in Boston's social circles, although Louisa could never figure out why. Then Louisa would go home and be thankful no one had tried to embroil her in any romantic scheme because she enjoyed what she thought had been her partnership with Parnaby Cobb.

Had she really been so naive as to think he would allow her to go on forever unmarried? No, she hadn't been naive—she'd waited at the beginning of each year starting when she turned sixteen for Cobb to announce she'd have a season. But that announcement had never come, and in truth, she'd not minded her spinsterhood, becoming more satisfied than resigned. Cobb had his unpleasant side, but at least she knew what to expect from him. Until recently.

Now she rode to the McPhee townhouse without any idea what to anticipate. Eliza had delayed the affair a day, dropped the invitee list to just include Louisa, and Louisa didn't even know if Claire was still engaged. Parnaby had said something about Eliza looking for a new suitor for her niece, so he must have meant Claire. Plus, instead of Louisa being in a superior position, she now found herself attracted to an Irish tinkerer with no family or fortune. Was that better or worse than a negro doctor? Or to someone of her class, did it matter?

Are we doomed to find a suitable match regardless of stature? And what of my ability? Is there such thing as a truly honest relationship?

She drummed her fingers on the wood of the carriage below the window and watched her surroundings change. Whereas Claire's parents' townhouse had been in an unfashionable part of town when she'd first been there and met Patrick six years before, the area had shifted, and more of the upper-class set had moved in to be close to the park and away from the miasma of the river. The homes around the park had been cleaned up, and the park itself sported new trees, planted the previous autumn and showing their first buds. Or at least thinking about it, their branches knobby.

What will my next form be? Reluctant wife? Runaway? She slumped back in her seat and fingered the locket through her dress. Would she have a choice? Could she force Parnaby to give her one? Was she brave enough to use her ability on him?

The carriage rolled to a stop in front of the McPhee townhouse. Someone had painted it a more cheerful color, and the window boxes held plants that would tolerate cold well. All in all, it looked like a place where a young woman should be able to dream of her beloved, but when Louisa stepped from the carriage, the force of the house's sorrow hit her. Now the yellow seemed of forced gaiety, and upon closer inspection, many of the plants in the boxes sat limp and wilted.

This house is holding its sorrow. A movement in the window to the left of the front door caught her eye, and Louisa thought she saw Allan McPhee.

She stopped, her hand on the rail.

Impossible. He died several years ago.

She couldn't remember when, only that Boston had mourned its lost tinkerer, but Louisa hadn't paid much attention at the time beyond wondering what became of Claire and her injuries. She inhaled the sharp, frigid air so she'd stop trembling and made herself continue up the stairs.

One ghost is tolerable. Two in one day? Entirely inappropriate.

As if he'd heard her thoughts, he vanished.

A knock on the door brought the Adams' butler to it, and he let her in and showed her to the parlor, where tea was laid out on a tray between two armchairs. He took her cloak, but Louisa opted to keep her shawl. Although a coal fire burned in the grate at the side of the room, she could tell it hadn't been going for too long due to the chill that still hung in the air. The government rationing of coal reached the highest classes. She wanted to bundle up in a chair with large cushions that would embrace her, but of course the formal furniture in the room had been built with more care for aesthetics than comfort.

Louisa had never thought much about armchairs before, but after having seen Patrick in his drab surroundings without the comfort of anything cushioned, she couldn't help but think that they didn't look as bad as she'd remembered. Not that she could lean back and get comfortable in her bustle and petticoats, not to mention the corset, which she always had her maid lace as tightly as possible.

She was so busy pondering the chairs with their minimal padding that she didn't hear Eliza come in.

"Claire will be down in a moment," the older woman said. Louisa spun around, her heartbeat dancing in her throat again.

"I'm sorry," Eliza said, obviously unrepentant. "Did I startle you? You young women are so delicate nowadays."

Louisa smiled over clenched teeth. If she'd learned anything about herself in the past few days, it was that she was not *delicate.* "I was deep in thought."

Eliza shook her head. "And that's another problem. Since

when do young women follow thoughtful pursuits? Claire would make all our lives easier if she would just stop thinking so much."

Louisa cocked her head. Would she have previously agreed with Eliza? She didn't know, and she certainly didn't want to unpack her assumptions about women and their roles with Eliza Adams. Louisa's life felt like enough of a mess she didn't want to show it to anyone else.

"Perhaps she just needs a diversion." Louisa hoped her non-agreement would be perceived as implied agreement. She could use a mind like Claire's—or perhaps Claire could help Louisa out of her own pickle. With that realization, Louisa recognized Claire would have the advantage in their conversation.

"Just so." Eliza stamped her approval on Louisa's idea with a sharp nod. "And I have just the thing for the two of you. I received your stepfather's note that he finally thinks it's time for you to marry." She shook her head and looked up with a resigned sigh. "I can't imagine why he's delayed so long. You're still very attractive, but you're lucky. With your mostly unknown heritage, there's no telling when your beauty will turn, so the sooner we get you married off, the better."

Louisa didn't know whether to thank Eliza for the compliment, take offense, or challenge the notion that she should marry quickly.

"Goodness, Miss Adams, I don't know what to say." She smiled like a silly coquette, or at least the silly coquette she used to be.

Had she truly admired Eliza Adams?

"Don't say anything. Just have a seat, and I'll see what Claire is up to. She shouldn't keep her guest waiting like this."

Louisa wondered how Claire managed to live with the odious woman. But then, Louisa had tolerated Parnaby Cobb and his strange moods and uncomfortable directness. Instead of sitting, she wandered around the parlor and drifted more closely to the fire. Rather than becoming warmer, the air chilled until Louisa retreated, rubbing the gooseflesh on her arms and pulling the shawl more closely around her. She had the sense that if she were to look in the mirror on the mantle, she wouldn't find herself alone, but she didn't want to see another ghost. Instead, she moved back to where the tea service had been set up.

That was odd. She touched the side of the teapot and was relieved to find it hot. A noise made her turn.

Claire McPhee stood in the doorway, a wary expression on her face. She twisted a ruby ring around the third finger of her left hand. "Hello, Louisa. Thank you for coming." Her voice sounded huskier than Louisa recalled, and she wondered if Claire was ill. Or perhaps she had been crying, judging from the swollen areas under her eyes and red nose.

"You're welcome. Are you well?" Louisa approached Claire and held a hand out. "Come, have some tea. You'll feel better."

Claire shook her head. "I'm not terribly well, but it's nothing catching. Thank you."

It occurred to Louisa that her acquaintance had been in an asylum, and Louisa had no idea how to interact with someone who had hysteria. There were no articles in ladies' magazines titled, "How to Talk to Your Neurotic Friend." Should she cajole Claire into eating something? Claire looked to be of a healthy weight, but her skin appeared sallow. Or should Louisa try to speak only of cheerful topics?

"Don't worry," Claire said, as though she could detect Louisa's uncertainty. "I'm not going to have a hysterical fit or anything like that."

Louisa nodded but waited for Claire to sit before she did so. A maid appeared to pour their tea and serve the little sandwiches and cakes. Louisa, who hadn't eaten since breakfast, had to remind herself to take dainty bites in spite of her stomach's embarrassingly loud insistence that she eat faster.

"How are you?" Claire asked, then with a sly glance through her eyelashes, "I hear you're in the market for a husband."

Louisa shrugged and swallowed the bite she had just taken. "Not exactly, but I suppose women like us don't have a choice."

Claire's eyebrows rose. "Meaning you don't want to marry?"

Louisa wanted to say no, but her mouth formed the words, "Not necessarily, but it depends on who the suitor is."

"And do you have someone in mind?" Claire cut a piece from one of the tea cakes, which she had been toying with on her plate. "Your smile says you do."

Louisa shoved the image of Patrick and the memory of their kiss—not the chaste one—from her mind. Her cheeks heated. "If I do, I'm afraid it is someone entirely inappropriate." She looked up to see the first genuine smile Claire had ever given her, at least that she could recall.

"I know the feeling." The words, spoken with sincerity, melted some of the awkwardness between them, and Louisa felt more connected to Claire than she had before. Formerly they'd been thrown together by Eliza Adams's and Parnaby Cobb's friendship but had little in common.

Louisa sighed. "And yet your aunt wants to match us with young men of commerce." She gestured to Claire's ruby ring. It seemed innocent in its small size. She couldn't resist asking the question, "What happened with the negro doctor?"

"His name is Chadwick Radcliffe, and..." Claire shook her head and looked over Louisa's shoulder. Louisa followed her gaze and found Eliza had entered the room with a woman who looked like the shadow of Claire's mother. Eliza held a notebook, and a maid hovered about outside the room holding blotting paper, pen, and ink.

"So it seems your stepfather wants to give a St. Patrick's Day ball on Friday, Louisa," Eliza said. "He does like to present a challenge. Let's discuss the guest list. That way you and Claire can make sure there are young men there whom you would fancy."

"I'm not sure you know any of those," Claire said. Louisa mentally applauded Claire's forthrightness but wanted her not to antagonize her aunt.

She touched Claire's wrist. *"Let me handle this. I'm accustomed to playing the game with pushy elders."*

She wanted Claire to get the message but didn't expect her understanding to be of a verbal nature.

Or to receive a message back, *"Very well. I have difficulty not responding to her when she's being ridiculous, and I'm still overwrought from my journey and kidnapping."*

"I'm sure it will be fine," Louisa said with a sharp look at Claire. "Who did you have in mind?"

"Kidnapping?"

Thankfully Eliza didn't seem to sense the exchange between Louisa and Claire. "The Denhams have two sons who are as yet unmarried, and their father is making a fortune building railroad tracks in the West. Then there are the Boyles, a fine old family, and their eldest son just broke off his engagement to the Johnson chit..."

Louisa listened to Eliza relate the latest gossip, which of course Louisa knew but had never expected to apply to her. Meanwhile, she found that when she attuned to Claire, she could read the other girl's thoughts.

What sorcery is this? She knew she had an ability, but she hadn't considered the possibility in others.

The rest of the tea passed in a blur, and when Louisa found herself in the front hall waiting with Claire for Louisa's carriage, she couldn't have described it to anyone.

"I'm very sorry about her pushiness," Claire said and stood aside as the butler helped Louisa into her cloak. "That's how she's always been."

"I..." Louisa shook her head. "I'm sorry, I'm not feeling well. But please come to tea tomorrow. I suspect you and I have much to discuss." *"Like our escapes."*

Claire nodded. "I would be delighted to." *"Can you really help me?"*

Louisa smiled and squeezed Claire's hand. "I'm very happy to do whatever I can." She hoped Claire could sense her limitations. The other girl's nod of understanding said she did.

"Tomorrow, then."

Louisa's carriage pulled up, so after a quick hug, she departed. As she rode away from the townhouse, she couldn't help but think that no, she'd really no idea what to expect. But she had plans to put into place before the following day. If she and Claire were to escape their respective households and disappear, she would have to be canny about it.

———

Once he reached a shadowed alcove, Patrick glanced around the hall. The man still hadn't moved. He knew Cobb would have more than one layer of security, so what would the next hurdle be? Men on the main floor? Patrick needed to find a different way out, then. He doubted he could just waltz out of the building. Hell, he could hardly waltz, although he wouldn't mind trying with a certain Miss Cobb.

Focus, ye daft bean.

Older buildings like this often had secret passages, but the plaster walls looked new and he didn't have time before the guard woke to try to find where one could be. Was there a back stair? He tried the door behind him, which opened to a hall, but Patrick couldn't tell whether it led out of the building. Its musty smell told him not likely.

The man on the floor in front of the dungeon stirred, and Patrick clutched at his pocket before he remembered he had the gun in his hand. Although he'd prefer not to use it.

And that his notebook with his calculations was still on the workbench. He'd been in such a happy fog he had forgotten it. But did he have time to retrieve it?

The guard sat up and rubbed his eyes, then checked for his weapon.

At least now my mind is clear. Or was it? Normally decisive, he hesitated, torn between getting his notes and trying to escape. And scolding himself for his carelessness.

Even if someone found his notebook, it was unlikely they

could do anything with his notes, which he wrote in a shorthand only he could understand. He hoped. And he wouldn't have a chance like this again.

Patrick slipped into the hallway and locked the door between him and the guard, whose rise to consciousness had accelerated once he reached for his weapon and found an empty holster. Maybe Patrick shouldn't have taken the gun, but he needed something to defend himself with. Whatever had happened to him and the guard—and his stumbling steps that almost sent him careening into the nearest wall told Patrick he wasn't necessarily over its effects—he would have to wait to investigate it. Hopefully Farrell had told him the truth, that the neo-Pythagoreans would be helpful in that regard.

What little light seeped beneath the door he'd just locked waned as he crept through the hall, and soon he blinked against the darkness, one hand on the weapon and one on the wall feeling for a way out. He was still below street level, so he knew he would have to find a stairwell. The situation reminded him of how Claire had told him and Chadwick that the aether had guided her through a subterranean tunnel to safety after an attack on Fort Daniels.

"Why can't you be helpful like that for me?" he muttered. Then he squinted—*is that a soft glow ahead?* He sidled toward it, his weight shifted away so he could run if needed. His mind sifted through Claire's tale for helpful details.

Another odd occurrence during the attack was that the other inhabitant of the house Claire stayed in had been injured, and then supposedly died, but her body had never been found. A ghost had referred to her as an "old one," but had never clarified what that meant. Patrick, Chadwick, and Claire had all seen golden creatures—not ghosts, exactly—but beings, and Mrs. Soper—the woman in the house—had been one of them, or so Claire had thought. Now the negro servant stood at the end of the hall and grinned at Patrick, her arms crossed and her smile glowing.

"Now you're a sight for sore eyes, you brute. Have you managed to charm that young lady yet?"

Patrick stopped about two yards away from the apparition. "Do creatures like you even have eyes?" he asked. "What are ye, anyway?"

"As someone from a country where the mystical is seen as the mundane, you have plenty of options to choose from. Or have you filled your brain with so much science you've forgotten your roots?"

"It's been a long time." But he recalled tales whispered around the fire on long winter evenings. That seemed an existence far removed from his current circumstances. But the aether would make a great addition to the fairytales of his homeland. Between dancing statues, the magical light that seeped into souls, and creatures of light with their own agenda, he was well on his way to developing his own mythology. Or to a very interesting conversation with Iris Bailey, whenever he saw her again. She would probably know exactly what kinds of beings they were dealing with.

As for his own past, his grandmother would have been proud of him for combining magic with science. Or was that what he'd done?

Mrs. Soper crossed her arms and fixed him with the stern stare he recalled so well from their time together at the fort. "You have an interesting concept of time, but then you, mortals typically only focus on your tiny lifetimes. Have you not learned at all from your experiences, that there are larger problems afoot?"

"I'm not sure what you mean, but right now my main problem is getting out of this building."

The handle of the door jiggled, and then someone pounded on it.

"Then you should go up the stairs." She gestured to a rectangle of blackness on the wall across from where he stood. "And, Irishman, do be sure to accept help where it's offered.

Sometimes you need to be the one rescued. It helps to keep the energy of the universe in balance."

"I'll keep that in. mind. Thank you." He edged toward the stairs, his heart pounding along with the blows to the door separating him from imprisonment or worse. He knew better, though, than to turn his back on a supernatural creature and definitely not to risk the appearance of rudeness by leaving before dismissed.

"You're welcome. Now go."

He nodded and darted into the stairwell. He almost tripped up the stairs but caught. himself. A crash echoed down the hallway. The noise grew into a rumble, and he coughed on the dust that blew up the stairs behind him with enough force to sand whatever skin was exposed.

What did she do?

When he reached the top of the stairs, he heard footsteps and darted into the shadows just before the door opened. A clerk in a vest and with rolled up shirtsleeves peered in with a startled expression. Then he wrinkled his nose and waved the dust away from his face.

"What happened here?" he mumbled.

Patrick remained as still as possible, but the man's eyes widened when he looked in Patrick's direction.

"The hallway collapsed," Patrick said with as much urgency as he could muster around the dirt in his throat and gestured down the stairs with the weapon. "The other guard is trapped down there."

"And the prisoner?"

Thank gods, he doesn't know who I am.

"Still in the dungeon as far as I know."

"Right. I'll get help." He turned and ran off. Patrick strode down the hallway the other way and out of a back entrance.

"Good, there you are." Someone grabbed Patrick's upper arm. "Nicely done with the dust—it hides the red in your hair and beard, at least most of it."

Patrick jerked his arm away and turned to face Paul Farrell. The man stood without a cap, which reminded Patrick to pull his from his coat pocket and put it on. He also wound his scarf more tightly around his face.

"I'm not going back down there." He showed Farrell the gun before putting it back in his pocket and keeping his hand on it.

"Oh, heavens no. There's someone who wants to meet you."

The cold air bit into Patrick's cheeks as the wind whipped down the narrow street, reminding him that freedom might not always be comfortable. He couldn't stand there arguing—someone in the building would figure out he'd escaped and come after him. But he didn't want to end up captive somewhere else, either.

"I'll come on one condition," he said. "That we meet at a hotel or somewhere else neutral. I'll not be anyone's prisoner again."

"Oh, that's funny. We're all prisoners, don't you see? Captives of fate." Farrell laughed, a high-pitched trill, and Patrick clapped a hand over the other man's mouth. He wouldn't be able to hold him for long, so he released him once he stopped shaking and moved toward the nearest intersection where he could see a crowd of moving pedestrians he could lose himself in, presumably just another laborer.

"You need my help," Farrell said. "It's not a problem for you to accept it. I can bring you to safety."

Patrick hesitated at the similarity between Farrell's words and those of the aether creature.

"There he is," someone shouted. Farrell grabbed Patrick's arm again, this time in a grip too strong for Patrick to dislodge.

"Frying pan or fire?" Farrell asked.

"Neither, you bastard." Patrick did manage to wriggle away, but men in the crowd moved in his direction.

"Guess it'll be the fire, then."

They dashed toward a carriage parked at the next corner. Patrick balked when he saw the symbol painted in black on the black door so only those who knew it or saw it in a certain light would notice it. The same symbol Farrell had tattooed on his wrist—that of the neo-Pythagoreans.

He clutched his weapon tighter. They could try to capture him, but he wouldn't make it easy.

"You mean the neo-Pythagoreans are going to offer me safety?" Patrick asked. Farrell shoved him in.

"Don't be an idiot. They want to offer you a deal."

Patrick refrained from pointing out that he wasn't the one who'd accosted another man in the middle of a street in broad daylight and shoved him into a creepy carriage. Or perhaps Patrick was the dolt for letting him. He could rationalize his behavior by saying he was still shaken by the encounter with Mrs. Soper or the strange effects of the aether—he still had a lingering sense of euphoria in spite of the circumstances—or the fact he hadn't been fed since the night before, and that not a hearty meal by even poor Irish standards.

But as usual, as Chadwick would point out if he was there, Patrick's curiosity had gotten the better of him again. Whatever the reason, he found himself in another pickle.

On the other hand, a pickle would be right tasty about now. On some bread with rashers and a good cheddar. His stomach growled.

The windows had some sort of substance over them so he couldn't see much outside, only that they passed through some sort of tunnel. When had that happened? He shut his eyes against the dizziness.

"You continued with the aether experimentation, didn't you?" Farrell asked. He sounded like he spoke from the top of a well, the words floating down to Patrick like feathers.

"I had to come up with something so Cobb would let me live."

"What did you do?"

Ach, you can't help but be the tinkerer, can ye?

"I made it happy." A sound like a giggle escaped him, and he swayed with the movement of the vehicle, which had picked up speed.

"You can't be serious. The harmonics are too dangerous. It's killed people who have pushed it too far."

"It likes me." If his encounter with Clarice Soper had been any indication, it liked him a lot. Why, he didn't know.

Reluctant to follow that train of thought lest he end up as hysterical as his carriage-mate, he asked instead, "And how did you get down there?"

"Yesterday? I was still working for Cobb, so the guard let me in."

Patrick peered at him through eyes that swam like he'd had a few too many drams of whisky. "No, earlier. When I was working. You appeared and looked like you wanted to say something to me."

"I was thinking of how to get you out of the basement." He looked up, his forehead a staircase of creases under his unruly mop of hair. "And then I felt a strange pull." He rubbed his wrist where the tattoo was. "This burned. I felt I was in two places, but not for long." Now instead of glittering, his eyes took on an onyx-like flatness. "And I can assure you, this is not my madness talking."

Patrick nodded and swallowed around the dust in his throat. To this point, Farrell had been neurotic but predictable, an affable loon. Now he appeared the type of predator that could have worked with Parnaby Cobb for years.

And Patrick was stuck in a carriage with him.

He recalled, then, how back in Paris, Farrell had used opium smoke with other ingredients to make Marie spill her secrets. As his hand fell limply out of his pocket and to the seat behind him, he cursed his curiosity.

But a pickle would still be nice...

CHAPTER TWENTY-ONE

Terminus, 12 March 1871

When Davidson alighted from the carriage at Mrs. M's tea room, he looked around as he paused to let his leg adjust to bearing weight again. No mechanical birds flew in the sky, and no one in the crowds on the sidewalks stood out as potentially threatening. Most wore their dark winter attire, but here and there a glimpse of color came through, mostly ladies taking advantage of their first chance to show off their spring frocks, although cloaks concealed most of the dresses themselves.

Henry wondered for the thousandth time what that sort of seasonal shift would be like in the domestic arena. He imagined reading the paper by the fire on a brisk spring morning and having a conversation with a beautiful dark-haired creature aglow with the echo of the year's new season of life, and perhaps with a new life of their own growing in her belly.

"Henry, put down your newspaper and tell me what you think of my new dress."

"It's lovely, my dear. The little roses at the hem are a nice touch."

"Thank you, Madame Cotisse is a marvel, isn't she? Do you think it's too chilly outside to wear it?"

"Not as long as you put on your cloak. Now come give me a kiss..."

He smiled at the imaginary memory of the life he hadn't chosen, and although the day had warmed to early spring temperatures, he shivered. Sometimes these images were so clear it was as though he peered into someone else's life. The woman was always the same, with fetching green eyes, dark hair, and skin just on the fashionable side of dusky.

Someone bumped him, sending a knife of pain through his injured leg, and he cursed under his breath. No, reading the newspaper by the fire was not for him.

He limped into the tea room, and a young man in a gray and white striped spring suit gestured for Henry to follow him.

"They're expecting you." The man's words, spoken quietly and threaded through the conversation around them, never failed to chill Henry. As they walked through the main dining room with its tables just far enough apart for the ladies' skirts to not share street dust, Henry focused on not stepping on or tripping over anyone's new frock. But his heartbeat's tempo increased as he approached the lace-curtained French doors at the anticipation of what awaited behind them.

The young man knocked on the left hand door, head cocked. Then with a nod, he opened it and gestured for Henry to enter.

Violet and Hobbes—he didn't know their real names—sat at the table with a full spread of food, two teapots, and three cups. One of the teacups, a dainty bone china, sat on a saucer in front of Violet, who wore her signature dark purple color, this time as a day dress, her blonde curls piled high on her head. At first glance, anyone would think she was just another debutante, but her wide summer sky eyes and full lips masked a formidable mind.

Her partner, Hobbes, clean-shaven and delicate-boned, sat beside her with another dainty cup in front of him. His reddish hair sat unruly like he'd been outside without a hat—or had been running his fingers through it. Henry took that as a bad sign.

Violet never gave away anything, but Hobbes could typically be read with some effort. He nodded to Henry and gestured for him to take a seat at the third set place.

Violet poured tea for herself and Hobbes and put the teapot back on the table before serving Henry. She sat and fixed her tea, then folded her hands in front of her. Henry couldn't help but think that the pink damask wallpaper and lace curtains made for the prettiest potential execution chamber he'd ever seen.

"How is the search for Chadwick Radcliffe going?" she asked. Her voice, almost musical, hid the subtext of the question.

"He is safely at our headquarters." *There, start on the high note.*

Hobbes nodded again, not unusual. Typically Violet did the talking.

She then asked, "In what condition?" Her sharp glance up at Henry through her eyelashes, a perversion of female charm, told him she wouldn't allow evasions.

"Alive and well, although bruised and exhausted. He is asleep there now."

"With the help of one of Colin's draughts, I assume?" She helped herself to a *petit four*.

"Yes."

"So your men found him?" When she took a bite, Henry again found himself surprised at the lack of point or fang. He'd often thought she'd be a good vampiress.

And here was the tricky part. He couldn't lie to the two of them—too much danger in being found out—but she had an uncanny ear for omissions.

"No. He arrived this morning at our headquarters. He said he was given their description and address by his rescuers, who released him early this morning."

Violet and Hobbes exchanged an alarmed glance. "Then you shall have to vacate immediately," she said. "That is supposed to be a location known only to us and you. Who were these rescuers?"

"The neo-Pythagoreans."

"And why didn't you or your men rescue the doctor?" Her hand hovered over the teapot she hadn't served from.

Henry knew his life teetered on the precipice, and he thought about his lovely ghost. Perhaps he could live out his fantasy of a normal life in his afterlife. "Cobb's men had him well-hidden. They used a decoy police van to throw my men off his trail, and the countryside is so broad they were unable to locate him themselves."

"A decoy police van? Didn't someone have a bead on the true one? Those things are designed for carrying criminals, not maneuverability, Henry." She touched the second teapot's handle.

"These moved unlike any we've seen before." His mouth dry, Henry wished for something to drink, but he held on to the thought he hadn't been given the poison yet.

"And how did you know Radcliffe was in such a vehicle?"

"I followed a mechanical hawk, which took me to a back alley."

"Alone?" Violet's perfect eyebrows climbed her forehead.

"No, with one of the other men."

"A mechanical hawk…" Hobbes tapped his lips with the end of a spoon. As always, the higher pitch of his voice surprised Henry. "Who do you think it belonged to?"

"I'm not sure. At first I thought it was Cobb, but he wouldn't have been so careless as to lead us straight to Radcliffe."

Violet wrapped her fingers around the handle of the other teapot, and Henry's forehead dampened. "And then what happened?" she asked. "Don't leave anything out."

Henry complied, although he didn't tell them about the foreman's attempted rape, only that he'd been tackled by another man, which had led to his leg injury.

"His story confirms our intelligence that Paul Farrell is now working for the neo-Pythagoreans," Hobbes said after Henry finished.

Henry nodded. "I believe that to be true. They also have

some sort of electrical power that allows them to appear and then disappear." He told them what his men had experienced that morning.

Violet waved her hand and Henry took a breath. "That's a common stage trick, using some sort of static power to throw off the audience's perceptions. Your men were fooled, although it is impressive that the neo-Pythagoreans were able to stop them in exactly the right spot for it to work."

"This organization is fascinating." Hobbes used the tongs to take a couple of finger sandwiches. "You've been tracking them for years, Henry. What are your thoughts?"

That I hope you won't poison me. But instead he said, "It's difficult to tell what their goals are other than to interfere with the development of aether technology."

"I agree." Violet hefted the teapot she had poured from. "Considering Paul Farrell had ties to Cobb—and still may—and is now involved with the neo-Pythagoreans, it is especially important for you to capture him and bring him to us."

She still hadn't served tea to Henry, and he knew his life hung on his answer. Perhaps he could still figure out a way out of this mess, to keep his word to the neo-Pythagoreans and satisfy his employers. He was the one with the most knowledge of the man and the organization, after all.

"Now that we have Chadwick Radcliffe in our custody, we plan to leave for Boston as soon as we can."

"We have an airship you can use," Hobbes said. "It will be ready for you first thing in the morning."

Violet poured Henry some tea, and he allowed his middle to sag in relief, although he didn't move what they could see of his torso above the table.

"Do help yourself, Henry." Violet waved to the plates of pastries and sandwiches and looked at him through her lashes with a sly smile. "Although there's no reason to act like this is your last meal."

———

"I'm not going to do anything. And we're not leaving until you open that box." Lieutenant Crow's guard reached for her weapon, but with a swift kick, Marie disabled her firing arm. The guard held her wrist and glared. Crow reached for her own holster but stopped when Marie stepped toward her.

"I can do a lot worse." Marie laced her fingers and stretched her hands. "And I've been itching to practice."

"You've broken it," the guard said.

"No, just bruised it. Iris, take their guns."

Iris complied. She didn't like having the firearms in her hands. They felt heavy with the weight of the lives they could take or ruin, so she handed them to Marie, who backed up so she could keep everyone in sight.

Iris glanced at Langlois. He lounged against one of the tables, his arms folded. Iris guessed he wouldn't become involved unless the artifacts were in danger. *Smart man.*

"We're not doing anything or going anywhere except back to the hotel to fetch the afternoon telegram." Iris wished again she could be taller and more intimidating.

"Or even better," Marie said. "I believe we were discussing Lieutenant Crow opening the box."

Iris grinned at her friend, who had felt through their bond that Iris craved to know what was in there and why it was so protected. Could it be the key to solving the final mystery of the aether?

Crow held her hands out, her eyes wide. "Let's not be hasty. Perhaps we should go next door and have tea, my treat."

"No." Iris gestured for Langlois to pull the crate from the closet. "You brought us here to open it, so let's do it. As an initiate of the Archaic Mysteries, you should be able to get past it."

"Help me," Crow hissed at her guard.

The guard shook her head and continued to massage her wrist. "You got yourself into this."

As Langlois dragged the innocuous-looking crate from the storeroom and then, with a grunt, lifted it and placed it on the nearest table to them, Iris tried to ignore the sensation of a thousand angry wasps buzzing around her, their insistence on punishment loud in her ears. She didn't have to touch the object to know who had sealed it, and when she closed her eyes for some relief, she saw a dark robed figure silhouetted in front of a fire raising his or her hands.

A voice of nondescript gender promised, *"You may steal our secrets, but you cannot un-know what you discover."*

No, she didn't want anything to do with what was in there, but she also didn't want it to fall into other hands.

"Say your incantation or pray to whatever god you like," she told Crow. "Just do something to make it stop."

The lieutenant nodded. Sweat dampened her forehead, and she whispered something too quietly for Iris to hear, other than to make out it sounded like old Greek. The angry wasps reduced from a thousand to a hundred—still enough to be terrifying, but less intense. When the sensation had reduced to just one, Crow leaned against the table, her eyes closed.

"They didn't tell me it would drain me," she said and slumped to the floor. Her guard caught her with her good arm, and Langlois jumped in to help carry her to a chair.

Iris swallowed against the pressure of the guilt in her chest. *Ruthlessness doesn't suit me.*

"So now what?" Marie asked. She still held the weapons at the ready, and Iris wondered how many times she'd done that before when she'd worked for Cobb.

"We open the box."

Langlois took a crowbar and pried the lid off. Iris watched as he cleared the straw, and then she couldn't contain her curiosity further.

In the box lay clay tablets, and a ring with a large green stone was nestled among them. Iris didn't touch anything for fear of being tugged into the past. Instead, she focused on the tablets and recognized the language as Greek from the Archaic period. One repeated word stood out to her—*soul*. She murmured as she translated, thankful she'd brushed up on her rudimentary knowledge while in the Ottoman Empire.

"Just as Eros rends the fabric of light, the music of the spheres repairs it. The souls of men are caught in the middle of two great forces. These secrets are to tip the scales of soul to set them free, balance, or transfer them. Woe to he who uses this for his own purposes, for no man can see the full tapestry…"

She looked up at Langlois.

"What did you find in the temple, Madame?" he asked.

Iris sank to the bench, recalling the cruel-looking metal implements she'd unearthed. Now she knew what they were for. "Tools to extract souls and formulas to loosen them. Mathematical ones. My husband recognized the numerical patterns as Pythagorean."

"But why?" Marie asked.

"The Pythagoreans believed in the transmigration of souls after death," Langlois said as he put the kettle back on the burner. "But this is the first I've heard of them wanting to control the process."

"This must have belonged to a very specialized cult." Iris stood on shaking legs. This discovery could make her career, but at what cost? Before she'd met Parnaby Cobb, she wouldn't have thought that men capable of wanting to wield such awful power existed. "Asia Minor was an area in constant flux during that time with city-states warring against each other, outside empires trying to take over… What if the priests of this cult went to a local tyrant or even an emperor and promised to move his soul before he died so he could live on?"

"And what does this have to do with the aether?" Marie cocked her head. "It can affect emotions, but souls?"

"What are we but our emotions?" Iris put a hand to her

heart, which thrummed under her fingers as a million ideas raced through her brain. "What other force is more powerful than logic? It's the oldest force of all, this Eros."

"And then what do we do with this?" Langlois mused. He put a steaming cup in Iris's hand. "Drink. It's very strong English tea."

"He didn't put anything in it," Marie said. "I watched him."

Lieutenant Crow stirred and half-sat. "As for what we do with it, we destroy it. That's what the neo-Pythagoreans want, for these secrets to remain hidden."

"Do your initiates know how to do this, to transfer souls?" Iris asked. She didn't miss how Crow hadn't included herself when she mentioned the cult.

The pause before Crow answered almost made her scream under the weight of the horrible possibilities. "No, that knowledge has been lost until now."

"Thank gods." Iris stood. She wanted to read the rest of the tablets, to discover the procedure, but she hesitated. She recognized that the processes named therein could cure the worst pain of all—grief—but at what cost? The loss of life? The souls would have to go somewhere. Into animals?

Egyptian lore came to mind then, about how the pharaohs were treated as gods, and cats had nine lives. What if their lives weren't their own? What if this knowledge had spread to Egypt with conquerors that had come through Anatolia and Persia and had brought it with them? But without all the pieces.

"For no man can see the full tapestry," she repeated. "Or woman."

Dizziness overwhelmed her as her thoughts swung back and forth—preserve or destroy?—the consequences of each, and—most frightening of all—would she have taken advantage of it to save her own father if she'd been allowed the chance?

"I need to think on this further," she said and looked at Lieutenant Crow. "Do you promise not to harm the tablets until we can have a rational discussion?"

Crow nodded. "But do you trust me?"

"I'm not sure. But I can't stay here and jeopardize my group's primary mission for this sidetrack."

"The two have more in common than you think," Crow told her and stood. "For what do you think Parnaby Cobb is after?"

"He wants to monopolize a new power source," Iris said. "Have you not heard of the aether weapon?"

"But what's more formidable than something that destroys men?"

Iris recalled the therapeutic aether device Chadwick Radcliffe came up with to help their friend Amelie Lafitte. What would a man such as Cobb do with that type of influence? "He wants something that can control them."

"And if he could control what happens after death, he would have the same power as a god," Marie added. "For Parnaby Cobb, more power is better."

Crow nodded. "Now you're getting it. I don't believe in the transfer of souls, but to control a man's emotions—his heart—is to control his life. Langlois, hide the box again. Mrs. Bailey and I will return tomorrow with a decision. I'll leave my guard here to ensure the crate's safety."

The guard glared at Crow but said nothing.

"I'll help with your wrist," Langlois said. "And the hotel next door has a wonderful shepherd's pie."

Iris wondered if he wanted the excuse to have some himself. "Very well, then. Let's get back to the hotel. I need to know what our instructions are."

When they walked outside, Iris pulled her cloak around her, but her hairs still stood up on end. The carriage rolled up, and now she saw the neo-Pythagorean symbol painted in black on the door. It had been invisible previously.

"You drive around with that on there?" Marie asked. She'd hidden the firearms in her cloak, but Iris knew she still had one trained on Crow just in case.

Crow grinned. "Most don't notice it, but you'd be surprised

how large our organization is, especially here. And we're not the only ones."

Just before she closed the door, a messenger ran up to her and gave her a slip of paper before disappearing into the crowd. Crow opened it and smiled.

"Good news," she said. "We have both your Doctor Radcliffe and Mister O'Connell in our custody."

The door to the carriage shut and produced a final stop to her announcement. Iris sat back and shook her head. It seemed she would have to trust the enigmatic Crow after all, if only to get her friends back. Or...

Iris looked at Crow. "That's fantastic news. However, I'm not going to help you further until I see that they're safe."

"I told you, you'll have to trust me."

"And then you tried to get me to open a box that very obviously had some sort of protection curse on it." Iris shook a finger at Crow. "That's not very trustworthy of you. No, you're going to have to do better than that. Right, Marie?"

Marie nodded. "Right. We need to see for ourselves that Patrick O'Connell and Chadwick Radcliffe are safe, and we need to talk to them to ensure they're not being held against their will."

Iris once again thanked whatever gods were handy that Marie had a much more strategic mind than she, being better with piecing together what did happen rather than what should happen.

"I'm going to have to check with my superiors. What time do you want me to fetch you tomorrow for the museum?"

"It depends—what time do you want to bring our friends to us?"

"Or you to them."

Iris shook her head. "You want our help, Lieutenant Crow. You're going to have to give up something for it. If you truly are interested in stopping Parnaby Cobb as you say you are, then you'll have to cooperate. We're a much stronger group all together."

"And if that frightens you," Marie added. "It should. Because I can tell you're lying." She inclined her head. "Partially."

"Fine," Crow spat. "I'll discuss it with my superiors and leave word at your hotel for you. At the very least I can produce O'Connell."

The carriage rolled to a stop at the hotel. Two dark-coated forms detached themselves from the crowd at the front, and Iris smiled when she saw Edward and Johann. "Very well. We look forward to hearing from you and to seeing our friends again."

The driver opened the carriage door and handed Iris and Marie out.

"We were getting worried," Edward told Iris when he reached her and took her hands in his. "We were about to go to the museum looking for you."

Iris glanced at Marie, who was getting a shockingly close public embrace from Johann. "What?" Marie asked and playfully tried to bat him away, but he held her. "We weren't gone that long."

"No," Edward said and gestured for them to follow him inside. "But we did see one of those spy ravens. It's Paul Farrell's design."

Iris and Marie exchanged concerned glances.

"Which means Cobb is interested in something here," Johann told them. "And I suspect that's Marie." He tucked Marie's hand into the crook of his arm. "Hence why we're moving hotels as soon as we can get packed."

"I'll have to send a telegram to Davidson from the new one, then," Iris said, recalling her own telegram that had gone astray. "I don't know that we can trust anyone here."

But she stopped by the front desk just in case something had come in that afternoon.

Indeed, the clerk handed her a folded piece of paper that read, *Have doctor. Be there soon. LFATB*

Iris smiled and turned to tell the others the good news, but they were huddled by the window looking outside.

"It's back," Edward said and turned to Iris."The raven. It's perched across the street."

"Then we should leave." *And hope Davidson hasn't left with Radcliffe yet. Otherwise he'll never be able to find us.*

CHAPTER TWENTY-TWO

Neo-Pythagorean Compound, Salem, 13 March 1871

When Patrick awoke, he found a soft blanket under his hands rather than burlap, and a pinch told him he lay upon feathers rather than straw. He sat, rubbing his beard, and found himself in a bedroom with blue-patterned wallpaper, curtains of some plush material, and a large mahogany bedstead. Tan brick made up a mantle and fireplace that housed a merry little blaze that had been going for a while if the temperature of the room was any indication. The whole place appeared masculine, but he noted the lack of curtain pulls, fire-stoking tools, and any implements on the dressing table that could be used as weapons.

Even worse, he found his braces and shoes gone.

And how do they expect me to hold up my trousers, then?

He rolled off the bed and stood, waiting for the room to stop spinning. When it did, he walked toward the fire, where he found a tray in the shadows to the side. It held a loaf of sliced bread and artfully arranged pieces of cheese and meat. No utensils. Or pickles. There was also a steaming pot of tea.

Holding his pants up, he lowered himself into the chair and pulled the tray to him. He put two lumps of sugar and a splash of milk in the cup provided and poured. The floral scent told him whoever held him captive liked good quality tea.

He was about halfway through his meal when a knock on the door brought him to his feet, his trousers to his knees, and the tray to the floor. The teapot and cups spilled but bounced on the tile.

What in the hell? Pants forgotten, he picked up the cup. It felt like it was made of bone china, but it was a substance much tougher. He couldn't even scrape the edge with his nail.

The door opened, bringing him to himself, and he bent over to retrieve his pants, but he overbalanced and joined his repast on the floor. He looked up to see a servant, and he held the cup out.

"I seem to be havin' a spot of trouble. Would you mind fetching some more tea?"

"That depends," the man, whose graying mutton chops contrasted the youthful lines of his face, said in a brogue to match Patrick's. "Will you be drinkin' it or lyin' in it? If it's the latter, I can draw you a bath. Much cleaner that way."

"I don't care what you do as long as I can get something to hold my trousers up." Patrick tossed the cup aside and maneuvered to his knees. He didn't care if the other man saw his red-haired thighs. If they disturbed him, it served him right.

No braces? Some servant he is.

But the man hauled Patrick to his feet with surprising strength, then wrinkled his nose.

"All right, laddie, it's definitely a bath for you."

Now that Patrick wasn't quite as hungry, he had to admit the man had a point—Patrick was redolent of *eau de dungeon*. Patrick held his trousers up while the servant went to a panel in the wall and knocked a complicated pattern. The wall opened to reveal a bathing room with another servant and a large copper tub of steaming water.

"Get yourself cleaned up. Soap's in the tub. It's a good thing you're bearded since I can't offer you a shave."

"Judging from your own face, I'd say that's a good thing," Patrick muttered, but he appreciated his fellow Irishman's sense of humor. "Where am I, anyway?"

"You're at the estate of The Lady. She's the leader of the Pythagoreans in this part of the country."

"You mean neo-Pythagoreans?" Patrick asked. He walked into the bathing room and shed his clothing. "Burn those if you like. As long as you give me something else to wear, of course."

The man who had opened the panel from the other side spoke. His accent matched his dark skin, and Patrick wondered if he came from the Ottoman Empire. "Our tradition has a direct lineage to the Master himself."

Patrick didn't hear any more of the speech because he'd stepped in the tub and immersed himself in the water over his head. He hadn't encountered many bathtubs in the world big enough for him, and he wondered how he could get on these men's good sides to acquire one. Not that a nomad like himself needed much, and a large bathtub would be hard to travel with.

The plug lacked a chain, so he emerged and washed the dungeon grime off himself. He hoped, anyway. Had Louisa's mum followed him? Would she be able to tell her daughter where he'd gone? When he'd taken his chance to escape, he hadn't thought much beyond the moment. Not his typical way of approaching things, but his head had been addled by the aether.

"We've had some difficulty finding clothing in your size," the bath steward, as Patrick had started thinking of him, said and helped him out of the tub. Now Patrick recognized how weak he was from the half-starvation of the past few days, as moving the towel over himself taxed his muscles. When he put a robe on, his fingers clutched at the sleeves. Again, the garment lacked a belt, but there was enough of it to pull around himself.

Or maybe there was something in the food.

He stumbled into the bedroom and made it as far as the dressing table. His eyelids wanted to crash to his cheeks, but he wouldn't let them, not yet, even if the feel of the comb through his hair was soothing.

"Did you drug me?" he asked. "Or am I still working Farrell's infernal smoke out of my system?"

The Irish servant paused in his combing. "I'm not aware of you being drugged, lad. Sometimes exposure to a large aether-burst can have effects like this. And delusions. Hence the precautions we took."

"And why there are two of you."

"Yes, exactly. We've heard of your strength and couldn't take any chances."

Patrick nodded, his head weighing more with each movement. The servants helped him to bed and left his robe on. He sank into the sheets and rolled on to his side, his hand finding the corner of the mattress. In that instant between awareness and darkness, he formulated his plan for his next escape.

When Claire arrived for tea, Louisa ensured none of the servants would bother them. She'd thought about meeting Claire in her private drawing room, but since they didn't know each other that well, Louisa opted for a less intimate but also not too formal setting. But when the maid showed Claire into the library, she didn't expect the other girl's broad smile as she squeezed Louisa's hands.

"I've heard Mr. Cobb had a large collection of books, but I hadn't dreamed it to be this extensive."

Louisa cocked her head. Her particular talent sometimes didn't distinguish subtleties, but she hadn't heard any sarcasm, so she took Claire's words as though they were truly meant.

"Please look around if you like. The maids are still assembling the sandwich trays."

"Thank you." Claire clasped one of Louisa's hands in hers and then walked to the nearest bookcase.

Louisa followed her. She liked the library and found the smell of the leather bindings and paper to be soothing, but she didn't know why. She had so many questions to ask, but she hadn't found any magazine lessons on "what to do if you think you've heard someone's voice in your head" or "how to open a conversation with someone who's been abducted." Of the two topics, she decided asking about Claire's kidnapping would be less awkward, although Claire hadn't stated it expressly.

"We didn't get much of a chance to talk personally yesterday, so I'm glad you were able to come," Louisa ventured.

Claire looked up from the book she had pulled, *The Compleat History of Steam in the Nineteenth Century*. "I am, too. I find this city to be a lonely, friendless place since I've come back. I don't know how you stand it, although you seem to have more freedom than most women of our class." She looked up with a certain degree of challenge in her light blue eyes.

Of all the replies Claire could have made, Louisa hadn't expected that one.

Although I should know by now Claire McPhee isn't a typical young woman. She has a medical degree, after all.

"How was your trip back to Boston?" She clenched one fist in her skirt—she hadn't meant to ask a direct question—and she braced herself for Claire's blurted answer, which was likely to be unpleasant.

Claire closed the book and returned it to its gap. It slid in smoothly, and Claire adjusted it so it wouldn't stick out any more or less than the other ones. Rather than spitting up a response, she asked a question.

"Miss Cobb, may I be frank with you?"

The words, although gentle, hit Louisa like a blow.

Is that what it's like when someone feels one of my questions? And why didn't she answer mine? But it was refreshing to know someone could challenge her. Well, two someones. There was Patrick, after all.

A gentle knock on the door heralded the maids entering with

a bounty of small sandwiches and pastries, all beautifully arranged and presented on Cobb's silver dining service. Louisa wanted them to hurry, but she breathed deeply, smiled while they arranged everything just so, and shook her head when the head housekeeper asked, "Is there anything else you need, Miss?"

"No, thank you, Mrs. Smoot."

"Shall I pour the tea for you?"

Louisa put a smidgen more force behind her words. "No thank you."

The older woman checked everything over one more time and finally exited after saying, "Just pull the rope if you need anything." Just before the door closed behind her, she muttered, "Young women having tea in a library? Well, I never..."

Louisa gestured for Claire to sit in one of the wingback chairs she'd had arranged around the standing tea trays with the food and the small round table on which the tea service sat. Claire did so and arranged her dark blue skirts. Louisa thought she recognized the outfit from several years before but didn't say anything about it. Instead, she wondered what it would be like to not care if one had a new set of dresses for every season and felt somewhat overdressed in her new green satin day dress with Brugge lace trim, which she still arranged to fall prettily when she sat.

"Tea?" Louisa held up the pot.

Claire nodded, but she held her bottom lip between her teeth.

"And of course you may be frank with me." Louisa decided to reference their silent conversation from the previous day. "Otherwise, how can we help each other?"

Claire released her lip, but otherwise her expression remained the same. She didn't look at Louisa as she took the freshly poured cup of tea and placed it on its saucer on the small table beside her. Louisa handed her a plate and a dainty pair of tongs.

"It seems unfair," Claire said as she served herself. She finally looked up at Louisa, her gaze more forthright than a woman's should be. "We have this meal, and then we'll each have dinner this evening, and we're expected to remain slender."

Louisa used the natural delay caused by the motions of serving herself to ponder her response. She felt that Claire was deliberately making her feel uncomfortable, but to what end? She decided to try another question, but with a lead in.

"Oh, I'm familiar with the rules." Louisa gestured to the plates in front of them. "We'll each have a few of these, and although I've not eaten yet today, I'll stop myself at one of each kind of sandwich, a *petit-four*, and a small piece of lemon cake. Although I'd prefer chocolate." She shrugged. "I don't know what it's like to strain my corset. Tell me, Doctor McPhee, have you ever eaten your fill?"

Claire's eyes went shiny. "Yes, at Fort Daniels after the victory and after I returned. And thank you for using my professional title. It gives me some hope that you see my accomplishments, my value as something other than a pawn in my aunt's strange games."

"She's trying to pull me in, too." Louisa leaned over the arm of her own chair and reached for Claire's hand. "We have too much at stake to be anything but frank. You implied something yesterday about being kidnapped. Please tell me everything. I need to know the full extent of what I'm up against."

Claire took Louisa's hand, and again Louisa felt the words in her mind. *"But can I trust you?"*

"Yes, as long as I can trust you."

They dropped their hands and returned to studying their food when a man's footstep outside the door heralded a sharp rap, and then Parnaby Cobb entered.

"Stepfather." Louisa moved to put her plate aside, but he stopped her with a wave. He held a leather-bound book in his other hand, and Louisa put a hand to the pulse at her throat. It looked like he held Patrick's notebook.

But then what had become of Patrick?

"Louisa, Miss McPhee, please remain seated. I'll only be a moment." He nodded to each of them, and Louisa didn't miss Claire's wince. "I'm glad you're both here. I've received some disturbing news, and I'm here to let you know Ms. Adams and I have decided to move the timeline of the party up. Rather than Friday, we'll be holding it tomorrow evening, and we expect you to make your decisions about your future husbands on Wednesday." His lips curled into a bow that resembled a regretful smile, but Louisa knew better. She decided to play along.

"But my new spring party dresses won't be ready," she said with a pout. "What am I to wear?"

"And I don't have any," Claire added. "I didn't need such frocks at the fort."

Cobb's left eyebrow made a skeptical twitch—he knew they weren't stating their true objections—but he grinned, and Louisa put her teacup back on its saucer and braced herself. She only saw that number of teeth beneath his moustache when he was about to pounce like a lion on a mouse.

"Never fear, ladies, for I've rallied the city's best *modistes* to work all night to make sure you're as lovely as you could possibly be. Miss McPhee, your aunt has given her permission for you to stay here tonight so you can be on hand for adjustments."

Claire nodded, her eyes wide. "I'm not sure what to say."

"You may thank me tomorrow." He nodded to each of them. "Don't eat too much—you want your dresses to show off your girlish figures, after all."

He left, and Louisa picked up her teacup with trembling fingers. After a bracing sip of the bitter liquid, she looked at Claire, who gazed down at a cucumber sandwich with a bite taken from it.

"What news could they have possibly gotten?" Louisa asked.

Claire blinked as though waking from a dream. "Chadwick or Patrick must have escaped. That's the only reason I can think for them to be in such a rush."

"But neither of them pose that much of a threat to either my stepfather or your aunt," Louisa pointed out. "They have no social significance or standing."

Claire smiled, and the warmth in it made Louisa's heart lift with hope. "No, but they're terribly clever, and they have a group of talented friends." She held out a hand, and Louisa took it.

"*So what do we do?*" Louisa asked in her head.

"*We do what we can to escape, and if that doesn't work, we turn away all the erstwhile suitors so they can come up with a plan.*"

"*But we have to let them know!*"

A scraping sound at the window startled Louisa. She walked over to it and looked out to see a gold—no, brass with some tarnished edges—butterfly at the window. The sense of being spied on made her look down, where she saw an automaton looking back up at her with its blank eyes. With a gasp, she stepped back and drew the curtains, fumbling with the sashes.

"What was it?" Claire asked.

"An automaton. Escape might not be as easy as we think."

CHAPTER TWENTY-THREE

Somewhere over the Eastern States, 13 March 1871

The airship steward swore to Henry that they kept the passenger compartment at a steady temperature no matter how cold the air outside was, but Henry didn't believe him. The further north they flew, the more he felt the chill to his bones. His leg, although better from Radcliffe's treatments, ached around the wound.

After Henry complained about the chill for the third time, Radcliffe put a hand on Henry's forehead.

"You're not feverish," he said. "How are you feeling otherwise?"

"Fine." He had to admit that he was peevish at the methods by which Radcliffe had been delivered to him and the threat that still hung over him. Should he go back on his word to the neo-Pythagoreans or should he risk his own life and career?

Is there some way I can satisfy both?

Henry had left Colin in Terminus along with the others to dismantle what was left of their headquarters, then try and track down the rest of Cobb's operatives. Radcliffe had given them a good idea of where he'd been held, and they agreed they would need the entire team, minus Henry. He suspected they'd worked well together before he arrived, and they didn't enjoy having to deal with him anymore than he did with them. Not that they'd quarreled, but they'd not coalesced into a good team. As typically happened with Henry, he worked best alone. But now that he had a dilemma, he wouldn't have minded someone to bounce some thoughts off of. He looked out of the window and pondered the winter's blue sky.

Radcliffe sat on the other side of the table from Henry and pored over a newspaper, his third that morning. The airship—built for speed, not comfort—had a bare commissary with a small locker of food, a barrel of water, and a burner should they wish to make tea.

The doctor had a certain calm presence about him, Henry could give him that. But could he give Henry the sort of advice he needed?

A rustling of the paper made Henry glance at Radcliffe, whose gray eyes met Henry's. "If Doctor McPhee were here, she would suggest that you may benefit from talking about whatever is bothering you. Perhaps then you would better progress with your healing."

He spoke his beloved's name with calm resignation. He'd been in this situation before, Henry knew. Henry knew all about the strange little troupe brought together by Parnaby Cobb, the aether that bound them and the mysterious cults—the Clockwork Guild and the neo-Pythagoreans—that followed them. But for the first time since inserting himself into their midst in Paris, he didn't know how best to help them.

And that was the problem. His job was to assist them in their scientific developments so they'd draw out members of the international organizations he studied and targeted, not to make deals with said organizations for their safety, putting his own life in danger.

"Doctor Radcliffe, as wise as Doctor McPhee's words are, the situation is more complicated than you realize."

The other man waved to their surroundings. "We've got time.

As I recall, this trip will last several more hours, and that's with an estimate of favorable winds."

So Henry explained what he could, at least as much as he could without betraying his organization. He described to Radcliffe how he'd followed Cobb and Farrell from Paris, had infiltrated Cobb's guard, but had never been able to get close enough to acquire the evidence he needed to prove that Cobb was working with the Clockwork Guild and put the man behind bars. He'd put Patrick in position to pass Henry information but hadn't expected that Cobb would put the Irishman in a dungeon to keep him away from his stepdaughter, Louisa.

Radcliffe shook his head and filled Henry in on their history, brief as it was. "I doubt anyone saw how powerful that one kiss was, especially Patrick. I wonder if he's finally caught the bug. You can't prepare for every circumstance, Inspector."

"No. That's what happened in Terminus."

Radcliffe's face went still, his eyes haunted, but he gestured for Henry to continue.

"We tried to rescue you between the train and prison, but we failed." What Henry hoped to gain from admitting this, he didn't know. Some sort of absolution? "And I cannot tell you how much I regret that."

Radcliffe nodded and looked beyond Henry to the sky. "I appreciate your efforts."

"We tried to find you after, but you were too well-hidden. So then, when I was given a chance to bargain for your safety, I did."

"And what was the bargain?"

Henry forced his spine to remain straight, but inwardly he cringed. "I had to agree to allow Paul Farrell to escape should it come to a final confrontation."

The doctor cocked his head, apparently considering. "That didn't go over well with your superiors, I imagine."

Now Henry did allow himself to slump, the weight of his secret too great. "They don't know about the bargain, only that the neo-Pythagoreans assisted us with some sort of advanced technology."

"I see." Radcliffe folded his hands on the table in front of him. "Well, then we need to come up with a plan."

Henry shook his head. "I don't work well with others, although I do appreciate the offer. That's what got me into this mess to begin with."

"Ah, but you've not worked with us." Radcliffe tapped the paper. "Remember—we've overcome bigger. We'll fetch Patrick from that dungeon and Claire from her aunt's house, and then you'll see. We make a formidable team."

"At least give me a few minutes to think this through." Henry stood to pace around the room, but his leg objected, so he fell back into his chair. "Quietly. Sitting here."

"Take all the time you need." Radcliffe picked up the newspaper in front of him. "But remember, once time is lost, you can't get it back."

———

At their new hotel, which wasn't nearly as nice as the previous one, the four of them shared a room with two double beds and—the main appeal—one window. Iris had taken the early shift keeping watch at the window for signs of the steam raven, but her sleep continued to be interrupted even after she snuggled into bed in Edward's arms. First, just as she felt she drifted off, he had to leave their sleeping embrace for his turn to watch. He tucked a pillow between her arms this time so she wouldn't hurt her shoulders. She had only dipped in and out of Morpheus's well while Edward was away.

Then it was Marie's turn, and she and Johann had a whispered argument—he insisting she needed her rest and her telling him that she would be fine, she'd handled worse when she worked for Cobb. Then Johann told her she didn't need to be in view of the window, which she finally acquiesced to. The exchange brought Iris back to her childhood, to her parents' whispered conversations when they thought she slept.

Usually he lets her do what she wants. Why's he being so protective now?

In spite of the dingy state of the window, the morning light managed to find Iris through a gap in the curtains. She blinked awake, unsure if the burning in her eyes was due to the light or the dismal night of sleep she'd gotten. Johann sat by the window, his violin case open on the floor and his bow in hand. When Iris rolled away from the light, Edward stirred, and soon Marie woke, too. They took turns using the washroom before descending to breakfast.

"Mrs. Bailey?" the young clerk asked. He looked no more than sixteen or seventeen, and his eyes brightened with interest when she nodded. "A French gentleman left a package here for you." He pulled it from beneath the counter and leaned closer to whisper as he handed the box to Iris, "I'm not sure if I should say this since ladies are of a delicate constitution, but I think it moved."

"Thank you," she said and tipped him a few cents. She tucked the smallish wooden box against her waist and felt the contents shift. At least that was what she hoped she felt.

It's not moving, it's not moving...

But she had seen statues dance, so she knew it was possible.

No one said much at breakfast, so the meal passed quickly, and soon Marie was headed out for a walk, Johann with her. Iris and Edward sat in the lobby in a little alcove opposite the front desk while they went upstairs to grab cloaks.

"What do you think is going on with Marie?" Edward asked.

Iris shrugged. She had a theory, but she didn't want to ask— the memory of her own miscarriage still hurt too much. Edward patted her hand.

"Once this is over, we can settle somewhere. Perhaps once we've had a chance to rest and recover—"

"Oh, let's just focus on what we need to do." She didn't want him to say it. What if she couldn't get or stay pregnant? Her parents had only had her, after all.

Iris suspected Marie and Johann wanted some privacy, so she could be patient, but whatever was in the box tugged at her awareness like an insistent child.

"What is it?" Edward asked and gestured to the box. Iris appreciated his change of subject.

"I don't know. I suspect Langlois from the museum sent it." She and Marie had related their adventures to their husbands, who had insisted they be included on the next trip.

"Did it come with any sort of explanation?"

"No, not that I can tell. There may be one inside."

"What else can you determine about it?"

Iris smiled, grateful that Edward, being a scientist and therefore a skeptic, didn't question her unique ability. "I don't know. I haven't tried anything yet."

His blue eyes—the famous Bailey blue eyes—sparkled. "What, you, resisting curiosity? Why, Mrs. Bailey, when did that happen?"

She swatted his arm, a warmth pooling in her belly at his teasing. There was a time, not too long ago, when he never dropped his serious scientist persona. These moments only happened with her and Johann, Edward's best friend since childhood.

"Since we became involved in this strange game," she murmured close to his ear and felt him shiver. Perhaps they would need some privacy once Johann and Marie left for their walk.

They appeared as if Iris's thoughts had conjured them, and indeed, they both had a rosy glow and walked as close together as they could.

"Well, we're off," Johann said and tipped his hat. "We'll be back in about an hour. I can't take being stuck in that stuffy room any longer than necessary."

"That's fine." Iris embraced Marie. "You two be careful."

"We will." Marie shifted her cloak so Iris could see the steam pistol at her waist. "I don't normally like them, but I'm not opposed to carrying a firearm when circumstances call for them."

"Then be extra careful," Iris admonished.

After they said their goodbyes, Iris and Edward went up to the room, where Edward drew her close.

"Iris," he breathed into her hair.

"Edward," she said, but the contents of the box shifted again. She put it on the bed and turned back to him, but he held her at arm's length.

"I know what it's like to be close to an exciting discovery. I'm not going to keep you from yours. Do what you need to do, and we can play later."

"Thank you." She kissed him on the cheek. "Please keep me from being gone too long."

He put a hand on her shoulder, and a hint of his old anxiety flitted through his expression. "Always come back to me. Promise me that."

She rested her cheek on his hand for a moment. "I promise."

They sat side-by-side on the bed, and Iris removed her gloves. She pressed her fingertips to the box and concentrated on it. She saw Langlois hastily packing it while cursing in French too rapid for her to understand more than a few words. One of them was "thief," another "guard," and a third "safekeeping." Iris guessed that he'd sent whatever the box held to keep it from being taken by Crow's guard.

She opened the lid, and the note on top of the straw said as much. After a deep breath, she dug around in the straw and pulled out the ring she'd noticed the day before. It had a large green stone set in an intricately carved base. At first she thought it was some sort of material that tarnished, but when she rubbed a finger over one of the carvings—some sort of worm that looked like it was biting its tail—the discoloration came off and proved to be soot or something similar.

"That's beautiful," Edward said. "May I?"

"Please. Tell me what you think before I read it."

He held the ring up so he could use the sunlight to see the raised shapes. "I'm not sure, but it seems to be a bunch of animals, not all real. I've seen a configuration like this before, in the Ottoman Empire, but I'm not sure where, exactly."

"Was it in our temple?" Iris asked. She took the ring back, and now that he mentioned it, she agreed that the animal shapes —portrayed with amazingly detailed precision—looked familiar. Some of the little creatures even had tiny jewels for eyes.

"No, but somewhere close." He frowned. "I can't place it."

Once the metal heated to Iris's touch, she felt a certain vibration, subtle but present. Could the clerk have sensed it? Her father had had a similar talent to hers, so she knew she wasn't unique. But she'd thought such talents belonged mostly to women. Or was the power of the object so strong others could feel it?

"Do I dare read it?" she asked Edward. "I can tell it's strong, but I also feel that it came to me with a purpose."

"Then do what you need." He squeezed her shoulder. "I'll be right here."

CHAPTER TWENTY-FOUR

Neo-Pythagorean Complex, 13 March 1871

When Patrick next woke, he guessed from the change in the light coming from the windows that several hours had passed. No one waited for him, so he rolled out of the bed and tested the door—locked, of course. A meal waited for him, but he shook his head. His stomach growled, but he suspected the food to be laced with something to keep him fatigued and compliant. The strange taste at the back of his throat told him his breakfast had contained something, and his stomach rolled. Unfortunately the wall leading to the bathing chamber was closed, and he couldn't get it to move.

Stupid, stupid, stupid... He walked the perimeter of the room looking for another possible escape, his steps providing the cadence to his self-recrimination. He should have gone back for his notebook. Perhaps he would have gotten another opportunity to escape from his known prison in a known location. As for his current situation, he didn't know whether he was in the country or the city, and even if he did manage to leave the estate, he didn't know which way to go.

At least I can get out of the room. He returned to the bed and pulled the corner of the sheets back to reveal the mattress.

As he'd suspected when he felt it, the manufacturer had fastened the corner creases of the cover with large pins to reinforce the cheap thread they'd used. He pulled the pins out and replaced the sheet. Then, with his teeth, he bent them into the shapes he needed to pick the lock, which responded to his touch like a lover.

He grinned at the analogy, simultaneously wishing for Louisa and glad she wasn't there to share his imprisonment and humiliation. He still didn't have pants, after all.

He eased the door open, and a glance in each direction told him he was alone...almost. A movement in his peripheral vision revealed that Louisa's mother stood there watching him.

"Don't you dare give me away," Patrick whispered. "I have friends who can get rid of the likes of you." He didn't know with certainty, but he suspected Marie's mother had some friends or relatives who could help get rid of a pesky ghost.

She shook her head. "I'm here to help you, you red-headed fool. He's got your notes, and he's planning something terrible for tomorrow evening centering around Louisa." She wrung her hands, her expression distressed. "As much as I hate to admit it, she needs you."

"Oh, does she?" Patrick crossed his arms. "And how are you here, then?"

"I don't know. Something about the aether loosened my connection to the dungeon and my bones." She floated to a door and pointed. "There are trousers and other things in there."

"And then what?" Patrick eased the next door open, which showed him it was the bathing room he'd been in. A suit of clothing was laid out, a true gentleman's ensemble complete with top hat, gloves, shoes, and...*Ugh, a cravat.* Patrick grimaced.

"Put it on, and hurry."

He darted into the room and motioned for her to turn around. "I don't care if you're not innocent. I don't need your opinions on my dressing. And that's not what I meant." He spoke in a low voice as he dressed. "Once I stop Cobb and rescue Louisa, what then? Will you continue to harass us?"

He tied the cravat in a simple knot. *A cravat. How ridiculous.* When he turned to see what the ghost would answer, he caught a glimpse of himself in the mirror. If he hid his unruly hair, which had never responded to any barber's attempts to tame it, with the hat, he could pass for a gentleman.

Louisa's mother tapped a finger on her lips. "If you manage to clean up so well, there may be something to you after all." She sighed. "And I admit I did not choose wisely, so I will let my daughter make her own decision."

"Thanks, I think." Patrick muttered. "Now get me out of here."

She floated through the door. He opened it, again checked the hallway, and was careful to shut it and to make sure the door to the bedroom was also closed and locked. There was no point in making it obvious something was amiss. He wore an evening dress ensemble, so he guessed no one would be there to check on him until later.

A grandfather clock showed him the time—four o'clock. *Tea time.*

The ghost led him along a maze of hallways, sometimes holding up her hand at intersections. He would hide however was convenient—behind a statue, in a recessed doorway, and once behind a suit of armor.

Am I in a museum or a house?

Finally the grandeur of the passages lessened, and the spirit led him down a wooden staircase into a carriage bay, which sat under and behind the house.

"The stables are out that door and over a small hill," she told him. "Don't get distracted by what you see when you go outside —you need to hurry."

He nodded and darted toward the door. He tried to run as quietly as possible in his gentleman's shoes, but they pinched, and no matter how he contorted his feet, his steps echoed off the walls. He finally reached a door up an incline beside a set of doors that looked like they belonged on a barn, not a fine house. When he slipped outside he found himself beside a temple. It pulsed with some sort of power, and the sun reflected off its white marble walls. A wave of disorientation nearly brought him to his knees.

"Keep running." The ghost was behind him, and the cold that surrounded her snapped him out of the lull. He tried to appear to casually saunter to the stables, which he now saw. Servants darted to and fro as though preparing for a large party, but intent on their tasks, they ignored him. Other gentlemen directed them, but they, too, seemed not to notice him.

"What's going on?" He asked the shimmer to his right.

"They're preparing for some sort of ritual, and they're under pain of death if they don't accomplish their tasks." She snorted, an odd sound to come from a ghost. "They're no better than Cobb."

Patrick made a note to ask her more about how she died, but first he needed a means to leave.

"The horses won't like me being in there, but if you can handle them, you can use the distraction to steal one."

"I'm not a horse thief," he muttered, but he was already a wanted man by more than one party, so he supposed he didn't have that much more to lose.

Where the hell was Davidson, who had gotten him into this mess?

As Maureen promised, the horses rolled their eyes and fidgeted when she and Patrick entered the stables. The only person in there was a young man, who shoveled out a stall.

"You, boy." Patrick put on his haughtiest English accent. "I need a mount."

The stable boy shook his head, but he glanced at the horses, some of which became more agitated by the second as the ghost wafted by them. Patrick guessed only he could see the ripple in the air.

"The boss said no one's to leave before the ceremony," the boy said in a nasal New England accent.

"Well, as you can tell, there's something very wrong. I need to go into the city for some special herbs for tonight."

"Yes, sir, I'll call someone to get you a carriage."

"No, don't. That will take too long." He looked down at his clothing with a regretful sigh. "I shall sacrifice my attire to the ride. And the more quickly you move, the more quickly the horses will settle."

The boy nodded and darted about, getting a saddle and tack ready. But whenever he approached a horse, it would back away or rear. Patrick sighed and held up his hands. The ghost took the hint and wafted outside, and the animals calmed enough so that the boy could get one ready.

"You must be one of her more powerful wizards," he said, awe in his tone. He backed away from the saddled horse, his eyes as wide as theirs had been.

"Thanks for your trouble." Patrick wished he had a coin or something to give the kid.

"It's an honor, sir." He bowed.

Patrick mounted the horse and trotted out of the stable, leaving through the open doors at the back. He caught sight of the ghost on the road ahead and hoped she had enough sense to stay ahead of him but not too close. He didn't need the horse to get spooked and take him in the other direction.

She led him to a break in the hedges low enough for the horse to jump. He hadn't done it since he was a child, but his body remembered where to tighten his hold and, the animal, a bay gelding, responded. Patrick held on as it sailed over the greenery and landed easily on the dirt road on the other side, adjusting his seat accordingly. He patted the horse on its neck.

"You've been wanting to do something like that all day, haven't you?"

The horse tossed its head, and Patrick smiled and allowed the ghost to lead him into the city. By the time he arrived, the fresh air had cleared out the rest of whatever had been in his system.

"Now what?" He joined the stream of traffic into the city. Signs pointing the other way indicated he'd come from near Salem.

Fitting.

———

As often happened when Iris opened the deeper parts of her mind to an object from the long past, she felt that she fell through time. Sometimes she had to push through the impressions left by more recent touches and handling, but the ring had its own agenda, pulling her faster and farther down a dark tunnel until her feet met a hard surface, and she took a wobbly step. She no longer held the ring, but oddly the vibration she'd felt in it now thrummed through the floor and air around her, making her try to pop her ears.

All right, pay attention to what you see and hear.

She blinked into the dimness and mentally catalogued what she could sense with her archaeologist's mind so she could record it later. Smells—damp earth and sulfur, almost like a match but not quite. Touch—hard floor, rough-hewn, and the same for the one wall that met her tentatively reaching fingers. Taste—dust, dryness, maybe a slight hint of damp, but inland, not seashore.

When her eyes adjusted to the very dim light of the place, the pattern of the light's dance on the wall made her frown with its familiarity.

How is this possible?

She made her way around objects, silent as a ghost, her progress not marked by footsteps or the swish of her skirts. That was another oddity—in her visions she typically inhabited someone's perspective. In this one, she moved through the place alone and incorporeal, the distance between her current self and her body sitting on the hotel bed with Edward seemingly infinite.

When Iris found the source of the light—a box made from some sort of crystal on the floor in the corner—she gasped. Inside a golden opalescence writhed.

"Aether?" Iris whispered. Her query echoed back to her but with more of a hiss. She could almost make out the word, "Eros."

"What is this place?" She looked around. "Who's here?"

This time the darkness swallowed the words, but the light increased until she had to look away. At first she thought she saw the after-image of the lamp in her vision, but no, a dark shape stood in front of her and watched her with glowing golden eyes. Iris nearly tripped moving back, but since she didn't have skirts to hinder her, she managed to get as far away from it as she could, at least until her back met stone.

That was another thing to notice—she had enough form to be held by the walls.

"Do you not recognize this place?" The creature's voice—male—had a foreign accent with rolled *r*'s and sibilant *s*'s. She'd heard echoes of it in her travels to the Ottoman Empire, and she placed the echoes as an ancestor of the current language of the area.

With that recognition, she lifted the aether lantern and held it aloft. As though it knew her desire, it brightened to reveal the place she stood in—the temple she'd excavated in the Ottoman Empire. Carvings on the wall had held the key to deciphering the scroll she'd been given for safekeeping in Paris. Except this time, newly hewn stone surrounded her, the objects in it gleaming and the lettering on the wall deep, sharp, and fresh. She tore her gaze away from the parts she and Edward had guessed at and looked at the creature who spoke to her. It, too, had brightened with the aether, and now golden filaments raced over its head, neck, and torso and disappeared beneath its beard and robe.

"I do recognize it," she said. "But why am I here now?"

"Do you hear the rushing noise outside?"

"Yes." It continued to press on her no matter how hard she tried to ignore it or tell herself she didn't have physical ears. But now she stood in her excavation clothing, and she guessed if she touched her hair, it would be back in its typical severe bun, so she must have taken on some sort of form.

"That is the sound of the world being remade, the gods erasing mankind due to their sins."

"And who are you to know this?" Iris's cheeks flamed with excitement—was the spirit being talking about the Great Flood?

"I am one of the magi left behind to warn those who will come after. There are a few of us Old Ones left in your time. Some have decided to live among you. Some, like me, are but echoes of the past that come forth when needed."

Iris cocked her head. *Ancient beings? Impossible.* "But then how is this place possible in my time? The Great Flood was before Abraham, who lived thousands of years ago."

The magus gestured to the lantern. "This captured bit of spirit has many abilities, including that of bending time. It will have burned out when you find this place, but it preserved the walls and implements for millennia."

"How?" Iris looked at the aether biscuit. It seemed so simple.

"That is not for you to know, for time grows short for you to be out of your body. I have a warning for you—you must not allow the magi of your time to use the aether spirit to manipulate men any further. And you must, at all costs, not allow it to be used for darker purposes such as separating men's souls from their bodies."

Iris shivered, now aware of the chill in the chamber. "Is that what Cobb is after?" But she'd known somehow he didn't care about a new power source. Or he did, but not of energy. He wanted power over men's hearts.

And women's.

"I do not know what your enemy wants, only that I need to

give you this message. And caution you that it will begin with a blood sacrifice."

With fingers that shook from the cold of the chamber and fear for what may come, Iris replaced the aether lamp where it had been. "Then I shall return to my time and warn the others."

"You have been put together by the magus for your minds. Now you must use them to defeat him."

Iris straightened and nodded. "I will do so." The image of the room faded, and she opened her eyes to find herself on her back looking up at Edward's concerned blue eyes.

"Thank goodness." He gathered her close, and she held on to him to anchor herself in the present. Something tickled her upper lip, and she tasted something metallic. When she sat up and put a finger under her nose, she found blood.

"How long was I out?"

Edward handed her a handkerchief, and she tried to clean her face and hand.

"An hour," Marie said from behind her. "We sent for a doctor. You were barely breathing, you were going cold, and your lips were turning blue. Then your nose started bleeding."

Iris leaned on Edward. He practically thrummed with panic.

"I was afraid you wouldn't come back," he told her.

"I promised I would."

Marie edged toward the door. "I'll go tell Johann you're all right. Unless you feel you need a doctor?"

Iris shook her head. "No, but thank you. The only doctor I want to see right now is Radcliffe. I have some questions for him." She recalled him appearing briefly during one nocturnal excavation when she and Edward were testing the aether underground in the temple. Perhaps he had some knowledge of the mysteries the magus had referred to.

CHAPTER TWENTY-FIVE

Airship over New England, 13 March 1871

Henry considered Radcliffe's offer all the way to Boston. Could he trust the troupe, as he thought of them? They certainly didn't have any reason to help him. But they recognized how Paul Farrell was a threat—he'd gone after Marie, one of their own, after all—and between the terribly clever Bailey couple and the resourceful Bledsoes, they had more brain power than many university departments.

Most importantly, Radcliffe had as much invested as Henry did. In the doctor's case, his beloved was in danger. In Henry's case, his life was at risk, but he'd observed how Radcliffe loved Claire, had gone halfway around the world to see if there could be a glimmer of hope for them, and had risked everything to get her back. Henry would have liked to think he'd do the same for his beloved if given the chance. Or if he had a beloved.

Either way, the team in Terminus wasn't invested the same way Radcliffe and his friends were. Part of Henry felt he would be taking advantage of them, but another part acknowledged the advantage would be in having a group of people who cared as much about the mission as he did.

So once both their ears popped with the descent, he said, "All right, I'll accept your help."

Radcliffe looked up from the book he'd picked up after finishing the newspaper. "I thought you might."

"Good." Henry relaxed into his chair. He'd been afraid Radcliffe would change his mind.

"The first thing, then, will be to find Professor Bailey and the others. Do you know where they are?"

"Yes, we've been in contact the whole time." He handed Radcliffe the telegram he received early that morning, that they had moved hotels. "We can go to them once we arrive."

"Good, and Patrick?"

Henry sighed. "As far as I know, we'll have to rescue him, too."

"If he hasn't rescued himself already." Radcliffe shook his head. "We'll figure that out when we find the others."

When the airship reached the airfield, twilight already darkened the sky and lengthened the shadows. The captain and crew helped to unload Henry's and Radcliffe's trunks—Henry had at least rescued that for Radcliffe—and turned right around, planning to fly all night to retrieve Violet and Hobbs.

When Henry approached the office to see about summoning a cab to take them into the city, a woman in uniform intercepted him.

"Mister Davidson?" she asked. "I'm Lieutenant Crow. I believe you're expecting me?"

Henry took in the tension around her eyes and mouth and the dust on her uniform. Something disturbed the woman, but he didn't have time to dally. Although, how did she know his name and that he would be there?

"Do I know you?" he asked.

"I've been working with Mrs. Bailey and the others, and I'm to bring them to you."

"I see." Although he didn't. Iris hadn't indicated they had a confederate in the city, and something about the woman seemed off. "Thank you, but we'll find our own way. I'm sure you can appreciate my need for caution."

"I can also bring you to Mister O'Connell."

Now Henry crossed his arms. Whoever this woman was, she knew entirely too much. He thought about shooting her, but there were too many witnesses. Thus he would have to find a way to take her aside, question her, and then eliminate her.

"Fine, you can give us a ride into the city, but I insist on sitting up front with you." He'd noticed the burly guard, who moved strangely. "And you leave the guard."

"Lieutenant—" The guard approached them, his mouth tight at the corners with building protest, but Crow held up a hand.

"It's fine. Get a cab into the city."

"But not until we're well away," Davidson warned.

"Right." Crow made a shooing motion. "Go. I'll meet you at the place we agreed upon."

The guard nodded and helped put the trunks in the carriage under Radcliffe's supervision. Before Davidson ascended to the driver's bench, he ran his hand over a dent that looked like it had recently been painted. Indeed, the surface was still sticky.

"Did you hit something?" he asked and climbed up to sit beside Lieutenant Crow.

"Something hit me. That's part of the problem, as you'll see." She started the steamcoach, and Davidson admired the sound of the engine. He hadn't heard one so well in tune in weeks, not since going South and setting up his operation there. Or had that only been days?

"Part of what problem?"

The door closed, and the guard stepped away.

"Doctor, are you all right in there?" Davidson called. He'd hated for Radcliffe to have to ride alone, but he refused to give up a degree of control.

"I'm fine," was the reply. "There's enough light in here for me to read my book."

"This is a finely appointed carriage," Davidson commented.

He noted how Crow's eyes roamed the woods surrounding the airfield.

"It belongs to my organization, not the air service, but the neo-Pythagoreans."

Davidson leaned away from her and reached for his weapon.

"Don't be foolish," she said. "I'm trying to help you. As you can imagine, we want to stop Parnaby Cobb as badly as you do. He's taken our mysteries, added modern science, and perverted them for his own aims."

They turned from the airfield drive on to a wide road. The smell of the sea, which Henry had noticed upon leaving the airship, diminished. Now the air had the snap of winter in it.

"And what have you done with Mister O'Connell?"

"He's no longer in that dungeon, if that's what you're wondering. We have him. He's comfortable."

"But another prisoner."

She shrugged. "He is not easily contained, as you may imagine, but yes, we're keeping him safe from Cobb and his men."

Another rhythm contradicted the chugging of the steam engine, and Davidson drew his weapon. A horseman approached them and slowed when he saw them. He tipped his hat to the lieutenant, who stopped the steamcoach.

"I'm sorry to interrupt you, ma'am, but I have urgent news for you." He leaned in and murmured in Crow's ear. Henry strained to catch what he was saying, but he could only get "escaped" and "searching...frightened stable boy." He also handed her a packet of something.

He smiled but kept his weapon handy. He guessed from the expression on Crow's face and what he'd overheard that O'Connell had escaped. He confirmed that when the rider tipped his hat, turned his horse, and galloped back the way he'd come. "Not easily contained?"

"I'm not going to lie to you, Inspector. Yes, O'Connell seems to have slipped away from our temple."

"Then it's particularly important that we go into town." He

gestured for her to resume their trip, and she did. "What's in the envelope?"

She handed it to him. "If this doesn't convince you that Cobb is planning something, I don't know what will."

Henry opened the packet to see an invitation to a gala he was throwing the following night. He noticed it was addressed to "The Ladye of the neo-Pythagoreans."

"And who is this?" he asked.

Crow shrugged. "Someone high up in our organization. No doubt Cobb wants to show off something. I'm guessing it will be his latest aether invention."

"But it says it's to celebrate the engagements of his step-daughter Louisa and a friend." His intuition told him that friend was Claire McPhee. "We need to go to that gala."

"Then you're welcome to my, er, the invitation."

"Your invitation? You're the 'Ladye'?"

"Don't be silly. A woman that powerful wouldn't be chauffeuring a difficult inspector and a doctor around Boston."

Davidson laughed. "Difficult, huh? I've been called worse."

Crow's lips curled into a grin, and he couldn't help but notice the attractiveness of her smile with the shrewdness that never left her eyes.

"I'm sure you have. Now that we're approaching the city, would you mind telling me where we're heading?"

Henry hesitated. Why had Iris moved hotels? Had it been to get away from Crow? If so, he didn't want to endanger his friends further, and he had a sense he couldn't trust the striking Lieutenant.

"I thought you knew." He gestured to the city. "This is a big place, but you immediately headed for this road."

She nodded but didn't take her eyes from the road. "Well done, Inspector. Yes, I do know where we're heading, although I won't be welcome."

"And why is that?"

"Because Mrs. Bailey doesn't trust me. As well she shouldn't."

"Then I'll have to be careful as well."

She graced him with a sideways glance, and he saw her eyes were hazel, a more interesting shade than the green he typically imagined.

———

The ghost led Patrick on his now-exhausted mount to a hotel in an area of the city that, although not seedy, made him glad the trip had smudged his fine clothing. A few other riders had given him curious glances, but that was the benefit of a large city—people had a wider range of what they considered odd.

He dropped the horse at the hotel stables and went to the front desk. When the young man asked him if he would like a room, he hesitated. He didn't have any money in his finery, and he didn't want to take a room he couldn't pay for.

"I'm here to see Professor Bailey," he said.

The clerk checked the book. "Ah, I see. Give me a moment, and I'll send a message to him."

Patrick stood aside as he helped another customer and took in the surroundings. He wanted to ask Maureen how she knew where his friends were staying but he didn't want to be seen conversing with a ghost. He already stood out enough in his soiled attire, sure his cravat—damn thing—was hopelessly askew.

The chug of a steamcoach engine outside the door caught his attention, and he moved to a window to get a closer look. To his surprise, Inspector Henry Davidson sat on the driver's bench with a young man in uniform. And to his delight, Chadwick Radcliffe alighted. He moved stiffly as though he'd had a rough time of it and looked around.

Patrick grinned. *This will be fun.*

He dusted off his hat and clothing as best he could, put on his gloves, and straightened the stupid cravat. A quick check of his reflection in the mirror over the lobby fireplace told him he looked more respectable than he had any right to. He strode outside and observed the unloading of the trunks.

Patrick stiffened his upper lip and said in his pretentious English accent, "Would you mind hurrying that up? I need to hire this steamcoach for an engagement this evening."

The valets did move slightly faster, but the driver, whom Patrick now saw was a woman, waved him away.

"This coach isn't for hire, sir."

Davidson turned toward him then, and his eyes narrowed as though he should recognize Patrick, who startled himself with the depth of the anger that emerged.

That's it, you bastard. Wonder for a minute. It's the least you deserve for putting me in this situation. For he recognized that if Davidson hadn't handed him over to Cobb, he wouldn't have been imprisoned twice, starved, and drugged. Or had Louisa held just out of reach and dragged away from him.

Or found her again, but he didn't want to admit that.

Radcliffe looked up from his book, and his eyes widened. He hid his laugh with a cough, but Patrick couldn't help his grin. He should've known his friend would recognize him.

"Then I'll hire on this dark gentleman. He looks like he might have some useful knowledge, but only a little."

"You Irish arse," Radcliffe said, and Patrick took his hand. They embraced as much as two gentlemen could without being accused of buggery.

Davidson's eyes opened, and the woman's narrowed.

"Mister O'Connell?" Davidson asked. "You look quite the gentleman."

"Yes," Radcliffe said, barely containing his laughter. "Who stuffed you in a cravat?"

"I did." Patrick tipped his hat. "Don't I look dashing?"

"No." The woman vibrated so hard with rage she would have turned the aether red with her emotions rather than the reverse. "How did you escape? And with those clothes?"

"A magician never tells his tricks, Madame," Patrick said.

"And shouldn't you arrest her for admitting she was involved in my imprisonment, Inspector?"

"In due time," was Davidson's infuriating response. "We should go in. I'll get rooms for us."

Of course he won't do anything useful.

They followed Davidson inside, leaving the porters to deal with the trunks. Patrick reminded himself to be grateful for a few things, namely the benevolent spirit and that he had Radcliffe back. Although…"Where's Claire?"

Radcliffe's smile vanished. "Eliza has her."

"Still? Oh, shite." He'd thought Claire would have managed to escape if Chadwick had, but he should have known not to underestimate Eliza Adams.

Radcliffe nodded. "We have a lot to catch up on."

"Patrick? Chadwick?" A petite blonde woman had emerged from the stairwell followed by a taller brunette and two men. "It is you!"

They all embraced, and it felt like Paris all over again. Previously Patrick would have reveled in the adventure of it all, but not with his best friend's love at risk.

Soon they were seated in the hotel restaurant, which they had to themselves since their group was large and the space small. Patrick noticed the woman in uniform had disappeared with her impressive vehicle, but Davidson remained. They all caught up on their stories, and then turned to Davidson.

"So what's the story?" Marie asked. "You delivered him to Cobb, but he escaped, then got captured, and then escaped, and you're just now getting here?"

Davidson looked into his beer, and Patrick derived some satisfaction from his embarrassment. "I was caught up in a situation in Terminus trying to retrieve Doctor Radcliffe."

"Yes," Iris said. "We met your Claire. She's as wonderful as you told us, and her aunt as awful."

"And she's in danger," Davidson told them. "Cobb is holding a gala tomorrow evening, supposedly to find a husband for his stepdaughter, but I suspect it's for more sinister purposes and that Doctor McPhee will be there."

Davidson's words chilled Patrick. "He can't force her to marry." But he knew Cobb could.

Davidson slanted him a pitying glance. "Then we need to figure out how to disrupt this gala, keep him from putting Miss Cobb and Doctor McPhee in danger, and prevent him from unleashing some sort of aether manipulation on the innocent."

"How would he?" Iris asked. Patrick noticed the large antique ring she wore over her gloves.

"He has my notes," Patrick admitted. "And Paul Farrell working for him."

"Oh, gods." Marie put her cup back on its saucer. "Your aether knowledge plus Farrell's talent with automatons could be disastrous."

"Could and will be," Davidson agreed.

"So what do we do?" Iris looked at the group.

"We're going to have to work together," Radcliffe told them. "Otherwise, we're all lost."

"Wait, I thought I was supposed to be the one creating the suspense," Patrick said. He ducked the clam shells the others threw at him.

"He's right. Chad, not Patrick." Iris leveled a curious look at the doctor and then relayed a tale of meeting a strange being in an ancient temple. "He said we have to stop Cobb at all costs."

———

Patrick left the group early after they had gotten most of the plans for the gala figured out. Exhaustion from his long ride had overtaken him once he'd eaten, and he'd gone up to the room he would be sharing with Chadwick. Just like old times, except not.

He should've figured things would eventually come to a head with Cobb, especially since he'd been pulling the strings since the beginning. If not for Parnaby Cobb, he and

Chad would never have gone to Vienna, which resulted in them being in the north of France. They wouldn't have been nearby when Iris, Marie, Edward, and Johann had dropped from the sky in a defective escape compartment from Cobb's airship the *Blooming Senator* and had required their help.

He removed his clothing and washed up as much as he could with the tepid water that came from the washstand faucet. He wanted a nice, long soak like he'd had earlier that day, but he acknowledged beggars couldn't be choosers when it came to hotel amenities. And still, it was much better than he'd had in the dungeon, and he wouldn't trade his freedom for what he'd gotten in the neo-Pythagorean estate.

That reminded him—they'd been preparing for some sort of ritual. Was it coincidence that it was happening the night before Cobb's gala? If Patrick had learned anything from his experiences, it was that there were no coincidences.

Then what sort of energy is in the air tonight?

He crawled into the nearest of the two beds, rolled over, and went to sleep.

He hadn't been asleep for long when a strange sensation in his middle woke him. He rolled away from it, but it pulled at him through his back. When he tugged back, he found himself squeezed through a cold tunnel, and opening his eyes revealed a golden light as though he was surrounded by aether. It faded to reveal Louisa's bedchamber.

She lay in bed in her nightgown, her hair in a braid. Her eyelashes lay in dark semicircles on her cheeks, and he wanted to touch her, but something about her looked pale and exhausted, so he only stood there and watched until she rolled over with a moan and opened her eyes. When she saw him, she pulled her covers over her chest.

"Patrick? What are you doing here? They'll kill you."

"I don't know how I'm here, but I don't think it's physical." He sat on the bed beside her, and she scooted over to make room, then put a hand on the other pillow, which showed the indentation of another person's head.

"Who was there?" Patrick asked, a cold ice sensation sliding down his gut. Surely she couldn't have been married off already.

"Claire McPhee. She's staying with me. They pulled her away for a midnight dress fitting." Louisa rubbed her eyes, which were red. "They're not letting us sleep for more than an hour at a time."

Patrick took her hands. "Do you know what Cobb is planning?"

"Only something that involves the aether and the major young industrialists of the city." She squeezed his hands and whispered, "And the automatons."

He couldn't help but kiss the tremble from her lips. Her mouth softened beneath his, and he gathered her to him.

"I'm going to be there with my friends. We'll get you out of there."

She pulled away. "Don't worry about me. Keep him from doing what he's going to do with the aether."

"But I do worry about you. And there are more concerned than just me."

"I'm not important. Save the rest of the city." The glazed look in her eyes told him she'd been given something to add to the effects of sleep deprivation.

"But you're important to me." It struck him then, that he could love her. "Am I important to you?"

She looked at him with wonder. "Of course you are."

"Then stop saying you're not."

She nodded, and two tears splotched the sheets below her chin. "It's sometimes hard to believe I am when every aspect of my life is controlled by someone else."

"Just wait. After tomorrow, you'll have freedom. You'll be with me. I'd take you with me now if I could."

"So you can control me?"

"So I can give you your freedom if that's what you want."

The sound of a door opening told Patrick that Claire returned to Louisa's chamber.

"I don't know what I want." Louisa yawned. "But I'm guessing someone wants me to wake up soon. But you'll be here tomorrow night, promise?"

"I promise, even if you can't see me, I'll be there."

He kissed her one more time and kept his hands above the covers even though he wanted to explore her body beneath the bedclothes. The sensation of being sucked through a cold membranous tube and then deposited back in his own bed caused him to wake, shivering.

Was that a dream? He pulled the thin bedclothes around him and noticed Chadwick now snored in the other bed. *In case it's not, I'll be sure to tell the others in the morning.*

CHAPTER TWENTY-SIX

Cobb Townhouse, 14 March 1871

"Mama, if you're here, let me see you," Louisa whispered. She stood beside Claire on the grand staircase leading down into the ballroom and welcomed guests. They came in small groups as carriages emptied, and Louisa didn't miss the appraising glances from the young men—and their mothers. All of them looked at Louisa and Claire with curiosity, comparing the two of them. Louisa could almost hear their thoughts as the same sequence of expressions flickered over each face—*Why are these two on the market now, not even having a season? Not that it matters—they both have family fortunes. Which look would I like my grandchildren to have, Miss Cobb's dusky beauty or Miss McPhee's golden looks? That one's too smart, though, and she's been to an asylum...* And then with a nod, they'd move on.

Louisa knew she had the purported "advantage" in the situation, but she couldn't ignore Eliza Adams' influence. She stood beside the girls and watched over them, chiding them whenever one of them yawned. They'd been granted a few hours of sleep that day, but not nearly enough.

No spirit appeared at Louisa's request, and she nodded to the next guest, biting back yet another eruption that wanted to be a yawn. What was she to do? Her feet ached, so she excused herself.

"I'm going to check on the refreshments," she told Eliza and Claire. "Miss Adams, would you mind receiving guests in my stead? I'll make sure to talk to them later."

"Louisa, I don't—"

But Louisa was already heading down the stairs. A backward glance told her Eliza frowned at her, but she quickly turned to the next group who arrived. Louisa wondered if she were to ask Eliza if the older woman wanted to be the mistress of Cobb's household, what she would say. Of course Cobb kept Eliza guessing. To marry her would be to risk losing her loyalty to the boredom older couples often developed with each other.

She shook her head at that train of thought. Of course she and Patrick wouldn't have the chance to be bored—they'd have too many adventures together with his friends. Claire had told Louisa about them, which had been what Chadwick Radcliffe had told her. The lady archaeologist and her brilliant aetherist husband, the actress and the violinist—they sounded fascinating and not at all the type of people she should associate with.

Which makes them all the more appealing.

A movement caught her eye, and she almost stepped aside in time to avoid Bentley Drury, the younger son of a diamond magnate. He wore his family's business on his hands and cravat pin, and his finger sparkled as he lifted Louisa's fingers to his lips. She suppressed a shudder.

And here is everything Patrick is not. I doubt Bentley's been outside of Boston more than twice.

"Why, Miss Cobb, may I say you look ravishing tonight? That shade of purple is quite becoming."

Louisa did have to admit the *modiste* had outdone herself with Louisa's gown of lavender, which brought out her coloring and fit her tightly in all the right places. However, she didn't want to get into a conversation with Bentley about it.

"Have you ever seen a purple diamond, Miss Cobb? I could give you all the jewels you like."

She stepped back. "I'm afraid that decision isn't up to me." She couldn't keep the bitterness out of her voice, and the twinkle in his eye told her she'd given him false hope that she would choose him if she were able. "Excuse me, I must check on some things."

"You're a wonderful hostess, as always." He bowed, and she ducked into the crowd, murmuring hellos and managing to avoid any other unwanted conversations.

She looked over the refreshment tables and the punch and champagne fountains and saw the servants kept things replenished. Something strange about the wainscoting caught her eye, and she moved closer to see a rubber tube ran along the walls and over the windows. She followed it, skirting along the edge of the room, again balancing politeness with avoidance, and reached the other side, where musicians warmed up. Just below the stage, several men set up an aether device like Patrick's. She cleared her throat and glared at Paul Farrell, who directed them.

"I knew you were still working for him," she snapped at him when he came over to her. "You set me up."

Instead of looking guilty, he shrugged. "This night will have many surprises, Miss Cobb, hopefully some of them pleasant to you."

She tucked the corners of her lips into a frown like she'd seen her mother do so many times when Louisa knew she had better not do one more thing to upset her.

"I don't trust you. Never have. And I will do everything in my power to disrupt whatever my stepfather has planned."

"Then it's a good thing you don't have much power, isn't it?" With that, he turned back to his work.

Frustrated tears built at the base of her throat, and the tired, itchy feeling in her eyes wanted to be released, but she held on to her composure, turned, and walked away. She grabbed a glass of champagne from a passing waiter, but she only took a sip to cool her throat—in her current state, alcohol would increase her risk of losing control. She gave it to another waiter with an empty tray who paused just a little too long to be proper. A second glance didn't enlighten her as to why he should be so familiar, but she was tired. He'd probably worked for them before.

"Don't worry, Miss Cobb. Help is on the way."

She blinked, but he had turned away. *Artemus?*

She gathered up her skirts, intending to chase him down, but a flash of orange-red hair and beard caught her attention. The tall man moved into the shadows behind some potted plants, and she followed.

Patrick, Chadwick, and Henry tied up the guards they'd overpowered and stashed them in the alley beside the house. Patrick shook his head at the idea of calling it a townhouse—although it stood tall and close to its neighbors, it backed up to a bluff over the river, and the symphony of glasses and conversation from the balcony above told him the guests enjoyed the view. In spite of the previous weekend's cold weather, the day had been balmy, and clouds had held the warmth close to the earth beyond sunset. It was too warm for the season, but then, the whole situation felt wrong.

"Ready?" Chadwick asked. Patrick and Henry nodded, and Patrick hoped the grappling hooks he'd made that day would be as good as the one he'd fashioned at Fort Daniels. He and Artemus Malloy had improved the design for a slower wind, so he and the others shouldn't end up crashing into the walls.

They donned their hooked gloves, wrapped their cloaks around themselves, and raised the grappling devices, sighting the lip of the roof. It was a narrow shot, but three clinks told them the hooks had found their targets. Patrick wrapped both hands around the handles, pressed the lever, and although the gears' actions were slower than before, it still nearly tugged his arms from their sockets as it lifted him in the air.

His cloak took the brunt of the scrape up the side of the building until he could get purchase with his feet and walk up it. Then he used the clawed gloves to pull himself over the small wall around the roof. The others clambered over soon after him, and they stashed their cloaks and grappling guns behind a chimney.

"As I suspected," Henry said. "Not guarded."

"Good. Then let's get to the party." Radcliffe straightened his cravat.

Patrick swallowed against his—why did men insist on wearing such ridiculous things?

Henry found the trap door that led from the roof into the attic. Patrick wondered how it was unlocked, but he supposed Cobb didn't think someone would break into his house from the roof, which was far enough away from the neighbors' that even the best jumper wouldn't be able to make it over the gap, and most thieves didn't have his technology.

They descended through the halls, and once again the ghost of Louisa's mother guided them. However, she faded as they got closer to the party.

"What's happening?" Patrick asked her.

"I don't know. There's a force pushing back at me. I—" And she disappeared.

"That's strange." Chad glanced around the corner. "I think this is a stairwell to the main level. Well, gentlemen, shall we crash the party?"

"Yes, but wait for my signal before you do anything." Henry checked his watch. "Doctor Radcliffe, if you see a chance to make it out with Doctor McPhee, take it. I'm not going to hold you to your promise to help me with Farrell if you have the opportunity to escape with her."

"I gave you my word, Inspector, and I intend to keep it." The doctor's gray eyes flashed. "Don't make me prove your suspicion of others."

"He's stubborn like that." Patrick inclined his head. "But it's always worked out."

Footsteps made them dart into the nearest room, a broom closet. The door to the room next to them opened and shut, and a man's voice came through the wall.

"Is everything ready with the aether device?" Cobb asked, and Patrick had to quell the wave of anger that engulfed him when he heard Cobb's voice. He wanted to punch the man in the face and tell him... Well, he just wanted to punch him and not waste time with explanations.

A hand on his arm brought him out of his rage fantasy.

"Yes, Mister Cobb. The demonstration should be enlightening."

Ah, Farrell. You never stopped working for him, did you? Your neo-Pythagorean friends will not be happy about that.

"And have you picked out a willing victim?"

The next voice to speak was a woman's, and Chad tensed beside Patrick.

"Bentley Drury approached Louisa earlier," Eliza Adams said. "He's rich and not too smart, and he likes to be in control. He should be able to take her in hand."

"Excellent. And I could use his father's wealth and access to diamonds. Brutus, come here."

The heavy footsteps made the walls of the closet shake, and in the dim light, the whites of Henry's and Chad's widened eyes showed.

The automaton.

In their plans, the metal men were the unknown variable.

"It's magnificent, Parnaby," Eliza said. "How are your experiments going?"

Farrell cleared his throat. "Our experiments are going well. It's been out and about a few evenings watching certain individuals, and it only came back with a dent once."

"The problem is that it doesn't act with free will, but we shall soon rectify that. Some knowledge has recently come to light thanks to a contact I have at the Museum of Ancient Art and Artifacts. The neo-Pythagoreans believed in the transmogrification of souls."

"Parnaby, you don't mean..."

Patrick wondered if Chad was smiling at the horror in Eliza Adams' tone.

"Yes, I do."

"I didn't think you were serious. By victim, I thought you meant someone to marry Louisa off to."

"Not exactly, although I think she would appreciate having an automaton for a husband. He would be as intelligent and infinitely more useful than that Irishman she's infatuated with. As for you, your usefulness to me has ended."

"You're dismissing me?" Taffeta ruffled, and Patrick imagined that Eliza stood, puffing herself up in anger.

"No, you know too much. Consider this your final sacrifice, assistance for me to begin the transmogrification process."

"What? No. No, you can't, I won't stand for—"

Patrick didn't hear the rest of the sentence. The three of them, unwilling to let a woman be harmed, even Eliza Adams, rushed out of the closet, and Patrick ran right into the automaton and bounced back into Radcliffe.

"What in blazes—?" Cobb exited the office, and he wiped a knife on a handkerchief, which came away stained dark red. "And what do we have here? Oh, this is too perfect. Davis, what are you doing here? I didn't know you were back in town."

Henry stood to the side, his gun drawn, and gestured to Patrick and Chad. "I arrived this evening, came to report to you, and found these two snooping around. I was bringing them to you to ask what you want to do with them."

"Good man."

Patrick scrambled to his feet and reached for his weapon, but Cobb shook his head and pointed to Farrell, who had a gun trained on both of them. Two more guards appeared, also with weapons, and Patrick and Chad held up their hands as they were searched and their weapons confiscated. Henry watched, his arms crossed but still holding his weapon.

"And did you come to rescue your ladyloves?" Cobb asked. "I'm afraid you've failed. But before I kill you, I want you to see what happens to them. Then I can have the satisfaction of knowing that they saw you die just before they met their own fates."

The guards moved Patrick and Chad along. Patrick walked through a cold spot, and he wondered if Louisa's mother had come through.

Or that's Eliza Adams's soul unable to make it out just as no others can make it in.

Either way, he hoped Henry could manage a way to get them out of their pickle before they joined her.

If Claire were to be honest with herself, she would be cursing both Louisa and Eliza for leaving her to perform the function of greeting the guests.

Finally the stream trailed off, and she smiled wanly at the last group. A short brunette woman accompanied by a tall man with a mop of curly blond hair, a tall blonde woman, and another blond man, this one bearded, approached her with familiar smiles. They emanated eagerness and joy at seeing her again.

She blinked—was it just her fatigue? No, these were the people from the airship, the ones who had tried to rescue her.

"What are you doing here?" she asked, too exhausted to worry about social niceties.

"We're here to stop Cobb," the shorter woman said. She wore a dress of dark blue, and when Claire looked closely, she saw the clever cosmetics they all wore to change their face contours. Before Claire could reply, she hissed as though burned and shook her right hand, on which she wore a large antique ring with a green stone.

"What's wrong?" The man Claire remembered as her husband caught her elbow.

"Something just happened. I'm not sure what, only that it's bad."

Claire caught the edge of her worry, which was backed with deeper knowledge than the rest of them had.

"Come with me," she said. "Let's have some refreshments, and maybe we can find someplace to talk."

They walked down the stairs, and Claire nodded tiredly at those who smiled at her. The swirl of emotions—some positive and encouraging, but most heavy with scorn, curiosity, and criticism—weighed on her as she passed among them. It was like walking on the bottom of the ocean would be, surrounded by water so it should be invisible to her, but pushed to and fro by it.

"Iris, look at the aether," Edward Bailey said. "I've never seen it that color. It's blood red. And there's a heartbeat?"

Indeed, now that Claire had been alerted to it, a steady pulse, like the heartbeat of a great being, flowed beneath the conversations and other noises, forcing them to comply with its rhythm. Glasses clinked, men barked with laughter, and women spoke in phrases that matched it. When Claire tried to move out of step, it forced her back with an invisible wave.

"What is it?" Claire asked, grabbing hold of Iris's arm. "What's happening?"

"I don't know, but I suspect something has been awakened." Her face went pale when she looked to the left of the musicians. "Oh, no."

Claire followed her gaze, and had her heart not matched the pulse, it would have stopped.

There stood Parnaby Cobb, and he was accompanied by two guards holding guns at the temples of Patrick O'Connell and Chadwick Radcliffe.

The musicians finished the piece they played, and Cobb held up his hand for silence.

"Friends and guests, thank you for joining us for this auspicious occasion, as it not only marks a new occasion for my family with the betrothing of my stepdaughter Louisa, but also for the world at large. I was going to wait until after dinner before unveiling my latest technological advance, but I thought it would be cruel to make you wait, particularly as we have two volunteers who need to be taught a lesson."

———

The man with the red hair and beard turned around, and Louisa's hope deflated. Her sleep-deprived mind had leapt on to the hope that Patrick had come to take her away from the party and everything it represented. This man, while he could have been related to Patrick, was only a Boston Irish shipping millionaire. Not a bad thing of itself, but she nodded politely at him and turned back to the stage, where she saw the Irishman she'd been hoping to encounter, but in danger. She clenched her fists over the knot of dread that had just pulled tighter in her stomach—he stood with one of Cobb's guards, who held a gun pointed to his head.

And the dark man being held by the other guard is Claire's Chadwick.

Louisa darted through the crowd, which moved toward the stage, and found Claire, no longer on the stairs but standing in an alcove with a group of people who did but didn't match the descriptions she'd given of Patrick's and Radcliffe's friends.

They could be in disguise, which would be smart of them.

The tall blonde woman turned to Louisa and winked, and Louisa almost did lose control of her tears in relief. *Marie's here.*

If anyone could help Louisa, it was the eminently resourceful maid and actress.

No, just actress, she reminded herself. Marie was no longer

her maid, as much as she'd wished for her. Marie had escaped and moved on beyond the influence of Parnaby Cobb.

A certain throbbing stayed in the air even after the musicians stopped playing, and Louisa's pulse beat along with it in her ears and at her wrists. *This must be what an infant hears in its mother's womb, that steady life-giving thump that echoed throughout its own body.*

But what was about to be birthed? Louisa didn't think it was something she wanted to experience.

Cobb stepped forward and made his announcement, and when he gestured for Louisa to come to him, she obeyed, her feet moving of their own accord in time with the pulse. She didn't want to—all her instincts said to run—but she couldn't stop herself. A glance around revealed that some of the women had uneasy expressions, but most of the men's eyes followed her, including Patrick's.

"What happened?" she mouthed when she got closer.

"Eliza," he replied.

It figures.

She looked around for the woman, but didn't see her. That was odd—this seemed the perfect opportunity for Eliza to gloat at her and Cobb's power over everyone, especially Louisa and Claire.

Louisa's feet stopped when she reached Cobb's side even though she tried to keep going. He put his hand on the small of her back and murmured, "You feel it, don't you? The heartbeat of the god, who is waiting for his goddess."

"You're insane," Louisa said. "Whatever it is, make it stop. If you're trying to frighten me into marrying one of these popinjays, it's not going to work."

"I'm not trying to frighten you, my dear. In fact," he said with a grand gesture, not breaking contact with Louisa, "I'm trying to ensure everyone has a good time. Mister Farrell, why don't you turn the aether to the joyful frequency?"

Farrell nodded and adjusted a knob on the engine that

created the pulse for the aether. It complemented the rhythm already in the air, and the aether turned a rose color, then darkened again. Now Louisa saw the color change in the rubber tubes that carried the gas through the ballroom, lining the walls and trapping all those in their influence.

A wave of peace and joy passed through Louisa, and she relaxed. Cobb smiled and removed his hand from her back.

"See what I mean?" He asked. "Enjoy the feelings, folks, and remember the sensations. You're going to need them in a few minutes."

Louisa fought the euphoria. She'd learned never to trust Cobb in a good mood, and she sensed something more sinister was coming. She closed her eyes and reached into that part of herself that would not be lied to.

Is this truly what I'm feeling?

No. The sensation of a cloud lifting led to the dull terror that she'd started with, and she opened her eyes. Claire stood with tears running down her cheeks but a huge grin on her face. The two women with her held hands, their faces pinched masks of struggle.

"And now let's have some fun." Cobb raised his hands, and the happy murmurs died down. "I believe many of you are here to vie for my stepdaughter's hand?"

A masculine cheer rose from the crowd.

"Then let the young men who would like to court her come forward."

Louisa wanted to tell them to run, both that she didn't want to marry any of them, but, more importantly, she didn't want them to be hurt by whatever Cobb planned.

Heavy footsteps behind her told her that Cobb's automaton had arrived as well.

About forty men in ages ranging from young bucks just out of Harvard to older widowers lined up. Cobb looked them over and then pointed to one.

"You there, come closer."

Louisa groaned—he'd called over Bentley Drury, who practically pranced to the front of the line. In the aether light, his pink and black waistcoat almost glowed.

"You're Alvin Drury's boy, aren't you?" Cobb asked.

"Yes, sir."

"You may not be aware, but marriage requires a lot of sacrifices. That's why I haven't done it much myself." He paused for a smattering of laughter from the audience. "What are you willing to give to marry her?"

Bentley looked at Louisa. "I'm ready to give her my heart, sir."

"Hearts are a dime a dozen. Go to any resurrection man, and he can find you one. Dig deeper, son."

He put his hand on his chest. "I would give her my soul."

The rhythm quickened, and something stirred the air around them.

"Your soul, you say?"

"As long as you're not the devil, sir."

Cobb clapped him on the shoulder. "Oh, no, don't worry. I'm not the devil." Then the mirth fell from his expression. "I represent something much older. And worse."

CHAPTER TWENTY-SEVEN

Cobb Townhouse, 14 March 1871

When the rhythm started, Iris turned to Marie. "Does this seem familiar to you?"

Marie nodded. "It's like the statues in the Marquis's Monceau palace. Except now the guests are the statues moving to the rhythm."

"Yes." Iris put a hand on her chest, wishing for her own heartbeat not to be caught. "It's the pulse of the god."

Then Cobb had appeared with Patrick and Chadwick—but not Davidson—and Cobb had called up his daughter. Iris groaned—not only had Patrick and Chadwick gotten caught, but the girl wore purple, the color associated with the god Eros.

What do we do? She grabbed Edward's hand. "You have to figure out how to disrupt the aether system. He can't be allowed to manipulate all these people."

He nodded, squeezed her hand, and melted into the crowd with Johann trailing behind.

Of course Cobb steered the crowd's emotions next. Iris and

Marie held on to each other, anchored by the ring to keep from being swept up in the collective euphoric feelings.

It was then that Iris knew exactly what kind of trouble they were in and what she had to do. "First comes manipulation to shake the souls loose, then transmogrification. I have to reach back," she told Marie. "Using the ring."

The rustling she heard could have been the women's taffeta gowns, but she didn't think so. She'd heard the wings of Eros before.

"How far?" Marie kept a careful eye on Cobb in case he recognized her.

"Farther back than I've ever gone. And I might not come back." She swallowed around the lump in her throat. "And if I don't, tell Edward I tried, and that I love him."

Marie turned to her. "No. There has to be another way, Iris. You'll destroy him, not to mention yourself."

"And if I don't succeed, we'll all be destroyed. Cobb has Patrick and Chadwick. Davidson has deserted us. And if Cobb does what I think he's going to do, the old ones will become angry and start the world anew."

Indeed, the ring hummed with the echo of the great flood that had destroyed the world in the past.

"Then I'll end this." Marie let go of Iris's hand and lifted her skirt to reveal a garter holster.

Iris batted Marie's skirt back down. "Don't be a fool, Marie. He has guards all over the room. They'd fell you before you got off a shot."

Iris had never seen Marie back down before, but thankfully she did this time.

"Right, but we have to do something."

"May I make a suggestion?"

They turned to see Lieutenant Crow wearing a beautiful royal blue gown standing behind them.

"Lieutenant, we didn't see you come in."

Crow nodded to each of them, seemingly unaffected by the

cool welcome they gave her. "I'm sorry I couldn't join you earlier. We had to clean the grounds of the house from the ritual last night."

"Right," Marie gestured to the stage, where men lined up. "Fat lot of good that did. You didn't prevent anything."

"No, it was more in preparation than anything else to open a door for the Lady, and while she gave us signs that she was willing to aid us, we didn't have enough power to pull her through." She glared at Iris. "And we lost the item that linked us to the past and her ancient worship, not that it would have mattered."

"What lady?" Iris asked. Then she recalled the images she'd seen in the shrines of the neo-Pythagoreans. "You mean Psyche?"

"Very good." Crow clapped, the sound muffled by her white gloves. "You're finally getting it."

Iris would have been insulted, but her mind was too occupied with putting the pieces together. "Eros in this case isn't the cupid god, it's the god of chaos from before the original pantheon, isn't it? One of the old gods that makes it into the stories of many cultures." She twisted the ring. "And the lady, the goddess of all living things, of order, matches and opposes him."

"Yes, exactly. But we lacked the people with the talent to call her. But you with your ability to touch the past, Madame Bledsoe with her talent to project, and Doctor McPhee with her own ability to sense and change emotions are the triangle with the best chance."

Claire turned. Iris could tell she'd been listening, but she still hesitated to take her eyes from Radcliffe. Now that Claire stood closer, Iris sensed the ring enveloping her in its rushing, keeping her from feeling the aether pulse.

"Thank gods," Claire breathed. "That was overwhelming."

"Do you agree to help, Doctor?" Crow asked.

"You mean we have the chance to end this? But at what cost?" Claire inclined her head toward the stage. "We've been at a crossroads of power before, Patrick, Chad, and I, and everything has a price."

Crow's smile vanished, and for the first time, she looked vulnerable. "I don't know. No one has done this before. No one has needed to."

Cobb's announcement cut through the rhythm, and the automaton clamped the young man by the shoulder. His grin, which had been fading, vanished.

"Never mind," he squeaked. "I don't want to marry Louisa. You other gents can have her."

"My stepdaughter wants a husband she can control. What better than to trade your soul for the automaton's?"

"That's not possible," Patrick said. "Those things don't have souls."

"Thanks to your aether work and Paul Farrell's genius with them, they do."

The crowd murmured in disbelief, but the rhythm and the happy feeling that still influenced them kept them from objecting.

Crow gestured for Iris, Marie, and Claire to move together. "If you're going to do something, now's a good time."

Indeed, Iris saw the shadow looming over the stage. The aether had gone a deep and disturbing shade of red, like spilled blood. The rustling sound grew louder until it echoed the aether with the sound of its beating.

Iris, Marie, and Claire joined hands, and Crow chanted. Iris's hands heated where they touched the other women's faster than she would have expected. She closed her eyes so she wouldn't see the eerie red glow and focused on the ring. Since Marie held her hand, Iris could only pinch the ring between her fingers, but it was enough.

Iris fell away and tumbled about. This time when her senses alerted her she'd arrived, she opened her eyes to a familiar location—the chapel under the Porta Maggiore in Rome. Street noise echoed around her, but muted due to her subterranean location, and its lack of rhythm gave her a reprieve. Sunlight came through a shaft above, and dust motes swirled around her. The entire place held a sense of expectation.

The aether device that had started it all sat on the altar. When she touched it, a soft noise above her startled her. The frieze of Psyche and Eros had come alive, and she saw that Psyche wasn't embracing Eros as much as she contained him.

How did I miss that the first time? I've sketched that scene a hundred times.

"Can you help us?" Iris asked.

The goddess turned to look at her with blank eyes. "Why should I, Mortal? The forces of chaos in the world ebb and flow in their natural rhythm."

"Yes, but the world isn't supposed to end now, not according to the symbols on the ring. This zodiac alignment won't happen for another hundred and fifty years or more."

Psyche inclined her head. "So you are clever, Mortal. I have heard whispers of you from those who travel the river of time. But what am I to do?"

Iris gestured to Psyche's arms. "The primitive force of Eros is emerging in our midst. We need you to capture him and bring him back to where he came from."

"And is it always a woman's job to catch and restrict her mate? You make me sound like a snake, not a woman."

"No, it's not." Iris wanted to stamp her foot at the being's stubbornness.

What does she want? We don't have time for these riddles.

"Then what? Think about your own husband, little one, and don't think I haven't seen the shadow of sorrow in your eyes. Don't let your many griefs blind you."

Iris fought not to look away, to hide her losses from the blind but seeing eyes of the goddess. "Marriage isn't a job. It's work, yes, but it's two people doing their best to help the other one succeed to their best potential."

"And...?"

Iris clenched her fists over the searing pain in her belly. But she wasn't pregnant again. "And to forgive them for what your own pride says they've done wrong." She dropped to her knees, the remembered pain of the miscarriage echoing through her body, the loss—which hadn't abated—through her soul. Tears streamed down her face. "Is this my price for your help? My child?"

"You must all pay a price, and you are the fortunate one in that you have already taken care of your debt. Is it worth it to you to save your world from destruction?"

The magi's words echoed through Iris's pain and soothed her. *At all costs.*

"Yes. I believe I speak for all of the others."

With a dusty crunch, the goddess emerged from the wall, the rest of the frieze melting away. She stretched, her eyes still a pair of blank orbs, and her smile had all the warmth of a wolf eyeing an incapacitated sheep.

"Then bring me to my vessel."

———

Claire wanted to go to Chadwick, but Iris held her hand on one side, her eyes closed and a line of concentration between her brows. Marie held Claire's other hand in a grip just shy of painful, and a blank expression with eyes closed, but Claire felt the strength and support flow from Marie to Iris.

Claire would have gotten the message even if she hadn't been able to perceive emotions and intention—she wasn't going anywhere. It reminded her of the strange connection she and Louisa had.

A glimmer of golden light caught the corner of her eye, but when she turned her head, no golden creature stood behind her.

Marie jerked, and Claire braced herself against Marie flinging her head back, her entire body rigid. Claire wanted to free her hands but couldn't. She and Iris kept Marie from falling backwards into a large fern.

"What's happening?" Claire asked Iris, who had opened her eyes and watched Marie warily. She would have felt more encouraged had Iris exuded a better balance of fear and hope. As it was, fear won out.

"The goddess is coming."

A force like that when two strong magnets match their opposing poles pushed Claire and Iris away from Marie, and they landed in a heap of satin and lace. The emotional tide around them shifted from the brittle remains of the euphoria to a cool breeze of wonder, but then strands of terror threaded through it.

Marie glowed golden, and she straightened. Her blonde wig clung to her and seemed to have lengthened. When she opened her eyes, they lacked pupils and irises. Wings sprouted from her back, but not the feathers associated with angels. Rather, she sported leathery white bats' wings.

"Um, Iris, what did you do?" Claire untangled herself and stood.

Iris did likewise. "I summoned Psyche to come and contain Eros."

Marie/Psyche made her way through the crowd, which parted, toward the stage. Some made signs against the evil eye, and some crossed themselves.

The shadow that had been growing over the stage collapsed in on itself and revealed a naked man with a sculpture's body and black feathered wings. He grabbed Parnaby Cobb around the neck with one muscular arm. Claire would have enjoyed Cobb's loss of haughty expression, but she feared for Radcliffe, who was being held too close to the tableau. It would take only one surprised move from the guard to blow Chad's brains out.

"Psyche, what are you doing here? I thought you were trapped in Rome."

"I have come to find you, husband." Psyche—the longer she

stayed, the less there was of Marie—opened her arms. "These humans seem to think they can tame you. Tame us."

"Uh, oh," Iris breathed. She looked back at Crow, who stood aside with a smirk. "You knew this would happen, didn't you? You broke down the barriers last night to her coming back."

Crow shrugged. "As if the capitalists and millionaires are worthy stewards of this earth. It's time for us to welcome the old forces of chaos, clean things out and start over."

Iris's betrayal and disappointment stabbed Claire's awareness. "You said I could trust you." Iris clenched her fists.

"And yet I kept doing untrustworthy things." Crow snorted. "And you're supposed to be the smart one of the bunch."

Her self-satisfied smirk turned to rage when Johann grabbed her hands, and Edward tied them.

"We'll take care of you later," Johann promised. He frowned. "Where's Marie?"

Claire rested a hand at her throat, where his panic echoed in hers. "She's been taken over by the goddess Psyche," Claire explained. "We were tricked."

"Marie!" Johann rocked forward, ready to run, but Edward grabbed him. Johann struggled. "No, you idiot. I have to go to her." He swallowed. "She's pregnant."

"Stop, we need to think about this logically." Edward looked at Iris, who nodded. "What's keeping them here, both of them?"

"Claire, can you sense the energy?" Iris asked.

Claire nodded. She took a deep breath and willed for the emotional energy to show itself. She'd never done it before and didn't know what to expect, but faint lines appeared, connecting husbands and wives and—*scandalous!*—lovers.

Claire shook her head. That was not what she needed to see.

Then there were the lines that connected Eros and Psyche to each other, both anchored by the aether, which blurred the objects and people around them.

"It's the aether generator. It's bending time and—" She

gestured, unsure of what to call it. "But they're not entirely in this time."

"Then we have to disrupt the aether," Edward said. "I couldn't find a vulnerable point in the peripheral system, so we'll have to go for the main channel."

Iris nodded. "Which means we'll have to get close to the dais."

"Fine with me." Johann hadn't taken his eyes off the spirit that possessed his wife.

A banging on the upper landing revealed that some of the guests had tried to escape and found themselves locked in. Claire and the others used the distraction to get closer.

Golden figures emerged from the walls like Claire had seen at Fort Daniels. One of them looked familiar—Mrs. Soper—who approached Claire.

"There's something keeping all but the strongest spirits out," the old one said. "But calling the goddess created enough of a crack for some of us."

"Can you help us?" Claire gestured to the stage. Psyche approached her lover slowly.

"I can't intervene. This is your show, child. But..." She waved her hands, knocking the guns away from the guards that held Patrick and Chadwick.

The two of them freed themselves from the distracted guards and took their weapons. They all convened behind the raised dais, and Radcliffe locked Claire in a kiss.

"Are you all right?" he asked.

"Me? You're the one who spent the night in a Southern jail." She caressed his cheek, careful of the bruising.

"I was more worried about you. At least your aunt—"

"Ahem," Edward said. "If you two will monitor the situation. Doctor McPhee, let me know if there's any major change in the emotional situation on the platform. Johann, I need your and Patrick's help getting past the men guarding the aether. Iris..." He looked at her with such love Claire couldn't keep the smile off her face, and his next words surprised her. "See if you can reach Miss Cobb, let her know what's going on. She's been watching us and seems to be a sensible young woman."

"She is," Claire said. "I can vouch for her."

"Good. Gentlemen, with me."

CHAPTER TWENTY-EIGHT

Cobb Townhouse, 14 March 1871

After the guards took Patrick and Chadwick away, Henry made his way toward the ballroom, but a tall figure caught his eye.

"Paul Farrell, you are under arrest," he said.

Farrell turned around, and to Henry's irritation, he only grinned and shrugged.

"I happen to know you made a bargain with the neo-Pythagoreans. You have to let me go."

"I don't have to do any such thing."

"Oh, really?" Farrell gestured behind Henry. "I wouldn't say that to Lieutenant Crow if I were you. She's armed, and we work for the same people."

Henry turned to see the soldier wearing a reddish purple gown that set off her eyes and dark hair. It had flowers embroidered around the hem. The dainty decorations did nothing to diminish the deadliness of the weapon she aimed at him.

"I would let him go if I were you, Inspector."

Henry turned to Farrell with a shrug. "Fine, but do me the favor of answering one question for me."

Farrell nodded.

"You don't work for either Cobb or the neo-Pythagoreans, do you? Who's paying you?" A glance at Crow told him she didn't know—her eyebrows had drawn down in confusion.

"Isn't it obvious to a man of your intellect, Inspector?" Farrell saluted. "I'm with the Clockwork Guild."

The bullet from Crow's gun met drywall. Farrell disappeared, and she cursed.

"How did you know?" she asked.

"His motivations didn't make sense. Cobb wants the gods to appear. The neo-Pythagoreans want to keep their secrets, as you know. Double-crossing either side would be too dangerous. But he's managed to do that and escape."

Crow cursed under her breath. "You're not the only one who's been wanting to catch him. Trust me, Inspector, this won't be the last time we meet."

"I'm looking forward to it." And, surprisingly, he meant it. The golden flowers embroidered around Crow's hem caught the light as she whirled and left.

No matter what Violet and Hobbes thought of him for Farrell's escape, he now had a new and very valuable piece of information for them. And hopefully he would still have a job and his life, especially now that there was a very interesting woman in it.

———

Parnaby Cobb's face turned red, then purple with the pressure of the god's arm at his throat. Louisa tried not to watch but couldn't help it. In her peripheral vision, she caught sight of Claire and the others moving her way, but she returned her attention to the god and his goddess, who had taken over Marie. At least that was what she thought they were. Claire had explained some of what her fiancé had been up to before he found her again and the strange events that had occurred in Europe.

That will never do. Marie's worked too hard to be free of others' control.

Louisa edged away from her stepfather, but the god released him, and Cobb fell to the floor, gasping for air. Eros and Psyche embraced and kissed. Bentley Drury still stood there, his shoulder in the large metal hand of the automaton. He'd decided to remain quiet, at least.

When Louisa looked toward the crowd again, she saw they'd dispersed, or were trying to. The only person who remained was Iris.

"Do something," she whispered, but the words reached Louisa's ears.

Of all the things Iris could have said to her, those words were the worst, and Louisa's resolve crumbled. She had tried to do several somethings and had failed. She'd messed up Patrick's escape. She'd gotten herself and Claire stuck in this situation. And now somehow she'd ended up with her favorite maid—and, if she were to allow herself to think it, friend—possessed by a goddess.

"I can't," she said, and the warm tears on her cheeks underscored her frustration. "I've only messed things up so far."

Iris gestured to her chest, and Louisa looked down at her own, where she saw her locket had come out of her bodice and glowed silver. She remembered her grandmother's words, then.

Embrace your destiny.

But what is that? What do I have?

She looked down at Cobb gasping at her feet and thought of the one thing she'd never asked him because getting an honest answer would risk her entire life.

"Parnaby," she said and nudged him with her toe so he looked up at her. "How did my mother die, really?" She put the weight of her talent behind the question, and his face reddened, but not for any physical reason.

"She had typhoid," he said, and then he spoke more quickly, the words gushing from him, "and she was getting better, but she was going to take you away, so I had her poisoned and her bones hidden in the dungeon where we put Patrick O'Connell."

The sound of taffeta crunching made Louisa aware that she clutched her skirts in her hands. "And why are you doing all this now?"

"Because I want to have power over Boston's elite." He put a hand over his mouth, but he couldn't stop himself. "And I want to be immortal through the power of chaos and control what happens to souls when they die."

The two gods released each other.

"Foolish mortal," Psyche said. "I can feel the hatred for you from my vessel. And I can feel the anger of the people you've manipulated with false promises." She tsked. "You've played god enough already, have you not?" She looked up at Louisa.

Louisa caught the hint. "Haven't you?" she asked.

"Never," Cobb said. He struggled to his feet and stood defiant. "No matter what you do to me, I shall always pursue what I deserve."

"And then we shall escort you to Hades to let him determine that." Eros wrapped Cobb's upper arm in his large hands. "Beloved, shall we?"

The aether pulse changed, and the two gods became transparent.

"Yes, our source is waning." Psyche took hold of Cobb's other arm. "And I grow weary of this vessel. She has too many ties here." She put a hand on her belly. "And a child—how marvelous."

They faded, then, taking Cobb with them. Marie, back to being a brunette, swayed, and Louisa and a blond man helped her to the floor.

She opened her eyes, which were back to their normal appearance.

"What happened?"

The man took a breath and pressed his lips to her forehead. With a sound that was somewhere between a sigh and a sob, he said, "The greatest performance of your life, my dear." And then he clutched her to him.

Louisa turned to see Patrick standing beside her, and she stood and folded herself into his arms.

"You're a brave woman, Louisa Cobb," he said.

"And you're a brave man to agree to take me on." She looked up at him with a grin.

"Oh?"

"Yes, because now that I've rescued you and your friends, I fully expect you to take me away from here and go on adventures with me."

"Oh!"

She waited a moment and asked, "Is that a yes?"

"Well, lass, since the gods listen to ye, I would have to say I'd be a fool to say no."

And then he kissed her.

"Well, I guess we'll just have to accept this, Eliza," the ghost of Louisa's mother said from the side of the stage.

"Yes, well, sometimes you can't get in the way of true love. By the way, I've never felt lighter." The ghost of Eliza looked at her hands. "But what are those girls going to do without my guidance? There are weddings to plan, after all."

"They're very resourceful, as you can see. I'm sure they can figure it out."

Louisa heard them and motioned behind Patrick's back for them to go away. She was ready to take full charge of her own life and whatever adventures her great Irish love would take her on.

CHAPTER TWENTY-NINE

Cobb Townhouse, 14 March 1871

"I'm never going to be welcome in those high society circles again," Louisa said. She rested her head on the arm of the chaise lounge as Patrick massaged her foot. He shook his head—he knew she didn't care.

"You never know," he told her. "You could be the spring's sensation—the girl you can't lie to."

"Oh, there's plenty the guests want to keep hidden." Claire gazed up at Chad, whom she leaned against. "You wouldn't believe the interesting things I saw."

"Isn't that part of your job?" Chad asked.

"Yes, but unfortunately I'm not allowed to say anything."

The others laughed. Iris leaned against Edward, and the smile that played around her lips said she would be rewarding him later for taking charge in the ballroom at the end and changing the aether frequency to one that wouldn't sustain the appearance of the gods.

Johann wasn't letting Marie out of his sight for more than a few minutes, although she had recovered her strength quickly. Perhaps she had enjoyed her brief stint as a goddess.

Claire and Chad gazed at each other like lovesick fools, but Patrick didn't blame them for it. They'd been through enough they could be as foolish as they wanted. As for him...

Every time he looked at Louisa, his cheeks stretched into a grin of their own accord, and he had to admit that he, tinkerer and connoisseur of other men's problems, was smitten. And the cheeky girl had essentially proposed to him in front of gods and everyone, so he was stuck with her.

Truth be told, he didn't mind.

A commotion from the front of the house distracted him. A round of quick eye contact among him and the other men made everyone sit up in preparation to stand. Before they could, the door opened, although they were shocked as to who came through.

"Davidson, you bastard," Patrick said. "What are you doing here?" He would have gotten up and punched the idiot, but Chad motioned for him to stay seated.

"Let's hear him out," Chad said.

Henry held his hands up. "I'm sorry about you two being captured, but one of us needed to be free to take care of things. I do apologize, though. But I have big news."

"Oh, do tell," Patrick said and muttered, "This had better be good."

"It turns out Farrell wasn't working for Cobb or the Pythagoreans. He was an agent of the Clockwork Guild, who now has your aether knowledge. My bosses have come up with a plan to deal with them, but they say I need help." He looked at each of the women in turn. "I need someone with expertise in and a connection to the past. Someone with a talent for subterfuge. And a couple of someones who can sniff out motivations and lies." He then shrugged. "And you gents can come along for the ride."

"How dangerous is it?" Johann asked.

Patrick snorted—of all of them, the violinist was typically

the least risk-averse, but the events of the day had shaken him. Plus there was the baby on the way, and who knew what effect the goddess had had on the child?

"It depends on the day. But I can promise it will never be boring. What do you think?"

Everyone looked at Iris. Patrick shook his head, but imperceptibly. When they'd all met the petite lass, they'd underestimated her strength. Now she was their *de facto* leader.

She twisted the large gold ring with the green stone around her finger.

"I can't say that this has anything to do with my unique abilities, but I definitely feel that this isn't finished. I'm fine helping out if everyone else is."

"Let's do it," Claire said. "Otherwise things will become boring rather quickly."

"And I'll hang in there as long as I can." Marie grinned. "I don't plan to be confined for too long."

The others agreed. Patrick listened to their plans and smiled, glad they'd be together for a while longer.

Now if he could just figure out how to get rid of the two old ghost biddies in the corner... He needed to write to his grandmother, who would have some advice for him. She'd want to know all about Louisa, and he would finally have a grand tale to tell.

Author note: Thank you so much for reading Aether Rising! I hope you enjoyed it. When I started the series, I had no idea Patrick would end up being such a fan favorite, but I'm glad he did. If you enjoyed it, or even if you didn't, please consider leaving a review. Reviews help readers to find books since they help ranking and give proof that other people read and liked it.

This is the final book in the main Aether Psychics series, but Henry Davidson still has many stories to play a part in, so I hope you'll continue reading his adventures in the Henry Davidson Mysteries, the first of which is The Art of Piracy. You'll get to see some familiar characters as the series progresses. Please keep reading to learn more.

Inspector Davidson Mysteries
Book One

She unknowingly holds the secret to his immortality. When airship pirates attack, will their budding love go down in flames?

Alternate France, 1871. Art historian Veronica Devine dreams of putting her late husband's betrayal behind her, so she's grateful for the somewhat distracting mission to transport a valuable collection from a French chateau across the Atlantic. But before her voyage even begins, she's attacked by thieves and saved by a mysterious stranger.

Luc, the Marquis de Monceau's, fate is bound to an enchanted ancestral painting. After fleeing the Prussian invasion, his survival hinges on protecting an alias that preserves the rumor of his death. So when the beautiful woman he saves insists she has permission to remove his portraits, he has no choice but to escort her aboard a luxury airship.

Within the confines of the majestic vessel, Veronica and Luc soon discover they have more in common than a love of art. But cryptic messages, a clockwork automaton, and conniving passengers threaten to ground their romantic aspirations.

Will Veronica and Luc unravel the mystery of the masterpiece before dark forces from his past send their ship into the depths?

The Art of Piracy is the opening novella in the imaginative Inspector Davidson Mysteries steampunk romance series. If you like colorful characters, action-filled adventures, and intriguing settings, then you'll adore Cecilia Dominic's suspenseful drama.

Buy *The Art of Piracy* to paint the skies with love today!

Available from most online retailers. Or, if you prefer paper, you can order it through your favorite local or online bookstore. It's available from Ingram Spark, and the ISBN is 978-1-945074-52-3

Chapter One

Veronica Lillet Kindred shaded her eyes and looked up at the chateau. It appeared to be a typical opulent French manor, not one that deserved to have tales told about it of ghosts and strange occurrences. But the horses had gotten more nervous as they'd approached, and her crew quieter.

She didn't know any of the men that well, but they'd started the morning boisterous enough to the point of boasting that they'd capture the first spirit they encountered and put it in a glass jar. Then they'd bring it back to Paris and start doing séances, mediumship being a better paying profession than requisitioning and moving art.

The boasting had turned to nervous fidgeting and whispered repetition of rumors.

While Veronica had no doubt that men committed the sort of horrors that could produce specters, she didn't believe in ghosts. Still, something about the house felt...wrong. Like someone had taken the harmony of the place apart and put it back together with a note out of tune. Or something like that. She could never exactly describe the things she felt, only a sensation akin to the internal thrum at a concert when the instruments played loudly. Ironic since she'd only ever been passable at playing the pianoforte and singing, her first love being art. She'd learned during her time as an art history apprentice in London to pay attention when something stuck out as different. That's why Léonard Basquet, famous art historian and dealer, had sent her on this errand.

Focus, Veronica...

Even now her fingers twitched to sketch the archways and soaring lines of the chateau's windows and walls, but she quashed the feeling. Even if she had the time, she doubted the drawing would come. She hadn't been able to put pencil to paper and produce anything useful since Peter's death, and she doubted her once-prodigious talent would return now. Besides, there was no time for such frivolity. They had a shipment to assemble and an airship to catch.

"Allons-y," she said with as much authority as a young woman could command over a group of rough men. They muttered under their breath but complied, no doubt motivated by the bonuses they'd been promised. She pulled out her list and studied it. *Only about ten pieces*, she read for the hundredth time. *Enough to start a collection. I'll trust your good taste as to what to select. -Léonard*

A big responsibility. But hadn't she been waiting for the past four years for something like this? And it came along with the chance for her to return to Terminus in triumph, not as the disgraced girl who'd secretly married her headmaster and been widowed six months later.

The foreman took out an ornate key that looked like it came straight out of a fairy tale and applied it to the padlock on the large wooden front door. Although the rest of the chateau might boast modern upgrades, the Marquis had apparently decided to keep the old door, which was pitted and studded with iron. The squeak of its hinges lingered into a sigh that seemed to come from the depths of the house. With a shiver, Veronica wondered what sort of monster might emerge, but several seconds passed with no signs of life within.

No one wanted to go in first, so with a huff, Veronica led the way. A switch on the wall made gas lamps flare to life. So the Marquis *had* updated his property. Good. She hadn't relished the idea of using a torch or candle to illuminate the dark middle of a house filled with priceless objects. She feared setting something irreplaceable alight, or—the worst horror—burning the place down.

As the lights in the grand entrance hall flared to life, Veronica wondered if burning down the chateau would, indeed, be the worst horror. The place had obviously been evacuated quickly. Dust covered chairs that had been overturned and iced moribund shapes on the floor that at first looked like animals but turned out to be scraps and articles of clothing. As Veronica and her crew followed the directions to the library, their movements kicked up the fine powder that swirled and eddied, making phantasmic shapes and casting faint shadows that tricked her peripheral vision. Underneath it all, the sigh that she'd heard when the door opened lingered and vibrated with its sense of wrongness.

Even so, she couldn't help a slight grin at the fact she led the way. The team of five burly men had fallen in behind *her*, and she congratulated herself on taking charge and showing courage.

See, Uncle Thaddeus, sometimes charging right in can be a good thing.

When they opened the double library doors and flipped the light switch, Veronica caught her breath. Two levels of books surrounded a large space anchored on the eastern wall by a fireplace, above which hung a large painting of Psyche and Eros in flight. The young god turned his face away, and Psyche gazed longingly at him. Veronica snorted. She knew that look. She'd *had* that look. Now she knew better.

"All right, down to business. Maurice and Gaston, you pack the crates. Lefoux and Armand, y'all, er, you follow me and bring the pieces I select to them. Carnais, stand guard." That last came out of her mouth almost involuntarily, and warmth crept into her face. Would they think her stupid or merely cautious? So far nothing had threatened them, at least not openly.

Carnais didn't argue, although someone muttered that muscle wouldn't protect them from whatever lurked in the chateau.

Veronica walked around the library on both levels and examined the paintings that hung between bookshelves, getting a sense of them. The Marquis' family had had eclectic tastes, although themes ran to the classical. She found a smaller Psyche and Eros, this of the young woman kneeling in front of piles of grain as the ants helped her sort them and Eros standing with his mother in the shadows in the background.

"This one." She indicated the painting. Although she found it annoying that Eros colluded with his mother in torturing his bride, she also felt a stab of satisfaction. Why not? That's what men did, wasn't it—hide things from their beloved that would tear things apart? Tear *them* apart?

She brought herself back to the moment with a shake of her head. There was no time for self-pity. That was all in the past. She had art to requisition.

Veronica chose several more, including a Flemish landscape, a pre-Raphaelite languishing nymph, and what looked like a military tableau. Also a couple of small statues. Sadly they didn't have room or weight allowance for one of the gorgeous large kouros. The Archaic Greek statues' graceful white forms would have fit beautifully in a gallery. Too bad one of them appeared to be damaged. They had hinged limbs and could move, but thankfully they remained still. She didn't think her crew would have appreciated it if they had gone into their stereotypical motions.

She had room for one more picture and returned to one she'd been drawn to but couldn't see the obvious value of. An eight-by-twelve inch painting of a small boy sat in a frame on one of the center tables. It looked to have been painted at least a hundred years prior, but no artist's mark helped her place it or its worth. The child wore a blue ruffled suit and held a dimpled golden ball.

When she picked it up, the energy around her increased in pitch and tone before falling into a hush. A noise from one of the upper galleries startled her, and one of the paintings she hadn't selected crashed to the floor, leaving an empty spot on the wall. Worse, there were two holes at eye distance about where the portrait's eyes would have been.

She shivered. Were they being watched?

The disturbance had spurred the men into action. One of them snatched the painting from her hands and put it in the crate with its fellow pieces. The crew murmured back and forth in French too fast for Veronica to catch, but she understood the meaning—they wanted to get out of there, and soon. She agreed. Whereas a phantasm or ghost would have been interesting, the thought of a person watching them? That was downright creepy.

***

Luc de Marcels, the late Marquis de Monceau, had not shuffled off the mortal coil in an airship accident, as was generally assumed. While he didn't mind the anonymity his presumed death had granted, he did resent having to lurk around his home like a ghost. Especially since it felt like something watched *him*.

At the moment, from the relatively hidden vantage point of a painting's eyeholes, he observed a dreadfully composed young woman direct a group of ruffians to pack up *his* art in crates destined for who-knew-where. Paintings that had hung in the library for generations were being taken down and packed away like so much bric-a-brac. He would have stopped them but dared not be seen, for many reasons. There had already been one close call when the girl had examined the painting he hid behind, and he had almost not replaced the strip with the portrait's oil-painted eyes quickly enough.

The woman had taste, he'd give her that. She passed over paintings and statues he knew to be less valuable. Not that he had any sort of natural eye for art, but family lore had specified which works were to be taken if the chateau needed to be evacuated quickly. Admiration warred with irritation as he observed her. And while he was no longer a gambling man—his last wager had cost him an eye and his good looks—he bet one of the paintings that ended up in the straw-packed crates would be the one he sought.

He again cursed his father for not giving him specifics as to which painting would unlock the Monceau legacy, a legendary magical force originally harnessed by a wizard in the dark ages. He didn't need to sell any of the art. No, to do so would mark him as a thief and expose his true identity, which would lead to his being tried for treason.

They were almost finished, but she paused by one of the few pictures in standing frames, this one a painting of Luc's great grandfather as a boy. Or at least that's what he'd always been told. It had been painted by some no-name peasant artist and had little worth beyond family sentiment and history, but she lingered over it. What was she playing at? Did she truly not know what she sought?

Or, worse, did she? Could she know something, be more aware than he? It was possible, he conceded as he stepped back. He'd seen the artwork in the library so many times he'd ceased to *see* it. She looked at it for the first time, and he couldn't help but envy her.

A crash made him jump backward, and he guessed the portrait he'd been looking through had fallen. Icy sweat covered his skin. Something in the house wasn't happy about its desecration, and the sound of fluttering wings made him dash through the secret passages and down into the kitchen, behind which he'd tied his horse. He cursed at himself under his breath for his foolishness but didn't linger inside.

Those sounds and the constant feeling of being observed by something that had just awoken hungry had driven him from his home in the first place and on to that cursed airship. He suspected what he'd seen in the library indicated that Mademoiselle Art Thief would be departing France on a nice steamship. He'd have to follow her and find out.

His horse, Noir, made no sound as he approached. He'd trained the animal well, and together they quietly picked their way through the now-overgrown gardens. Seeing the estate's gradual decay made his heart hurt—his mother had been so proud of the grounds especially. He paused to watch the men load the crates into a carriage, and the crew arranged themselves, ready to depart. The young woman had just climbed on to the driver's bench beside the burly gentleman Luc had identified as the crew's foreman when a dark shadow painted the scene in shades of tar. He looked up to see the bulk of an airship descending, figures dressed in black dangling from ropes. Dark cloths covered the bottom halves of their faces, and each wore a black cap.

Now Luc cursed audibly and mounted his horse.

"Go, you fools!" he shouted at the woman and her crew, and they didn't hesitate. The carriage lurched forward, the man yelling at the horses to move their lazy rumps. The airship pursued them, and Luc calculated their odds. If the carriage made it down the drive across the lawn and into the Forêt de Monceau, the trees would protect them. Luc only needed to keep the pirates from landing on the conveyance.

Luc held Noir's reins with one hand and urged his stallion forward. Noir obeyed, his burst of speed telling Luc the horse had been cooped up for too long. Luc unholstered his pistol, took quick aim, and shot at the pirate who was closest to the carriage. He prayed his shot would be high enough not to hit the carriage's drivers or occupants, and when the pirate fell, he knew his aim had been true. For once. He would deal later with the sickening certainty that if the bullet hadn't killed the man, the fall surely had.

Halfway to the forest, the carriage wobbled, and Luc sucked in a breath—would it lose a wheel? No time to worry about that problem. A bullet whizzed by his ear, and he urged Noir forward so they'd be under the airship and in its shadow, hopefully harder to target. He shot at the next closest pirate to the carriage and missed. That one fired back at him, but the motion of the airship made the ropes sway and twirl, and his bullet went wide. Still, Luc tried again.

Triumphant shouts brought his attention forward, and he saw the carriage disappear into the shadows of the trees. The pirates ascended their ropes, and Luc guessed—hoped—they'd given up. With one last burst of speed, Noir entered the forest, and its coolness enveloped them.

***

"And then he yelled, 'Go, you fools!' and shot at the pirates and kept them from capturing us." Veronica illustrated the scene with broad gestures, and Léonard grinned. Well, at least *he* found the situation amusing.

"And obviously, you did 'go,' fools that you were," he prompted.

Veronica took a deep breath to calm the thrumming of her heart at the memory of the close call. Her eyes still stung when she thought about the wind and dust in them, and her fingers ached from clutching the side of the wagon, and then the reins, so tightly.

"It was harrowing," she admitted and took a sip of wine. "Utterly ha-arrowing." She didn't care if a slight Southern accent had crept into her words in spite of her effort to use overly proper English, as she'd been taught in London. It happened when she'd drunk too much wine or had become overly exhausted. Or when upset, like now.

How could her mentor just sit there and laugh and shake his head?

"So you made it to the forest, then? And back to Paris?" He sounded utterly delighted.

"With my eyes on the sky the entire time once we came out

of the trees," she snapped. Finally, the pressure built in her chest to the point she had to exclaim, "At least you find this amusing! Do you know what it's like to have a ship full of pirates on your heels? In a rickety wagon with a barely competent driver? I had to take the reins from him or he'd've knocked us into a tree or overturned the stupid thing."

Gaston hadn't been pleased, and they'd spent the ride back to Paris in uncomfortable silence. None of the men would share their impressions with her in spite of her desire to give Léonard a complete accounting of the incident, so she had to fill in as many of the details as she remembered.

"Yes, as a matter of fact, I do." Léonard's expression snapped back to its customary somber demeanor when discussing serious matters, which for him typically consisted of alcohol or art. He ran the fingers of his right hand along his fashionably trimmed gray beard. "But the situation you describe is unusual."

"What do you make of it?" she asked. She'd often wondered about his past and how he, a man of upper years, had ended up teaching at King's College and collecting art in London. She knew it had something to do with the political unrest in France and him not being favored by the Emperor Napoleon III, hence why Léonard had finally been able to return. Napoleon III had been killed in the battle that ended the Prussian siege, and then the new government, after some turmoil, had taken over. But she'd never found out what Léonard had done to attract the emperor's dislike. Not that it mattered now. She'd come to find that the French nobles were easily insulted.

"It's rare for pirates to attack a house, but perhaps they were there for the same reason you were."

Veronica couldn't help a slight grin. "To requisition pieces of art to set up a new gallery in a city in the former Confederate States?"

"No, silly girl, and you know better. To loot the house. Perhaps they saw you and your crates and decided they wanted whatever you had."

Veronica sighed. "It seemed to be more than that. I can't tell you how I know..."

"You just do," he finished for her. During their five years of her working for him, he'd come to respect her intuition and her artistic eye, as he called it. It was why she'd moved from secretary to assistant to protégé. He leaned forward and put a hand on hers. "You know that if my old bones had been able to take the rough roads out to the estate, I would've been there."

She patted his hand with her free one, then brought both hands back to her lap. "I know, Léonard. It's just that..." She shrugged, unable to put all her feelings into words, so she settled on, "I thought this would be an easy assignment. Go to the disgraced, dead, and heirless noble's house, grab some art, and bring it back to Terminus."

She couldn't add, 'And show my family, especially my uncle, that I'm a capable, intelligent person who can make it on my own.' She'd never spoken of her family or her own disgrace to Léonard. She supposed they each had their own secrets.

"You know this may not be the last of it," Léonard said, and she looked up from her sole meunière.

"What? Why not?"

"Airship pirates roam all the oceans, including the Atlantic. You'll never see them—they're much too clever and good at using color, light, and shadow to their advantage. If there was something at the Monceau place they wanted, they won't stop until they get it."

Her intuition tickled the back of her brain. "What are you not telling me, Léonard?"

"Nothing, dear girl, nothing. I've given you all the information I have. It's up to you to do the rest. You proved yourself admirably today, especially after your driver was shot."

A sensation akin to electric shock made Veronica still. She hadn't mentioned that was why Gaston had been unable to control the horses—his left arm had been made immobile by a bullet to the shoulder, which he had only realized after the excitement and terror of the situation had passed. Thankfully the rest of the crew had all been veterans of the recent fighting and knew basic battlefield wound dressing and care, so he hadn't bled out. Or on the crates, and there was no danger of damage to their contents from seepage.

"More wine?" Léonard asked. "It sounds like you could use some to calm your nerves."

"Please," Veronica said and held out her glass. She forced herself to smile and pretend everything was all right, but she knew with certainty that Léonard held something back. And if it put her life in danger, that was one thing. If it imperiled her future triumph, well, she'd make sure that wouldn't happen.

At least he hadn't asked her to marry him again.

Facebook: facebook.com/CeciliaDominicAuthor

Cecilia's books available everywhere e-books are sold. Look for paperbacks in select online and brick-and-mortar stores or ask them to order them for you from Ingram.

If you'd like to keep up with her and her writing, and to get *Noble Secrets*, the *Aether Psychics* prequel novella for free, please sign up for her newsletter using the link listed above.

*Want to see where the Aether Psychics started? Check out **Noble Secrets**.*

A dangerous man from her past.
A handsome duke in her present.
Secrets that threaten their future.

After tragedy hits and danger moves in, Pauline Danahue flees London, searching for sanctuary and a way to start over. A job at a small university provides the escape she needs. Keeping recalcitrant professor Edward Bailey on task after a shattered heart renders him broken and destroyed becomes her daily routine. But when the same vicious man from her past sets his malicious sights on Pauline, her safe haven comes crashing down.

Duke of Waltham, Christopher Bailey, never counted on the gentle commoner, Miss Danahue, to save his brother—and himself—from broken pasts and a lifetime of mistakes. But she does just that. As their love blossoms, danger closes in, threatening Pauline and Christopher's lives. Together, they are forced to face their biggest fears, revealing secrets that could ruin them both.

Noble Secrets is available from most online retailers!
If you prefer paperbacks, you can look for it or ask your favorite bookseller to order it with the following ISBN: 978-1-945074-53-0

Or, if you want to read Noble Secrets for free, sign up for my author newsletter:

https://www.subscribepage.com/CeciliaDominicbackofbook I hate spam and promise to keep your email safe.

NOBLE SECRETS

Chapter One

Department of Aetherics, Huntington University, 4 July 1862

Pauline looked up from her newspaper. It was still early, and she'd been enjoying the summertime quiet, but the sound of men's voices ascending the stairs—presumably attached to her bosses—meant it was time to get back to work. She folded the paper and put it in her large reticule so no one would see her reading it. In spite of the university being a bastion of learning, it was frowned upon for the staff—well, female staff—to engage in intellectual pursuits.

She turned on the steam kettle and set up the tea tray, turning in time to see four men walk into the front hall of the department.

Dean Hartford led the charge. Pauline mentally ticked off what he would want - Earl Grey, extra strong. Two blueberry scones. No butter. Then the chairman, Harold Kluge, the same but with only one scone. Then the blond gentleman. He looked familiar, and Pauline's intuition said he would only want tea. The same for the fourth one, who—

The deep blue of his eyes and his tired smile made Pauline want to lead him to a chair, fluff his pillow, and put a nip of brandy in his tea. She shook her head. He resembled Edward

Bailey, a young professor whose genius had allowed him to take a faculty position at an early age, but she'd never had that kind of response to the finicky academic, who liked his sugar cubes split.

"Pauline, tea in the conference room, please," the dean said. His normally booming voice was subdued, which only heightened the tension in the air.

Pauline fixed everyone's tea the way they wanted it that morning and arranged the pots for balance. She ignored the twinge in her shoulder when she hoisted the tray. That pain emerged at the most inconvenient times, and she shook off the memory of the large hand grabbing her by the upper arm and slamming her against the wall. That had been another girl in another life.

She paused in front of the closed conference room door and huffed. How did they expect her to carry the tray and open the door? She couldn't even knock with her elbow for fear of upsetting the very full teapot with the extra strong Earl Grey, and she dared not call for fear of annoying some faculty member in some office on the hall.

She would have to go back to her desk, offload some of the items, and come back. Before she turned, the door swung inward, and the blue-eyed young man took the tray from her so quickly she squeaked.

"Sorry," he mouthed.

"Quite all right."

"...able to work?" Chairman Kluge was saying. He shot an annoyed look at Pauline. "Please serve the tea without comment, Miss. This is a serious discussion. As I was saying, Your Grace, we have a patent application underway for a new aether isolating device, and Professor Bailey is indispensable to the process. If we delay, I fear those snobs at Oxford will beat us to it."

Your Grace? Pauline looked at her savior with curiosity. He seemed young to be a duke, but then it all clicked into place.

Of course! Professor Bailey had an older brother, and he was the son of a late duke. As she was new in town, she still sorted through the tangle of titles and identities.

"I'm concerned as to his mental welfare," the duke said. "You know he's always been, well, Mother describes him as quirky. Different. Sensitive. He's had his first heartbreak, and it's going to keep him from being able to work efficiently. He is inclined to just stop what he's doing and stare off into space."

Pauline poured the tea and listened with interest. She liked Professor Bailey just fine but recognized he was an unusual sort, very much in his own head. Considering her experience had been with men who preferred not to think too much about what they were doing and to whom, she appreciated his intense focus on his work.

"I still don't understand how she could have thought he was you, Christopher," the blond young man said. He lounged with a languid air, and he raised his eyebrows when Pauline handed him his tea fixed exactly as he liked it. She mentally kicked herself—she should have remembered to make a show of asking, but she was distracted by his familiarity in calling the duke by his given name.

"Lucky guess," she whispered.

He grinned, and she looked away, her face heating. She knew his sort—he would be one to make a big show of attending to a woman's desires, making her think she meant something to him, and then leaving her cold in the morning. She rotated her shoulder against the pain that had become a stubborn needle at the top of the blade.

The duke didn't answer the question of how the professor had been mistaken for him. "The important thing is what to do with him now. He would have gotten his heart broken eventually, so it's good he got it over with."

"You make heartbreak sound like a disease," the dean said.

"Isn't it?" the blond man asked. "That's why I avoid it."

"Yes, Maestro, we're familiar with your romantic philoso-phies," Chairman Kluge snapped. "Let's get back to the matter at hand. How are we to keep Professor Bailey on track with developing the device?"

"It sounds like you need someone to watch him and ensure he's working, not mooning about," the dean mused. "A babysitter, as it were."

"It's a good thing he's a genius," Kluge muttered. "Maestro? Are you free this summer?"

"'Fraid not, old chap." The blond gentleman hoisted his teacup. "Got a full summer concert lineup."

"I wish I could help," the duke put in, "but I have an estate to run."

Pauline edged toward the door. She felt the tide of opinion shifting, and she certainly didn't want to get roped into watching the moody professor. She'd babysat enough men in her time, and the thought of attending to a finicky academic made her stomach fold in on itself and the needle of pain in her shoulder twist into a knife.

"Miss Danahue's duties are light at the moment with so many of the staff being away for the season," Chairman Kluge said. "She can help out."

Pauline stopped, her hand on the door handle, and said in her sweetest voice, "Of course I'm happy to, but are you sure you don't need me for other things?"

"No, that seems to be the best solution," the dean said. "You will watch Professor Bailey and ensure he finishes the aether isolating device development and patent application."

"I'd greatly appreciate it," the duke said. Pauline sensed his deep exhaustion.

She nodded and forced her jaw to relax as she smiled, hoping it looked genuine. "Of course, Your Grace."

———

When Christopher left the Department of Aetherics, he paused and rubbed his eyes, which itched from lack of sleep. It had been a few long days. First there had been the cryptic telegram from Edward saying that everything had gone wrong and he wasn't coming back from the seaside because it would be too embarrassing. Then Christopher had gone to fetch him at the behest of their mother, and they'd arrived back so late that he had slept little before coming to the meeting at the University.

But if he were to be honest, guilt had kept him up during the brief time he'd had to sleep, poking his chest with its needle-sharp claws every time he tried to drift off.

"Are you all right?" Johann Bledsoe, a violinist and Edward's best friend, stood beside him. "I'd forgotten how intense those academics can be."

"Just tired." Christopher wondered how much Johann remembered of the party and the disastrous prank he had played on his own brother. "Do you need a ride back to the country?"

"Thanks, but I'm keeping a low profile with the family. Plus the first summer concert is this evening."

"Right." Christopher's mind couldn't keep up with the days since the first part of the week had distorted in carnival mirror fashion. "At least you have the option to lay low."

They walked toward the park that the university had designated for the use of steam vehicles. Christopher's driver sat with the steamcoach reading a book.

"Do you think Miss Danahue will be able to keep Edward in line?" Johann asked. "She seemed a clever sort, or at least resourceful."

Christopher didn't want to say what he'd thought of the young secretary. The beauty of her face and the haunted look in her dark eyes had been the first things to truly pierce his brain fog that morning. Part of him was glad she'd be watching Edward because it would give Christoper the excuse to watch her.

"I suppose we'll see," he said. They'd reached the lot. "Now if you'll excuse me, I'm going to Waltham Manor to try to set my mother's mind at ease."

"Right." Johann tipped his hat and walked toward town.

Christopher got into the coach and settled into the cushions. The vehicle rolled forward, the sound of gravel under the wheels smoothing to the hiss of the inlaid rails of the street. He wished he could as easily leave behind Johann's earlier question. Christopher knew how Lily Cavender had mistaken Edward for him, and the knowledge fed his guilt.

The chuffing of the steamcoach's engine and the fresh warm summer air coming through the windows lulled him into a fitful sleep, but all too soon he arrived at the manor.

The coachman opened the door, and Christopher alighted. Waltham Manor loomed over him, its dark stone echoing the sternness of the slate gray sky. A few drops splashed him as he dashed to the front door, and a rumble of thunder chased him inside.

"Did you get everything straightened out?"

Somehow his mother always knew when he would be home and waited for him in the front hallway. She leaned with both hands on her cane. The gloom from outside appeared to have seeped in, and the grand staircase stretched into the darkness of the upper landing. The family portraits' eyes glowed when lightning flashed.

Christopher rubbed the grit from his face and sneezed. The steamcoach's wheels kicked up less dust than a team of horses, but it had still been unwise to keep the windows open. He'd meant to close them once the vehicle left the cobblestones of town with their smooth inlaid tracks for steam-powered coaches such as his, but he'd been enjoying a dream of a pretty secretary.

"Christopher?"

He snapped out of his dreamy—or nightmarish—fog. "Yes, we agreed on someone to babysit Edward. Kluge won't even charge for it."

"When does a university administrator pass up an opportunity for money?"

Christopher chuckled. Although she was ill, the duchess maintained her sharp mind.

"Since he's concerned about a patent application Edward's been working on. They're trying to beat Oxford, whose aetherics department is going to submit something similar."

"And who will be watching Edward?" Her gray eyes lit with a flash from outside.

"A secretary. Pauline Danahue."

The duchess wrinkled her brow. "I don't know that name. She's not from the area, is she?"

Christopher saw where that conversational track was going, and irritation flared in his chest at the thought of going back and making different arrangements. "It doesn't matter. She's the department secretary, and she's competent."

"You know I'm concerned about your brother and his fragile emotional state." This time the flash of lightning emphasized the thinness of the skin around her eyes.

"Don't worry about it, Mother. I'll check in on Miss Danahue. You need to rest."

He took her elbow with a gentle but firm hand and settled her in the parlor. He ignored the musty smell that lingered no matter how often they opened the windows. The doctors had all agreed—the duchess would likely not make it to Christmas, although Christopher knew she was stubborn enough to live longer just to prove them all wrong.

"Now if only I could get you settled," she said as she reclined. He fluffed the pillow behind her and covered her with a blanket. In spite of the warmth of the house, her touch chilled him as though all the heat in her body was going to her middle, where cancer ate at her.

"Don't worry about me. I'll marry when the time is right."

"This place needs a woman's touch, Christopher. And the townhouse—it's shameful how you and Edward have turned it into a bachelor's haven." The corners of her mouth tightened, the only sign she ever gave that she felt the gnawing on her insides to the point she couldn't ignore the pain.

Christopher rang the little bell that stood on the table beside her.

A maid carrying a tray entered, and Christopher mixed a few drops of laudanum into his mother's tea. He handed it to her and supported her as she drank.

"You'll not distract me from this conversation," she said, but her words slurred as she continued to speak. "I'm going to hold a ball a week from tomorrow, and I'll invite all the eligible young ladies. Except Lily Cavender, of course. Deceitful twit." Her eyelids fluttered, and she murmured, "A grand ball. Surely you will find someone who suits you. You're being stubborn like your father..." Her breathing evened, and Christopher smoothed the iron gray hair back from her face.

"And you," he said. He kissed her forehead and gave the laudanum bottle back to the maid. He followed the girl into the chief housekeeper's small office.

"Is she really serious about this ball idea?" he asked Mrs. Selby, who had run the household since he had been a child.

The older woman nodded and gestured to the lists on her desk. "I'm afraid so, Your Grace."

Christopher sighed. "You and I both know she's not well enough. Has Doctor Phillips been consulted?"

"She was having a good morning when he came."

"Of course she was. Or she was putting on a good show."

Mrs. Selby lifted her shoulders in a shrug of surrender, and she looked down, but the wetness in her eyes was apparent. "I don't have the heart to refuse her anything right now, Your Grace."

The irritation flared again—both at the housekeeper for humoring his mother's wishes to push him into a marriage he didn't desire and at the doctor for allowing the duchess to shorten her already waning days with the effort.

"Just keep it reasonably sized," he snapped, then added to soften his words, "for her health. She'll want to greet everyone personally."

The housekeeper nodded. "I know you're worried about her. We all are. I'll do what I can."

Christopher knew his mother well enough by now. She'd get her way with the ball, but he didn't have to bow to her will with a wife. Edward's experience had shown him what those noble girls were made of—deception and cunning—and he wanted none of it.

Edward has his work at the university. Why can't I be left alone to manage the estate as I see fit?

"Will you be eating dinner here?" Mrs. Selby asked. "I can tell Cook if you are."

"No, I just needed to check on Mother and reassure her. Edward is back at the townhouse, so I'll go back there and make sure he eats. Tonight is also the first summer concert."

He took the smaller steamcart from the stable and waved off the driver. "I need the time to think, and driving will help," he said.

"Yes, sir. Be careful—the roads are muddy."

"Will do."

He'd intended to enjoy the fresh-washed look of the trees and shrubbery on the roadside, but his thoughts echoed the rhythm of the engine.

What do I want in a wife? Do I even want one right now? Women are a bloody lot of trouble for the effort you have to put into them. What would happen if I kept driving, down through London and to the coast?

But the thought of another long day on the road made the idea of escape a fleeting one.